A. A. Jameson

Wish

Published by A. A. Jameson in 2021
defduf@gmail.com
ISBN 978-0-9568675-1-3

Susan

Wish

Everyone he had ever known was there, laughing as he ran slowly past, mocking faces turning to follow him to the edge. He dived out into space.

As he sank towards the sparkling surface of the sea the laughter faded, became the sighing of waves. His wings beat the air, calmly at first, then with increasing urgency: he'd almost brushed the water before he slowed then began to rise and move forward. Up, up, and his confidence grew. He banked to sweep smoothly back over the beach onto which the slow-moving waves pulsed hypnotically. Below him his shadow followed a line of footprints in the sand.

They applauded and waved. He smiled affectionately down at them, passing over their heads in a long glide. Rapid beating and he rose again, higher still, through woollen clouds, leaving the world behind. Exhilaration flooded him: a tilt of a wing and he swung into the snapping wind; the smallest flexing of muscle and he soared free of the clouds. He searched the skies for others, but he was alone.

Abruptly the ecstasy left him and he found himself struggling to slow his sudden descent. His wings beat frantically, then slowed, stopped. He sank towards the sea, feeling foolish, staring dully at the glassy waves that would carry him to the beach. In the distance figures moved forward across the sand. As they approached those in the lead dropped to run on all fours.

I. April

The peregrine sailed on stiff wings high above the remote valley folded into the Welsh hills. Flicking from side to side the grim black-on-white mask searched the still skies for the tremble of life, tiny flexings of wings and tail steering the muscular body in patient circles. A jet flashed silently into a neighbouring valley followed closely by its roar. As the unearthly rumble faded slowly into the west, the harsh, rapid chatter of the peregrine pierced the reverberating hills.

Far below, on one of the south-facing slopes of the valley, a rough wall of stones had been raised against an overhanging rock buttress, providing some protection against the continual winds and none against the almost continual rain.

'Your bird just shouted at the jet, Geoff.'

The man at the wall lowered binoculars and turned to a figure struggling with a stove.

'Geoff?'

'Bloody wind.' Geoff struck another match, and the blustering sound of the primus stove began. 'Got it.'

The man at the wall peered up into the sodden skies. 'It's still circling around up there. Not scared.'

Geoff took no notice. 'Bloody wind. Bloody rain.' A rattle of falling rocks came from further up the slope as a sheep lost its footing. He glared towards the skyline. 'Bloody sheep.'

'Sheep.' The second man stared at Geoff for a moment, then returned to his study of the hunting peregrine. A fresh sheet of drizzle spattered into the shelter.

'Shit!' gritted Geoff.

Eventually the water boiled; Geoff made tea.

'Nige.'

A mug was balanced on a flat rock, steam whipping away in an almost straight line.

'Thanks.' Nigel drank quickly, watching with amusement as his brother fumbled with a tobacco tin. In contrast to his own, Geoff's face was bearded and weather-beaten, his hair a mass of corkscrews. The hot tea had steamed up his spectacles and his mouth worked as he frowned down at tobacco blowing from numb fingers.

Nigel grinned. 'You look like the original Wild Man. Except for the specs.'

Wish

Geoff looked up sourly, licking a cigarette paper. 'Hmm.'

A faint piping sounded from the opposite slope and a grey shape swept in to land high on the rugged cliff-face that dominated the whole valley. Nigel squinted into his binoculars while his brother sucked at burning tobacco and stared morosely at the ground.

'Looks as though one of them's brought in a kill. Can't say which though, or what it's got.'

Geoff sighed and moved on hands and knees to pull a notebook from beneath an anchoring stone. Taking a pencil from the spiral binder he blew on his fingers and began to write.

Nigel lowered his glasses. 'Have a look Geoff, see if you can tell.'

Geoff replied without looking up, slurring the words as his lips gripped the cigarette. 'No need. It'll be a pigeon.' Abruptly a blast of wind plucked the cigarette from his mouth and whisked it over the wall.

'Shit!'

'What's up?'

Geoff's eyes rolled. 'What a godforsaken shithole! Nige, roll me a ciggie.' He passed over the tin. 'My fingers don't want to know.'

Taking the tin, Nigel crouched behind the wall and pulled off his gloves. 'Oh come on. It's not that bad. A few months just watching birds fly around.' A sudden shiver shook him, and he held the tin steady until it passed. 'Some of us have to work, you know. OK, so it's a bit cold now and then, agreed. Bit wet. Bit … quiet. Character-building, though, I expect.' He sniggered. 'Anyway, it's your study. You chose it, after all.'

Geoff took the roll-up and got it going with the third match, while Nigel rolled another for himself.

'And there's bound to be a social thing, isn't there? Meeting people of interest?'

Geoff snorted. 'Like who? Bloody sheep?'

'Well,' Nigel smiled happily as he popped his cigarette into his mouth, 'I should think that when the weather gets better -' he raised his voice over Geoff's objections '- when the weather gets better, there'll be plenty of people trekking about around here. Big tourist area. All those nubile little hill walkers …' he took the cigarette from his lips and licked them '… hills alive with sweaty rucksack girls. Boots and shorts. Compasses, maps. They'll be lost too, half of them. Wanting directions. And let's face it, you're the main attraction round here. No competition. They'll be dangling on your every word won't they? You're the one with the big telescope.'

Geoff smirked. 'Not much chance of that.'

A crow called harshly as it was swept overhead. Seconds later its mate followed, and the two black shapes dwindled quickly to the east.

'I've been here three weeks and I haven't seen a soul.'

'Well, you've got this chap coming up from London tomorrow. Maybe he's got a sister. Bit of company, anyway. Any idea what he's like?'

'Not really. Clive knows his mother. Says he's alright.'

'Must be a bit of a fanatic to do it for nothing.'

'Guy's on the dole. Probably bored out of his skull.' Geoff flipped his cigarette butt into the wind. 'As long as he pulls his weight. And he will.'

'If he likes it as much as you do, you'll be lucky if he doesn't get straight back on the train. I'd love to stay myself of course, but you know how it is. Got to get back to the grind.' Nigel thrust his hands back into his gloves and raised his head cautiously above the wall. 'It's stopped.' From the skyline opposite heavy white vapour rolled down like smoke. 'Getting a bit misty though.' Geoff muttered something unintelligible behind him. The valley seemed suddenly to have become utterly still; even the wind had died away. Looking out into the cold grey silence Nigel shivered again.

'Where's that bird now Nige?'

Nigel swung his binoculars to the sky where the peregrine had been describing its endless circles.

'Gone.'

For the umpteenth time, Geoff tugged the cuff from his watch as he paced the cold concrete of the station floor. He didn't need to look at it; he knew the time. People waited, huddled in twos and threes on the benches, faces blank with resignation. Litter flapped by the side of the tracks; pools of scummy water wrinkled in the niggling wind. Again Geoff fired a glance at his wrist for the benefit of a passing station attendant, who raised his eyebrows in sympathy. The man began to whistle, and stopped to open a door through which the bars of an electric fire could be seen glowing a dull orange. He went inside, still whistling, and the door closed. Geoff glared off down the empty track.

Wish

Eventually a sluggish yellow spot developed against the washed-out chlorine colour of the hills. Houses sprawled either side of the tracks as the train rolled, with no great hurry, through the outskirts of the town. Geoff strode forward to stand with arms folded. He had ample time for another glare at his watch.

Doors flew open, banging as the train finally wheeled to a halt, and passengers emerged. Most looked as it they'd forgotten they could walk. They were crumpled in a way suggesting the whole train-load had been asleep for hours and had just been roused unexpectedly. Geoff regarded them with disdain. Students shouldered past, loaded down with bags and cases; timid old folk waited uncertainly at the back for the crowd at the ticket barrier to disperse. A figure pushed through them: bearded, longish lank hair, battered black leather biker's jacket, haversack.

Geoff clucked to himself. 'Surly looking bugger.' As he got closer Geoff saw the man was the taller by a good three or four inches. He scowled up at him.

'Are you Alver?'

The heavy features were set in a wary expression.

'Yeah. Geoff?'

Geoff nodded, and there was a pause. Neither offered a handshake.

'Come on. You're late.' Geoff turned and marched towards the exit, where Alver caught him up as he fumed behind a scrum of haversacks and guitars. 'Bloody students.'

Outside Geoff motioned to a red sports car with a soft black roof. Alver's eyes travelled its length.

'Pretty swish.'

Geoff withdrew his hand from the door and stepped back. 'Not really.' His voice took on a braying tone. 'MGA, actually.' He cocked an inquisitive eyebrow across its roof. 'Seen one before?'

'Never even heard of one.'

'Yes. Earlier version of the MGB.' He became uncertain. 'You have heard of that?'

'Oh, yeah.' Alver thrust out his lower lip and nodded.

'Good. Well, throw your bag in the back then, Alver. Door's open.' Geoff dropped gracefully into the driver's seat and started the engine.

'Good trip?'

Once clear of the town the road was almost deserted, and Geoff swung the car stylishly around the bends as they began the climb into the hills. After a short, unsuccessful foray on the subject of cars, Geoff switched to the matter of his study.

'Well,' he gave Alver a sidelong glance, 'are you familiar with these birds at all? Peregrines?'

'Only from TV.'

'Oh, they're great birds. You'll love them. Terrific fliers.' He slammed into a lower gear to take an uphill corner. 'Terrific killers, too.'

From his window Alver watched the green and black of a fir plantation slide by on the other side of a flimsy-looking fence. 'Yeah. Looking forward to it.'

Geoff nodded. 'I've been here since mid-March, doing it all myself. More or less. Had my brother down this last week, but mostly it's been a pretty lonely job. Pretty grim. Some rough weather, you know?' He looked round and smiled brightly. Alver was staring straight ahead.

'Look out!'

Geoff stamped on the brake as a lamb wandered, bleating, across the road just beyond the bonnet. On the grass verge its mother looked up with heavy-lidded eyes, interrupting its relentless chewing to issue a stuttering belch. The smoky-blue lamb trotted back to thrust its head up into the swollen udder, tail jiggling as the milk flowed.

'Bloody stupid animals, you wouldn't believe ...'

The car started forward again. Geoff turned to Alver. 'Something you'll learn to get used to,' he bawled above the sound of the engine, 'sheep.'

As the miles swept by Alver gazed at the folded green hills that spread away into the distance, at the nearly black, geometric plantations that chequered the uplands, and the smaller woods of skinny oaks and ash clinging to the lower slopes. All the while Geoff pointed out areas of interest, producing slippery Welsh names with evident relish.

At length Alver turned from the rolling countryside. 'What will you want me to do then?'

Geoff's hands fanned briefly on the wheel. 'Well, just help out, really. I need help with the observation - there are two birds, I can't follow them both at once, you know? You take the notes, that's most important. Absolutely everything those birds do goes into those records. If you see one of them take a crap, it goes in.' He flashed a grin. 'Don't worry, I'll tell you just what to write. Dictate. And you'll soon get the hang. Also, you make sandwiches every night to eat the next day while we're at the site. Look, buzzard.'

A large brown bundle of feathers detached itself from a telegraph pole and flapped heavily away over the trees. Alver turned in his seat and craned his neck to follow as the bird gained height, well behind them now, and began to float easily on wide, fingered wings. When he could see it no longer he turned back and nodded.

'Must be about the biggest bird I've ever seen. Flying, I mean.'

'Right,' agreed Geoff. 'You'll see plenty of those. Tourists think they're eagles. Not that there are any yet. Tourists.'

Houses were now very few and far between and the hills had a more desolate air. Distant ridges showed hard and black against a sky drained of colour.

'Brace yourself,' said Geoff, and a second later they rattled across a cattle-grid, then he wrenched the car into a side track which led off through twisted oak trees. The ground was heavily rutted from a month of such manoeuvres.

They pulled up in one corner of an enclosed area of rough pasture, where a grimy blue and cream caravan stood, one end resting on a neat stack of grey concrete blocks.

'This is it.' Geoff jumped out and disappeared inside. Gripping the car's roof for leverage, Alver held the door open with one knee and pulled himself up, finally emerging backwards. He stood and stretched.

Apart from bumping sounds from the caravan the silence was sudden and heavy after the constant drone of the engine. A sheep moaned: several stood around cropping the small field enclosed by a dense, tangled fence of hawthorns. More pale smudges moved slowly on the hillsides.

From somewhere near the wood came a volley of sharp, high-pitched whistles, and a moment later a man appeared, wearing a long waterproof and carrying a stick. At his heels trotted two black and white collies, darting shifty looks towards the caravan. A reddened face beneath a grubby peaked cap gave Alver a guarded look rather like those of his dogs, then a curt nod. Alver nodded back as the farmer made his way to the small cluster of buildings at the end of the track.

'I assume you do have some bins?' Geoff was framed in the doorway.

'Do what?'

'Bins. Binoculars.'

'Oh. Yeah. Sure.'

Inside, the caravan was cramped and dingy. A smell of dust and cooking hung comfortably in the air.

'That's your bed. There's a compartment underneath where you can dump your stuff. Through here's the kitchen.'

Cooking equipment hung neatly from hooks on the wall, variously sized saucepans in graded sequence. Small herb-filled bottles lined a shelf over a tiny, scuffed plastic basin; jars and pots gathered in the shadows of a cupboard set above a small working surface.

'Oh,' said Geoff, pausing. 'I'd rather I did all the cooking myself, if that's OK with you. The thing is, I'm vegetarian.' He stared challengingly at Alver, who nodded but said nothing. 'Actually, I'd rather meat wasn't brought into the caravan at all, really. Just the way I am.' He chewed at his bottom lip, awaiting a response. 'Do you … er … do you eat meat?'

'Course.'

'Oh, I see.' Geoff nodded energetically. 'Nothing wrong with that, of course. Lots of people do. Most of them, in fact.' His fingers rearranged the neat rows of herb pots. 'Tell you what though, I bet over the next couple of months I can make you forget all about the stuff. Meat.' He flashed Alver a boyish grin. From somewhere on the hills came a muffled *baa-aah*.

'You're saying I get to do the washing up, is that it?'

'Makes sense, doesn't it? There's never very much. And no animal grease. It is a lot easier than cooking, after all.'

Alver grunted and turned away, flopping down next to his haversack on the shabby red mattress which was to be his bed. He closed his eyes and lay his head back against the wall.

Geoff followed him through and stood, hands in pockets looking about as if inspecting the place for the first time. He drew back his lips and began a tuneless whistling, rocking gently from foot to foot, then stopped and cleared his throat.

'Is … er … is that alright then?'

He was just about to repeat the question when Alver's eyes opened a fraction. For a second he stared, as if surprised to find Geoff standing there. He nodded.

2. May

By the time April passed into May the routine was established. Half an hour before dawn their alarm would shatter the silence, provoking a chorus of nervous bleating in the field outside. There would be time for a quick breakfast of muesli, which Geoff bought in large plastic bags from the town. Alver would munch steadily, eyes half-closed, whilst opposite Geoff whistled as he sliced banana into his bowl. By the time first light filtered over the hills to the east they were waiting in the shelter, and recording would begin. During the long day, one or the other would wander off occasionally for a break, but the site remained under continuous observation. When it became too dark to watch any more they would return to the caravan, where Geoff would cook, humming and whistling along to his radio in the kitchen while Alver assembled sandwiches on a breadboard balanced across his knees. They would eat, then Alver would see to the washing up, usually finishing to the sound of Geoff's steady snoring. After a sleep of four hours, they would start again.

It rained almost every day and the cold was unrelenting, growing most intense in the still hour of pre-dawn when they had to jog up and down the hillside to keep warm, stumbling in the darkness. Earlier in April it had snowed, and the slopes had been as hard as the iron-grey rocks. Spectacular hailstorms had swept the valley, sending the two of them cowering beneath the overhang, yelling like drunks in the hammering din.

Geoff had an outsize waterproof cape for overwhelming rain, but it proved not quite outsize enough for them both, and they had to take shelter in the car. They would sit there glumly, watching the heavy white mist rolling down from the crags, blotting out the view by slow degrees. Rain ran in through gaps where the soft fabric roof met the window frames. They plugged the gaps with tissue, which became waterlogged and fell into their laps, interrupting bouts of uncomfortable, fitful sleep. On these occasions Geoff did not pretend to be amiable and preferred to feign unconsciousness. Alver would gaze abstractedly into the mist, or open one of Geoff's books on his lap and study pictures of birds and flowers, waiting for the steady drumming of the rain to ease.

Now the rain had passed, leaving the sky a washed-out, dirty grey. Darker sheets of cloud hung on the western horizon.

'Look at that lot.' Geoff scowled at the skies and lowered himself carefully onto his folded cape. 'What a bloody country. I'm not kidding - the whole bloody Irish Sea is constantly being recycled over this place.'

A raven gave a gruff dog-bark as it passed along the ridge behind the shelter; the muffled reply of its mate came moments later.

'Cig Geoff?'

'No thanks.' He frowned, 'Oh, alright ... go on then,' and pulled one from the gaudy blue packet in Alver's hand. 'Wish you'd smoke something else though.' He caught the matches and crouched in the lee of the rock wall, puffing furiously to get the cigarette alight. 'They stink.' He gasped for breath.

Silence returned as Geoff went back to reading his sodden newspaper, pulling a gaily-striped woollen cap down over his ears. Alver faced the cliff, his attention on the bird perched on a high crag over the skyline. For the first time in a month the pattern of behaviour of the birds had altered. Where one bird or the other had remained on the nest always, calling when it was ready to be relieved, now the male, or tiercel, stayed away from the ledge except to bring prey, which the falcon would leave the nest to take from him in a noisy aerial exchange. This indicated that the eggs had hatched, at about the time Geoff had predicted.

A high, keening note came from the bird on the crag, an eerie sound in the heavy silence. Alver made a note. All the most prominent features of the cliff-face had been given names, mostly by Geoff, to make recording easier.

Geoff took off his spectacles and wiped them. 'I've been meaning to ask how you ... how do you manage to sign on the dole, if you're here all the time?'

'Oh, a mate does that for me. Sends me the money.'

'Hmm.' Geoff replaced his glasses and twitched his nose to settle them into position. 'That's not quite legal, is it?'

Alver turned to study him. 'So?'

'Oh, nothing. Just wondered, you know? How ... easy it was. Doesn't bother me. Why should it?' He grinned.

The head of a sheep appeared over a low point in the wall, ridiculous against the grey sky, lower jaw moving, then dropped from sight again.

Alver nodded. 'They've got their hands full. You ought to see those places.' He fell silent for a moment. 'Yeah. You only have to sign on once a month, where I was. They can't cope.'

'Yes, I can imagine. So you'll only miss a couple anyway.' Geoff's manner became serious. 'That bird still there?'

'Yep.'

'I'll just check.'

Near the beginning Alver had spent almost two hours recording the presence of a small, pale rock near the top of the cliff-face, giving Geoff some editing work to do on the notes.

Satisfied, Geoff went back to his paper. 'Don't know why you don't use the spare bins Alver.'

'These are OK.' Alver spoke over his shoulder.

'What make are they anyway?'

'Just binoculars.'

'What though?'

Alver shrugged. 'Anonymous.'

'Hmm. You want to invest in a good pair,' advised Geoff smugly. He flourished his own. 'West German. Best you can get. Leitz.'

'Right. And how much were they?'

'Oh, about three fifty, I think. I didn't pay that of course. Father knows someone.'

Alver turned and raised his own pair. They made a faint clinking sound. 'These cost a fiver. In the pub, before I left. Things look big enough.'

'Yes, well.' Geoff pulled down his ski cap. 'If you ever want a good pair, let me know.' He returned to his paper.

More rain arrived from the west, drifting into the valley in long, almost vertical columns, and they were forced once more to retreat to the car. Alver lifted out sandwiches misshapen by the haversack and glanced idly though the morning's notes as his jaw worked. Reflected in the damp pages was a day of brief glimpses of birds dropping over the skyline, sitting motionless for hours at a stretch, or simply disappearing. Their infrequent calls were all recorded: a muffled chatter as the tiercel attacked something on the moors beyond the valley; muffled shrieks in the mist.

'Don't see how you're going to make any sense out of this lot.' He sucked smears of cheese and peanut butter from his fingers.

Geoff, who preferred his sandwiches with an added layer of jam, provided glimpses of a vivid churning as he replied. 'Don't you worry about that.' His words were indistinct, then a lump travelled down his throat and he smacked his lips. 'This is just the data-collecting stage. I'll soon knock it into shape. Bit of research, dollop of statistics, few diagrams. When the young get big enough to see I'll get the telescope set up, make a few sketches as they develop ...' He waved vaguely with his free hand, 'Nothing to it,' and tore another bite from the sandwich.

'How long d'you think it'll take? Can you work it out?'

'What? This part? Simple.' He slapped his fingers free of crumbs and brushed at his lap, then moved noisily in his seat. 'It's all predictable. Science, you know? Well, laying was completed around 1st April, OK? According to Brown, incubation begins after the laying of the penultimate egg and hatching occurs 30-32 days later. Right. It looks as though hatching started today, second of May, which is about right. Again, according to Brown the young should leave the nest after 35-42 days, so the first should go anytime after the first week in June. There're probably three chicks, so they should all be in the air within the first three weeks of June, all being well. Simple.'

'And then you're finished with them?'

'Correct. Roles and behaviour at the nest-site.'

Alver looked thoughtful.

'What's up?'

'Nothing. Thought it would take longer, that's all.'

'Fraid not.' Geoff seemed amused. 'Assuming all goes well. And it will.'

A sudden gust sent rain spattering against the roof. On the other side of the windscreen grey flowed into green.

'You haven't really told me what you did, before the dole, I mean.'

'Oh, this and that. All sorts.' Alver turned to look through the streaming glass.

'Yeah, I know, that's what you said before,' said Geoff testily, 'but what exactly?'

Alver shrugged. 'Like I say. Nothing very unusual. Factories, building sites. An office, once. Few pubs. Post Office.'

'Which one did you have longest?'

'Computer operator.'

'Really?' Geoff chewed thoughtfully at a forefinger. 'That's interesting.'

Alver slowly shook his head, his eyes dull. 'It's not.'

'No? Well, what attracted you to the idea of this then? Not everybody's idea of fun. Glad you did, of course,' he added quickly.

'Something I haven't done before, a change, you know. Something different. I've always liked birds, watching them, flying.' He turned to Geoff and half smiled. 'Matter of fact, I like it here.'

'Really? Great.' Geoff nodded dubiously.

Late in the afternoon the sky brightened, and they watched from the shelter as the tiercel streaked off to the west in pursuit of a lone pigeon. In the binocular field the two dots merged, drew apart, then merged again as the male peregrine grasped his prey.

'Bang!' shouted Geoff, punching the air.

The bird carried his kill down onto a grassy slope and bent to his work. White feathers drifted in a broken line out over the rocks as the notched beak tore them from the racing bird's breast. Red smeared the hooked and notched bill as the peregrine paused between tugs, one big yellow foot planted on the corpse, to direct a black-eyed glare at his surroundings.

When the tiercel had taken enough meat to satisfy himself he wiped his bill carefully on the grass and lifted into the air, carcase trailing from those brilliant yellow feet, and floated across the cliff-face with an urgent, keening cry. The falcon appeared, falling silently from the nest ledge to follow in the wake of her mate, gradually drawing level as he slowed, and turned on her back to snatch the pigeon in a welter of shrieks.

There was a vague impression of movement on the ledge as the falcon fed the young, while Geoff dictated and Alver scribbled.

'Celebrate with a ciggie.' Geoff took out his tobacco tin, as he always did after a kill, and sat down contentedly with his newspaper. Alver was trying to locate the tiercel again when Geoff gave a spluttering snort.

'Hey, get this.' He brought the page closer. '"Birds hit the Big Time." That's the title. "A new get-rich quick scheme is sweeping the land – chick napping." He looked up and gurgled, then went on. '"The chicks are those of the peregrine falcon, and teams of bird-lovers from London and the Midlands are setting out to scour the mountains of Scotland and Wales where this magnificent bird of prey breeds. The reason? Oil-rich Arabs are offering as much as £2,000 per chick, and hawk-eyed entrepreneurs are swooping in for the kill. After all, why rob banks when a weekend's work could net as much (there are usually three or four chicks per nest)? Although it is illegal (the peregrine falcon is a protected species), fines are likely to be chicken feed compared to the pay-off. Footnote: To the Arabs, falconry is the national sport, and falcons from Britain are prized above all others because of their greater size and power. Aren't we always telling you British Birds are Best?"' Geoff slapped the paper down on his knee. 'What a bloody paper! If it wasn't for the crossword ... Chick-napping!' He gurgled again and waved the paper at the hills. 'Watch out for the Kray twins coming over the skyline.'

Alver glanced at him sharply, then his face relaxed into a grin. 'Well, six grand, for what, half an hour's work? Not bad.'

'Couldn't do it yet, anyway,' declared Geoff. 'They'd need to lift them just before they fly. There're ready for training then. Still, I don't suppose 'crooks' would be aware of that.'

'Where would you take them?'

'Me?'

'Them.'

'London,' replied Geoff wisely.

'Where though? Harrods?'

'Oh, these people know.' He gestured vaguely. 'I have heard,' he continued, turning to follow the flight of a crow, 'that guys go out, early in the season, and watch the birds. And these guys know what they're doing, you know? They work out where the nest-site is, maybe late March, just as the eggs are laid, then they put a cross on a map. Over the weeks they build up a few crosses, then they can either sell the map, or send out their own 'teams of bird-lovers' at the right time of year. No time wasted clumping about searching just when everyone expects them to. Just straight in and out.' He looked significantly at Alver. 'They're rare birds, and this one's a pretty well-known site, you know? We'll have to keep our eyes open.' He sniffed. 'After all, it's my thesis we're talking about.'

The evening wore on, becoming steadily more settled. Curlews called on the moors, and Geoff spotted the tiny, weaving shape of a house martin high overhead making its way westward.

Soon afterwards Alver began flipping small stones at targets within easy reach. Without lifting his head from the book he was reading, Geoff made irritable clucking noises at each clattering shot. Alver selected steadily larger stones.

In the evening hours the light began to fade, gently washing colour from the slopes and crags of the valley. The threat of rain had withdrawn again to the west, and the sky was clear.

The click and clatter of Alver's shots tailed off as he got to his feet and stood against the wall, placing his hands on the cold broken stone. At some point the wind had died away completely, and now all was still. Only the harsh calls of crows sounded in the silence. Furrows creased his forehead as he swung his gaze slowly the length of the valley, wide grey eyes peering into the gathering evening. His lips moved: 'The sea above us.' It was said in barest whisper.

'What?' Geoff stood and shook the dirt from his coat. 'Hoo! Getting a bit nippy.' He moved to the wall to stand next to Alver.

'What was that you said?'

Alver shook his head. The soft piping notes of a ring ouzel drifted down from the tumbled rocks, and Geoff glared up into the darkness. 'If there's one sound that really gets up my nose .... ' He began to pack the rucksack. Soon it was time to go.

Clive Rowland lived in a tiny village hidden in the hills crowding down to the flattish strip of land bordering the coast. The houses, solid buildings of chiselled grey stone with faded bricks the colour of cheese set around doorways and windows, stood in two rows facing one another across a narrow street: a bleak grey gully among the unchecked miles of rolling upland and small, shaded woods.

Clive's time at the house, which he had named *Diolch I Duw*, or 'Thank God', was limited by his job. When there he would drive out into the hills with his folding chair and painting equipment, producing watercolours of the surrounding countryside throughout the seasons which he took back with him to Bristol to sell. Occasionally an acquaintance in the nearby town would show one in the window of his art shop. They were generally described as mournful, Clive's paintings; the skies were seldom blue. For a while he'd produced brighter pictures, but had slipped back into the older, more comfortable style. His favourites, all in this older style, hung on the walls of *Diolch I Duw*.

Clive's job as lecturer in art at a college in Bristol offered undemanding hours and a flexible, relaxed routine. Much of his time was spent drinking with the students in the union bar of the nearby university, and it was here that he had first met Geoff, who now, thanks to Clive, had a pair birds to study for his thesis, a caravan to stay in while he did it, and an assistant. He also had somewhere not too far away to go for a hot bath and the occasional meal.

The flat electric buzz of the doorbell cut across the noise from the TV screen and Clive bent forward to turn down the volume before going to answer it.

'Good evening Geoff. Just watching a bit of television. Come on through.'

Geoff followed him into the living room in his socks, having left his walking boots in the car. He dropped into a padded arm chair.

'Scotch?'

'Great.' Geoff stared at the screen.

Clive poured from a bottle of Famous Grouse into two heavy tumblers.

'The water should be piping hot. I've had it on for a couple of hours now. How have you been managing while I've been away?'

'Oh, I've managed. Great.' Geoff took the drink, making a show of licking his lips. 'I'm ready for this.'

'I expect you're hungry too. I could make you an omelette when you get out of the bath, if you like.'

'Oh, thanks but no thanks. I have to cook when I get back.' While he spoke his eyes were fixed on cavorting cartoon figures. 'Foghorn Leghorn,' he murmured into the whisky.

'So Alver's arrived, has he?'

'Yeah. He's up at the site now. I'm going to pick him up before it gets dark.' He sniggered at the blaring television.

'How are the two of you getting on? Look, I'll switch that thing off.' He made a movement towards the set.

'No no,' Geoff thrust out a hand. 'It's OK. I don't mind.' He turned to face Clive, his eyes flicking every now and then to the screen. 'Alver? He's alright, I suppose. Bit of a surly bugger though. Getting a conversation out of him ... well, he's not exactly the life and soul, is he?'

Clive sipped his scotch between puffs at a cigarette. Greying hair was styled to hang down over one eye, at odds with a fifty year-old face.

'Well, I've never actually met him personally you know. I'd like to very much. You must bring him round one evening.'

Geoff stared at him distractedly. 'Hmm? Yeah. What? You don't know him? You know his mother, right?'

'Yes, a lovely lady. That was a long time ago.' His gaze dropped to the floor. 'Before Alver came along, as a matter of fact.' He looked up again, but Geoff was watching Foghorn Leghorn. 'While I was living in London, oh, years ago. I had to spend some time in hospital there. I got to know her then.'

'That long ago?' Geoff asked the TV screen. 'But you still keep in touch?'

'Always have. Letters though, that's all. Haven't actually seen June for years. I did go to visit, once – they live in Manchester now – but ... well, her husband made it fairly apparent I wasn't to go back again.' Clive gazed into space. 'So we write.'

'Jealous type then?'

'Yes. It seemed as if I represented a part of her life that he wanted to pretend had never existed. Of course, June explained, apologised ...' He frowned into his empty glass. 'Men are often like that – jealous of a woman's past. As you know, I'm sure.'

'Yeah.'

Clive straightened in his chair and lit another cigarette. 'But you're getting on alright with Alver?'

'Yeah.'

'I'm glad about that. For June's sake, really. Actually, she's been quite worried about him. Twenty nine and he doesn't even look like settling to anything. A succession of meaningless jobs, apparently -'

'Yeah.'

'Ah. He showed such promise as well, when he was younger. I thought it might do him good to get away from London for a while. Such a terrible, terrible place. It can destroy people. Do you know his mother hasn't seen him for ages? ... they live up in Manchester you know ... she only hears about him through Leon, his brother.' There was a pause; Geoff stared at the screen.

'Sorry, I'm going on a bit. Another drink Geoff?' Clive got to his feet.

'Not for me Clive. I'll run the bath.' He jumped up and left the room. 'You have one though,' his muffled voice instructed from the bathroom.

'Very kind,' Clive murmured to the empty chair. The sound of running water started as Geoff padded back into the room.

'Go on Clive … you were saying?'

'Ah … yes. His mother gathers he's been rather depressed lately, so I thought of you, your project here, he could help you, and it might do him good as well. The hills, open countryside, fresh air, you know … away from the pressures of the city.' He gulped at his fresh drink and swallowed, closing his eyes briefly. 'It can work wonders,' he muttered almost inaudibly into the glass.

A quiz show had succeeded the cartoons. As the grinning compere swaggered onto the screen Geoff snorted and swivelled in his chair to face Clive.

'He hasn't been married or anything then? He hasn't said much, and I didn't want to ask.'

'Oh no. There was a girl, a few years ago. Everyone thought … but they split up, rather unfortunate circumstances, his mother was very upset.'

'What happened?' Geoff leaned forward.

Clive waved a hand. 'Oh, you know how these things are sometimes. It can be quite a messy business … when people who care for one another … June says it didn't seem to bother Alver much, but I shouldn't be surprised if he's one of these types who doesn't show his feelings.'

'Yeah. A surly bugger.'

Geoff marched back to the bathroom. The gurgling of water stopped, then started again. His voice was muffled. 'She seems to tell you a hell of a lot, if you don't mind my saying so, considering she hasn't seen you for all these years. Alver's mother, I mean.'

Clive took his drink and leaned against the wall next to the bathroom door. It swung shut as he began to speak, sending steam rushing into the room.

'Yes, I suppose she does.' He chuckled dreamily. 'I don't think her husband knows we keep in touch.'

A sucking breath came from the other side of the misted glass as a dim shape sank into the bath.

'He must do,' came the muffled voice. 'He must know your part in Alver coming here.'

'I don't think so. Geoff?' Raising his voice, Clive faced up squarely to the steam-misted glass. 'You must promise not to tell Alver what I've just told you. Just to be on the safe side. It might get back to June's husband … I wouldn't want to cause her any trouble. Alright?'

The reply was inaudible.

'Alright Geoff?'

'Course.'

The staccato hisses of Geoff's version of whistling started up, punctuating the echoing sounds of splashing.

Clive walked slowly to the bottle of Famous Grouse and poured another drink, then sat on the edge of his armchair staring blankly at the flickering screen. The face of a contestant frowned in close-up concentration, and Clive raised his glass with a rueful smile before swallowing.

3. The Farmers

As May advanced, day by day the lines of the valley softened imperceptibly under a green fuzz of plant growth. Grey veils of rain still drifted in from the coast, but the sun's influence between them grew steadily, drawing the chill from the rocks in the afternoon and touching the cliff-face with shadows. Shrill brown and white sandpipers had arrived and bobbed nervously on the flat stones of the stream. More martins appeared, high against the clouds as they hawked flying insects after the long toil of migration. A cuckoo appeared, but was gone the next day. Tiny flowers emerged in the grass; butterflies of blue, white and orange danced above them, winking out of sight whenever a cloud passed in front of the sun. In the valley bottom to the west the dead oaks of the winter carried glossy olive leaves on branches crusted with lichens. Droning bees wandered the slopes.

On the cliff-face the first traces of whitish blossom appeared among the leaves of the small rowan tree which marked the nest-ledge. The tiercel now brought three or four kills a day to the sitting falcon, and occasionally they would make a joint attempt on a flight of racing pigeons. No intruders were tolerated now, and the falcon particularly was ferocious in driving off crows, ravens and buzzards. The chicks, huddled out of sight in a shallow depression scratched out of the thin soil, were never left untended for long. Pigeons provided almost all the diet, with the occasional thrush or starling; the tiercel brought in one of the sandpipers, a limp brown and white bundle, legs trailing. Often the kill was unidentifiable, a shapeless bundle of feathers or a hunk of red meat, plucked raw. Carcases and remnants were hidden among the rocks, the peregrine pushing them deep into crevices with bill and forehead, to be retrieved when hunting was poor. Although small groups of birds could arrive at any time, certain days were pigeon-racing days: purposeful flotillas of forty or fifty birds would appear from the west, on a course taking them straight across the valley. On some days two hundred pigeons would pass within sight of the cliff-face and its eyrie. Wet days, though, when nothing flew but the crows and ravens, were far more usual. At times, when the wind dropped for a few moments, the faint cheeping of the young carried across the valley.

Wish

Geoff and Alver stood against the wall watching a fox on the far side of the valley as it moved among rocks about two hundred yards from the cliff.

'Cheeky bugger,' breathed Geoff. 'It's after the kills.' As if it heard him the fox stopped and raised a sharp, rust-and-white face, ears pricked. It sniffed the air deliberately then went back to poking about among the boulders. Suddenly it flinched back against a rock, lips drawn back in a snarl, ears flattened. Almost simultaneously there came the crackling scream of a peregrine.

'Hoo! They don't like foxes do they?' Geoff was grinning.

The tiercel circled low overhead while the falcon attacked, both birds chattering incessantly. By now the fox had crawled into a hole where two flat rocks leaned together. The falcon dived, pulling out inches from the cringing fox when it seemed impossible, looping back up to her starting point then plunging down again, all the while chattering furiously. At the top of the loop, as she turned, she was flying upside down. Again and again the falcon dived, and then the tiercel was diving too, alternating his attacks with those of his mate. Backing into its hole the fox gathered itself then made a dash for another pile of rocks, then another, still pursued by the screaming birds.

They could see now it was an old-looking animal, with a straw-coloured saddle marking. In a series of short, crawling rushes it moved in stages up the slope until they lost it among the tumbled rocks. For a while they were able to follow its movements via the circling, diving birds, then a flicker on the skyline marked its escape onto the moors. The screams continued, growing fainter as the peregrines swept after it, then they stopped altogether. Soon the falcon reappeared to circle slowly several times over the cliff-face before descending to the eyrie.

'Excellent! Let's get that down.' Geoff rubbed his hands as Alver sat down with the notebook.

After taking down Geoff's meticulous dictation, Alver poured them both coffee.

'Thanks.' Geoff took a swig and reached for his tobacco tin. 'Who'd be a fox, eh?' He screwed up his face as french cigarette smoke drifted into it.

'I wonder what they think of us?'

'How d'you mean?'

Alver looked at the burning tip of his cigarette. 'Well, we sit here glued to them all day, every day, writing down everything they do. We've invaded their valley and their lives, but they've never so much as chattered at us, have they?'

'Don't know what you mean,' huffed Geoff. 'For a start, we never go closer than two hundred yards. We do not influence their behaviour.'

Alver nodded. 'Yeah. I know we're not supposed to. But that fox, it was further away than that.'

'We-ell,' Geoff drawled the word irritably and scratched his neck. 'That's quite a different thing, isn't it? Number one, it's a fox, which wouldn't mind nicking one of the young. Then it would be back for the others. Two, it was on their side of the valley, which might make a difference. Hmm.' He paused to consider. 'Might be interesting, that. Anyway, number three; it was their larder, where they keep grub for a rainy day.'

There was a pause.

'Anyway, what d'you mean, 'think'? They don't think. They just behave according to – '

'Brown?'

' – instinct.' Geoff scowled.

Alver flipped a stone; Geoff waited a moment then took up his newspaper.

'You know what I mean though.' Alver looked directly at Geoff, one eyebrow raised significantly.

'No I bloody don't. You're not making yourself very clear.'

Alver smiled and turned away. Another stone clattered into the nearby gully. After a few minutes awkward silence Geoff got to his feet.

'Just going for my morning constitutional.'

The route Geoff usually chose was well-trodden by now, and he had to be careful to remember the sites of his previous visits. As he walked his head was shaking and he muttered to himself.

He strode across a field strewn with the vertebrae and dung of sheep, although the only occupants were two black and white cows. They stopped pulling up swatches of grass with broad pink tongues to watch listlessly as Geoff marched past to a spot in one corner by a clump of gorse. After a few moments they lowered their heads once more, ignoring the squatting figure.

Geoff studied the pink bells of a foxglove where they had begun to appear low down on the stem. As he zipped himself up he made a cursory examination of the neat, steaming turds, then turned away and strode back the way he had come.

Overnight a soaking mist crept into the valley, reducing the crags of the cliff-face to vague shadows that came and went in the shifting gloom.

The two men huddled behind the wall as usual. Their watches told them it was mid-day, although it was no brighter than the early morning. A peregrine shrieked somewhere out in the whiteness. While the mist deadened the few bird calls and other anonymous sounds of the valley, the voices of the peregrines were harsh and somehow closer in the eerie half-light. Guesses at what each call indicated had had to take the place of observation.

Finally Geoff stood up, wiping his glasses. 'Come on, let's go for a drink.'

The Farmer's Arms, which they had visited a few times over the weeks, was a small, one-roomed pub in the nearby village. Small as it was, it was seldom more than half full: few people other than locals found their way up into the desolate moorlands and hills. Summer, they were told, was a different story. Tourists. Low tables and rickety chairs were scattered haphazardly, apart from an ordered group in one corner where the locals sat playing dominoes. Leaflets in Welsh advertising agricultural shows and markets papered one wall above an open fireplace; a dartboard hung on another. Behind the bar shuffled an old man with long, wavy grey hair, a cigarette permanently between his lips.

'Two pints please.' Geoff tapped one of the beer pumps with a forefinger. The old man cast around for glasses, like a customer who'd somehow found himself on the other side of the bar.

'I'll get these Geoff.' Alver pulled a crinkled note into shape.

They sat in the middle of the room, at a flimsy table which slopped beer from their glasses. 'Perfect', announced Geoff loudly as Alver leant down with a folded beer-mat. The faces of the old men looked up in a cloud of tobacco smoke in the corner, then the clatter of dominoes resumed.

'Clive's back at the weekend Alver. How about coming round for a bath? He's usually got some scotch, too.'

Alver blew out cigarette smoke and rocked back in his chair. 'Yeah. Why not?' He brushed lank dark hair from his eyes.

'You don't seem too keen.'

A shrug. 'I could do with a bath, I suppose.'

An argument swelled in the corner, two elderly voices chattering incomprehensibly in unison.

'Bloody clabber,' said Geoff round the rim of his glass. Then he frowned. 'It's supposed to be a very fine old language, I know that. Older than ours. A language of Nature, you know? Lyrical.' He frowned. 'It's just that, when you hear it - '

' – it sounds like the warm-up to a gobbing contest.'

The frown became a grin. 'Yeah.'

Alver took a pull at his pint. 'Beer's duff too.'

'Yeah.' Geoff was nodding, smiling broadly. He emptied his glass and belched. 'Same again?'

'Sure.'

Geoff brought two more. A domino-player stared through the shroud of smoke. His eyes went back to the game when Geoff looked across.

They drank in silence for a while, then the pub was suddenly full as a party of strangers pushed into the smoky room, incongruous in smart, bright clothes. Overloud English voices silenced the conversation of the locals, who laid their dominoes and muttered, shooting narrow-eyed looks through the smoke.

'Grockles,' sneered Geoff. At the back of the largely middle-aged group stood a girl. He rocked casually back in his chair. 'Still, they brighten the place up.'

The newcomers vacillated loudly over whether to have this or that while the old barman looked patiently from one face to another.

Alver gave them a look of contempt. 'Tossers.'

'Absolutely. Your round.'

'What? You finished already?' He drained his glass. 'And what happened to the two pint driving limit?'

Geoff smirked and held out his glass.

The English group at the bar chatted languidly as though in an otherwise empty living-room.

'Yes, and then we can travel down to St. David's,' piped a woman in blue. 'Tim should have brought the boat out by now.'

A middle-aged man with a moustache agreed. 'Absolutely. Spot of lunch first though. There's a little place Peter put me onto, well off the old beaten, you'd never know it was there. Fabulous sewin, he says, and the lamb of course ... ' he took in the room at a glance. Behind him the barman was muttering around his cigarette.

'Just going to water the horses.' Alver eased his way between the Home Counties, his boot finding a foot beneath it and sinking with his full weight. A gasp was followed by a muttered 'Really!'

Back at the table, Geoff was rolling a cigarette. 'You fish don't you?'

'Yeah. Used to, anyway. Don't seem to have done much for a long time ...'

'Heard about these Japanese fishermen?'

'What, you mean the cormorants?'

'Nah.' Geoff's head shook in a cloud of smoke. 'Anglers, I mean. They pay to fish.'

'So?' As he spoke Alver scratched his chin through his beard, sprinkling the table with tiny white scales of dead skin.

'I mean they pay a different amount depending on what they want to catch. S'true. If the Jap can afford, say, the price of a five pound carp, he hands it over.' Geoff leaned forward over the table clutching his drink as still more people crowded into the small room. 'Hoo! Everybody had the same idea as us. Anyway ... yeah, the Jap sits down, they open a little gate in the side of the pool, underwater, which connects with a tank containing the five pound fish, right?'

More men came in, of various ages but all obviously farmers, wearing the cloth caps and vaguely old-fashioned jackets of dull green or brown they favoured. Some carried sticks. The English group had now been herded to the furthest corner of the room: an occasional well-modulated voice or braying laugh still cut through the gradually swelling celtic burble.

Geoff pressed on, practically bellowing now. 'Must be a market or something. Bloody ridiculous. Anyway, err, these fish have been starved a bit, you know? One swims into the pool, and the little gate is shut. So the Jap fishes until he catches it. It's the only fish in the pond. You know?' He gurgled and swallowed. 'Then he goes home.'

'What if he doesn't catch it?'

'Refund.'

A Welshman who had been leaning steadily closer to catch what Geoff was saying straightened and turned back to his companions, wearing a faintly bewildered look. Another leaned back against Geoff's chair, in conversation with a man whose large, heavy-looking head nodded vigorously whenever he was addressed. His own voice was remarkably deep and resonant. Alver couldn't understand what was being said, but he stared at the man, who noticed and turned slightly sideways. He was repeating everything he said: a few words, then the same few words again, with no change in rhythm or emphasis. The man leaning on Geoff's chair would speak, and the large mouth would make a loud comment then repeat it, sometimes more than once. The large red face saw Alver was still watching and turned further away, setting the other farmer shuffling round against the back of Geoff's chair.

'That bloke's got a face like a TV close-up,' whispered Alver.

Geoff grimaced, making a discreet flapping motion with his hand, then leaned forward and spoke carefully into his glass. 'I suppose you've noticed the girl?'

'Yeah.'

'She keeps staring at you.'

Alver raised himself from his seat to peer through the murmuring groups of farmers. The girl had her back to him. He breathed out smoke and raised his glass, shaking his head.

'She was,' insisted Geoff. 'She must have just turned round. Do you know her?'

'Don't be daft. Who would I know round here?'

Geoff leaned forward. 'Well, ever since she came in with that bunch of grockles she's been staring over here. It's not me though. I watched when you went to water the horses, and her eyes were on you all the way. You're the one, Alver.' He took his glass and went to rock back in his chair. His head bumped the farmer's back and he looked up angrily, but the flow of Welsh continued uninterrupted.

'They need watering again.'

Alver made his way to the toilet, pushing through the huddled English to the door marked *Dynion.*

When he came out the English were clumping noisily from the room. Geoff turned in his seat and sneered them all the way to the door, then rolled his eyes towards the table in the corner. One old face twitched in what could have been a smile.

As Alver sat Geoff leaned forward. 'She's not with the grocks after all. Quick though, she's just about to leave.'

Turning casually in his seat Alver watched the girl as she crossed to the door. In the doorway she turned and looked straight at him. Pale eyes stared from dark, plain features; long black hair framed an oval face. Not a girl's face. Older. Then the door was swinging shut and she was gone.

Geoff nodded, smirking at the uncertain look on Alver's face. 'Well? You do know her after all, don't you?'

'No. She did remind me of someone though. Can't think who. No,' he ended decisively, 'I don't know her.'

'Well, it must have worked both ways, the way she was staring at you.'

'Yeah. Well it must have been two other people.'

'Bet it comes to you.' Geoff nodded again as he smoked. 'You should have said something.'

'Such as?' Alver stood up. 'Another drink, Geoff?'

Geoff waved a hand, his face fused to the glass. He drained it, banged it down on the table, which wobbled free of its propping beer mat, and belched. 'No more.' He fumbled at his wrist and stared at his watch. 'Hmm.'

Outside on the steps they heard the bolts slide into place behind them, then the renewed clatter of dominoes.

'In there all day, I shouldn't wonder,' said Geoff loudly, then hiccupped. 'Bugger!'

The valley dwindled as he rose effortlessly to where the wind sang in his pinions. His brain recorded the distant flight of a crow, the nervous movement of a rabbit in the gorse; the powerful, poised figure of his mate as she hunted the air below him. Behind his empty eyes the unhurried ticking of a reptilian patience awaited the spur of that irresistible, fluttering signal. Each twist of his head brought a different part of the valley floor and the air above it into the snapping clarity of his binocular vision. A splash of wrongness screamed from the slopes: a hole in the world. Long ago they had ceased to hunt over this place. It no longer existed. On the home ledge far below the cries began again. He swung smoothly round into the wind and searched on. Then an ugly sound. He started.

'Do what?'

'Should know this one. Greek goddess of retribution and vengeance. Seven letters.' Geoff chewed his pencil.

'No idea.' Alver focussed on the tiercel circling fifty feet above the falcon.

'Oh bugger it. I'm not in the mood anyway.' He hiccupped and thumped his chest.

'What do the Stars say today?'

'You and the bloody Stars.'

'Come on. They're a laugh.'

'OK, let's see. Gemini: "It's time for a celebration. There will also be changes in your domestic life. You should feel more settled about a lot of things. A visit to the seaside is likely." Same old waffle.'

'What about - ,' but Geoff was already reading out his own.

'Taurus: "Try to ignore your worries about the future and your relationship with someone close. Better times are coming. Enjoy yourself and make plans you intend to carry out in the summer." Baloney.' He fell silent. Alver smiled as he scratched in the mud with a stick.

Geoff roused himself. 'Hey, listen to this. Apparently,' he held the page closer, 'there was a bare-knuckle fight for the championship of England and Wales, held in "an open plot, somewhere in the Welsh mountains", last weekend.' He looked up. 'Wonder where?'

'Big place, Geoff. I mean, they stretch for miles, don't they?'

'Bet it was round here though. Wish we'd known.' He followed his finger 'Iago Roberts, the Radnor Bull, champion of Wales, met – '

'Who won?' The tiercel now circled alone. The mist had vanished.

'Hang on, hang on ... "Black Bob Webb of Essex. Spectators numbered over two hundred, many from London ... blah blah ... Rolls Royce, Mercedes ... expensive clothes, heavy gold jewellery ... wads of notes changing hands ... the air thick with Cockney accents ... The police arrived just after the scene had been vacated, as they often seem to in such cases." Yeah. Bet the Chief Pig had his money down. Oh, the guy from Essex won.'

'Hmm?'

'Black Bob, the guy from Essex won.'

'Oh. Yeah.'

'Well.' Geoff folded the newspaper and tucked it into the rucksack, at the same time taking out the toilet roll. 'It's me for a constitutional before I nod off.'

As the steady tramp of his feet faded Alver leaned on the wall and his eyes glazed. He sat alone on a cheerless beach on the east coast: cold blue sky, thin wind, the grey North Sea deserted, sluggish waves moving on the gritty sand. Small knots of holidaymakers shuffled doggedly up and down the beach. It was summer, then - June, July maybe. 'Taking off to the Sea for a while,' and here it was. The hitch-hike back to London still to come. He fell asleep.

A muffled thudding woke him. Three figures chased another along the shore towards him. They ran right at the water's edge, as if they were playing a game. But these weren't children. The three pursuers wore suits. The man in front, in jeans and T-shirt, and two of the others were in their twenties, the last man older. They caught him almost in front of Alver and began to hit him. All three swung at the doubled-up figure. Greasy black hair swung and jerked over the man's face as he was hit. It seemed impossible that there should be room for them all, but the punches and kicks rained in. They stood in the surf, grunting with the effort of their work. One swore and swore, his face red and contorted 'Slag fucking slag you fucking poxy slag.' A gold medallion swung at his chest, a man of squat power twice the age of the others. His fist swung into the man's stomach as he swore, each blow measured, unhurried. Something gold, a ring, caught the sun in a glinting arc. They stepped back, the body slid into the water. Still they swore and kicked, then stopped, panting and red-faced. The powerful man came up the beach. His voice was a hoarse bellow. 'Nobody saw nothing!' The silence filled with the sea and gulls crying, and panting. 'Anybody says different, they get the same as 'im.' The brutal smeared voice of the east end that Alver knew so well. The man backed away glaring. He adjusted his jacket, turned, strode after the other two.

Alver looked cautiously around. A figure moved away, at the corner of his vision, like a shadow. In the sea the crumpled jacket and trousers moved, but it was the rocking of the waves as the tide came in. He was quite sure the man was dead.

He found a pub and watched a mirror behind the bar as he drank. In this mirror he had first seen Dawn.

A sheep thudded past as Geoff returned.

'Anything doing?' He clambered over the wall with an effort and slumped down on his cape.

'No. I'm dying of thirst though.' There was no coffee left. 'How about some water from a mountain stream?'

Geoff sucked in his breath, shaking his head. 'I wouldn't do that.' He looked suspiciously at the hills. 'Eighty per cent sheep's piss. And the other twenty's probably lead. Don't forget it runs right past that disused mine at -' Here he produced a long, phlegmy Welsh word.

'Oh yeah.' Alver sat down reluctantly. 'I suppose you're right.'

'Still,' Geoff said, clasping his hands behind his head, 'You've been living in London. You're probably riddled with lead already from the petrol fumes. Cabbages as well. You eat cabbage, don't you? I read they concentrate the stuff in their leaves. How long since you left Manchester? Still, I don't suppose it's much better there.'

Alver's eyes were on a buzzard as it wheeled over a distant ridge.

'Yeah. You've probably got a brain full of the stuff. Tell you what, when you go on that trip to the seaside, don't go swimming. You'll drown.' Geoff sniggered and sat up. 'Come on, let's have another go at that crossword.'

Moments later they stood to watch one of the red kites that occasionally wandered into the valley as it floated by behind the shelter, each successive lazy circle carrying it further eastwards. Bigger even than the buzzard, it drifted on, huge dark wings flashed with white, forked red tail flaring in the sun as it angled and twisted to catch the shifting breeze. Alver watched until the bird finally blurred into the distance.

Geoff sat with the crossword. 'Here you are Alver, one for you. You're a football fan. "United's Martin." Six letters.'

'Buchan.'

'Great.' He filled in the answer, then gave Alver a sly glance.

'Thought any more about that girl in the pub then?'

Alver drew a weary breath. 'Woman, you mean. What's there to think? Just some woman.'

'Mmmm. Well, she hasn't been in there before.'

'Neither has that bunch of English snoots. And you won't see them again, either.'

'That's different. They were genuine grockles.'

'Yeah.' Alver looked away, muttering to himself. 'Not like us.'

The evening was well advanced and the mist had begun to creep back when one of the peregrines rose quickly from the cliffs with a strange, crooning call. From the nest-ledge appeared the falcon, to follow her mate upwards with the same soft cry.

On the opposite side of the valley binoculars were raised in anticipation. Other peregrines passed through the valley from time to time, and while most were driven off by the resident birds with screaming ferocity (more than they showed to any other bird or animal), some brought an entirely different reaction. The birds would rise eagerly, aware of the newcomer before it was visible even to binoculars, calling continuously with soft notes quite unlike their normal harsh screams. The three birds would then fly together, not with the purposeful strokes of everyday flight, but elegantly, without haste. In a rippling line they would soar and wheel, dive and make passes at one another; two would tangle claws and fall together as the third followed them down, then they would separate and race skyward again, calling all the time.

On the handful of occasions it had occurred it had usually been at this time of day – dusk - and had continued until the birds were lost in the gloom.

Shadowy shapes swooped and flickered in magnifying eyes as soft, ethereal cries floated on the evening.

'Can you see a third bird Geoff? I can't.'

Indistinct against the darkening sky, the peregrines fell, spinning like leaves.

'Visibility's lousy. What we're seeing is three birds, two at a time.'

'Hmm.' Alver's binoculars creaked as he pushed at the focussing wheel.

The two birds rose steadily, wings stroking the air with exaggerated deliberation, growing smaller and smaller. Geoff started to pack the rucksack, but Alver continued to watch until the wavering specks merged with the evening.

'I'm sure there's only two.' His voice was a whisper. 'How is that? There must be another one. Has to be. Why can't we see it?'

'Come on Alver, let's get moving.' Geoff peered at his watch. 'Twenty two-oh-seven. You can note it all down when we get back to the van.' He held out the rucksack for Alver. 'Come on. I'll knock out some savoury pancakes with cabbage. Don't drool. Guaranteed lead-free.'

'I can still hear them.' Alver's head was cocked to one side, his eyes closed. Geoff paused, then thrust out the rucksack again. 'No you can't. Come on.'

They made their way along the dimming slopes, scattering ghostly clusters of sheep. In the rocks below the ring ouzel tried a few tentative notes, but fell silent when Geoff glared into the gloom.

'Funny,' mused Alver as they trudged, 'how they like some birds and not others.'

'Nothing funny about it. It's simply one of their offspring from a previous year passing through.'

'Hmm.' Alver smiled in the darkness. 'You think so? They were really having a great time though, weren't they?'

'Yeah.' Geoff's voice was heavy with sarcasm. 'They were having a great time. Yes Alver. Quite. I'll be sure to mention that.'

As they reached the car Alver gazed up at the night sky. 'Another misty day, by the look of it.'

Geoff grunted as he dug in his pocket for the keys. The leather of his seat creaked as he swung into it. He paused, then snapped his fingers.

'Nemesis.'

'Do what?'

'The Greek goddess of retribution and vengeance. Nemesis.' He turned the key and the engine caught at once. 'Knew she was in there somewhere.' His fingers went to a switch and the track sprang into view as the headlamps snapped on. Fence-posts loomed to either side. Further off, where the light failed, the eyes of sheep glittered in the dark.

4. The Sphinx

The lizard waddled across the rock, sluggish but intent. Filmy lids slid across beady eyes as it neared the edge; then it was over, flopping onto the heather, long bony toes scrabbling for a grip.

Alver reached down and replaced it in the middle of the rock. 'Determined little bleeder.'

Legs working before they touched, the sinuous grey body started immediately for the edge again. A pattern of stripes and bars beaded the dark parchment skin; tiny claws scratched tiny sounds from the rock. Again Alver retrieved it as it toppled. Later, when the sun got up, the reptile would flicker across the heather like light itself, impossible to catch.

He leaned back against the cold stone and gazed out across the waving brown sea of heather. Forgotten, the lizard catapulted from the rock as if the swollen nerve in its head could no longer see beyond its edge. The heather rustled and it was gone.

The outcrop sat on the brow of the hill to the east of the watch-point, and much higher. At dawn, with the light in the east, the hulking rocks suggested some massive, brooding creature, but as the shadows advanced with the sun so the illusion slipped slowly away. By mid-morning the Sphinx, as Geoff had named it, was an unremarkable hump of rock on the skyline. Beyond the rough slopes of heather and grass, north and east into the distance ranged line upon line of hills, growing successively bluer and less distinct.

In the eye of Alver's binoculars an anonymous smudge on the slopes below hardened into the buttress and piled grey stones of the shelter and in it Geoff, his head just visible as he crouched behind the telescope. A single peregrine circled over the cliff, dark and tiny.

Alver's gaze lifted from the one familiar valley to the crooked, shadowy lines of countless unknown others among the distant hills. To the north the ranges lifted much higher, harsh-looking grey-black ridges beyond grassy slopes mottled with the pale grey of sunlit rock. The highest, most distant peaks had been dusted with white for much of April.

A buzzard wailed, the only sound but for the breeze which was stronger up here, plucking and slapping at the scrubby clumps of heather and gorse. Alver lay back in the heather behind a weathered slab, the tough woody branches yielding beneath his weight.

Slowly it grew warmer. Drowsiness overcame him as the sun moved slowly in the sky and the air filled with the dusty buzzing of grasshoppers. He smiled at a small rustle somewhere out in the tangled heather, then the smile faded as his face went slack.

In a place where it was always dark a shadow took shape and grew. Birds flew to meet it. Soon it blotted out the sun. Alver's eyes snapped open.

A kite floated overhead, black against the sunlight. Leaning lightly on the breeze it turned its head to study him.

'Not dead yet,' he murmured. The great bird's tail flared as it allowed the wind to carry it away and out of sight beyond the hill.

Alver was approaching the shelter when both peregrines left the cliff, climbing rapidly, as a faint ticking noise in the air grew steadily louder. Geoff jumped to his feet behind the wall and started waving. The sound swiftly became the clatter of helicopters as two huge grey and olive machines swept along the valley, below the height of both the shelter and the nest ledge.

'Buggers!' screeched Geoff. A figure waved behind a window.

'Two hundred and fifty feet, you irresponsible twats! Not fifty!'

The noise was cut short as the helicopters vanished round a bend, but the reverberations lingered. Geoff fumed on. 'Right! They'll hear all about this! It's against the law. They shouldn't be any lower than two hundred and fifty feet! That's the limit.'

Faint chattering from the cliff-face subsided as Alver clambered over the wall.

'That must just apply to the planes Geoff. The jets.'

'It applies to every bloody thing!' He still glared after the departed helicopters.

'But they have to land sometimes, don't they, helicopters? Rescues? How can they do that if they've got to hang around at two hundred and fifty feet?'

'Hmm.' Geoff made a quick sweep with his binoculars. 'They've calmed down already. Interesting.' Taking the notebook, he began to write. 'It's OK. I'll do this.'

Alver settled in and shortly began pitching stones at a piece of sheep's skull showing white on a grey pile of rubble.

'Don't use all the stones, Alver. I'll need some for the next time those buggers in the helicopters come along.'

'Maybe we could make some sort of weapon.'

The wind swung from the north back to the west, and the sky once more became a racing grey mass of streaks and patches. Rain spattered down at irregular intervals, never quite enough to send them to the car but sufficient to cause discomfort and turn the trampled ground of the shelter gluey.

During a break they watched through the telescope as the falcon fed the young. The powerful grey and cream adult bird now used the lip of the ledge instead of going in towards the back, pulling flesh from the carcase held beneath one yellow foot and offering it with a slight tilt of the black-striped head. The downy white chicks were now visible, but their number was uncertain. Each appeared to eats its fill before the falcon moved on to the next. Afterwards one threshed the air with stumpy wings, although as yet no feathers were visible. The view blurred then dissolved as more rain coated the lens.

Late in the afternoon they spotted a sheep perched on a ledge high on the cliff-face. It was one of the scrawny animals that passed their lives in the uplands, scratching food from the bleak moors and gullies. Unshorn creamy coats and dangling tails gave them the appearance of dogs as they scrambled among the rocks. By comparison the sheep of the lowlands looked overfed and plodding. The sheep on the cliff had followed a patch of grass out along the ledge, nibbling as it went, moving more and more slowly as the ledge narrowed, until it could go no further. Through the telescope its jaws could be seen grinding mechanically, bulging eyes gazing disinterestedly ahead. Two hours later it was still there.

'Why doesn't it back out?'

'Because it's a sheep,' said Geoff smugly. 'Why else?'

'So?'

'Have you ever seen a sheep walk backwards? No. And you won't. Sandwich?'

'Ta.' Alver took a mouthful and reluctantly began to move his jaws. 'How about something different tomorrow? Peanut butter's alright – '

'This is the best peanut butter you can get,' Geoff spoke indistinctly around a mouthful of food. He had brought his peanut butter with him, several jars of it, from Bristol.

'Yeah, I know that. But every day? How about ham – no, not ham – cheese and tomato, something like that? Eggs?'

'Not eggs,' said Geoff darkly.

'Alright, not eggs. Cheese and tomato then.'

'With jam.'

Alver swallowed.

Without binoculars the sheep was a pale smudge near the top of a sheer grey wall. Two birds tumbled against the sky as a peregrine dived at a larger, tattered brown shape which fled wailing over the skyline. Alver took the notebook and licked the stub of pencil, speaking as he wrote. 'Be quite something when they're all flying about.'

Geoff grunted.

'Watching them learn to fly. That'll be something.'

'Well, it'll mean the end of this pissing rain, for a kick off.' The floppy top of his striped woollen hat hung damply to one side. 'As soon as they're in the air it's finito. They can watch each other learn to fly.'

Alver studied the busily munching, determined face.

'So you can tell all your mates back home you'll see them in a month's time.'

'Do what?' He turned back sharply, then his eyes narrowed. 'Christ, it is, isn't it? A month. I thought it would ... it would ... It doesn't seem very long.'

Geoff levered off the lid of his tobacco tin. 'It's not,' he beamed. 'What'll you do, when you get back to civilisation?'

'Oh ... something.'

'Back to computers?'

'No. Something different.' He looked away. 'What about you?'

'Knock this thesis out, of course. Bit of research, won't take long. Then kiss this country goodbye, for a month or two anyway. Somewhere nice, in the sun. Greece, maybe.' He watched his cigarette smoke as it was caught by the wind and dragged over the wall. 'I've got a lot to see and do. I'm only twenty three, not an old man like you.' He darted a grin at Alver, who stared thoughtfully at the ground.

'What job will you do though? Will you do more with peregrines?'

'No thank you. Egyptian vultures, maybe. Something that's got the sense to live where it's warm. No, only kidding.' He glanced sideways at Alver. 'As a matter of fact, I thought I might cross over into your field. Computers.'

'Yeah, you are kidding.'

Geoff shook his head. 'Nope. Why should I be? Systems though, not quite what you were doing. Get a job anywhere, abroad, plenty of money. I want to make my pile and get out by the time I'm forty-five, tops – all set to start the next century in a state of applied leisure. That's the plan.' He sat up. 'Right now though I'd be satisfied just to be somewhere that's got women instead of bloody sheep.'

On the cliff-face the forlorn pale shape was motionless.

'What about you then Alver? I expect there's a girl awaiting your return from the wilderness?' Geoff slid a look around the rim of his spectacles.

Alver gave an unintelligible grunt. He tossed a stone, then picked up another. 'Not exactly.' His arm swung. The wind had dropped and the stone fell into the nearby gully, faint echoes adding to its clatter. 'Don't know how you can look so far ahead. Anyway, what about this woman of yours? What was her name?'

'George,' smirked Geoff. 'Georgina. Everyone calls her George. Yeah, there's definitely something going on there.' His face changed. 'Trouble is, while I'm down here out of circulation, there's this creep at the Uni who'll try to move in. Actually, that's one of the reasons I'm trying to get her to come down for a day or two. OK?'

Another stone clicked and the piece of bone jumped.

'Hey, save some for the flyboys. That's OK with you then? If George comes down? It's only fair to warn you. OK?'

'Sure. Be nice to see a girl.'

Geoff blinked across at him as he polished his spectacles then replaced them and looked at his watch. 'Just time for an evening constitutional.'

Alver nodded vaguely. As the footsteps faded, his eyes unfocussed.

Surrey rolled past as he kept the motorcycle to its rocketing course. The fast lane, M23. Hands clenched on the handlebars, his whole body in a fight with the wind. One hundred miles an hour and Dawn hammered on his back slow down. The road led straight in front, no curves, and the white needle crept to one-oh-eight, one hundred and ten miles an hour. He was flying. To either side the mirrors blurred with vibration. All he could do with the machine now was point it. If he let go, they would be blown off. A curve and he eased the throttle forward. The exhilaration and terror faded. His body ached as it strained forward, but now there was nothing to strain against. He could move his head. Dawn's voice, a thin, faraway sound. He flipped up his visor and turned. 'Enjoy that?' An inaudible answer. He shouted again, but still couldn't hear her answer above the roar of the engine, which was drowned by the rush of the wind. At seventy he flicked the indicator and moved into the middle lane. A dawdle. A clear blue and white English day as they passed into Sussex. The sign read Brighton 19. Dawn could not warm up. Wandering the seafront at his side, her arms folded, face set and pale. An occasional brave smile and I'll be alright in a minute. A photograph as she sat on an upturned boat: blue jeans, long blonde hair, black leather; underneath, a black bikini, but it was too cold, crabs in the sea, and he swam alone while she watched. An icy ordeal. In the pub they sat wordless, each staring into different space. Say something. She could think of nothing, didn't feel quite with it. Take no notice. I'll be alright. He studied her lovely face, finding it vacant and child-like. The blue eyes of a doll, lips pale and too full. Men watched. Drink up and get your leather on. He pushed the heavy motorcycle from its stand and the front tyre flattened. It had been stabbed. Youths in parkas lounged against scooters and jeered. No spare inner tube, no repair kit. It was late and the shops were shut and it was cold. Dawn cried then, blubbing miserably on a wall on the seafront, but he shouted at her until she stopped. She was cold. Let's find a bed and breakfast. They spent what cash they had in the warmth of a pub near the sea, then stayed on the beach till morning. The mods came into the pub, there was a fight. Afterwards his left hand wouldn't close properly. The beach was very bad, and there was trouble with the police. When the shops opened they hadn't spoken for eight hours. Dawn shook with the cold as she signed the cheque. While he worked she sat with her hands gripped between her thighs and stared out over the English Channel. Another motorcyclist stopped and offered to take her back to London on his BMW. Finally he had finished. He itched with sweat, and blood showed in the oil on his hands. As they approached the outskirts of London he reached back, patted her thigh. Later that night she agreed she'd behaved badly. I'm sorry. I'll get better. Let me make it up to you.

When visibility finally failed that night, the sheep was still high on the cliff, stranded on its ledge, unable to go back, fading with the light into the grey of the rock.

After the evening meal Geoff stood undressing by his neatly turned-back bed while Alver did the washing up.

'Excellent cauliflower cheese!' His lips smacked loudly in appreciation. He was nude as he slid between the crisp, white sheets. 'Goodnight.'

''Night.' Alver rubbed wearily at the plates, wincing at the squeaking sound made by the dishcloth. The fitful light thrown by the hissing mantle caused heavy, dancing shadows, making the clean plates appear dirty. Black-eyed bean skins clogged the plughole. As he worked to remove them his chin sank slowly to his chest, then jerked up again with a jolt. A chorus of honking came from the geese at the farm while he rubbed his eyes. Rain began to patter softly again on the roof.

He looked around to get his bearings. In the shadows beyond the light of the little kitchen his sleeping bag seemed humped into the shape of a sleeping body. Picking the blankets from the floor he dropped his jeans and jumper in their place and went back into the kitchen, shutting his eyes as he turned off the light, then opening them to make his way to his bed. Geoff's steady snores already filled the cramped darkness.

For a while Alver lay gazing at the stars, then idly started to masturbate, his hand moving sluggishly. The geese called again and his hand quickened, then slowed once more as his cheek sank into the pillow.

Next morning when they arrived in the valley the sheep on the cliff was gone. Two days later, on the 20th May, they discovered that the shallow scrape in the earth behind the sloping ledge held not three eyasses but four.

Geoff jumped up from the telescope and punched the air. 'Bang! Four young! Cleared the three point four mean!'

'Great. That'll mean an extra day or two as well, won't it?' Alver smiled at Geoff's beaming face.

'Hmm. Yeah, I suppose it will. Still, can't be helped. That's assuming they all fly of course, that they don't get nicked or anything. What an outstanding pair of birds!'

The tiercel sat motionless on his usual vantage point, a grizzled chunk of rock thrusting out into space from the top of the cliff that Geoff had named the Fist.

Geoff sat down with the notebook, then looked up. 'This calls for a celebration.'

'What, the Farmers?'

'Stuff the Farmers. Tonight, why don't we go into town?'

'Mmm. The bright lights eh?' They were both grinning.

When they left the valley that evening there were still several hours of daylight remaining, but Geoff wasn't worried.

'Their routine's pretty well established now. I'll be able to cover it alright, in the notes. Nothing for you to worry about.'

On their long, winding way down through the hills Geoff slowed and stopped the car at a narrow side-road walled with ash and hawthorn. He fingered his beard as his foot pushed gently at the accelerator. 'Hmm. Wonder if old Clive would fancy a jar?'

Alver said nothing, and Geoff reached down for the hand-brake then paused. 'You don't mind, do you? He did say he wants to meet you. After all it is because of him that you're here. Me too, come to that. In a way.'

'Where would he sit?'

Geoff leaned back, reaching behind the seats to clear books and boxes to one side. 'It's a decent evening for once. I'll take the roof off. You can sit in the back here and Clive can sit in your seat, rest those poor old bones he's always complaining about.'

The car swung into the side-road then stopped again. 'If that's OK with you?'

'Sure.'

Alver sat in the car outside the silent grey house while Geoff went inside. Nothing moved apart from a smoke-coloured cat stalking the gutter. Moments later Geoff appeared, with Clive, pulling on a jacket, behind him. Alver pushed open the door and climbed out.

'Alver. Delighted to meet you at last.' Clive smiled broadly and thrust out a hand.

He took it and nodded. 'Clive.'

Geoff worked his way around the screws holding the roof in place. 'Won't take a minute.'

Presently they were cruising through the outskirts of the seaside town, then the town centre itself, the narrow, shadowed streets ringing with the cries of gulls on the seafront.

Alver pointed at a sign. 'There, Geoff. That's good beer. You can park up on the front.'

Geoff steered the car to a stop in front of a wall of tall, pastel-painted Victorian guest-houses. Gulls squabbled noisily on the rooftops.

Before climbing out, Clive turned in his seat. 'I see you like your beer then Alver?'

'Not just that. I've had enough of being perched up here like a prat.'

Geoff was already pushing open the door of the pub. A handful of people sitting in silence on stools at the bar looked up as they entered.

'What're you on tonight then, Clive?' Geoff's voice boomed in the small quiet room.

Clive pulled out a wallet. 'Let me get these, Geoff.' He smiled hesitantly at the guarded faces of the locals.

'No, it's OK. You can get the next one.'

Alver had disappeared to the toilet. Geoff lowered his voice a fraction. 'Don't forget, Alver's on the dole. He hasn't much money.'

Clive nodded emphatically. 'Right Geoff. I do appreciate that, you needn't worry. I'll have a pint of bitter, then, if I may.'

Alver returned and the three of them drank in restrained silence for a while before Alver whispered, 'This place reminds me of the Farmers.'

Geoff's voice was louder. 'This place makes the Farmers look like Las Vegas.' Voices murmured in Welsh at the bar.

'Beer's different class though,' added Alver. 'Everybody else seems to be drinking the mild. Have to try that.'

'Yeah. We'll have to come in again sometime.' Geoff placed his empty glass on the table.

They walked up a windy street lined with shops, all of them now closed, as Geoff described to Clive the discovery of the fourth eyas.

'Fascinating. I really must come up there to see you. And them, of course, the birds. Perhaps I should bring my paints.'

The next pub was more lively, and a Space Invader machine stood in one corner. 'Civilisation!' crowed Geoff, making straight for it.

'What will you have Alver?'

'I'll get these Clive.'

'No, I insist. Bitter, is it? Or mild, isn't that what you said, back there?' Alver hesitated, then peered along the bar. 'That was back there. Guinness will do, please.'

They found comfortable chairs at one of two tables in a small alcove. A steady rumble of whines and thuds came from the corner where Geoff stood, fingers twirling and stabbing. Clive took his drink across to him then threaded his way back between the tables.

'Cheers then Alver.'

'Cheers.'

Their eyes dropped as they raised their glasses and swallowed.

'Well, and how are you liking the open-air life up here Alver?'

'Fine. Bit wet, but I don't mind that. It's a good place, I like it.'

They smiled at each other and sipped their drinks. Clive leaned forward and motioned with his head towards Geoff's tense figure.

'He's not so bad, you know.'

'Who said he was?'

'Oh, nobody, nobody. Ah, Geoff and I know each other very well, and he's a smashing chap, but he can get a little, well, bossy, sometimes. He likes to have his own way, does our Geoffrey. I'm sure you know what I mean.' He winked as Geoff loomed over the table.

'Any tens, you two? Or fifties?'

Alver hid a smile with his glass. Soon the machine was rumbling again.

'Have you seen your mother lately Alver? How is she?'

'Oh, she's fine. Cigarette?'

Clive pulled one from the blue pack, then studied it. 'Ah. French.' He read the name from the packet with a flourish, '*Gitanes*,' and snapped a flame from his lighter. 'Their word for gypsy, isn't it?'

Alver shrugged. 'Is it? Gypsies? No, I haven't been in touch with home for a while, as a matter of fact. I'll have to give them a bell.' He blew out smoke. 'How come you know my mother, anyway?'

Clive glanced across at Geoff. 'Didn't she say anything ...? About me?'

'Just that you were a friend from a long time ago.'

'Yes, that's right. It was when I lived in London, oh, years ago now.'

'Hmmm?'

'I had to spend some time in hospital. That's where I met your mother.'

'What was the matter with her?'

Clive looked flummoxed, then began to push a beer mat round the table. 'Nothing, nothing at all. She worked there, actually. As a nurse.'

'Really?' Alver stared at Clive through a film of smoke. 'I didn't know that. I didn't know she was a nurse. Funny, she's never mentioned it. I thought, well, I thought she'd only ever worked in offices.'

'It was a very long time ago.'

'Hmm. How long? I mean, before … was I around?'

Clive gave a chuckle. 'No, you weren't around. As I said, a long, long time ago. You're making me feel old now.'

'I wonder why she packed it in? Nursing? I'll have to ask her about it.'

'No no, I shouldn't think she'll want to be bothered about things that happened way off in the dim mists of time. Obviously it didn't suit her. She didn't do it for long anyway, as far as I know.'

'I know London pretty well. Which hospital was it?'

Clive looked into his glass at the swirling beer.

'Oh, Alver, I can't remember. A small one, out in the countryside somewhere. Not actually in the middle of London.'

'Oh. Well, anyway. Obviously you must have kept in touch off and on for me to be here now. Thanks for that Clive. I appreciate it.'

Clive's hands fluttered. 'Quite alright. Glad to be of help. And it is a lovely part of the world, isn't it? When you get to know it, as I do now – '

Geoff barged into a seat between them and looked from one to the other, light glinting on his spectacles.

'Whose round is it then?'

While Alver was at the bar there was a sudden increase in the noise around him. A body slumped onto a stool next to him, and a flushed, grinning face mumbled apologetically.

'A grand match!' shouted the barman above the hubbub. The man on the stool nodded deliberately, his eyelids drooping and his grin lop-sided. Geoff scowled across to the corner where men pulled tables together in front of the Space Invader while others took out guitars.

'Oh no! A Welsh bloody folk club! Pain and grief!'

Clive's hair flopped down over one eye. Cigarette in one hand and drink in the other, he moved it with a boyish toss of his head. 'I think there's been a rugby match, Geoff.'

'Hmm.' Geoff's attention had moved to the next table, where two young girls had just sat down. They murmured to one another while darting looks around the room. One noticed Geoff watching and looked down at her drink.

The jangle of guitars began as Alver returned with the drinks, and loud voices were raised in rousing, incomprehensible song. A small knot of people made a constricted attempt at dancing.

'Bloody clabber,' muttered Geoff, and one of the girls giggled into her hand. Clive got up and edged his way round the table, then struggled out of his black leather jacket and tossed it back onto his seat.

'Just going to turn the old bicycle around.' He wandered off among the lurching figures.

'I see he's on the whiskies already,' observed Geoff, leaning back in his chair.

Alver shrugged. 'When you get to his age you can't take the volume.'

'Clive can, don't you worry.'

'He seems like a reasonable bloke.'

'What, old Clive? Yeah. He's a laugh.' Geoff lowered his voice. 'I feel a bit sorry for him, actually. I mean, I hardly know the guy, but he doesn't seem to have any friends, always hanging around with students back in Bristol, you know?'

Alver nodded.

'Whenever you go in the bar, there he is. Bit lonely, I suppose. Still, if that bothered him he wouldn't spend so much time up here.'

'I like him.'

Geoff wasn't listening. At the next table two colourfully dressed youths had taken seats opposite the girls. Their voices were loud and drawling.

'Listen to those two pillocks,' whispered Geoff, from the side of his mouth 'pretending to be Americans.'

Men stood about in small, noisy groups, arguing and laughing, while cigarette smoke formed a cloud the length of the bench where the women sat in an unbroken line beneath a closed window, bending forward or leaning back as they chattered. The men were young or middle aged, and mainly burly, in red or black rugby club pullovers with a badge and initials at the breast; most had long sideburns and sported dignified beer bellies. Above the music, which nearly everyone now sang along with, came the bellow, 'Did you hear what Terry Holmes said at half-time?'

At the next table a girl's voice squealed, 'Canada? My cousin lives in Canada, in Calgary.'

The place was packed and noisy now as another Welsh song was followed by one in English, about the Rhondda valley. Everyone but for the scattered pockets of slightly embarrassed-looking English sang along. People stepped to one side, still singing, to make way for an old man in cap and spectacles who tottered slowly past collecting glasses, smiling and mumbling to himself, his dark jacket shining dully under the lights. One of the drunks who sat with his head on his arms was prodded upright and handed a banjo, which he took dazedly and began to strum like a madman as the room sang *Freight train, freight train, going so fast.* A body huddled quietly on the floor in a corner.

'What's everyone having?' Geoff's face was flushed and determined.

Clive leaned anxiously forward. 'Are you sure you should, Geoff? Don't forget, you are driving, and - '

Geoff snatched his glass. 'Whisky, is it, Clive?' He disappeared into the crowd.

Clive stared at the jostling figures and shook his head ruefully. His hair once again hid one eye.

'A bit different from the Farmers,' shouted Alver over the noise. He passed Clive a cigarette. 'I suppose they did win? It's hard to tell. Bit different from our football fans, isn't it?'

Clive was rapt as the voices swelled. 'Just listen to those voices, Alver! Doesn't it lift you quite out of yourself?' His mouth moved to the words, although no sound came. *For I've got silver in the stars, and gold in the noonday sun, and gold in the noonday sun.* He smiled wistfully then leaned forward to snap his lighter.

'I understand your brother's doing very well for himself, Alver.'

'Oh?'

'Yes. Your mother mentioned something about it. Television isn't it?'

'TV, yeah. Leon's doing alright.'

'What about yourself? I mean, do you have any idea what you'll be doing when your work here finishes?'

Alver rocked back in his chair and gazed across at the guitar players, smiling helplessly at one another as they played.

'Oh, not really. Something.'

'Ah, you'll be staying in London, will you?'

Alver shrugged. The room was singing *Me and Bobby McGhee.*

'Perhaps you'll go back to Manchester?'

'No. Not Manchester.'

Clive tossed back his hair and leaned forward, his lined, slightly glistening face straining as he shouted. 'It's just that, if you wanted to make a change, you know, you could try Bristol. It's a nice place, it really is. All the amenities of a big city without all the pressures. Much, much nicer than London. You could stay with me, I've a flat there … until we find you somewhere of your own, of course. A job, perhaps. You know what they say. 'It's not what you know, it's who you know. Geoff's there as well, of course.' He picked up his glass, saw it was empty. 'London's a terrible place.' His head shook sadly. 'Brutal.'

'Thanks Clive. I'll see. Very good of you though, considering we've just met.'

Clive's eyes locked on Alver's. 'I … we're all here to help each other, Alver, aren't we?' He looked away again. 'Well, see how things go. Something may come up for you.'

'It usually does.'

'You will bear it in mind, though?'

'Sure.'

Geoff returned. 'Bloody bedlam. If you're a regular you've only got to glance at your glass twenty yards from the bar and they're falling all over themselves to serve you. There you are, Clive. A treat.'

'Ah. What is it, Geoff?' Clive held the glass to the light, head on one side as he peered at the clear, yellowish liquid.

'Don't worry, it's whiskey. Sheep Dip, they're calling it. Tried it before?'

Clive gave a tight smile, looking uncertainly from the glass, to Geoff, to Alver. He shook his head. 'No, but thank you Geoff.'

There was a slightly less noisy pause between songs. On the next table the two girls and the Canadians talked in subdued voices.

Geoff's eyes slid sideways as he drank, then he sneered, leaning across to Alver to whisper, 'Now they're pretending to be interested in Welsh folk-dancing. I mean, as if.'

Clive leaned forward, looking from one to the other, and started to speak, but the guitars started up again and he closed his eyes and sank back into his chair.

'How's the Sheep Dip, then?' bawled Geoff.

Clive nodded and raised his glass. The room sang, *I feel so broke up, I wanna go home.*

Geoff took out his tobacco tin as he turned to Alver. He indicated Clive with a tilt of his head. 'Well, what else would you get for the man who'll drink anything?'

As the tempo of the guitars increased, a figure slumping against the mantelpiece was tapped on the shoulder with a clarinet. Swaying upright, he took it and licked his lips, then put it to his mouth. Music tumbled out as his fingers flew over the keys; people alongside him clapped and stamped as he played. When the song finished he handed back the clarinet and slumped once more over the mantelpiece.

On a stool at the end of the bar perched the old man in the dusty, shiny suit, his feet dangling above the floor, his head nodding, a faint smile playing on his wrinkled, stubbly face. The landlord moved cheerfully among the tables himself, a curling black pipe clenched jauntily between his lips, empty, froth-ringed glasses crammed between his fingers.

The two girls got up and left with the Canadians, and their places were taken by an elderly couple who sat in silence, staring into space, sipping their drinks, oblivious to the noise.

'What it's like to be married,' observed Geoff in a low voice, then more loudly, 'Come on, Clive. Time for one more.'

Clive's head jerked. 'Ah, yes, of course. My round, I believe.'

The clarinettist surfaced again for a faster song. Midway through he struggled frantically out of his rugby club pullover and threw it through the smoky air towards the window, where one of the women caught it, shook it out and folded it neatly, placing it on the still behind her without interrupting her singing.

Clive brought their drinks, went back for his own.

Geoff hiccupped. 'Bugger!' He wiped a hand across his mouth. 'Every time I have more than two pints - ' another hiccup.

'Drink your pint from the wrong side of the glass,' suggested Alver.

'Crap!' Geoff held his mouth tightly closed as his body lurched. 'Bloody old wives' tale.' He stood to let Clive in.

'Oh, Clive,' he began as they sat down, 'We'd like to come round for a bath next week, both of us. So that's two nights. Say Wednesday and Thursday, OK?' Without waiting for a reply he leaned back in his seat with his drink, staring off into the whirl of bodies and smoke. Clive saluted solemnly.

When Alver laughed, Geoff shot a suspicious glance back at Clive, then hiccupped. 'Bug-ger!'

As they left, Clive touched Alver's arm. 'Your mother ... she is alright, isn't she? I mean,' his slightly unfocussed grey eyes looked straight into Alver's, 'really alright?'

'Yes, of course she is.'

'Good, that's good. She's a wonderful lady ... your mother. Tell her ... no.'

'I'll tell her I saw you, and that you asked after her, OK?'

'Yes. Yes, that's it.'

The night was still and black as they climbed into the hills; without the roof the amplified sound of the engine throbbed in the silence and the frame of the car shook. At one or two bends the car slithered, causing Alver to sway in his raised position behind the seats.

'Steady as she goes there Geoff.'

Geoff spoke around one of Clive's kingsize cigarettes. 'Just making the journey a bit more exciting for you, nothing to worry about. Actually I'm an even better driver when I've had a drink. S'true.'

Below them the town was now a sprawl of cold white and orange lights in the blackness. In the back, Alver sang softly as he stared up into the night. 'I've got silver in the stars and gold ... '

Entering Clive's darkened village they passed the chapel, grey and grim in the moonlight, and the small graveyard.

'Liveliest place in town,' said Clive in a stage whisper, waving a hand at the scattered headstones.

Not a single light showed in the village; as they said their goodnights they found they were whispering. From somewhere in the night came the sudden hoot of an owl.

'Next Wednesday, then,' whispered Geoff.

Clive nodded. 'And we must have another night out together, sometime. I've thoroughly enjoyed myself. Even the Sheep Dip. Goodnight.'

The leather seat creaked as Alver lowered himself into it.

'Goodnight Alver.' Clive leaned closer. 'And do think over what I said.'

Alver nodded at the pale, serious face. 'OK Clive. See you.'

Just outside the village Geoff pulled in abruptly and switched off the engine.

'Just have to dip my sheep.' He gave a snigger punctuated by a hiccup and jumped out, slamming the door behind him. Sheep moaned in the darkness as the two men urinated side by side into the hedgerow.

'Nice bloke, Clive,' said Alver as he shook himself.

Geoff hiccupped, sending water spraying into the air. 'Yeah. He's a laugh, old Clive.'

Though here there was no wind, higher in the hills it still blew, and over the moors, a distant, almost imperceptible rushing in the night, one long, restless sigh.

Geoff shook his head and chuckled as he slammed the door. The engine fired and they moved off.

5. Food for free

Geoff dictated as he squinted into the telescope. 'Fourteen twenty. All four eyeasses visible, one wing-exercising. No feathers visible yet.' He looked round pointedly until Alver threw his last stone and began to write.

'What's to eat tonight then, Geoff?'

'Thought I might knock out some savoury pancakes. There's a bit of spinach left, plenty of black eyed beans.'

'Plenty.' Alver nodded resignedly to himself. 'I'm off for a constitutional then.'

Geoff grunted as he fiddled to adjust the telescope's focussing wheel.

After a lengthy walk Alver found a place beneath a line of stunted hawthorns at a field's edge, each tree bowed away from the west and its ceaseless winds. As he crouched the buffeting of the wind was cut off abruptly, and in the silence his eyes glazed. There was Dawn, laughing among a group of other students, stopping as she saw him, her eyes shining. At his feet a large, black beetle moved slowly over the grass, knobbled black legs rising and falling laboriously. When it was almost out of reach he picked it up, holding it inches from his face.

'Places to go, beetles to meet eh?'

Jointed black antennae waved sluggishly as the legs continued their mechanical, slow-motion march. A small blob of fluid appeared on the insect's face and grew; it was the colour of blood.

Alver recoiled, dropping the beetle and falling back against the trunk of a hawthorn, scrabbling with his hands for a grip. A movement caught his eye and instinctively he looked up to see a peregrine glide silently over. For an instant light glinted in a dead black eye, then the bird was gone.

He struggled back into a squatting position and cleaned himself. The beetle had disappeared. As he walked from the field he sucked fingers stabbed by gorse needles, ignoring the sheep that scrambled from his path or watched silently with blank, slit-pupilled eyes.

Afternoon passed quickly into evening. Small groups of gulls began to straggle inland, making for the reservoirs where they would roost for the night. In a fit of boredom, Geoff had once counted them all as they flew out at first light and again when they returned in the evening. The figures were identical.

He sat now making corrections and improvements to his sketches of the young birds. 'About halfway there now,' he murmured.

'Do what?'

'The eyasses. They're about twenty days old, halfway to fledging.'

The falcon had recently brought in a large pigeon, the young had been fed, and their squealing had died away. From the Fist the tiercel looked down into the valley, his crop bulging. Even a buzzard flapping wearily along the skyline drew nothing more than a harsh chatter.

'Geoff? Do you ever dream about flying?'

'You mean like a bird?'

'Yeah.'

'Don't think so. I dream about falling. Everybody does that though, don't they? Falling and spiders.'

'Hmm. Must be watching these birds every day, I suppose. I've always dreamed about it, but now ... it's nearly every night. Maybe it's the country air, more oxygen.'

'Beats walking, I suppose. Don't you ever crash?'

'Yeah, that's what usually wakes me up.' His hand felt around the patch of bare, dusty ground in which he sat. He moved the few feet to where the stones started again. 'It's a big place to fly around in, though.'

'What is?'

'Your mind.' Alver had taken a small, sharp stone, and was scratching the surface of a larger one.

'Yeah. More space in some than others.'

There was a sharp rushing sound as Alver hurled the scratched stone over the wall. The three clicks it made on the rocks of the gully rattled with echo.

'When you think about it, the world inside your head must be as big as the world outside.' He reached for another stone and began to scratch. Geoff grunted.

'All of us, everyone carrying around a world in his head, each as big as this one.' He waved at the valley, then sent the scribed stone curving into space.

'Yeah.'

'And each of those worlds is full of people, of course. I'm in yours, you're in mine, we're both in hundreds of others. All the people we've ever met carry us around in their world, somewhere. And we're in this one. Have you ever wondered whose this one is?'

'Depressing thought.' Geoff grinned. He glanced up at the bleak sound of a crow on the skyline.

'Everyone you know is in there somewhere, wandering about, and sooner or later you get to meet them all. Some of them maybe you've never even seen, only heard of.'

'In dreams, you mean.'

Alver smiled at Geoff and nodded slightly. 'In dreams, some of them.'

'Well if I see you flying past in my world, I'll wave.'

'I know you will.'

'And if you see someone falling through yours - '

'I'll wave too.'

Another scratched stone flew over the wall. 'Might not be you though. You said yourself, people are falling all the time, everywhere.'

'Yeah, well.' Geoff shook himself. 'You'll be meeting a few more prospective denizens next weekend. Some friends are coming down for the day. Maybe stay overnight.'

'From your college?'

'University, yes. Couple of blokes. And George, I told you about her.'

Alver smiled. 'Good for you, Geoff.'

'Well, in a sense. That prick James is coming as well. He's the one ...' He saw Alver's smile fade and nodded gloomily as he patted the sketches into a sheaf on his knee. 'Don't worry, they won't be wanting to sleep in the van.'

There was a pause, then he added. 'You know, there's nothing to stop you inviting people up here. As long as there's not too many. I meant to mention it before.'

'Right.'

'Your brother, for instance. What about him?'

'He wouldn't be interested, Geoff.'

'Oh? Well, anyone you like, really.'

As evening deepened the ring ouzel's mournful piping floated down unremarked from the dim grey gully to the west of them.

That night Geoff spotted a sheep tick on the back of Alver's arm, just above the elbow. A small dark body protruded above the flesh where the mouthparts lay buried, ingesting blood. After twenty minutes with matches, pins and a pair of tweezers, they had succeeded in digging out the body sac and most of the buried head, leaving Alver with a shallow, bleeding hole in his arm and two unretrieved dark specks just visible at its bottom. Geoff cleaned it and covered the mark with a plaster.

Rain began to patter down, and as they lay in bed the caravan rocked gently every now and then with the gusting wind. Geoff's snoring stuttered for a few minutes before settling to its usual steady rhythm. Alver stroked his penis absently as he waited for sleep. Soon his head fell to one side.

He soared high in brilliant air above a shimmering sea, every cell alive and exuberant. A rapid beating of his wings, then he banked to glide smoothly down towards the shoreline. Breeze tingled over him. People dotted the beach, and he knew them all. He shouted to them to look up, but heard only a wordless cry. Waves pulsed slowly towards the beach; figures stood where the waves ended in the sand. He shouted again, and one looked up, a square, dark face with a drooping black line of moustache. Turning, he skimmed low over the sea, seeing the silver flashes of fish. The waves were swollen, and roared as they thumped into the sand. His friends were distant dots on the beach, but for one who lay at the sea's edge. The waves moved faster as he swooped. A face tilted, and it was a girl. A woman. Grey eyes caught him as the sea roared; then silence, and he was falling, and had forgotten how to fly.

Rain drummed on the roof as they sat in the car. Alver dozed, making occasional mumbling sounds, while Geoff studied a book open on his knees, munching thoughtfully at an apple.

'Spot-on book this, Alver.'

There was no reply.

'Alver.' He prodded impatiently at him with the book.

Alver lifted his head and opened bleary eyes.

'This book,' Geoff gave him a quick glimpse of the cover. 'Spot-on. Tells you how to live off the land.'

Moving stiffly in his seat, Alver made a dry, cracked sound in his throat and ran his tongue around the inside of his mouth. 'What, rustling, poaching and that?'

'Nah. Berries. Leaves. Mushrooms, toadstools, you know? Seaweed. It tells you what to look for and how to cook it.' He waited for a response.

Alver rubbed his eyes.

'Well, I'm in anyway. Wrong time of year for the fungi of course, but I'm sure I've seen one or two of the other things in my constitutional territory.'

'Hmm. Thought you meant sheep. Eating sheep.'

With a last flurry the rain stopped abruptly. A figure appeared at the edge of the nearby field in a long, hooded overcoat. His voice carried on the wind as he shouted and whistled to the two sprinting collies. Sheep flowed together.

'In fact,' said Geoff, winding down his window and peering out, 'I think I'll go for a wander right now.' He climbed out then leaned back in, holding the door open. 'You must admit, a vegetarian diet keeps you regular. See you back at the site.' The door slammed. Slowly the squelching tramp of footsteps receded.

Pipits fell around Geoff in their song flights as he climbed; the grass on the slope was slick with water but he followed the sheep trails that cut diagonally across the gradient and soon he could look back and see no sign of the car. Orange-brown butterflies rose in spirals together, floating away on invisible currents as he approached. The sun had appeared and from the scattered woodlands came the slow swelling of bird-song.

He stopped in a rock-filled gully and bent to pat the ground at the foot of a large, weathered slab, then took the book from his pocket and sat carefully on it, resting his back against the rock. Within minutes the quiet, hidden gully echoed to the steady rhythm of snores.

Alver slid the last few yards to the shelter on his back, after the air-cushioned soles of his boots lost their grip for the umpteenth time. Inside he spread Geoff's cape over the sticking mud and assembled the telescope, focussing on the cliff-face as he squirmed into a comfortable position. The swivelling barrel moved in progressively smaller jerks as he located the spot he was looking for.

The falcon stood at the front of the ledge, the pale shapes of the young moving lethargically in the background. Magnified sixty times the stark black and white mask glared out from a grainy backdrop of grey rock. Touches of yellow around bill and eyes did nothing to relieve the primitive cruelty of the image. White breast feathers touched with buff and barred with grey hardly blurred the solid muscle beneath. Outsize yellow feet gripped the rim of the ledge; black talons glinted. *Flick* the mask glared straight at him, *Flick* it turned away. Somewhere out of sight the tiercel screamed. *Flick* and again the cold black eyes fixed him with a burning stare. An instant later the peregrine dropped from the ledge and beyond his circle of vision.

The drawn-out rumble of a distant jet hung heavily in the air as Alver jotted in the notebook, heavy features set in a frown of concentration. A clatter of sliding stones signalled Geoff's return. He leaned against the wall for a moment breathing deeply before he climbed over. In his hand he carried a white plastic carrier bag.

'And?' Alver nodded dubiously to the wall where Geoff had propped the bag.

'Man's right. The whole countryside's crawling with stuff you can eat.' He thrust an arm into the haversack and brought out the sandwiches.

'OK, I give in. What's in the bag?' Alver reached across and peered in, then recoiled. 'Nettles?'

'That's right.' Geoff gave him a challenging stare.

'Nettles sting you Geoff.'

Geoff sucked in a breath. 'Boiling destroys the formic acid,' he said patiently. 'They're supposed to be very good. Bit of onion, plenty of seasoning. Don't worry. Far better for you than baked beans.'

'What baked beans? Anyway, how did you pick 'em?' He watched as a tiny brownish insect appeared briefly among the leaves then disappeared purposefully back into the green mass.

Using the same heavy voice, Geoff explained. 'If you grasp the nettle firmly, the spines are crushed, and don't penetrate the skin. Therefore, you don't get stung.'

'Oh. It really works then, does it, this grasping them firmly?'

'Of course. Just a matter of confidence.'

'You used gloves.'

'Not necessary,' said Geoff briskly, diving a hand back into the rucksack. 'Apple?' He tossed one across and began to check through a list as he bit into a second.

Alver scratched his chin and cheeks, idly watching the white cloud of scurf as it drifted away. A movement on the opposite slope caught his eye and he swivelled the telescope to focus on a rabbit hopping cautiously among rust-coloured skeletons of bracken.

Geoff tossed away the core and looked up from his list. 'We're going to need a re-stocking trip into town soon. Anything special you want?'

'Just cigarettes.'

'Yeah.' He rolled the end of the pencil between his teeth. 'Wonder if I should get anything extra in for them at the weekend?'

'They can have my nettles.'

'They can get something to eat in the pub or whatever. Be easier, anyway. No, I'll just get our supplies.'

In the caravan they searched one another for ticks, but found none. While Geoff washed, Alver removed a boot and peeled off the sock to examine his foot. It was white, with what dirt there was collected fairly neatly between the toes. As he wriggled it back into the damp, dark sock he shouted above the noise of the radio. 'You go for your bath on Wednesday if you like Geoff. I'm not that bothered, really. I don't need one. A wash'll do me.'

Geoff thrust his head round the corner, wiping water from his face. Without glasses his eyes looked small and lost. 'But you never have a wash. Not a proper one. Anyway, I thought you'd like to see old Clive again.

Alver shrugged. 'We can go for a drink sometime, can't we?'

'Well, it's up to you.' He ducked back into the kitchen. 'Nothing like a good bath though.' The thin sounds of his whistling cut through the murky music-blare, then came the dull clank of pans as he started to prepare the meal.

Alver lifted his feet onto the bed and lay back, eyes closed. The music faded as Dawn leaned over him, set a plate before him. Steak. Glasses heavy with red wine; her face coloured with it. Her chin cupped in her hands, blue eyes shining across the table for him. He made love to her beside the half-empty plates and glasses. Silently, like a mime. She willed him to speak, he refused. She held him; he kissed her and shrugged free. The cooling meal, her little plans. He opened his eyes, his mouth a tight line.

'Here we go. Savoury pancakes, blacked-eyed beans, and nettles.'

Alver studied the plate.

'Come on, it won't bite.' Geoff forked a green mouthful towards his face. 'Mmm … not bad at all. Go on, try it.' He grinned happily, green shreds flecking his teeth.

Wish

Alver was sitting at the Sphinx when he saw the distant arrival of their visitors. It was a clear morning and visibility was good; the three coloured dots wavered uncertainly, then made straight for the shelter. He looked down at the grey pellet he rolled between his fingers, cast by a peregrine as it sat on the Sphinx: a pressed mass of indigestible material – splintered bones, a few feathers, embedded at one end a small metal ring from the leg of a pigeon. Somewhere a man waited for the pigeon with that number, and wondered why it was overdue.

Carefully, Alver placed the pellet in a small crevice in the rock, next to the two barred grey feathers that showed blue when they caught the light. Dawn ran her tongue around her lips, face pale in sleep. Jaw muscles moved as her teeth ground. Slack face of a child. Always sleeping, never dreaming.

Geoff explained in a loud, clear voice '... so they haven't brought in a kill for - what? - almost three hours. You should see something soon.'

'Your birds perform on time for you, do they Geoff?' The man gave a broad smile as he rested his back against the buttress at the rear of the shelter. He spoke languidly, his voice resonant and overloud. Drawn rakishly over the dark curls of his head was a coloured woollen ski-cap similar to Geoff's.

'Not exactly James, not exactly. But the eyasses require a certain mass of food per day, which means, more or less, a certain number of kills. The next one's overdue, that's all. Ah. Here he is.'

Alver clambered onto the wall.

'George, James, Derek, this is my ... er, this is Alver.'

There were nods and mumbles, and he finally dropped from the wall into the shelter and fixed James with a look until he moved away from Alver's usual place, shrugging to the others.

Derek cleared his throat.

'So while they're up there circling now, they're actually hunting?' He crouched at the wall with binoculars, while George and James shared the spare pair.

'That's right,' replied Geoff authoritatively. 'They're in neutral now, but you just wait till they get their asses in gear.'

George giggled and he grinned at her. 'What's the matter?'

'Nothing.' Her long blonde hair swung as she shook her head.

'And how long do you have to spend like this, just sitting around?' James's voice was a booming drawl. 'Must get a tiny bit … monotonous, no?'

'Oh, sometimes,' said Geoff cheerfully. 'You're lucky it's not raining. It usually is. We've had a couple of pretty bad days, haven't we Alver? Even so, when you get a storm raging in the valley it's quite an exhilarating experience. You really see the grandeur of the place.'

'I bet you're looking forward to getting back to civilisation though.'

George's was an open, slightly pudgy face, with eyes that went to slits when she smiled. 'There must be things you miss.'

Geoff looked at her and grinned. 'Oh, one or two things I suppose. On the other hand, here we're really in touch with reality. We see practically all the daylight there is, the air's clean, we see the seasons change. We're relaxed, aren't we Alver? Laid back, in fact. And healthy.'

'Cigarette, Geoff?' drawled James. 'Or have you given them up?'

Geoff reached over and took one.

'How about you, Alver?'

Alver shook his head. 'No. Ta.'

'I see you've still got the same prehistoric little car, Geoff.' James leaned across with his lighter. 'About time you traded it in for something a bit more grown-up, isn't it?' He smiled pleasantly.

Geoff scowled, one hand in his pocket as he waved the other, holding the cigarette. 'Nothing wrong with that car. As a matter of fact a guy wanted to buy it just last week. Offered me a grand, on the spot.'

'You should have taken it. On the other hand, the poor chap obviously wasn't very well.' James smirked at George, whose face shook as she suppressed another giggle.

Geoff started to reply, but George recovered and interrupted. 'What are the people like round here, Geoff? Do you get along with them alright?'

'Oh, they're alright. Very different … it's so slow, such a slow pace. It's obviously the people here who've got it right, though. We're too impatient. We don't take the time to enjoy the journey, just the destination.'

'Have you got to know anybody?'

'Well, no, not really. We don't have much contact with them, you know? The local farmer ... we get along pretty well with him.'

James tilted his face to blow smoke carefully into the air. 'These people you say go around stealing birds, Geoff, are they Welsh?' He leaned against the rock, hands clasped in the pouch of a chalk-blue fisherman's smock.

'No, English, most of them.' Geoff's bearded face became wary.

'I've even read that people are paid to protect birds against being stolen ...?' James directed another plume of smoke into the air.

'Yeah. That's right.'

'English again, no doubt.'

'Well,' Geoff shrugged, 'I suppose so.'

'So it's the English doing the studying, the English doing the stealing and the English doing the protecting. In someone else's country. It all seems very bizarre.'

All eyes were on Geoff, except Alver's which watched James coldly.

'You mean the Welsh would prefer to be left in peace?' asked George.

'Well, I would, wouldn't you?'

Geoff's brow furrowed as he sucked at the tobacco, but Derek interrupted before he could speak.

'One of the birds has shot off after something.'

They followed the flickering grey shape as the tiercel streaked westwards, Geoff shouting out a commentary. 'That's the male.' The bird suddenly clapped its wings to its body and dropped at breathtaking speed, then beat again, dropped, losing height rapidly in steps while gaining tremendous distance. Abruptly, a second bird was in the field of view. 'Racer!' The two shapes merged, then parted, 'Missed!', but the larger bird swerved with blinding speed and closed again, anticipating each desperate plunge and jink of its quarry like a shadow. Again the shapes merged. At the last possible instant the pigeon fell like a stone as the peregrine snatched empty air.

'What happened?'

Geoff ignored the questions as he searched the sky and rocks for the pigeon. The peregrine had shot skywards and now moved in slow circles, gradually losing height.

'It got away,' announced James in a consoling voice.

'Yeah. Not sure what happened there.' Geoff continued to sweep the valley floor with his binoculars. 'The pigeon must have had a bloody heart attack at the last minute. They don't usually miss easy ones like that.'

'Must be everyone watching,' suggested James, 'making them nervous.'

Geoff reached for the notebook. 'I'll do the notes on that one, Alver.'

Further down the valley a pair of ravens had nested in a steep, rocky gully, using a heavy pile of sticks perched high on a sheltered ledge. Their eggs, laid in February when blizzards and hailstorms swept the valley, had long since hatched, and now the two crow-like young flapped heavily along the skyline, the two adult birds gliding easily above. The four huge black birds were driven off by the falcon in a welter of screams and agitated croaking. She returned towards her perch on the Fist, swerving at a hawthorn to dislodge a crow and send it hurrying off down the valley.

Alver watched the tiercel as it gave up searching for the missing pigeon and swept in a long curve to drop onto the grass of the Larder slope. Moving awkwardly on the uneven ground it lifted one large yellow foot and planted it deliberately before following clumsily with the other. After a few moments' inspection of the rocks it thrust forward its head which disappeared into a crevice to re-emerge with a dark mass dangling from the bill. There was no leaping effort as the bird lifted easily into the air, the carcase now trailing from hooked black talons. Muffled shrieks sounded as the larger silhouette of his mate appeared, grappling briefly with him to take the prey. She circled once in front of the cliff-face, forcing the young to a frenzy of piping before dropping lightly onto the ledge among them.

Alver lowered his glasses as George was talking, her hair swinging with the movement of her head, and Dawn's hand crushed cigarettes and packet, dropped them to the floor, No more. And later, sitting in a chair, legs crossed, arm crooked to point the cigarette at the sky, soft lips parted to blow smoke. He smiled.

George smiled back. She was holding a bag towards him, 'Chocolate, Alver?' brushing away hair as the wind whipped it across her face.

'Ta.'

Her eyes followed his hand, and the smile dwindled. Alver turned the hand over. The body of a tick stood out from his wrist like a piece of grit. 'You little bleeder!'

'What is it?' George's voice quavered.

'A tick.'

Geoff bustled over. 'Another of the little buggers? They must be fond of you.'

'A tick?' George had got to her feet and was nervously smoothing down her bright red anorak.

'Don't worry,' said Geoff over his shoulder. 'They live on sheep, normally. Alver must remind them of one. We've only had two in all the time we've been here. Or rather he has. I think they must live up in the heather, when they're between sheep, as it were.' He peered at Alver's wrist. 'They're a bugger to get out, though.'

Derek eased Geoff aside and took the wrist. 'Yeah, I've seen these little bastards before. You have to make sure you get the whole thing out. Got any spirit, any whisky or anything?'

Geoff shook his head and pushed at his glasses with a forefinger. 'What for? You're not going to amputate?'

'It relaxes the thing's muscles, makes it loosen its grip,' explained Derek in a matter-of-fact voice. 'George? Got any perfume?'

'Yes. Do you want me to get it? It's in the car.'

'Tweezers as well, if you've got them,' shouted Derek after her. James had gone too.

A pale line appeared low in the western sky while they were gone, spreading slowly across the sullen grey sheet of clouds. The cold, streaming wind became fitful.

'*Youth Dew*,' announced James loudly as he and George neared the shelter. 'Should send the other ticks wild. Sheep too, I shouldn't wonder.'

Derek soaked some cotton-wool and held it over the dark stub for a couple of minutes, then gripped the tiny body in the tweezers, teasing it gently from the flesh.

'Got him.'

'Thanks, Derek.' Alver took the tweezers carefully and examined the tick.

Geoff leaned over. 'Here, try looking at it through the wrong end of your bins. It'll act as a magnifying glass.'

The three looked in turn while George and James glanced amusedly at one another with raised eyebrows. A ruby-brown body the shape of a bean trembled in the hard, shiny grip of the tweezers; beyond dangled a cluster of hooked limbs and mouthparts.

'Evil-looking little bugger,' breathed Geoff. He tapped the tweezers carefully on the wall then picked up a stone and ground the tick into the rock. A tiny smear of red showed where the body-sac had ruptured.

James leaned across to whisper something to George, who giggled and hid her face in her hands.

Geoff smiled enquiringly at them.

'Just telling George, Geoff, by the time you get back to Bristol you should smell ravishing.' James noticed Alver's stare and started to smile, then looked away.

A buzzard flapped in frantic circles, struggling to gain height as a peregrine shot from the cliff, its chatter harsh and cracked. The much larger buzzard rolled to present its talons, then righted itself and struggled on when the screaming shape had passed.

'What a horrible noise,' said George. 'It sounds so vicious. I don't know how you stand it all the time.' She gave a nervous smile. 'It gives me the shivers.'

Late in the afternoon two foxhounds appeared on the skyline to the east, trotting over the rocks, veering off every few yards into the heather following their noses, holding all the time to a westward line. Nearing the cliff they came under attack, but blundered on stubbornly along the skyline, flinching, the peregrines now hoarse with rage, and disappeared to the west, still apparently lost.

Geoff set up the telescope for George to watch the young being fed with a golden plover, snatched by the tiercel from its breeding grounds on the moors.

'Ooh, you can see red. Blood!' She looked up, her face a comic mask of revulsion.

'That's right,' chortled Geoff. 'Meat eaters, you know. Disgusting habit.' He rummaged in the haversack and brought out flask and sandwiches.

Seeing this, James dug in his pocket and brought out a set of keys.

'Hey, fetch the wine, would you Derek?' He tossed him the keys.

Geoff beamed as Derek climbed from the shelter. 'Excellent! Sandwich, anybody?' Made by Alver, only last night. Peanut butter and banana. George?'

'No, thanks all the same, Geoff.' A shadow of the telescope look crossed her face.

Geoff shrugged and moved across to crouch in front of Alver. He spoke in a low voice as Alver took a sandwich. 'Look, you wouldn't mind, would you, if we wandered off a bit early? This lot could do with something to eat, a drink maybe, you know?'

Alver nodded, teeth fixed in rough granary bread.

'I could come back later, pick you up in time for a drink, OK?'

'Sure.'

Geoff shuffled back and his voice regained its usual volume. 'Well,' he rubbed his hands together. 'What say we go for a bite somewhere, maybe a drinkie or two? In, say ...' he flourished his watch, '... oh, about half an hour? Fine.'

From somewhere nearby came a steady trickling sound as a sheep urinated. Geoff grinned apologetically at the others.

'What about the birds, Geoff?' asked Derek quietly.

'Oh, Alver's going to keep an eye on them for ... while we're away.'

The sky was now a calm, pearly grey, with no clouds and little wind. Geoff chatted with George and James, mainly about University, while Derek asked Alver questions about the peregrines. Eventually Geoff announced it was time they left.

As she knelt awkwardly on the wall on her way out of the shelter, George's anorak lifted and she paused for an instant, her bottom pressing at the fabric of her faded jeans. Alver licked dry lips. Then she moved again, and the female shape was gone.

He stood to watch as they made their way up the hillside. Dawn's lips curved in a dreamy half-smile. He lifted the plain blue smock. Nothing on underneath. A chair against the door behind them. As he bent, her nipples were spotted with white. Milk ... it's the drugs. Don't worry. Her hair gone, a lovely blonde skull. He pressed, forward and up, grinding against the wall, reading desire in the blank face, in blue eyes clouded with drugs. Averting his face to press, squeeze, pull. A bump at the door. Keep going. Another bump. Nearly there. A voice, Owen's voice. Dawn moved to answer, the same half-smile, reaching for the chair as he grabbed at his jeans. My medicine.

He rubbed at the small red smear on the rock where Geoff had crushed the tick.

'They said they'd be along about lunchtime, to say cheerio.'

Alver nodded as he scratched one stone with another.

'Sorry again about not getting back earlier last night.' Geoff fiddled with the haversack. 'It's just that we got talking and the next think I knew ...'

'It's OK Geoff. I know how it is.'

Geoff nodded, satisfied.

Another squally shower arrived on the niggling wind. They huddled under the buttress.

'What d'you think of them?' asked Geoff aggressively.

'George is nice. You're alright there, Geoff. Nice-looking, too.'

The tight expression relaxed slowly. His eyes regarded Alver seriously over the top of his spectacles. 'She's still quite young, I know, and she's got a lot to learn. She's a bit ... shy, still a bit childish, she giggles a bit, but I think, given time, I can really make something out of her.'

Alver cleared his throat, as if about to speak, but said nothing.

'What were you going to say?'

'Well, I was going to say, how would you feel if you overheard someone saying they thought they could make something out of you? A woman?'

Geoff started a laugh which turned into a coughing fit. He gave one final cough, spat and swallowed.

'Depends on what.'

'Yeah. But it's bound to be something you don't want to be.'

'Well, she can make a millionaire out of me. I don't mind.'

The rain had stopped again, but more ragged grey cloud hurried towards them from the west. Alver stood up and stamped his feet. Dark patches had spread over most of his combat jacket.

'I'm off to the Sphinx for a while.'

Geoff raised a restraining hand. 'No no, don't go yet, they should be here any minute. Stay and say cheerio.'

When they arrived conversation was tentative, and mainly between Geoff, George and James. Derek and Alver watched the cliff-face.

'Bed and breakfast alright, was it?' asked Geoff cheerfully.

'Oh, adequate Geoff, adequate.' James had donned a shiny yellow plastic anorak over his fisherman's smock.

'What about you, George? Everything alright was it?'

'Yes, lovely thanks Geoff. A lot of noisy farm dogs. They didn't seem to stop all night, but the lady was very nice. Welsh.'

'Good, good. Fine.'

'Oh, Geoff, you will apologise to Clive for us, won't you?' George bunched her hair and tied it behind her head as she spoke. 'Tell him we just didn't have time, but if we come again ...'

'Don't worry, I'll tell him.'

She patted and smoothed her hair and turned to gaze out over the vista of silent green hills and wet sky. 'I imagine, on a nice day, this is a lovely place to be an artist ...'

'And we all know Clive's an artist, don't we?' James gave a loud chuckle. He got to his feet and stretched, then rubbed at his back, groaning theatrically. 'Haw! The jolly old arse hurts.'

Alver looked at him. 'You shouldn't do so much talking then should you?' Their eyes met in the silence that followed.

'Yes, very droll,' murmured James, studying his watch. 'Well, children. Time we were going.'

After the goodbyes Geoff went off up the hillside with them, managing to hold George back a little as the others walked in front.

'Enjoyed yourself then?'

'Yes Geoff. It was lovely to be out in the open air.' She smiled up at him.

'Pity about the weather.

'Yes, but it was nice yesterday.'

They walked a bit further.

'Look, I'll be here for another three weeks or so, if you'd like to come back.' He slid a glance round the rims of his glasses.

George nodded slowly as she walked. 'I'd like that. If I don't have too much work, of course. It is getting very busy, just now.'

'There's a coach from Bristol, I checked. I could pick you up from the station.' He indicated James and Derek silhouetted against the sky above them. 'It'd be nicer, you know, if there were just the two of us.'

'And Alver.'

'Oh,' said Geoff with a dismissive wave of a hand, 'he's been on at me about a weekend off. He wants to go and see his brother or someone in London.' He leaned towards her. 'It'd be a bit more private, you know?'

The noise of the car's engine faded as he made his way back to the shelter, and they were left with the moans of the scattered sheep, the wind, harsh bird-calls. Cloud in heavy grey masses hurried over but the rain held off. An initial rush of conversation became sporadic, died away, and they sat for a while in an easy silence.

'Funny,' mused Geoff. 'I'm glad they came, but now I'm quite glad they've gone. Except George, of course,' he added quickly.

Alver lay propped on an elbow, scratching in the dirt with a stick. 'An invasion, Geoff,' he replied without looking up. 'They're OK, George and Derek anyway, but it's still a kind of invasion. They don't belong.'

Geoff reached for a notebook as squealing came from the cliff and a dark shape swept up onto the ledge. 'Here, this is supposed to be your job,' he murmured, grinning as he licked the stub of pencil. 'What d'you think you get paid for?'

Both adult peregrines stood on the ledge among the crowding eyasses. When the telescope was touched into focus both birds stood wrenching flesh from an anonymous carcase and feeding the young, which were now untidy bundles of grubby down patched with quill stubs. Already each one showed a version of the peregrine's fierce black mask.

Geoff sniggered as he wrote. 'I thought for a minute you were going to bop James one.'

'One more word and I would have. He's the kind of bloke you'd like to fill in just once, don't you think?' He pulled a cigarette from the packet. 'Tosser.'

'He only came because he's got a car, really. He's not really interested in birds or anything ...'

'Get away.'

Geoff made a gurgling sound in his throat. 'Last night, in the pub, he asked me what you were reading.'

'How d'you mean?'

He assumed you were at University.'

Alver muttered something under his breath.

Evening approached then lengthened around them; the patches of cloud grew smaller as the wind faltered and the sky became a wash of softer grey. A cuckoo called loudly several times from a nearby gully without showing itself, but as the light began to fail they saw its flitting grey shape in the dusk, making for the oakwood.

'Geoff?'

'What?'

'Next time you see James, wind him up.'

'Come again?'

'You know, get him going.' Alver's voice was quiet, deliberate. 'If he backs down, and take it from me he will, that'll be the end of any more lip from him. If he squares up, don't wait for anything, just bang him one. Same result.'

Geoff smiled. 'Yeah, be nice that,' he said, wistfully. 'But you just can't go on like that, unfortunately. It wouldn't make me very popular.'

Alver scratched one stone with another, flipped it. 'You'd be surprised.' The stone clicked as it bounced over the sheep's skull, a pallid speck in the general dimness, then clattered among the rocks of the gully.

Geoff picked up a stone and juggled it, then tossed it haphazardly over the wall. He chose another, straightening his back for a view of the skull. Free now of the myriad tiny sounds of the day, silence lay in the valley like mist.

'And Geoff?'

He stopped, his arm drawn back.

'Make sure George is around when you do it.'

Geoff relaxed his arm and nodded, tossing the stone in his hand. Spidery lines were scratched in a crude pattern on its surface.

'How …'

Alver turned to look at him.

'Nothing.' Geoff hurled the stone into the dusk.

'Time to go,' said Alver, getting to his feet.

6. Clive

Clive cracked eggs into a bowl. 'A shame they couldn't come round. Never mind, I'll see them next time, eh? We could all go for a drink.' He shouted through to Geoff who sat staring at the television.

'Yeah.'

'I'd like to have seen little George, particularly. A lovely girl.'

'Mmm.'

A hand held artificial flies to the eye of the camera as a river slid by in the background. 'These chaps,' explained a sleepy voice, 'are designed to imitate the natural … insects … flies that you see all about the river at the moment. We call these flies Ephemerids, because they're only with us … for a few days …' Shimmering specks danced above the oily water. '… and the largest of these is Ephemera … dancia, which anglers call the Green Drake …' an insect clung to a reed: slender pale body, filmy wings, long threads at the tail.

'Cheese and tomato alright Geoff?' Clive's voice sounded faintly from the kitchen.

'Fine, yeah.' Geoff leaned further forward on the edge of his seat. '… from the mud after as much as three years as a … dull, unattractive nymph … see him? There he is … not much to look at, is he? But …' the voice drifted gently away again, drifted back,'… just you wait and see … he'll moult once, shed his old skin, there he goes …' A Mayfly drifted downstream, turning slowly with the current … 'and this is the dun, but then he'll moult … a second time, and … there we are … a much more splendid creature altogether …' Water shivered around the floating insect as it flexed tiny wings, then it had struggled free and risen to join the other Mayflies in their dance above the river. '… thing is, you see, he only lasts a few days in our world … after all that time down in the mud … there he goes, poor chap … ' A flitting shape fell to the water, stuck there, travelled a few feet and vanished in the ripple of a rising trout. '… some don't even get the chance to try out their wings …'

'Here you are, Geoff.' Clive handed Geoff a plate and knelt to place salt and pepper at his feet.

'Excellent Clive, thanks.' He pushed at the omelette with a fork without looking at it. On the screen, the genial, white-bearded face discussed fishing tackle.

'Ah, do you fish, Geoff?' Clive took out his cigarettes, then thought better of it.

'Nah. Can't see the point.'

'Oh, trout's very nice. You can catch them in most of the streams round here, you know.'

'Can you. Well, thanks but no thanks.' He chewed and swallowed. 'Bet they're full of lead, the number of old lead mines there are round here. All the washings went into the rivers you know.'

A rod moved back and forth in a slow rhythm; from its tip a line curled and straightened, white against a green background.

'Very satisfying experience,' said Clive, sipping from a tumbler. 'Takes a lot of skill, you know … to drop the fly just where you want it, right on the nose of a trout.'

There was a brief disturbance in the oily flow, then the rod dipped and jerked against the sky.

'Geoff, are you sure Alver won't come for a bath?'

'That's what he said.'

A giant silver trout head loomed, eyes staring, gill covers opening and shutting '… name from days long gone, we call it the priest … presumably because, a long time, oh, years and years ago, the priest … was the last person a condemned man spoke to … here it is …' a short, cosh-like object was hefted in a clenched hand. There was a wet clunk. 'Of course, as in any … form of fishing, you have to make sure you have the right … lure.' The limp fish slid into a bag at the man's waist.

'Bloody barbaric,' murmured Geoff.

'Did he say why, at all?' Clive asked lightly, reaching again for his cigarettes as Geoff laid his empty plate on the floor. 'Alver, I mean.'

'Thanks Clive, nice omelette.' Geoff took out his tobacco and belched softly. 'Pardon. He said he wasn't bothered. He should be, he's starting to whiff a bit. Do you know he hasn't even washed his hair since he arrived?' He drew a cigarette paper across his tongue.

'Perhaps you should …'

'Look Clive, it's up to him, isn't it?'

'Yes, of course. Drink?'

'Be nice.'

As the credits rolled on the screen Clive looked up from the bottle of Famous Grouse. 'This music … the song, do you remember it from that night in the pub? Alver was fond of it, he was singing it on the way back in the car, do you remember?' His mouth framed the words *silver in the stars* as he tilted the bottle. 'Lovely words,' he murmured, pausing, bottle in one hand and cap in the other. The music faded and an advert sprang onto the screen. Rousing himself he screwed back the cap and handed Geoff his drink. 'Are you finding him any easier to get on with? You said he was inclined to be a bit … morose, if I recall.'

'Cheers Clive.' Geoff's lips puckered as he took a sip. 'Did I? No, we get on fine now. He's still not exactly motormouth, but, yeah, he's OK. When you get to know him he's … he's quite an interesting guy. He's got his own ideas, anyway.' He gulped at the whisky and grimaced. 'I think. A bit childish sometimes, though.'

'How so?'

'Oh, he just seems very naïve sometimes, some of the things he says, then other times …' He sniggered. 'He's OK.'

'Mmm … I'm glad you're getting on better together, anyway. In your situation it would be very unpleasant if you took a dislike to one another.' Clive was on his feet, examining one of his paintings on the wall: a tumbled rocky gully splitting a hill's green shoulder under a wet, racing sky. He nodded quietly to himself and sipped whisky.

'Yeah.' Geoff go to his feet, sneering at the television. 'Right. A nice long soak now. No rush to get back. Alver said he'll walk it and make himself something to eat.' He turned at the bathroom door. 'You can put that thing off if you like, Clive.'

Shortly after he'd left Clive's solemn little village, Geoff passed the huddle of cars and caravans that had been building up by the roadside for several days as gypsies filtered into the area. In the dark there wasn't much to see – dim lights in the caravans, the glinting eyes of restless dogs. When he'd gone past earlier he'd slowed down to inspect things, frowning at the grubby, staring children, the piles of rusting metal, the clothes drying on bramble bushes. He'd seen no men or women, although curtains had twitched as unhealthy-looking animals yapped and snarled while others trotted tirelessly on running leads, alert and soundless.

'Bloody shit-heap on wheels,' he muttered as he rolled past.

From the top of the hill Alver watched the headlights sweep round onto the track and flicker as they moved off through the trees. When the noise of the engine stopped he came to a halt and sat down at the roadside. Without the steady tramp of his boots the only ripples of sound to disturb the silence came from a car on a far distant road or a sheep as it stirred on the hill. Pulling down the zip of his combat jacket he lay on his back in the cool grass, breathing deeply, gazing at the cold silver stars in the night. Gradually his breathing became less ragged. A shadow flitted across the stars. They had walked the towpath by the Grand Union Canal. Dawn talked in a dull voice, and cried, and talked again, *I'm sorry … I couldn't help it … I was lonely … he made me laugh,* then fell into miserable silence, the tramp of feet. There was a tench, a black, slowly finning shape far down in the stony water. All the colour of her face gone with the tears. White plastic cups bobbing on the black canal beneath a hated factory window. *Why don't you say something … what will you do?* He watched as she packed her few things. A few records, clothes, college books, more tears. He held open the taxi door. *If … do you think … I'm so sorry Alver.* He slammed the door.

A flurry of sharp needle-squeaking came from the grass where a shrew scampered. He zipped up his jacket and got stiffly to his feet.

Geoff appeared in the doorway as he approached.

'We've had a break-in.'

'Do what?'

The window over Geoff's bed had been smashed; the caravan was chilly with the night air.

'What did they get?' Alver prodded at the crooked lines running from the jagged hole. A piece of glass fell, tinkling on a stone outside.

Geoff looked slowly around, hands on hips. 'That's the funny thing. Nothing, as far as I can see. You'd better check your stuff.'

'That won't take long.' Alver's clothes, stowed beneath the bed, were all there. His bike jacket still hung in the wardrobe. Fingering the black leather he turned to Geoff, who was working his way carefully through the few drawers and shelves.

'Alright here Geoff.'

'Can't understand it. My camera, the radio even … nothing gone.'

'Maybe you interrupted them when you came back.'

'Could be, could be,' Geoff pursed his lips in thought, 'but it's so cold in here, you know? As if that bloody window's been open quite a while.'

'Well, maybe the farmer wandered past then, scared them off.'

'Hmm. Maybe.'

'OK, a mystery then.'

'Well it's no mystery who did it,' muttered Geoff darkly.

'Who?'

'The bloody gypos. There's a gang of them parked between here and the village. I knew it as soon as I saw their bloody shit-heap on wheels.'

'How many of them?'

'Who knows?' He waved his arms as he went into the kitchen. 'They all creep about in their vans all day, don't they? Then come out at night, looking for stuff to steal. Could be dozens.' When he re-emerged he carried a sheet of cardboard, tape and scissors.

'Well, at least nothing's gone.

'Yeah.' Geoff knelt on his bed as he trimmed the cardboard. 'Let's just get this patched up. It's like the Antarctic in here. Bastards!'

A few stray honks came from the farm and Geoff paused.' Wonder if old Jones Bach did see anything? I'll nip up tomorrow and ask him.'

Alver wandered slowly about, touching the walls, the shelves. 'You should be able to tell if someone's been in here.

'How?'

'You should be able to sense it, you know, a person's presence.' He stopped in front of the wardrobe, frowning.

'And can you? Here Alver, hold this steady over the hole while I tape it down. Alver?'

'Yeah, OK.'

'What's up?' Geoff snipped a piece of tape and pressed it into place.

'Well, it's just that you don't expect to get burgled in a place like this. In London …'

'Were you then? Burgled, in London?'

'Yeah, we - '

'We?'

'Me and this girl I lived with …'

'Lose much?' There was a tearing sound as Geoff stripped more tape from the reel.

'One time we did, a hell of a lot. The other time, well, it was like this. I reckon I interrupted them.'

'Bastards. Bet your girl was upset.'

'Yeah. Not that time, she was … she wasn't there that time. The first time though, when they cleaned us out … her underwear chucked all over, you know. Yeah, poor old … she was in a shocking state. Kept a hammer under the bed after that.'

'Bet you wished they'd come back.'

'Too right.'

'Police do anything?' Geoff stood back from the window and nodded, satisfied.

'Nope. Too many murders going on that night.'

'You were insured though?'

Alver shook his head.

'Pain and grief. Well, that should do it. I'll have to tell Jones Bach he needs a new window. He can keep his eyes open from now on as well, even if he didn't see anything tonight. What're they all doing round here, anyway? The gypos?' Two tiny images of the gas mantle gleamed in his spectacles as he peered at Alver. 'I mean, what brings them round here?'

Alver shrugged. 'Work, money … the usual, I suppose.'

'Hmm. Well, from now on I carry what I can with me in the car. What about you?'

'I haven't really got anything. My motorbike jacket, these bins, for what they're worth. Yeah. I'll wear the jacket. This one's a bit grubby anyway.'

Geoff nodded in agreement as he watched the combat jacket pushed onto a hook in the wardrobe. 'Yeah, been thinking of getting a bike jacket myself, matter of fact.' There was no response. He made a pot of tea while Alver plodded through the routine of sandwich-making.

The tea drunk, the silences between comments grew longer. Eventually Geoff slapped his thighs and stood up. 'It's me for bed then. Aren't you having anything to eat?'

Alver looked up and yawned. 'Can't be bothered. Too knackered.'

'Well, it's after one,' grunted Geoff as he pulled off his jeans. 'Just time to cram in a good three hours.' He turned back the covers and climbed in, 'Goodnight. Or as they say round here, *Nos da, iechyd da.*'

'Yeah.'

For a while Alver sat slumped on the edge of his bed, head nodding, then he reached down wearily to unlace the heavy boots. He struggled out of his jumper and dropped it beside the boots. In jeans, T-shirt and socks he wriggled into his sleeping bag, pulled the few blankets into a mound on top of him, and was asleep before Geoff's snoring got into full swing.

Out of the blackness appeared a green rectangle of lawn surrounded by wavering buildings. As he walked slowly across it he felt a slight giddiness and knew that Dawn was there. She walked slowly, surrounded by children. Her clothes were elegant; her face had lost its hint of chubbiness, its features now more angular, sensual; a striking face, tanned and made-up as it had never been, hair a tight, blonde cap: a face transfigured. The so-familiar startled blue eyes watched his approach coolly; the lips, less full than he remembered and a dark vermilion, parted, and the words breathed in his head, *Alver you can't exist.* Something lurched inside him but he smiled and walked on. A boy at her side tossed hair from one eye and said, *You can't exist,* his voice clipped and indistinct. There was a dreamy giggling in the silence. A wall of darkness moved towards him, clear-cut against the light, and as it swept over him voices echoed stonily in his head. *Alver you can't exist.* Drifting into wakefulness he felt a feathery touch on his leg and reached down to crush a small, horny body; then he was asleep again.

A gorged buzzard flapped heavily away over the sloping fields through grazing sheep as Clive struggled over a gate in one corner. Two large boards held by a strap across his shoulders carried an assortment of papers, and tied to them an easel and a small folding chair added to his problems at obstacles such as the gate. At his hip a canvas bag contained paints and brushes, and a packed lunch. He stumbled into the field on one knee, then unloaded himself, placing his equipment carefully between the scattered lumps of dung, and took out a silky, wine-coloured handkerchief to wipe his face. Patiently he pushed hair back under a floppy, narrow-brimmed brown hat patterned with herringbone and bristling with trout flies. He gazed down at the corpse of a lamb, shaking his head sadly at the puny ribs poking through the gore. Tufts of dirty wool trailed off into the hedgerow among the bright yellow and blue flowers of celandine and speedwell.

Wearily, Clive shouldered his equipment again and pressed on. A blue-dyed lamb's hooves drummed the ground as it fled, bleating frantically, prompting a ragged chorus of bleats, moans and hoarse garglings. Clive tramped doggedly across the field. Two sheep larger than the rest, with black legs and faces and so fat they found it difficult to walk, hobbled away together, each waiting for the other if it got too far in front. A coloured stain in the sea of washed green caught Clive's eye and he changed course towards it.

Minutes later he rested against the dusty red bonnet of the MGA, mopping away the sweat that once again beaded his forehead and licked the hair poking from the hat into dark, sticky strands. He pushed the handkerchief back into his pocket, and after a resolute glance towards the skyline began to climb carefully up the rough, grassy slope.

It took him some minutes to locate the shelter, one huddle of grey among several on the broad green sweep of the hill. As he approached he saw the sudden movement of an arm, followed by the clatter of a stone, amplified and prolonged by echo.

'Well well.' Geoff was grinning as he stood to watch the last few yards of Clive's approach. 'Dr. Rowland I presume. You look a bit flustered there, Clive.'

Clive un-shouldered his boards and bag, passing them gratefully over the wall. He let go a long, wheezing breath.

'Thanks Geoff. Hello Alver. Yes,' he leaned his weight against the tilting layers of rock, 'I have had a bit of a struggle. I didn't realize you were so far from the caravan. If I'd known, I could have driven up here.'

'Might as well come in, now you're here. I'll get the coffee out.'

'Ah, that would be very agreeable.' He clambered awkwardly into the shelter and pulled a plastic sheet from the canvas bag.

'Many thanks, Geoff.' He took a mug half-full of coffee. 'Bit of the creature, anyone?' He held up a silver, leather-bound flask.

Alver grinned. 'Sure. Why not?'

Clive trickled whisky into all three cups. 'Well, you've certainly got an impressive view from up here.'

'Maybe you could do us a painting of the cliff.'

'Of course Alver. That's why I've struggled up here with my things.'

'Be better than a photo,' continued Alver, nodding towards the fissured grey wall of buttresses and crags with its straggling patches of grass and bracken.

'I'm glad you think so. The camera is a very useful tool, but somehow it never seems to capture what you really see. Don't you find that ...?' Clive looked at him and smiled. 'I must say Alver, you look rather menacing in that jacket, doesn't he Geoff?'

Geoff grunted, busy with the telescope. 'Come on Clive, before you get started I'll point out the nest-site and one or two other features that you should include.'

A thin, cold sheet of grey now masked the blue of the sky, blearing the shining disc of the sun and shutting off its warmth.

When Geoff's instruction had finished they made room in the cramped shelter for the easel and chair.

'Make it a good one, Clive,' suggested Geoff as he pulled stones from around the chair and passed them to Alver. Clive smiled and pushed hair back under his hat. His face was still a moist pink from the exertion of the climb. He started to reply but was interrupted by screeches from the cliff-face signalling a food-pass, followed by softer sounds as the falcon fed the young. Geoff scribbled in the notebook.

'I was just going to say, Geoff, that it all depends on the weather, really.' Already, working with swift, firm strokes, he had sketched in the jutting lines of the cliff, the smoother sweep of the flanking slopes. Alver peered over his shoulder. 'You start with the bones of the place, don't you?' Clive's lips twitched uncertainly as Alver moved across to the sheaf of papers held with a red sash. 'Mind if I have a look, Clive?'

'No, help yourself Alver. Not very distinguished though, I'm afraid. A few unfinished items, mostly sketches.'

Alver took the portfolio to his corner and began to leaf slowly through the sheets on his knee.

'Alver?' Clive was applying the first wash of colour.

'Yeah?' He looked up from a view of tumbled grey rocks, shadows, a spill of white water.

'I was expecting you to come round the other night, for a bath.'

'Oh, yeah.' He returned his attention to the waterfall. 'I didn't need it in the end. Geoff explained, didn't he?'

'Course I did,' muttered Geoff from the telescope.

'Well,' continued Clive, 'do you think you might both be able to come round for a meal? I'd like to repay you in some way for our night out.' He angled his head and applied a smudged line of rust-red where bracken ran along the side of the gully.

'That's very nice of you, Clive. Isn't it Alver?'

'Yeah. Ta Clive.'

'Good. Well, whichever day suits you, really. I've taken some time off. From work. I need a break. What do you think, Alver? Of the sketches, I mean.'

'I like them.' His fingers held a forgotten grey building falling into ruin at the edge of a desolate moor.

'You don't find them a bit too ... mournful, at all? A bit ... depressing?'

'No. I like them.'

'Good, good. As I say, there's nothing really up to scratch in there. Nothing really finished, I don't think. The people who buy paintings, they seem to prefer ... well, more cheerful pictures, or so I'm told.'

Geoff continued to scribble notes as he studied the young peregrines through the telescope. The most advanced eyas now showed tan coloured patches on its breast as it waddled to the front of the ledge, turned, and defecated neatly into space. All four eyasses flattened against the rock as a jet rumbled through a neighbouring valley.

'Who's this?' Alver held up a small pencil sketch of a girl's face.

'Mmm?' Clive looked round, then turned back to his work. 'Just a girl. No-one special.'

'Who?'

'Oh, just someone I knew years ago. I used to sketch people, in those days.'

'Who though? What was her name?'

Geoff glanced up from the telescope. 'What is this Alver, the third degree?'

As he spoke, Clive dabbed at the hillsides with watery green. 'Oh, I can't remember. Honestly, it was so long ago. It was a preliminary sketch for a portrait.' He smeared on a band of grey. 'I don't even know what it's doing in there.'

A dark cloud had appeared from the west and was eating its way steadily across the sky.

'What's the big deal?' asked Geoff.

Alver stared at the paper. 'Dunno. She seems to remind me of someone.'

'Yeah, a lot of them seem to do that.' Geoff grinned at Alver's sidelong look.

'Don't worry Alver,' Clive assured him, 'it couldn't be anyone you know. It must have been thirty years ago when I did that sketch.'

'Yeah. It's just something about the eyes, I think. You've caught a certain look in them. What happened to the painting?'

Clive's shoulders twitched in a shrug. 'I never did one. At least, I tried, but … I couldn't get it right. I stopped painting people; they always turned out wrong, somehow.'

The sun was now lost behind heavy ashen folds; a high keening note from the cliff-face rose eerily in the deadening gloom.

'Damn!' breathed Clive.

Geoff got to his feet and stretched, then craned over Clive's shoulder. 'Hmm. Not bad, Clive, not bad. Take a look at this, Alver.'

Alver moved across and stood next to him. He nodded.

'Unfortunately it's all changed, now there's a different light,' explained Clive, peering anxiously at the sky. A peregrine called again, the same thin, rising note.

Alver leaned forward and pointed, 'This bit's just right,' the shadowy face still held between thumb and second finger. 'The Fist.'

As he spoke a single spot of rain landed with a faint pat on the paper just beyond the tip of his pointing finger.

'Damn!' said Clive again, but more loudly. The water fell in a slow path down the painted cliff-face, steered by the tilt of the easel.

'Alver, please would you mind putting that sketch back with the rest, quickly. This is going to be ruined in a minute.'

'Sure.' He laid the square of paper carefully on top of the others, then paused, rubbing at his beard, head tilted to one side. Finally he laid the sheaf in place behind the sash and closed the cover.

'Well,' said Clive as he fumbled to dismantle the easel, 'there's no point trying to rescue this one now. Good job I'd only just started. I'll have to come back again.' He slid the paper from the wooden board.

'Can I have it? If you don't want it …'

'Well, if you like Alver, but I can do a much better - '

'No, I like that one.'

'Alright then, I'll take it home and touch it up this - '

'It's OK, I like it the way it is.'

'But the rain drop …'

'It makes it better,' said Alver firmly.

Clive straightened and regarded the picture quizzically. 'Why? I don't understand.'

'It just does.'

Geoff slid the telescope into its plastic case. 'Come on you two, hurry up. It's going to piss it down. Here we go,' he said, as a light snapped on and off in the sky. 'To the car, quick.' Thunder rolled over the hills like the booming of a colossal jet.

'There isn't room for me in your car, Geoff. Can I borrow that cape until it passes?' Clive's voice was querulous.

'It's alright, Clive, you go on up,' said Alver. 'It's not going to rain.'

'What?' Geoff sat astride the wall, telescope and haversack hanging from his shoulders.

Alver smiled. 'It's not going to rain, not here. I'm going up to the Sphinx to watch it. Should be good. I'll see you back here.'

'Well, OK, it's your funeral. Come on, Clive, get your a - ' He broke off as he saw Clive had already scrambled over the wall and was floundering up the hillside.

The air was still and heavy now, and shivered with tiny vibrations.

When they reached the car Geoff was shouting, although there was no wind. 'Shove your gear in the boot Clive!'

He slammed the lid and wrenched open his door as another volley of crashing thuds broke over the hills. Both doors banged shut and the noise was cut off; they sat with the heavy sounds of their breathing.

'See what I mean Clive? Bloody childish sometimes.'

'Is there much shelter, wherever it is he's going?'

'What, the Sphinx? It's just a bunch of rocks on top of a hill. Oh well,' the seat creaked as he dug for his tobacco tin, 'he could do with a wash.'

Clive nodded vaguely, his eyes on the lowering skyline.

At the Sphinx Alver climbed to his usual ledge and stood for a moment facing the west; then he sat, arms wrapped around his knees, gazing into the silent, shadowed valley. Light flashed as darkness flowed into the twitching air, and thunder crashed again; a tiny, repeated howling sounded in his ears. His head bowed. Hair floated in great, flaxen swatches, darkening as it settled into the water; blue eyes, glassy as they watched, her mouth a huge grin, her head tufted stubble. *Now I am cleansed.* She nodded. Her mother sobbed and shuddered in the arms of her husband Jack. *No need for that!* The voice was sharp, the grin ferocious. *He's here now.* Marion wailing *what's happened? Dawn, please tell us, Dawn,* her embracing arms avoided. *I've told you, you mustn't call me that, it's not my name.* Jack, pouring hatred, *what have you done to her you bastard?* then Dawn again, desperation struggling submerged in blue eyes huge in a naked face. *Call him by his real name then. You know it. Everyone knows it.* Brushing at herself, *the dirt, I must wash,* lock clicking in the bathroom door. He banged, his fist pounding, Please, Dawn, let me help. A click, the monstrous grin. *Ah! The Betrayer!* A finger dipped through floating hair, pointing water at his face. A dab at his forehead. *There! Now everyone can see!* A white door. Jack's bullying voice on the telephone, loud over the moaning of his wife.

A gust pulled at him, whipping hair across his face as he looked up. Thunder rumbled again, muffled by distance, and paler splashes were dissolving the blackness in the strengthening wind. Within minutes the hills rippled with racing shadows as the sun floated free.

Alver held the hair from his eyes, watching the darkness dwindle slowly to the east, then stared at the white marks of teeth on his fingers, and the colour that seeped into them.

Apart from the two of them the Farmers' Arms was deserted, but for the elderly barman and the handful of domino players in the corner.

'Don't they ever go home?' Geoff lolled in his chair against a wall and blew smoke. 'Hey, maybe old Clive should try this place. He gives it a go though, you have to say that for him. Did you see that dinky little hat, with all the flies? What did he look like?' He gurgled and swallowed beer. 'Good artist though. He'd have knocked out that painting in no time if it hadn't rained. Well, nearly rained.'

Alver was examining Geoff's latest sketches, made that morning. Number Four, the youngest eyas, was the only one still showing extensive areas of down. A frontal view showed a feathered breast and baggy down leggings, with an arrow to the legs labelled *yellow.* Side views showed large amounts of down remaining on the wings, with fluffy rings around tail and head. The most advanced eyas, Number One, had tufts of white clinging to a much darker, more bird-like body. A creamy bar tipped the already full-sized tail. The savage family face glared at him.

'These aren't bad either, Geoff.'

'Oh, a bit rough and ready. They'll do though, once they're touched up a bit.' Taking the glasses he got to his feet. 'Think we can manage just one more, then we really ought to be getting back. It's bound to clear up soon.'

The old man took the glasses without a word and shuffled to fill them. On the other side of the tiny window rain slapped the glassy grey street.

'Nice to have the rain back,' remarked Geoff brightly.

'Why yes,' the old man took a bit of cigarette from his mouth and blinked watery eyes. 'It's what it likes, isn't it?'

Geoff pursed his lips and turned to gaze at the bottles and shelves until the drinks were ready.

'Just looking at those peanut adverts,' he began halfway back to the table, 'behind the bar.' He made a growling sound in his throat and rolled his eyes as he set down the drinks. 'They're virtually pin-ups.'

'Yeah. Always blondes as well.'

'That's right. I like it best when you get one card overlapping the one underneath, you know? Chopping off the head, so you've just got The Body.' He gave a wistful shake of the head and growled again as he raised his glass.

'You're a bit of a one on the quiet, aren't you Geoffrey?'

Geoff smirked.

'Poor old George. Bet she doesn't stand a chance when she comes down here.'

The smirk faded. 'If she does. I still haven't heard from her.'

'Don't worry Geoff. You will. Christ, it's only been a few days since she left. Give her a chance.'

'That's right.' Geoff brightened. 'It hasn't even been a week yet, has it?'

'Come on - let's hear what the Stars say.'

'Yeah, right.' He spread the Daily Mirror on the table and turned the pages. 'Hmm … let's see … right, yours – Gemini: "Routine is getting you down and you're in the mood for a holiday. Life is looking brighter. Huh, should be mine, that one."' He moved a finger. '… yeah, Taurus: "Don't let yourself be taken in by people who are merely trying to take advantage of you." He looked up and prodded his spectacles further onto his nose.

'And that should be my one. Who is it flogging away all hours of the day for nothing?'

Geoff gave a half-grin. 'Yeah. Silly sods have got them mixed up.'

Voices were raised in the corner as the clatter of dominoes halted.

'They're always bloody arguing,' whispered Geoff.

'You can't tell though, can you?' Alver dug in his ear with a finger and examined the yellow and black matter clotted under his nail. 'Maybe they're cracking jokes.' He wiped the finger on his jeans.

A man opened the door and stood framed against the grey light, peering into the smoky room. Crossing to their table he looked from one to the other and settled on Geoff.

'That red MGA outside belong to one of you?' His face had sharp, middle-aged features, and a thin moustache.

'Yeah. It's mine. Why?'

The man pulled up a chair and sat down, his back to Alver. He wore a glossy, expensive-looking leather jacket. 'Why? Cos I want to buy it is why, my friend.'

Geoff gave a curt shake of the head as he sipped.

'Come on, you haven't heard my offer yet. A grand, straight.'

'It's not for sale.'

'But the motor's not worth half that.' The voice was loud, aggressive.

'It is to me.'

'It is to you as well,' said Alver to the man's back.

He half turned in his seat, his face belligerent, then got to his feet.

'Alright, alright. It's your motor my friend. Look, tell you what I'll do. Here's my card, alright? If you change your mind, give me a bell. Alright?'

'Sure.' Geoff frowned incuriously at the printed card.

The man hesitated, then strode from the room with a quick glance at the silently staring old faces in the corner. With a clack the door closed and subdued conversation returned to the dingy room.

'Amazing,' said Geoff, waving the card.

'Yeah. There's hundreds more like him down there though. Take my word for it.'

'Nah. I didn't mean the wide boy. I mean getting an offer of a thousand for my car. Just what I told James.'

'What, you mean you didn't, before?'

Geoff shook his head, beaming. 'I just said that to string him along … wind him up a bit, you know?'

Alver smiled back. 'Played Geoff.'

'It was, wasn't it? Come on, that's worth celebrating. Scotch?'

'Yeah. Why not?' Alver's chair scraped the floor as he stood up. 'Back in a tick. Spot of horse-watering.'

Geoff was tapping his glass on the bar.

Sitting in the semi-dark while his bowels worked Alver's fingers played absently with the beaded metal zip fastener of his breast pocket. It was crammed with paper. Carefully, he drew out the untidy wad and, balancing it on his knees, began to work idly through the assorted scraps, holding one occasionally to the dim light to study it. Old Underground tickets, a membership card for a snooker club, ticket stubs from a concert at Wembley; he smiled as he read through the grubby letter from Trinity House explaining the difficulties involved in the job of lighthouse-keeping; cards from taxi-firms in London and Manchester; a receipt for an inner-tube, £5.25; a cut-down photograph. He lifted it to his eyes and stared. Creased and shiny, Dawn's face smiled uncertainly at him from a narrow frame of grey sea and sky. Awkwardly he shifted his position on the toilet seat to free the beginnings of an erection, and the cards and tickets spilled to the floor. Nailed boots scraped on stone as he reached to gather them; a man hawked and spat noisily, then sighed as water spattered against the wall outside.

Geoff waited, perched on the edge of the rickety chair, his fingers drumming the table.

'There you are. You'd have been quicker going for the usual walk in the hills.' He motioned impatiently to Alver's empty seat. 'Come on, I was going to tell you about the kites, wasn't I?'

Alver sat down with a blank expression and reached for his drink.

'Well …' Geoff waved a hand at the offered cigarette, 'apparently, when the livestock's being castrated on the farm …' a face peered through smoke in the corner, '… you know, to promote an increase in growth rate, the farmers slip a rubber band, soaked in some chemical, onto the animal's doings, and when it dries and the band shrinks …' he waited for Alver's nod of understanding, then went on, '… so, as the band tightens, it cuts off the blood supply to the testicles - '

A sudden bout of coughing came from the corner, accompanied by an exchange of amused, world-weary looks. Geoff glanced across, then pulled his chair closer. 'So, they eventually just wither away and drop off, the testicles that is. Along comes the kite, and there's its favourite dish, just lying there on the ground, waiting. That's why, under a kite's nest, you find little piles of rubber bands.' He grinned triumphantly.

'Do you?'

'Yeah. Well, apparently. Pretty delightful, eh?'

'Yeah. Like jellied eels, probably. Cheers Geoff.' Alver knocked back his whisky in one gulp, drawing the back of his hand across his chin where the liquid ran into his beard.

From the doorway of the pub they watched ragged holes appearing in the wet grey sheet above them. Water raced down either side of the steep, cramped road, swirling over submerged gratings, but the rain was now a gentle mist. To the north shone a filmy rainbow, and a line of green ran along the tops of the hills where the sun reached under the cloud.

'Excellent!' Geoff trotted to the car and unlocked the door. 'Come on, let's go.'

Alver jumped in beside him and belched, then exhaled contentedly.

Geoff nodded admiringly. 'Nothing like a good eructation, is there?' The engine roared into life.

That afternoon they wandered down to the stream at the bottom of the valley, keeping a careful eye on the cliff-face, ready to turn back at the first sign that they were disturbing the birds. Water had been a part of all their days in the valley, a constant thread of sound on the fringes of awareness, but they found the stream to be deceptively distant from the shelter, and as they went on its rushing noise steadily swallowed all others; by the time they stood on its wide, stony banks they were shouting to one another.

'Everything looks a lot different from down here!' yelled Alver.

The familiar broad plane of light and shadow was now a sheer mass of hulking rock that soared upwards and outwards above them. As he looked up, Alver took an involuntary step back in the gloom of its shadow. He turned to Geoff and his mouth moved, but his voice was drowned in clashing water. To the east the Sphinx was a black nub on the skyline.

Geoff had taken off his climbing boots and socks and rolled up his jeans, and stepped cautiously into the stream. He stopped and shouted, and when Alver held a hand to his ear he grimaced and shook his hands in an exaggerated shiver.

A sandpiper flickered low over the water towards them, then swerved abruptly away in a volley of whistles. Geoff beckoned, pointing to the water and nodding, but Alver shook his head, mouth open in silent laughter. Shrugging theatrically, Geoff waded to the middle and turned to face the flow, frowning at the stream's vigour as it frothed and surged at his legs. He looked up to see Alver some distance away, one hand cupped to his mouth and the other pointing upwards.

Far above floated the black shape of a peregrine, inscrutable against the streaming cloud.

'He's keeping an eye on us!' bellowed Geoff, pointing first to the bird and then at themselves. Alver nodded and waved to indicate they should move back.

The way back up to the shelter was long, and after the first few moments they climbed in silence, eyes bent to the next foothold, pausing briefly at intervals before pressing on.

'Hoo!' sighed Geoff after several panting moments back behind the wall. 'It's a lot tougher coming back than it is going.' He grinned at his wriggling toes. 'Quite refreshing, that little dip. You should have tried it. Bloody cold, though, and the stones ... under the surface they're all coated with algae, slippery as glass, or ice.'

Alver lit a cigarette and sucked in smoke. 'It all looks so much different from down there, so much ... bigger. Did you see that rock sticking out, way up there, beyond where the bird was? That must be the Fist. No wonder they sit up there all the time.'

'Yeah.' Geoff was pulling on his socks. 'There's no life in that water though, you know. Apart from algae. Too cold, too acid. Too much lead, maybe. Not even weed, as far as I could see. Just algae and bloody stones.' He examined a mark on his leg. 'I even looked under a couple, but nothing. I'd like to see old Clive pull a trout out of there.'

'Yeah. Well, he's not short of flies.'

'You're supposed to use the one nearest to the natural one that's there already though. How many Green Drakes did you see down there?'

'Do what?'

'Green Drakes, Alver. Thought you were a fisherman. And it is May, just. Anyway, there aren't any trout.'

'Oh, they'll be there, somewhere. Small ones. So will the flies. You just didn't see them.'

Geoff began to reply, but something caught his attention on the slope below. 'Well, bugger me. Recognise our friend down there?'

Among the rocks of the gully moved a pale, blue-mottled racing pigeon. It stopped and pecked at the broken sheep's skull, then walked haltingly on past it. Through binoculars they watched the small head jerking with every hesitant step, the wide eyes staring; coloured rings jostled on each pink leg.

'The Return of the Missing Piddy,' announced Geoff. 'That's the one that had the heart-attack.'

The pale shape tottered from view behind a run of bracken.

'After all this time?' Alver lowered his glasses.

'Must be.'

'Well, it's got a long walk home.'

'Nah. It won't last long.' Geoff's voice was dismissive. 'How the bloody hell it's lasted this long. Stupid bird. Obviously it doesn't understand its role in life, which is to be a packed lunch for a peregrine. Now look at it. It's redundant. A bird that's forgotten it's supposed to fly. It'll be wasted on the first fox or polecat to come along.'

'It did look a bit dazed. I suppose it must be the same one? Still, he's lasted this long.' Alver put a hand to his mouth and shouted towards the rustling bracken. 'Good luck mate!'

'Any sarnies left, talking of packed lunches? Bugger off!' Geoff directed a grimace at a muffled machine-howl, its note building then changing abruptly seconds after the jet had passed high overhead and vanished into the clouds.

On a curl of peanut butter and jam squeezed from the bread an orange-coloured ant waved tiny antennae as it balanced.

'Meat, Geoff,' said Alver, passing the sandwich ant-first.

'Hmm. Only a pismire.' Geoff brushed the insect to the ground.

'What's that, more yacky-dar stuff?'

'Nah.' His cheeks bulged as he munched. 'Old English word that. Pismire.' He swallowed. 'Means ant.'

'Right.'

Across the valley one of the peregrines dived, chattering, at a sparrowhawk gliding slowly past the cliff-face, drawing a faint chorus of piping from the nest-ledge. The small grey hawk jinked to one side, evading the falcon's rush easily, and swept along the course of a gully a foot above the ground, twisting delicately in and out of the gorse and hawthorn, then shadowing the river back towards the oakwood.

As Geoff scrawled in the notebook he paused several times and studied Alver, chewing thoughtfully at the long bristles below his bottom lip. Finally he spoke.

'Alver?' When Alver looked up he resumed writing. 'Remember what I was telling you, about going away, when all this is over? The sun, you know?'

'Yeah.'

'A couple of weeks in Greece, maybe. Hopefully with George …'

'Yeah. Good luck there Geoff.'

'Mmm …' Geoff rolled the pencil between his teeth. 'You said something about there being a girl, back in London …' He trailed off, his eyes asking the question.

Alver grunted. 'Cigarette?'

'No, thanks. Well, I was wondering if you … fancied it, at all, you and your girl …?'

'What? Go to Greece? Me?'

Geoff wedged the notebook back under its rock. 'We could all go together, you know, as a foursome. I was thinking of going with some blokes from university, but …'

Alver smiled across at him. 'Thanks for the thought, Geoff.'

'Oh, money, you mean? We'd be camping, wouldn't cost much.' He picked up a stone and tossed it. 'Anyway, there's a couple of weeks to go yet. Think it over. You could get in touch with – well, see if this girl's interested. Think of it: wine, beaches, sea, sun, you know? Ouzo. They've even got peregrines.'

Smoke left Alver's mouth in a series of spurts as he chuckled. 'You want to be a salesman, Geoff. Forget the computers.'

'Yeah.' Another stone arced over the wall. 'I'm not too sure about that anymore, as a matter of fact.'

'Mmm?'

'Well, I've been thinking along the lines of conservation work of some sort, you know, the academic side, even admin, with some work in the field as well.' He glanced cautiously towards Alver. 'Some of those jobs are pretty well paid, the top ones. Anyway, money isn't everything, is it?'

With a faint smile, Alver nodded, then unzipped his breast pocket and reached inside. 'Found a photo. Thought it had … didn't know I had it.' He passed it across.

'This your girl, is it?' Geoff stared at the trimmed photograph, eyebrows raised. I'm impressed. What's her name?' His eyes followed it as he passed it back.

'Dawn.'

'Bit of a Corn Goddess type, isn't she? Dawn eh? You keep in touch do you? I hadn't noticed any letters.'

Oh, we're in touch all the time, really. We just see each other whenever we can. It's not nine to five.'

Geoff grinned. 'Know what you mean. Solid but loose, eh?'

'Something like that.'

That night, as Geoff's measured snores filled the darkness, Alver mumbled to a floating gallery of framed faces revolving in black space over ranks of naked, headless bodies. Some faces he recognised; all were familiar. From somewhere came an irregular, dreary clanking as curls of withered flesh rained softly to the ground between anonymous legs.

7. The lead mine

One by one six grey pencil-shapes sped out of the piled white cloud and slanted obliquely down, racing in silence ahead of their roar. One by one they winked out of sight behind the same long, yellow-green hill, then slid back into the sky a mile away, rolling over in a nearly vertical climb back to the clouds. One by one they vanished, and only their outpaced rumble remained, rolling sluggishly over the hills.

In the eye of the telescope rabbits relaxed and resumed their nibbling as the heavy sounds faded.

'That's the life,' Geoff sat back from the eyepiece and stretched, 'being a bunny. Your mission: convert vegetation into new bunnies.'

High above the slopes, one of two wheeling black specks drifted lower, passing from white to open blue.

'And be ready at all times to be converted into new buzzards.'

The black shape dropped further, hovered briefly, dropped again below the skyline, became a brown shape.

'Come on, Buzz.'

In the telescope the rabbits tensed, then vanished into the gorse in a flicker of white tails as the heavy brown bird plunged to within inches of the ground.

'Useless bugger. You're inefficient, you'll be phased out!' yelled Geoff.

Patiently, the distant buzzard regained height in labouring circles to rejoin its soaring mate.

'No worries about road tax or national insurance if you're a bunny, eh? Just get out there and eat grass. What d'you think?'

'At least they fit in somewhere.'

'Yeah. In between grass and buzzards.'

Alver shrugged. 'Not too long ago we were being converted into sabre-tooth tigers, weren't we?'

Geoff gurgled and tossed a stone. 'We're the next stage though mate, haven't you heard? We've moved on. Doesn't apply any more.'

There was no reply.

'Anyway, how do you fancy converting some dandelion leaves into more of yourself?' He grinned and patted the book which had supplanted Brown in the pocket of his waterproof jacket. 'Apparently they're quite bracing with a dash of worcester sauce. What d'you think?'

'Thought dandelions made you piss.'

'Nah. Only if you eat a field full. See if you can grab some when you go for your constitutional, if you like.'

'Mmm.'

During the afternoon the raven family tried to pass over the cliff, but they were spotted. The adults, black and tattered, missing moulted flight feathers, escaped onto the moors; the two juveniles were driven into a gully and grounded, and crouched dejectedly among the rocks, uttering the occasional dispirited croak.

'I did see Jones Bach, by the way,' said Geoff, watching one of the ungainly black birds as it hopped hurriedly between rocky hiding places. A screaming peregrine swept down instantly, wings closed, one yellow foot extended to rake the air inches from the croaking black shape. 'Hoo!'

'What did he say? Anything?'

'Well, apparently the gypos come down every year, doing odd jobs around the farms, you know?'

The second raven made a break for it, flapping low over the rocks back the way it had come, but the falcon was onto it and had it grounded again within a hundred yards. She circled back, chattering, to check the position of the first bird, then curved up to land on the skyline midway between the two.

'Clever bugger. Yeah, apparently what they do is they drift down toward Pembrokeshire for the potato-picking. The farmers rely on them. There's usually a few bits of minor trouble, nothing serious. Jones Bach reckons no-one wants any bother with them because they'd pass the word around and there wouldn't be any workers next year. I should think there's more to it than that though,' he added significantly.

'Yeah.' Alver scratched through his jeans at the inside of his thigh. 'Nothing much you can do. Just wait till they go away.'

The tiercel beat in from the west trailing the soft pink-brown corpse of a collared dove, and the falcon lifted from the skyline to meet him in a noisy exchange, taking the kill and circling down to the nest-ledge. A few minutes later the awkward black shapes of the ravens hurried off to the east, where the two adult birds met them in a clamour of croaking.

Wish

Alver trained his binoculars on the ledge, where one of the eyasses threshed strength into burgeoning wings.

'Bugger it!' Geoff's fingers trailed a white concertina of gummed-up cigarette papers. 'Can I have one of your smelly ones?'

Tossing him a cigarette, Alver stood up and pushed the pack back into his jacket. 'Well, I'm off for my stroll.'

Geoff nodded as he shielded a match. 'Don't forget,' he mumbled through a cloud of smoke, 'Dandelions.'

Alver paused, astride the wall. 'Yeah. Might be gone a while.'

'Oh? Well, there's no rush.' He waved his cigarette and smiled. 'Take your time. It's a nice day for it. Just the leaves Alver.'

At the top of the slope Alver turned in a slow circle, hands thrust deep into his pockets. It was a nice day. To the east, beyond the valley and the Sphinx the hills stretched away to a hazy horizon; northwards lay gentler, more open land, dotted with sheep and the white and brick-orange of isolated hill-farms sheltering in dark stands of conifers; the low coastal plain of the west was hidden beyond the humped shoulders of the valley; behind him and below, Geoff and the peregrines.

He set off, turning away from the track to the caravan and following the line of the valley where deep, green-grown ruts in the earth led westwards in the lee of the hill. After a few hundred yards the old path dipped below the constant wind to run past a long-deserted grey cottage. Its roof fallen, one grey wall leaning inwards, empty holes for door and windows, it huddled against the hill like a tumbled outcrop of rock. A little owl blinked cold yellow eyes from the rubble then was gone, a small bounding brown shape lifting over the hillside and out of sight. Banks of sombre green nettles and thistles crowded a once-cultivated plot, butterflies floating above them in the heavy air. Orange tortoiseshells rose with purple-black peacocks as Alver passed by, then settled again in the slumbering warmth.

A dark swathe cut across the path as water crawled in a thin film from the hill to disappear into a tangled mass of brambles and hazel. Alver jumped across, then bent to scoop up a twisted branch of gorse, blackened by fire, swinging it rhythmically as he walked. Blue eyes dimmed and closed as a thread of conversation was lost, and a finger beat time in the air, *one two three one two three,* and the eyes opened again, puzzled: *Who are you? You are mist. Tell me your name.* The track remained straight in front of him and the stick swung faster in time with his tramping feet. Magpies chattered and watched from a leaning hawthorn; white flashed in the scrubby gorse as rabbits hid. His boots slapped across a patch of streaming ground as the branch whirled faster in his right fist. Abruptly he slowed and stopped. The green line of the track curved off to the north, dipping towards marshy ground dotted with grassy hummocks. He took a deep breath and stretched, rubbing at the back of his neck as he shook his head stiffly from side to side.

A speck appeared in the sky ahead of him, and through binoculars he watched the dumpy silhouette of a wood pigeon flying in an unhurried straight line towards him, then veering suddenly when still a mile away and beating off to the north.

Lowering the glasses he turned to consider the green curve of the track and the straw-coloured tussocks of sedge, then he set off to the west on the long walk towards the skyline, over broken ground where dark stony earth showed through the poor grass.

Once at the top he was able to follow the line of the ridge, with the valley falling away on his left hand, the stream a pale thread among the stones at its bottom, and to his right the undisturbed miles of upland sheep walk: both horizons, to south and north, rimmed with the long march of the hills. A ragged grey sheet was spreading once more from the west as the wind streamed over the tops with a steady low moan. Black bird-shapes wheeled far away over remote ridges and hidden valleys.

The line of the hill soon fell steeply into a gully of tumbled rocks, bracken and gnarled, stunted hawthorn. At its bed ran a thin, stepped line of water. Alver scrambled down, disturbing a cuckoo which passed him in a flutter of grey and white and a staring yellow eye, then he was climbing again, clutching at grass and woody branches of heather as stones clattered down behind him.

At the top he was met by a push of cold air. Forcing tangled, sweaty hair back behind his ears, he looked down on the old lead mine.

From the hillside a great bite was missing, gouged away to leave a vacant grey face of sheared edges and slabs above a litter of dead rock. Small, drab patches marked the slow return of grass and bracken. Piled grey waste led in a barren sprawl from the workings to the mine buildings: a derelict, grey stone cottage of the sort he had passed earlier, and the vast, rusting, corrugated shell of the works themselves.

Alver started down the slope, carefully at first, slowly gathering speed until he was bounding through the scree, sliding to the bottom in a clatter of stones and dust. A few sheep watched from the skyline, but among the grassless grey hills of spoil nothing moved. He went forward brushing the dust from his clothes.

A long-disused track built of stones and covered in more of the whitish dust threaded its way between the spoil-heaps in a series of diagonals, a grim parody of the sheep-tracks that netted the hills. At each hairpin bend a flattened area extended where heavy machines had once rumbled and lurched as they slewed for the next stretch of the ascent. A dull clanking sounded fitfully on the wind.

From the top of the gully alongside the scarred rock face water fell, dropping from pool to pool, sliding out through the workings and making off towards the stream in the valley bed two hundred yards away. A pit, or shaft, lay among the spoil-heaps, a black hole, rubbish littering its sides, a crude fence of barbed wire wrapped around its rim. The rotten posts sagged inwards, as if about to fold quietly into the dark. Alver leaned over and dropped his stick, which touched the side once then hit the bottom with a dry rattle. He moved on.

Another building became visible, edging into view round the heaps of waste, beyond the small road that had once served the mine: gaunt, grey, rows of empty black windows in leaden stone; the place where miners had once lived. A cloud of jackdaws now swirled noisily in and out of the echoing rooms.

At the rusting hulk of the works Alver stepped into a sunless interior and walked towards the middle across a floor carpeted with dust and littered with fallen beams. Grey rags of cloud streamed in silence between rusting black corrugated sheets; a loose sheet clanked drearily. In the empty shadows gaudy packets and canisters marched along conveyor belts, machines slammed and pistoned, white-overalled figures bustled as the dust settled about his feet. Kneeling, he scooped a handful from the floor and ran it through his fingers, a dull, glinting sediment of dead metal.

The tumbled cottage showed through a gap in the sheeted black wall, lying beyond a flat, grassy green rectangle. Stepping carefully over an angled beam he squatted and rubbed his fingers through the curly mat of grass woven with miniature plantains.

One end had lapsed into rubble, but at the other the weathered tiers of cemented stone remained upright and solid, the slated roof almost complete. A rotting door leaned from a hinge, and Alver held it with one hand as he looked inside. The room was dark, stuffy, warm; a dull orange glow showed in the darkness. He drew back abruptly.

Slowly he walked around the building, placing his boots carefully between the scattered stones and slates. Eventually he arrived back at the doorway.

'Hello?'

His voice sounded flat and weak. He cleared his throat.

'Hello? Anybody there?'

Turning, he scanned the volcanic waste of dust and spoil, then lifted his binoculars to sweep the hillsides. Nothing moved. With a final look round he stooped and pushed the door slowly open.

Smoke from branches smouldering in the grate pricked his eyes as his feet sank in a soft layer of dirt. In one corner, indistinct in the dim light, gorse branches lay stacked against the wall. He reached behind him for the door and backed into the daylight.

The dreary clanking came and went on the mounting wind. Even the sheep had gone from the skyline as he searched the hills again; the view blurred as he shook in a sudden shiver. After a moment's hesitation he ducked back into the murky room.

Pulling the blue and white pack from his jacket he pushed a cigarette between his lips and lit it. He threw the match into the grating and crossed to the stack, pulling out one of the longer sticks. The crack as he snapped it across his knee was deadened by the thick air and the years of gathering dust.

Alver broke the pieces again then laid them on the dull embers and knelt in the hearth to blow; soon smoke curled from the grate as the wood caught, mingling with swirling motes of dust and dirt. Still kneeling, he held his hands to the warmth while he puffed at his cigarette.

In the corner something behind the shadowy tangle of wood caught the flickers of light, and he crawled over to pull it out. On a rumpled page a woman sat astride a motorcycle parked by the sea, breasts pushing at a tiny black and white dress which rode up pallid thighs as they gripped the silver machine. Bright yellow boots reached from her knees to stacked platform soles on the foot pegs. Alver's lips twitched in a faint smile and he nodded, flicking his cigarette butt into the fire. He turned the page, and the woman knelt on the seat, face hidden in a swirl of black hair, the dress now a ribbon of black and white cloth between hanging breasts and pale, pushing bottom; hands with painted nails gripped the black rubber handlebars. Slowly rubbing his erection, Alver laid the magazine on the hearth in front of the spluttering fire and reached across for another branch, snapped it, and lay the pieces in the flames. He unfastened he belt, glancing over his shoulders at the doorway, and lowered his jeans. Another page, as his hand began to squeeze rhythmically, and she sprawled naked on the beach in front of the machine, legs spread wide, pink tongue frozen as it licked red lips below narrowed eyes, hair a black fan on the sand. The movements of his hand became more urgent, squeezing, pulling, his eyes glassy as flesh rippled in the flickering light. He tugged at the zipper of his jacket pocket, his breathing ragged, and the photograph fell into his fingers. Hurriedly he dropped the blonde face into position above the quivering breasts and urging limbs; Dawn's half-smile flickered in the firelight as he squeezed and gasped, his semen spurting into the flames, hissing on the burning wood.

Alver knelt in the dirt of the ruined cottage staring blankly at the curling, dog-eared pages. With a sudden, convulsive shake of his head he snatched the photograph, pushed it back into his pocket. The door bumped against the wall behind him and he jerked around, fumbling at his jeans.

Cautiously he peered outside, his hands hastily buckling up his belt. The light had begun to fade from the sky and the mine was cold and deserted; the door bumped again as the wind rocked it on its solitary, rusting hinge.

He scooped up the magazine, turning first towards the stack of wood, then pausing and turning back to face the fire. Abruptly he tossed the magazine into the grate. The girl and the motorcycle writhed and dwindled in the flames as he snatched and broke another branch.

He went outside for a last look around, and returned to find the fire smouldering and almost dead. With a gorse branch he raked out the charred magazine and took it out into the fading light. Stumbling over scattered rubble he made his way to the sagging barbed-wire fence, and leaning over dropped the magazine into the darkness. Scraps of blackened paper fluttered up from the shaft as he walked hurriedly off along the dusty, zigzag track.

The next day the gypsies had gone, leaving the grassy roadside flattened and discoloured.

Geoff's lip curled as he regarded the scene from his car, muttering at the piles of refuse, rusting scraps and fire-blackened patches.

'Bloody shitheap.'

He turned up the radio and the car pulled away. As it rattled across the cattle-grid a sheep with a tattered fleece and a bald head watched from the shadows of the oakwood.

Ruts and furrows marked his usual parking place as the car stopped in a thin haze of dust. Geoff cut off the engine, let the radio run on for a moment as his head jerked to a chopping rhythm, snapped the switch and jumped out, banging the door behind him.

As he laboured up the hillside his lips framed words and his head nodded, eyes bent to the ground at his feet. At the shelter he tossed a large, blue and white carton over the wall.

'There you go Alver. They should keep you going for a while.'

He clambered in. 'Anything doing?'

'Nothing unusual.' Alver passed across the notebook then clawed at the cellophane wrapping the cigarettes.

'Hmm. Life as normal.' Geoff looked up from the notes. 'The gypos have gone, by the way.'

Alver nodded, pushing a cigarette between his lips.

Geoff took out his tin. 'God help Pembrokeshire, that's all I can say.' His fingers fiddled expertly with paper and tobacco.

'Come on, Geoff. You don't even know it was them.'

He looked up in surprise. 'Who else could it have been?'

'Yeah, but nothing was taken, was it? And you're going to hate all gypsies now, for the rest of your life, for something they might not have done.'

'Bloody right! Anyway, they've buggered off now, and good riddance.' He shook a match impatiently and threw it away, drawing deeply on the completed cigarette. 'Hey, look what I found.' Digging in his pocket, he produced a small paperback book and waved it in the air. 'A Welsh-English dictionary. We'll be able to understand the buggers at last!'

Over the cliff the two peregrines circled patiently, the smaller tiercel fifty feet above his mate. A faint swell of piping came from the ledge.

Before settling back against the rock with his book, Geoff made a show of looking round. 'Yeah, I think all the wet, grey days are behind us, you know? A gentle build up to the Aegean sun. Yeah, I'd almost say it's almost warm.'

Alver followed the falcon as it flickered over the skyline and reappeared moments later with the corpse of a small bird. 'Kill in, Geoff.'

Geoff dutifully took up the notebook and began to write.

The falcon swooped up onto the ledge, easing seconds later back into the air and drifting slowly eastwards before circling up through the blue to rejoin the tiercel. Eyas number one held the kill beneath one yellow foot at the front of the ledge, bending over and pulling with its bill as its siblings piped and struggled in the background.

Geoff finished his note-making with a flourish and replaced the book beneath its stone. He leaned back against the rock, the dictionary open on his lap. 'How about this then, Alver? It's a bird. *Bilidowcar.*'

Alver shrugged. 'Give in.'

'Cormorant.' Geoff gurgled happily and turned the page. 'An easy one then. *Twrci.*'

'Turkey.'

'Correct. You're getting the hang of it.' He placed a stub of cigarette carefully under a stone.

Alver smiled, watching as one of the circling shapes dived from its path to hurry a passing gull on its way.

'What about peregrine, Geoff? Let's hear peregrine.'

'Hmm, let's see ... *Hebog*. Huh, sounds like hedgehog. Hang on, there's another name. *Gwalch glass.* The blue hawk. Yeah, that's more like it.'

Alver mouthed the words. 'Blue hawk. Good name, that. Makes sense, anyway, a bit more than our name.'

Geoff glanced up. 'What, peregrine? That's a great name. Means traveller, or wanderer.'

'Does it?'

'Course. Surely you've heard of peregrinations?'

He shook his head. 'Same as gypsy then.'

'Well, similar, similar. Not such a bloody mess though.'

Alver chewed at his index finger as he stared at the distant birds. *You wouldn't understand* said Dawn's soft, husky voice. Smug female masks faced him, then turned in satisfaction to one another, their eyes blank.

'Alver, try this one. *Mosgito.*'

'Mosquito. Yeah, gets easier as you go.'

The call of a sheep began as a grunting bellow, cracked in the middle, and trailed off in a whimper. It was answered by a muffled belch.

'What's sheep?'

'Oh yeah,' responded Geoff in a heavy voice. 'Sheep. Let's have a look ... *Dafad*. Sounds right. A flock of *dafads*. Yeah.' He lay the book on the ground and prised open his tobacco tin. 'They'll never beat sheep, though. Come on, another.'

Alver scratched at his groin. 'Oh, I don't know ... cat?'

'Cat, cat ... *cath*. Dull. Another.'

'Lizard.'

'Lizard, lizard ... *madfall*.' He snorted. 'Ridiculous. Another.'

'No, give it a rest for a while, Geoff.'

Geoff's eyes blinked behind his spectacles. He nodded. 'OK.'

Alver trained the telescope on Number One, which had now managed, with an awkward combination of flapping and scrambling, to move into the heather several yards from the ledge. The dark face showed touches of leaden blue around bill and eyes as it moved jerkily to follow the flight of an insect. Piping sounded from the ledge as the falcon took in a golden plover and began to feed the young, and the eyas scrambled from the eye of the telescope in a blur of buff and dark tan.

'Bugger!' Geoff was looking to the west where heavy grey cloud advanced. 'Just when I was going to take my shirt off and get in a bit of practice sunbathing. Let's time it.' He checked his watch. 'About twenty-five minutes, I reckon.' Pushing the dictionary into his jacket he began to collect their things and pack them into the haversack. 'So what did you think of the old mine then?'

Alver grimaced.

'Yeah. Hard to believe it was crawling with people not so long ago, ripping the guts out of the place.'

'It's an ulcer.'

Geoff nodded. 'Did you see that sort of square lawn affair? You'd never guess what that is, or was.' He gurgled. 'A tennis-court. No really! Apparently the owner of the mine built it so the miners could relax between shifts. Clive was telling me. Imagine it! Filthy black guys prancing around knocking out baseline winners, and so forth.' He frowned and his eyes unfocussed. 'No, that's coal-miners, isn't it? Still,' his voice dropped as he leaned closer, 'Clive says that on a dark night, when there's a new moon, you can sometimes hear the ghostly thwack of ball on racket.'

The wind had strengthened, and the towering blue-grey bank filled the western sky. A ragged line of gulls passed overhead.

'This wind's stronger than I thought. It's going to be here any minute. We'd better head for the car.'

Alver looked at the sky, then at the cliff. 'You go if you like. I'll try it with the cape. The birds cope with it, so we should be able to.'

Geoff stared for a moment. 'Oh, you do agree that it's going to rain this time?'

'Oh yeah. Won't last long though.'

The first dull crumps of thunder rolled on the wind.

'Well,' Geoff flicked an anxious glance at the clouds, 'it would be of value to see how the birds react. Yeah, we can both squeeze in.'

Rain patted at the cape, then hammered, sluicing down the folds and onto the ground, rolling in a steady film under the wall and on towards the distant stream at the bottom of the valley. They huddled, knees to chests, holding the quivering olive sheet tight to the ground, one of Geoff's hands clenched around the head hole.

'Hope you're bloody right!' He spoke through gritted teeth, his voice tight in the din. Thunder split the air overhead.

Alver nodded, watching the shadowy trails running together, coalescing, flowing on over the membrane, as he heard the calm monotone of Owen's voice ... *You must understand, these conversations are part of the unreal world she's found ...* Studying steepled fingers, the clock ticking on the wall above him ... *and when they stop, she will have left that world and returned to the real one, or the one you and I think of as real ...*

'Hang on, I think it just might be ...' Geoff eased his grip on the opening and peered out, 'Yeah. Not much more left.' The drumming had subsided but was still continuous. He manoeuvred his binoculars to the small daylit window. 'Hmm ... they seem to have enjoyed it more than we did. The eyasses are just sitting out there, right at the front of the ledge.' Thunder crackled, muffled and halting. 'Excellent!' He grinned. 'And they don't even have capes.'

Later in the afternoon a kite passed slowly through the valley, sweeping at one point directly over the shelter. As it swung round in the air above them, two green plastic tags flipped forward, one just inside the angle of each wing, then disappeared again as the bird turned back into the wind and was carried east in another long curve.

'Bugger. Just couldn't quite read the number', breathed Geoff, lowering his glasses. 'Pity. We'd be able to recognise it for certain if it comes back. Looked peculiar, didn't it? When those two green bits shot out?' He grinned.

'Why do we have to control everything? To warp it to our way?' Alver's face was hard, his voice almost a whisper. He shook his head and turned back to face the cliff. After a long, slow scan of the rocks he lowered his glasses and lit a cigarette.

'What's for eats tonight then Geoff?'

'Well, I still fancy trying dandelions. I'll be going for a constitutional in a minute. Savoury pancakes and dandelions, how does that suit?'

'Why not?'

'You know,' said Geoff, getting to his feet, 'I'm surprised we haven't seen any people round here, you know? I mean, it's the end of May, June tomorrow, we're not that far off the beaten track.' He directed an accusing glance at the hills.

'I thought that was what you wanted.' Alver blew smoke.

'Yeah.' Geoff drew the word out as he paced a slow circle, hands in pockets. 'You'd think we'd get at least a couple of lost girl hikers up this valley though.'

'Maybe they can't find it.'

'They should buy a map. Anyway, old Clive found it alright.'

'He knew what he was looking for.'

'Yeah. Good old Clive. Wonder what he'll dish up when we go round for this meal. Apart from Scotch.' He swung one leg over the wall, 'Well, see you later,' then his clumping footsteps were receding into the blustering wind.

After a few minutes' wait, Alver worked a hand down inside his jeans, his body stiffening as he scratched. Finally satisfied, he withdrew the hand, sniffed at the fingers then stretched out against the rock, his boots rutting the sticky earth. With one hand propping his head, his eyes closed and his breathing gradually fell into a slow rhythm.

Later that night, Alver stood just beyond the wash of light from the caravan, splashing urine into the darkness. Geoff's figure moved behind the net curtains of the kitchen and tinny radio noise drifted from the open door.

'Five minutes.' The voice was muffled.

From the farm came an outburst of barking, which set off the geese. As the sounds died away, Alver knelt to examine a handful of small twigs lying across one another in the half-light. He reached a hand towards a snapped white end, then hesitated. Droplets of dew glistened already in the darkened grass.

'Come and get it!' A spoon beat briefly against a saucepan.

Alver stood slowly, then walked towards the light.

8. June

The driver took a pipe from his mouth as Alver stepped on board.

'Hello, how are you?'

Alver gave a tight smile and handed across his money.

Sitting upstairs, he was the only passenger as the green double-decker bus wound its unhurried way down through the hills, the driver singing softly to himself in Welsh and moving the gears with the ease of long practice. Flocked white cloud floated over the hills in a blue sky. Behind a sunny screen of ash a plantation slid by, dark and dead. A buzzard watched from a telegraph pole, head turning as it was left behind; a woman waved from the roadside.

He rubbed at the inside of a thigh while the bus stood outside a village post office and the chatter of Welsh drifted up from below. Beyond the cluster of buildings, where the grassy slopes became steeper, was the grey pock-mark of a disused mine. After several minutes the conversation ended abruptly and the bus rolled forwards.

A tractor turned slowly into a field of black and white cattle in front of them and glass rattled in the windows as the bus's engine strained to pick up speed. Alver glanced sideways at a vague reflection of himself. *They're in the air ...* A sudden look of cunning sparked in the blonde, sleeping-doll face ... *all around us ... She told me. They all know her.*

The bus swung onto a bridge. Below them the river was much wider than in their valley, but still shallow and stony, still weedless, rushing towards the flat western horizon.

Alver left the bus at the railway station, near where he'd first stepped from the train a month and half earlier. Behind him the driver, engaged once more in conversation with his other passengers, slipped a 'Goodbye now' easily into the impenetrable burble.

Moving though a swarm of children he rested against the station wall and lit a cigarette, gazing around at intersecting streets shuffling with cars and people. Colours jostled and surged against hard-edged stone and glass, engines ground and idled, voices babbled. A knot of blond-haired youths with huge back-packs stood outside the station, looking bewildered and cheerful. Pigeons curved through the air above the busy heads.

He crossed the road and bought a newspaper, then made his way through the bustle towards a black, white and yellow sign advertising the beer they'd tried the night Clive was with them: Banks's.

The door closed behind him on the glare and bustle, and he found himself in a cool, dim room, quiet with murmured conversation and the click of balls on a pool table. Assorted faces turned, then went back to their drink and hushed talk.

Alver bought a pint, pulled dark beer through an inch of white froth, and stood the glass on an empty table in the corner. He walked to the door marked *Dynion* and pushed it open.

In the small cubicle he loosened his belt and pulled down his jeans. A red patch, angry from his scratching, extended for an inch and a half below his genitals on the inside of each thigh; a thin yellowish line marked its leading edge. He sat carefully on the toilet seat to examine it, then leaned back against the piping, staring at the ceiling. In one corner a large, brindled spider crouched in a fog of silk, surrounded by a dusty litter of wings and jointed legs. A motorcycle snarled in the street. Alver got to his feet and fastened his jeans, then tugged at the chain.

A record thudded from the juke box as he slid onto the bench by his table. More people had crowded into the small room, bikers in leather and studs; a pile of helmets lay next to the door. Loud voices filled the bar with accented English, while the pool players waited impatiently to make their shots, exchanging loud Welsh comments which brought a tight smile from the barman as he flipped the beer handle over a glass. One of the bikers noticed Alver's jacket and nodded. Another record thudded out.

As he got up to leave, one of the regulars was reaching with his cue to tap the leather shoulder of a biker sitting on the end of the pool table. From behind the bar, seductive female faces peeped between inverted spirit bottles and leaning piles of cigarette packets.

'Fuckin mushroom-eaters,' grinned a wild face with a cross stamped between its eyes, motioning towards the table. Alver gave a half-smile and nodded as he pushed his way out.

When he found the doctor's surgery he stood outside, reading and re-reading the brass nameplate through the tramping crowds: Welsh names, the usual strings of letters. He glanced down at a sheet of paper from the notebook, scrawled with Geoff's handwriting, and allowed himself to be carried away by the next surge of pedestrians.

The sun had now hammered the haze from the air. To the north of the town the dark arrowhead of a hang-glider showed briefly below the wheeling gulls before dipping from sight behind the roof-tops. A wizened old lady got up from a bench as Alver approached and shuffled into the human tide; he took her place just as another moved forward from a shop doorway. Pulling out his newspaper he turned to the sports page, but snorted at headlines of cricket and tennis and laid it closed on his lap.

A huge motorcycle rolled slowly by, an immaculate mass of machinery finished in sea-green and gold with glittering chrome, the whispering note of its engine hardly audible above music from speakers set in the fairing. As Alver shaded his eyes a gauntleted hand rose briefly from its grip on the handlebar, and he nodded back. White-blonde hair spilled from the helmet of his passenger, fanning over black leather.

He watched the motorcycle disappear round a bend with the flow of the traffic, then took off his own heavy jacket and laid it across his knees, relaxing against the warm wooden bars at his back.

Idly he leafed through the newspaper. In the world there had been a murder in Yorkshire, an increase in the mortgage rate, a call for the return of the birch and the use of stocks. In America a lady doctor declared the Messiah was a woman. In Norfolk a rare bird thousands of miles off course had been chased cross country by hundreds of birdwatchers until, exhausted, it had been eaten by a cat.

He looked up as a police car swung onto the street, siren blaring, forcing cars into the kerb, accelerating round a corner and out of sight. Almost immediately there came a screech of brakes, and for several minutes the siren wailed at a steady pitch, then it stopped abruptly.

Alver's lips moved as he read his horoscope. "Gemini: Things are going well after a recent period of uncertainty, and will continue to improve. A good time to go shopping. He smiled. Your partner will be in good spirits, and will surprise you with his/her thoughtfulness. Expect a reunion with a loved one." A woman laden with shopping made as if to sit next to him, then changed her mind and plodded wearily on down the street. Alver grimaced and jerked his hand from his thigh. A face on the other side of the street caught his eye.

Jumping up, he pushed his way across the pavement and started into the road, stepping back as a Land Rover hooted him and waiting impatiently for it to pass.

Wish

'Owen?'

His shout was smothered by the noise of a green double-decker bus that rolled slowly by in front of him, blocking off his view. The driver nodded pleasantly through the open doors, lips drawn back from his pipe-stem in an affable smile.

The man had turned off the main road and Alver hurried along the kerbside, dodging lamp-posts and holidaymakers, pushing into the giggles and chatter and through to the relative quiet of the side-street.

Small groups of people moved among the parked cars; a radio played from scaffolding where men painted and sang. He walked slowly to where the street ended in a larger one running across it, looked carefully both ways over the sea of bobbing heads, turned and looked back the way he had come, then turned again, swinging his jacket over his shoulder.

Across the road the brassy nameplate gleamed, the letters picked out in white. Wiping sweat from his forehead he started towards it, then stopped; when a car hooted he turned round and walked slowly back to the main street. Not too far away, just beyond the main bustle, was another black, white and yellow sign.

This pub was larger than the last, and noisier. Alver sat in a corner and watched a group of students filling two tables pulled together. Two or three were arguing loudly while the others looked on, face poised for laughter. One of them, wearing a German army uniform, caught Alver's stare and looked away; another lurched to the juke box and leant against it, then pumped in money. A record blared out, all bass and thumping drums. Dawn flourished a sheet of paper. *Leon plus me equals you plus Cerys. I've worked it out … it's so easy. You can take people away …* pink lips twitched. *Everyone has a number.* Blue eyes watery and bulging from long nights without sleep.

He lit a cigarette. The students shrieked with loud English laughter.

Several girls sat at the two connected tables, most dressed carelessly in jeans and oversized jumpers. One, quieter than the rest, had neat blond hair and wore a short, green and white candystripe dress. Alver's eyes flickered after her as she moved toward the *Merched* sign on the wall. He noticed the youth in uniform was watching and stared back deliberately until the student lowered his eyes. When the girl returned Alver watched him stand up and make a remark to the tableful of uptilted faces, then guide her to the door as the laughter swelled again behind him.

He drained his glass and stubbed out his cigarette. For a moment he stared at the door, then took his glass to the bar. His first attempt to speak was lost in clogged phlegm; he cleared his throat and swallowed.

'Pint of mild, please.'

The barman took his glass without a word and held it under a nozzle, gazing disinterestedly across the room as he flicked the lever across and back again. A girl smiled over his shoulder as she slid from a wet, clinging dress.

'Thank you, that'll be fifty pence please.'

A hand reached over Alver's shoulder clutching a five pound note. He shrugged up the padded shoulder of his leather jacket, hard, and the hand disappeared.

'Packet of nuts as well, please.'

Another record thumped the air, and a youth in a wide brimmed purple hat danced his way back through the tables to his seat.

When Alver emerged at closing time the gangs of holidaymakers still trudged determinedly back and forth on an endless circuit of cafés, souvenir shops and amusement arcades. If anything, it was even hotter now. He pulled out the crumpled shopping list and barged into the crowd.

Traffic crawled patiently along the main street, pale faces peering from open windows; people milled in the shops as he queued for the things on the list. Back on the sweltering street a woman smiled and rattled a tin, and he shuffled away with a paper disc on his jacket reading *Samaritans: to help the suicidal and despairing*.

Eventually, he found himself at the seafront. Dropping the list into a bin he jumped down onto the beach and sat on a low stone wall. People littered the sand: a dozen or so shouted and splashed just offshore with a handful further out, bobbing heads where the sun sparkled on the sea; a small boat moved steadily out beyond them. Overhead gulls swooped and squabbled, dazzlingly white against the hot blue sky.

Lowering his jacket and bag of groceries, Alver sat beside them on the warm, gritty sand. He shaded his eyes to watch a tern, feather-white as it danced above the waves, ignored by the bathers, riding so lightly, so buoyantly, that it seemed its wings worked to keep it down, to keep it from soaring up and far away. Abruptly it fell, dropping into the sea among the cavorting bodies, rising with a flash of silver clenched in its bill.

Wish

He bundled his jacket to make a pillow and wriggled into the warm sand, folding his arms across his chest. Waves hushed onto the beach as children whooped and screamed.

As he drowsed his father loomed over him, yellowish-brown eyes faded and glassy in a solemn face, breath sweet with whisky. The muscles around Alver's mouth twitched, then he rolled onto his side, drawing up his legs and pushing his hands between them.

Feet thudded into the sand, going past him, heading towards the sea.

Geoff jerked upright at the sound of Alver's approach and began buttoning up his shirt, taking a quick look at a large red and yellow spot among the sparse hairs of his chest. Alver clambered over the wall and dropped beside him with a grunt.

'How'd it go then? What did the quack say about your back?'

'Oh, just a strain of some sort, so he reckons.'

Geoff snorted knowingly. 'Yeah. What colour are the pills?'

'No pills. He said it'll go away on its own.' He held out the carrier bag. 'Here's your stuff.'

'Excellent! Get everything?' As he rummaged through the contents he paused, frowning, then broke into a slow smile. 'Hello, what's this then?' He held up a bottle of Famous Grouse.

'Oh, I bought that. Help yourself though.'

Geoff beamed. 'Don't worry, I will. I'll go halves, OK? Good thinking.'

While Geoff worked through the bag, Alver studied the notebook then took out his binoculars to scan the cliff-face. On the ledge two young peregrines threshed in a bout of wing-exercising.

'Oh, excellent! Danish blue.' Geoff peeled back a corner of the wrapping and sniffed. His eyes rolled. 'Nectar! So,' he continued, dropping the cheese back into the bag, 'how was the big city? Expect you managed a drink?'

'Packed. Yeah, a couple.' He ran his tongue round the inside of his mouth with a look of distaste. 'In fact you can pass me that bottle.'

He took a pull and grimaced, then held it towards Geoff, who looked uncertain.

'Well, I was really thinking of when the weather cools off a bit …'

Alver shrugged, and Geoff's expression changed.

'Oh, go on then, why not?' He unscrewed the flask top and held it towards the bottle. 'I don't know, you and old Clive make a great pair.'

'Cigarette, Geoff?'

'Yeah, why not?'

For a while they drank and smoked in silence. The haze had returned to the air, but the sun still beat down, and grasshoppers churred on the slopes. A tractor worked somewhere beyond the hill at their backs. On the skyline a peregrine circled briefly and vanished onto the moors.

Geoff picked up a stone and sent it in a lazy arc over the wall. He cleared his throat. 'Had a letter today, Alver. From George.' He paused, then picked up another stone, rolling it between his fingers. 'She'd like to come down again … I told you she might.'

Alver flipped a cigarette butt over the wall. 'On her tod?'

'On …? Yeah, that's right. Bit more … privacy, you know?'

A faint chatter came from the moors, rising and falling on the breeze.

'When?'

Geoff tossed his stone. 'Next Sunday, actually. The sixth.'

He gave a sidelong glance.

'Played Geoffrey.'

'Yeah.' He grinned, and turned his face away to look off over the wall. 'Really looking forward to it, as a matter of fact.'

Alver gulped down whisky and reached across to trickle some into the flask top. The sound of the tractor fell away, then started up again.

'So, er, so that's alright then? Five days time. I know its short notice …'

'Sure.'

Geoff nodded to himself and sipped from the flask-top. He began to speak, but stopped as Alver pointed across the valley.

'Ever noticed those clumps of bracken over there? Shaped just like two sixes. Sixty-six.'

Geoff squinted in the direction of the pointing finger. 'I … think … Oh yes. Got it. Yeah, you're right. Sixty-six. No, never noticed it before.' He turned back to Alver, who was scratching in the dirt with a stone. 'Must have changed as the vegetation developed,' he offered. 'Developed. Become more apparent.' He sipped at his drink.

'Emerged.' Another sip. 'Er ... any idea where you might go, Alver, for the weekend?'

The question hung in the air. Alver looked up from the ground and focussed on him.

'London, maybe?'

'Nope.' He drew his heel through the marks on the ground. The drone of the tractor stopped abruptly.

'What, er ...'

'Manchester.'

'Oh, right, yeah. See your folks.' Geoff gulped whisky and broke into a fit of coughing. He wiped his mouth and blinked watery eyes. 'Is it a long time since you saw them, your folks?'

Alver nodded, eyes trained on a point somewhere near his feet. 'Yeah.'

'Well, George is arriving on the Saturday, matter of fact, so there's no need for you to rush back or anything, you know?' Geoff peered short-sightedly as he cleaned his spectacles. 'Fancy a bit of danish blue?'

As the evening stretched on, and the sounds of birds and insects faltered and stopped, so the noise of talk and laughter grew, echoing over the gullies and broken slopes. Geoff's anecdotes became longer and more disjointed as the level in the bottle fell.

Eventually he broke off, still laughing, and got to his feet. Vaulting the wall he made his way to the gully and retrieved the broken skull, balancing it carefully on a prominent rock, and returned, his face flushed. They continued to drink as they sent stones to rattle and leap around the skull, taking turns to replace the dwindling fragment of bone. The peregrines brought in kills to the three eyasses on the ledge and to Number One, which had again advanced into the heather. Slanting lines of scrawled symbols and abbreviations slowly spread down the page of the note-book; after an entry Geoff dropped the book impatiently to the ground and reached for another stone. Again there came the dull rattle of bone on rock.

'Your turn,' beamed Geoff.

'No. Had enough.' Alver gave a lop-sided grin. 'My arm's knackered.'

Geoff started up, then stopped and sank back. 'Yeah. Me too.' He gazed at the sky. 'We're in for another excellent day tomorrow. In fact, it's all going to be excellent from now on. I feel it. Every day, you wait and see.' He belched and gave a contented sigh. 'Not another drop of rain.'

Alver nodded deliberately. 'Good.'

'Yeah. I think I could quite get to like this sort of thing, you know? As a living.' He wrapped his arms around his knees. 'All that office scene ...' a hand flapped vaguely. 'This is what counts. Being in touch with things.'

A faint shrieking came from the cliff. Alver's slowly drooping eyelids snapped open, then began to droop again; his head sank forward. Geoff pushed himself unsteadily to his feet and stood with his hands on the wall. He swayed forward and a dislodged stone bounced heavily away down the slope, thudding on the grass.

'Who needs it?' he murmured. 'Come on, Alver. Let's have a smelly cig.'

Alver looked up, mouth set in a grimace, eyes rolling. 'A blue hawk,' he mumbled, pushing a hand into his pocket.

Geoff turned his back to the wall and slid down it, then reached across for the flask-top. 'How about inviting your brother up for a couple of days then?'

Lighting their cigarettes, Alver spoke deliberately, his lips moving with exaggerated care. 'I told you. Not interested.'

'Oh yeah, you did.' Geoff considered this. 'What is he ...? Clive did say, something to do with television, wasn't it?'

Alver nodded, blinking slowly. One side of his mouth drooped.

'Doing very well. According to Clive, anyway.'

Again Alver nodded. Geoff swigged whisky then sucked at his cigarette, peering out over the wall after the pale line of smoke. 'That some movement up there?' He moved on all fours to the telescope and fiddled with the focussing wheel before rocking back on his haunches.

'What is it?' asked Alver in a thick voice.

Geoff screwed up his eyes and rubbed them with his fingers. 'Oh nothing. Focussing seems a bit dickey on that thing.' He sank against the wall and beamed at Alver. 'Good idea, getting this.' He waved the flask-top in the air. 'Livens things up a bit. More cheese? Funny, I never used to like scotch.'

'No, ta. Had enough.' Alver's breathing whistled in his nose. *Alver?* The girl's face, hard and dark, a face wearing a woman's mask, eyes ... the noise of the pub faded. *Dawn has told me about you.* Grey eyes, the colour of lead. *She must have been beautiful, before you defiled her.* 'Who ...?' The face swam closer, or he turned away: she was gone. Owen's voice on the telephone, reassuring, *no, quite impossible, it couldn't have been, she ... no-one can just walk out of here Alver ...*

'You know,' said Geoff, once more at the wall, 'looking around from here it's easy to imagine nothing's changed for thousands of years. It could still be the Stone Age. The hills a bit rougher, maybe, vegetation a bit different.' He sipped, staring out over the valley as Alver's laboured breathing whistled behind him. 'Even before that, before Man took over. Wolves padding around the place, wildcats maybe, a bear or two.' He was muttering into the flask-top. 'No bloody sheep.'

'People,' grunted Alver.

'Well, yeah. A few maybe. Living in caves and whatnot.'

'What do they ...? Druids. Yeah, the druids.'

Geoff glanced round. 'Yeah. Welsh word that, as a matter of fact. Means men of the oak, I think.' He pointed to the west, to the wood on the banks of the stream. 'Down there – ' his voice broke in a hiccup, which became a giggle.

Alver struggled up and lurched into the wall next to him. Another rock thudded away over the grass.

'Hoo!' Geoff swayed back, face red now, eyes bright behind their discs of glass. 'How many did you say you had in town?'

Alver threw him a wild look as he rolled awkwardly onto the wall. With a grunt he fell to the grass and regained his feet, breathing heavily, a slick of sweat plastering hair to his forehead. Geoff giggled again as he watched Alver stagger towards the gully in a series of rapid stumbling steps punctuated with swaying pauses.

He reached the gully in a rush, on his knees in a clatter of sliding rocks. Propping himself unsteadily on one hand he lifted the other, two fingers extended, but the vomit was already in his mouth. Clotted, creamy liquid gushed repeatedly into the rock as his body heaved. Finally, panting, he convulsed with a spasm that brought only spittle, and clawed in a pocket for a stained grey handkerchief to wipe his mouth and eyes. He took a last deep breath, face grimacing at the steaming, dripping rocks, and got slowly to his feet. Dropping the balled handkerchief to the ground he heaped loose scree over the worst of it and turned to plod back up the slope.

As he clambered back over the wall he smiled shakily at Geoff, who was watching anxiously.

'That's better.' A faint bubbling noise came from his nose with each breath.

Geoff smiled too, but looked uncertain. 'You sure you're OK?'

'Sure. Just a matter of doing what your body tells you.' He made a smacking sound with his lips. 'Lovely.' Taking the bottle from the ground he took a gulp and smacked his lips again.

Geoff stared, his mouth hanging open.

'Go on then, Geoff. What were you saying? About the Druids …?'

'Er … yeah … well … just that, really. Just that you can easily imagine how it must have been. It's that kind of place.'

'Power.' Alver took another pull at the bottle, and lit a cigarette. 'Peregrines here all that time, as well.'

'Yeah. I imagine so.'

'Oh, they were.' He blew out smoke. 'It won't all be sunny, either.'

'Mmm?' Geoff frowned.

'Any more of that cheese then?'

As he passed it across, Geoff sniffed the air unhappily. 'Your chin, Alver …'

Alver nodded, rubbing his hand through his beard and wiping it in the grass. He bit into the rich white and blue segment. 'Wolves, wildcats, peregrines and druids.'

Geoff frowned and took a small sip from the flask-top. 'And now there's just the peregrines.'

'And us. First cloud.' Alver smiled at the ground.

Geoff had to screw up his eyes to search the sky. 'Oh yeah. The bugger.' He swirled his drink. 'So, what d'you think you'll be doing after this little lot's finished?'

Alver looked away. 'Who knows?'

'Well, don't you?'

'Not yet. I will though.' He shrugged. 'It's nothing to worry about'

'But you must have some plans?'

'Plans?' Alver scowled at the almost empty bottle resting against his leg. 'People having plans is what keeps that madhouse out there going.'

'Well yes. That's just the way things are, isn't it? Reality. No good pretending they're not. I mean, what's the alternative?'

Alver pointed across the valley without looking up. 'Sixty-six.' Ravens croaked to one another high over their heads.

Geoff's mouth opened and closed and he tilted the flask top, gazing at the brown-yellow film of whisky rolling over the plastic.

'I'm enjoying this,' said Alver in a quiet voice. 'This, now, here.'

Geoff's head, which had started to sink between his shoulders, jerked up.

'Yeah, right. Been thinking about that. What d'you think, on the last day, if we have a bit of a party up here?'

'We're having one now, aren't we? They just happen.'

'Well yeah, but I mean a proper one. Invite people. Bit of drink, bit of food. I'll get some people. George, Derek, Nige my brother – you'd like Nige. Old Clive would come along wouldn't he? You could invite who you like. Your girl, maybe? What d'you think?' He gurgled. 'Maybe some druids'll show up.'

'Sounds like the danish blue talking.'

'Nah.' Geoff was insistent. 'Be good.'

'Will you know when the last day is?'

'I'll know. No problem there.'

Alver lifted the bottle to his mouth, then held it towards Geoff. 'Just a trickle left.'

Geoff belched and held a hand flat over the flask-top, shaking his head. 'Nah. Had enough.' He swallowed another belch and gave a crooked smile.

Alver studied him. 'Two fingers, Geoff.' He drained the bottle and dropped it into the carrier bag, then got to his feet and trained his binoculars on the cliff. 'Getting a bit dark to see.'

It was also turning cold, as the line of the retreating day had long since passed over the shelter and on up the hill behind them. Sometimes they climbed with it, to stay in the warmth a little longer, but today it had crept over them unnoticed, and left them behind.

In the caravan Alver turned off the light and wriggled into his sleeping bag. Carefully, he turned to bring the ice-cold zip to brush against the insides of his thighs, which were burning. Just as he was drifting off Geoff muttered and wrestled over in his bed to face the wall. The muttering came again, then Geoff sat bolt upright.

'Mummy!' He stared around wildly.

'No.'

Geoff's voice was breathless and rushed. 'White rabbits, white rabbits, white rabbits.' He lay back on the bed, muttering in the darkness, then turned again to face the wall. After a few stutters he settled into a steady, rumbling snore.

Once, in the small hours, Alver's eyes opened and stared into the blackness, then closed again. He ran along a beach with two men. Ahead of them ran a further, shadowy figure. A soughing silence pressed at his ears. The man in front of them turned and threw up his hands in front of his face. A gull cried and Alver turned to see the figure lying further up the beach, as if asleep. Long black hair hid the face. Again the gull cried, and his arms swung, but he could not lift himself free of the clinging sand. A hand brushed back the hair, and eyes found him. Lips curved in a smile, but the eyes were the cold grey of the sea.

9. Leon

Clive worked methodically, chopping aubergine with short, measured strokes of a deep-bladed Japanese knife, his head moving emphatically at intervals to the swell of the Pastoral Symphony floating in the air about him, filling the dusty corners of *Diolch i Duw* with its serenity. At the end of each downstroke a pale, purple-rimmed disc was shunted neatly to one side before the blade lifted for the next. On the shelves and walls jars, bottles and tins stood in tidy lines, most of them dull with disuse.

The music soared, and Clive's eyes closed as his head lifted and he began to whistle. Abruptly he caught himself and frowned down in concentration at the blade nearing the end of the glossy purple pod; his whistling became distracted and tailed off. At the summons of the bell he dropped the knife and hurried to the door, wiping his hands on bottle-green corduroy trousers.

'Ah. Welcome, welcome. Do come in both of you, come in.' As he followed them through he apologised for the music. 'Not too loud is it?' he shouted. Geoff and Alver both shook their heads and smiled. 'Helps me when I'm working in the kitchen.' He grinned at them for a moment, then strode over to the record. 'Perhaps it is just a bit.' He turned it down. 'There. That's better.'

'Brought a bottle,' announced Geoff, standing it with a thump on the cabinet next to the Famous Grouse.

'Oh, you shouldn't have, really. Anyway, make yourselves comfortable. What would you like to drink?' Clive had already picked up the whisky, but noticed Geoff's uncomfortable expression. 'I've got ...' he knelt down and poked around in the cabinet, '... er ... don't often go in here, actually, I usually - ,' he grunted with effort as he reached to the back, ' – ah, here we are. Some vodka, some ...' holding a small oddly-shaped bottle to the light, he frowned uncertainly. 'Cherry brandy? It could be, I - '

'I'll have some of that wine, thanks Clive.' Geoff stood in front of the fireplace, eyeing the blank television screen.

'Ah. Of course. And for you Alver?'

'Whisky's fine for me, thanks Clive.'

'Good.' Clive braced his palms on his knees and pushed himself to his feet. He half-filled a glass and handed it to Alver. 'There you are. The water of life. I've a bit still to do in the kitchen. Won't take long. Oh, your wine – I'll just go and open it. Oh, what a big bottle, what is it? Valpolicella. Perfect choice Geoff.'

A moment later he reappeared with a glass of wine, free hand stroking the air as he handed it to Geoff, his head nodding dreamily with the rolling music. When he returned to the kitchen Geoff followed and leaned on the edge of the door, peering round it as he sipped his drink. His shoulders shook with a suppressed snigger, and he turned to beckon Alver.

Clive swayed as he chopped, a sound between a hum and a loud breath coming at intervals from his throat, his face set in a stern expression. The music began to die, and the blade dipped and swooped in ever more imaginative and emphatic gestures; a flurry of chops and a ring of courgette wheeled away across the floor and under the fridge. Clive interrupted the rhythmic swinging of his head to snatch a gulp from a tumbler on the windowsill, then reached for an onion. Alver took Geoff firmly by the arm and pulled him away.

The music reached its end and Clive appeared in the kitchen doorway. Geoff was already kneeling in front of the television.

'Ah.' Clive crossed to the record-player and stood there, hands in his pockets. 'Anything on Geoff? In particular, I mean …'

Geoff grunted and twiddled knobs. After a moment Clive reached and snapped off a switch, then picked up the Famous Grouse and disappeared into the kitchen.

Moving backwards on his knees Geoff felt behind him for his seat and eased into it. Animals peered disinterestedly through mesh and steel bars. 'History of zoos,' he muttered.

Alver stood with his drink and studied one of Clive's pictures hanging on a dark chocolate-coloured wall. A steam-engine wound through a rippled sea of greenery, a smoky white trail marking its wake.

'What do you think?'

Whisky breath. *Never give them your name.* Clive, half-smiling, sipping from his tumbler, watery grey eyes flicking from Alver to the painting and back.

'Be a lot better without the train.'

'Oh, really?' Clive sounded disappointed. 'I thought it was rather good. It's a narrow-gauge railway, quite a famous one.' He stood back from the wall and angled his head. 'Gives the eye something to work in to, a destination, in all that wilderness …'

Alver swallowed whisky and drew back his lips in a grimace. 'It doesn't fit ... the place itself ... it's not necessary. I don't think so, anyway. The rest of it's good though. You've caught the hills.' He paused and ran a hand through long, greasy hair. 'You've got the look of the place, the feel. Like the one you did of the cliff.'

'Ah. I'll do you another when I next come over. That was spoiled.' Clive pointed to the sky. 'You see, it's just about to rain. I only just - '

'Bloody country,' observed Geoff loudly over his shoulder.

Clive and Alver glanced across at his back. On the screen dark mounds of slaughtered buffalo lay in a swirling sea of dust. Clive grinned and rolled his eyes.

'Christ. Just take a look at that.' Geoff swivelled on his seat and waved at the screen. His voice was hard with disgust. 'Animals.' A faded green lizard lay wearily across painted papier-mâché mountains. Every few seconds its tongue thrust briefly from its mouth, but otherwise there was no movement. From its back, dark leathery wings drooped, bony finger-ends brushing the floor of a miniature valley.

Geoff's voice cut across the sound blurring from the screen. 'Sewing bats' wings onto lizards to make monster movies. Pretending they're dragons. Pretending they can fly. How bloody grotesque.'

Clive licked his lips fastidiously. 'The things people will do ...' He turned to Alver. 'People can be so inhuman ... I can understand anyone not wanting to have normal feelings. They can be destroyed ...'

The lizard's tongue flicked and the commentary stopped; flicked again and the scene was gone, and a pale, nervous-looking deer edged into view.

Shaking himself, Clive wandered back towards the kitchen, sipping as he went. 'Help yourselves to drinks. I shan't be much longer in here.'

Geoff leaned back in his chair, one leg swinging over the side. 'Yeah, what're you making, Clive?'

Clive turned in the doorway. 'Oh, a kind of moussaka, actually. A recipe of my own.'

Geoff's leg stopped swinging. 'What?'

Vegetarian moussaka, Geoffrey, all under control.' His voice held a trace of irritation and he muttered to himself as he ducked back into the kitchen.

Alver leaned over the back of Geoff's chair. 'Just lay off Clive, OK?'

Geoff swung round aggressively, met Alver's gaze, just inches away, and drew back. 'Oh, don't worry. He knows I'm only joking.'

Nodding, Alver pushed himself upright.

'We get on fine,' added Geoff in a hoarse whisper as Alver moved away.

In the kitchen Alver topped up his glass with Famous Grouse and wandered around, picking up and examining jars of dried beans, herbs, little pieces of pasta shaped like seashells.

'You've got a lot of stuff, Clive.' He wiped the dust from his fingers onto his jeans.

'Ah, yes. I suppose I have, really. One collects things, over the years.' His tongue poked between his lips as he poured a thick, creamy-looking sauce into an earthenware pot full of chopped vegetables.

'Looks good, Clive.' Alver licked his lips uneasily, looking away from the pale, splashing liquid. He considered his swirling whisky for a moment, then tilted back his head to drain the glass.

'Let's hope so.' Strands of hair were sticking to Clive's forehead; as he lifted the heavy pot he vainly tried to dislodge them by blowing. 'Could you open the oven door for me please, Alver?'

He crouched and pushed the pot onto a shelf then swung the door shut.

'I used to be quite good. Don't get much opportunity to cook for people nowadays. Let's hope I haven't lost my touch, eh?'

'I'm going up to Manchester at the weekend.'

Clive straightened slowly. 'Oh, I am glad Alver. Your mother will be so pleased.' Taking the offered cigarette between his lips he stared at its end as Alver held out a light, then took it from his mouth, his eyes unfocussing in a cloud of smoke. 'You must tell her ...'

'I'll give her your regards, yeah.' Alver gazed around the kitchen in the ensuing silence, arms across his chest, empty glass in one hand, cigarette in the other. 'I'll tell her what a nice place you've got.' His gaze returned to Clive. 'She'd like it here.'

Clive's lips twitched and he turned to study the oven. 'It should be ready in about half an hour. Something like that.' Lifting his glass he drained it and bustled from the room. Alver leaned back against the sink, watching cigarette smoke drift slowly up to the cobwebs netting the ceiling. A moment later Clive reappeared. 'I forgot, the bottle's in here. Come on, Geoff thinks we're neglecting him.'

After the meal Geoff and Clive got into a lengthy discussion of various students and staff-members in Bristol. As Alver climbed the stairs their voices rose and fell, first together, then Clive's alone, then Geoff's swamping bellow of scornful laughter. In the soft, pinkish light of the toilet the inflamed area of his groin looked duller; better, almost. He studied a calendar while urine splashed noisily into the bowl. May showed the starry gulf above them. He stood back from it, frowned, then hawked and spat into the bowl and pulled the chain. As the noise of moving water subsided, Geoff's strident voice again drowned Clive's downstairs. Taking the calendar from the wall, Alver turned the page and replaced it. June's was a dark scene, a horsed knight and dragon dwarfed by sinister-looking, fantastic foliage; unpleasant shapes hung back in the shadows. A ring was drawn in ink around one of the dates, and Alver leaned forward: Sunday, June 14th.

He stood for a moment on the landing, listening to the excited, unintelligible burble of voices, then stepped quietly to a part-open door and gave it a push: Clive's bedroom, dim and still. A faint smell hung in the air, a mixture of after-shave, slept-in sheets and stale clothes. On a low table by the bed stood several paperbacks, a heavy glass ashtray, a beer mat, a small, framed photograph. Alver bent closer. His eyes narrowed as his mother smiled out at him, dark-haired and slim, the years stripped from her. Clive stood next to her, his face unlined and cheerful, his hair brushed back, dark and glossy. His mother wore a white tunic. In the background stretched a lawn, and beyond them part of a sprawling Victorian building, rows of tall windows in red brick. Voices swelled again downstairs, and Alver straightened up. Owen's voice … *in her best interests, just for a while. Your visits seem to disturb her … we'll contact you when there's been an improvement*. Then Jack's face, thrust forward, eyes glaring, temple throbbing. Alver ignored him. 'Does this mean you've an idea what the cause is?' Owen's mouth opening, Jack's voice bellowing, *Course he has, we all have! It's you, you no-good, work-shy, big-talking bastard! Led her so far up the fucking garden path and left her there, fucked her up so she doesn't know who she even is any more … Now fuck off! And if I ever see your face round here again I'll break your fucking back!* Marion began to sob as he faced Jack. 'You're an old man, Jack. Be careful.' The fight, the feel of his fist sinking into yielding gut, the running down flights of stairs demanding keys from startled figures in white; staring, giggling women in pale blue smocks; then the last key, the last door, and beyond it the real world of bustle and indifference.

Alver stared at his fist, and slowly forced it to unclench. He went back downstairs.

'There you are. Thought you'd got lost.' Geoff was red-faced as he lay back in the armchair, legs crossed. 'We have the first recruit for our party. Clive.'

Clive beamed at Alver from a large cushion on the floor. He pushed back his hair and nodded. 'I think it's a jolly good idea. Mind you,' he continued, looking suddenly serious, 'a lot will depend on the weather. It's the same with everything round here. Still, Geoff assures me it'll be gloriously sunny. What do you think, Alver? You're our weather expert, after all.'

Dropping heavily into a chair, Alver stared hard at Clive for a moment, then picked up his glass of wine. 'I'll tell you when it gets nearer the time.'

'Maybe Leon would like to come ...'

'Wouldn't be interested Clive.'

Clive persisted. 'Oh, but surely, if you asked him, after the London rat-race ...'

'He belongs in the rat-race.'

'Oh, Alver. That's not a very kind thing to say.' While Clive spoke, Geoff studied Alver over the rims of his glasses.

'He wouldn't want to know, Clive, OK?'

For a second, it looked as though Clive was about to argue, but instead he reached for his cigarettes, passing one across to Geoff. 'Well, of course. You know best.'

Alver swirled wine around his mouth, gaze fixed on the thin trail of engine-smoke over the woodland.

Clive followed his gaze, then cleared his throat. 'Geoff tells me you expect the first young one to fly next week, maybe even over the weekend - '

'Nah,' interrupted Geoff, pulling his cigarette quickly from his mouth. He grinned at Alver, who had turned with a look of surprise. 'Not this weekend. Early next week. Won't happen till you get back.' He took a long pull at the cigarette and settled back, exhaling with a flourish. 'Wouldn't dare. Next Tuesday. That's my prediction.'

From his position on the floor between them, Clive looked from one to the other, but neither said anything more. 'So it will soon be all over, then ...' His voice quavered a little, and he coughed discreetly. 'Any thoughts, Alver on ...? No, of course. No rush, is there?' Hair had crept back over one eye.

Geoff made a show of looking at his watch, and waited for Alver's nod. He got to his feet. 'Well, Clive ...'

'Oh.' Clive rocked from side to side on the cushion in an attempt to get up, then put down his drink and hauled himself upright using the arm of Geoff's chair. 'Are you sure?' Dark, spreading spots led in a line down the velvety brown material of his shirt.

Geoff nodded vigorously, his mouth full of wine. He swallowed and held out the empty glass. 'Got to be back on the job bright and early in the morning. It's alright for some.'

'Yes, yes of course.' Clive smiled hesitantly at each of them, then bent down to pick up his drink. As he straightened again there was a small but distinct popping sound. 'Ah.' His grin became rueful. 'The old knees aren't what they used to be.'

'Dry joints,' said Geoff lightly. As he set off up the stairs he muttered. 'Surprising really.'

Alver turned to Clive. 'Thanks for the meal Clive.'

'Oh, not at all. Wasn't too bad, was it?' His eyes flicked towards the ceiling. 'It would have been even better with meat though, wouldn't it? I don't think I could become a vegetarian, you know. Much as I dislike causing suffering to animals ...'

'Clive?'

'Mmm?'

'If you and my mother were so fond of each other, why did you ever split up?'

Clive's face went suddenly slack, and he lowered his eyes. 'Oh ... we were fond of one another. Very fond. These things happen though ...' he gave a dry chuckle, 'or don't happen. One of you meets someone new, someone more ... Anyway, it was all a long time ago. It's difficult to recall things clearly now.' He managed a half-hearted smile, eyebrows raised.

Alver nodded solemnly. Upstairs the toilet flushed.

'My fault,' muttered Clive, raising his glass as he turned away. 'My fault.'

'Didn't ... wasn't there anyone else?'

'Oh yes. Well, there was a girl, for a time. She ... wasn't very good for me.' He gazed at the picture of the train. 'Such a long time ago though.'

Geoff bounded down the stairs and into the room.

'Righto! Off we go then.'

Clive stood on the doorstep as they climbed into the car. Doors slammed and Geoff shouted. 'Give you a bell then, Clive. About the party.'

'Yes,' Clive shouted back, then with a start lowered his voice to a hoarse whisper. 'Yes.' In the silent grey building next door a light came on at an upstairs window.

'Cheers Clive.' Alver spoke over the wound-down window.

Clive nodded, his eyes wandering from the square of light to Alver's pale, intent face.

'Yeah, bye Clive' bellowed Geoff. After a few preliminary bursts on the throttle, the car roared along the narrow, darkened street and off into the night.

For some time after the engine noise had faded Clive stared after it, then he turned, and after a quick glance next door stepped wearily back inside *Diolch I Duw*, closing the door quietly behind him. A minute or two later the light next door winked out, and the darkness was complete.

The falcon lifted into the air and floated easily out over the valley, pulling at a feathered corpse dangling from her talons, throwing back her head to swallow. Black eyes watched from black and white masks on the ledge. The youngest eyas, Number Four, still carried tufts of down around the tops of wings and legs but the other three were becoming daily more difficult to distinguish. Number One, once more in the heather run away from the ledge, turned awkwardly to follow the flight of a bee, showing a back slaty grey in the sun between dark chocolate shoulders. Two hundred feet above lingered the circling black point of the tiercel, sharp against a white-dappled blue backdrop. Once in a while the soft bubbling of a curlew sounded from the hidden moor land.

A kite wandered into the skyline and the soaring black dot fell chattering, blurring white and blue, striking the air feet from the carrion-bird and looping up to attack again. A scintilla of green showed for an instant as the wind caught the kite and carried it away.

Alver followed the tiercel in its climb back to its station high above the cliff, then shifted to study the ledge. Two eyasses stiffened briefly as a farmer whistled his dogs in a field beyond the hills. For ten minutes more he watched the hunting peregrine, propping his back against the rock buttress at the rear of the shelter, until eventually the bird beat away to the south and did not return. Alver pulled himself to his feet and scrambled over the wall, setting his feet to the zigzagging line of sheep-walks that led to the Sphinx.

Long before he reached it he had shrugged off the heavy motorcycle jacket and slung it over his shoulder; at the end of the climb he stood for several minutes bent over, hands on knees, breathing deeply with closed eyes. At the end of each sucking breath there was a small scraping sound in his chest. Pushing himself upright he coughed and spat into the grass.

The Sphinx looked over him. He ran a hand slowly over the rough, sun-warmed surface, frowning up at the blind grey face looking out over the valley.

For a while he studied the flickering, stop-go runs of the hunting spiders in the heather, and grasshoppers clambering in the grass and bracken to begin their dusty afternoon buzzing. He lit a cigarette, watching the smoke crawl away over the heather and disappear. A pipit rose jerkily from the slope, shrilling alarm, then it too disappeared and fell silent.

Alver's hand now held the photograph. He lay it carefully beside him and stared at the unhappy, smiling face. Slowly, the expression slipped from his face; his eyes went blank. A hand moved, pushing blindly at his groin.

Abruptly, he jerked the hand away and plunged it into the heather, his face contorted. Throwing himself flat on his back he gazed with blurring eyes at the slowly-moving clouds. His hand, clenched tight around a knotted branch of heather, strained upwards, slowly tearing it from the earth.

A crawling line of cars stretched along the winding coast road, some pulling caravans, all crammed with children, uncles, aunts, dogs. Radios blared, children fought and sulked, aunts sat quietly knitting. Red-faced men muttered, fingers drummed on steering-wheels.

'Bloody grockles,' sneered Geoff as he sped past, one hand on the wheel, hair whipping out from his skiing cap. He cut in sharply behind a caravan, bringing a blast on the horn from the car behind. 'Bollocks!' he muttered, glancing at the mirror. A red-faced man turned angrily to his wife, punching a pointing finger at the open red sports-car.

'Bollocks!' repeated Geoff to the mirror. 'Get back to that there Brummagem.' His inaccurate midlands whine caught in his throat and he had to cough several times to clear it. He began a staccato, tuneless whistle as he pulled out again and roared past carloads of faces watching with envy, malice, anger and resignation. With an extravagantly wide sweep he swung out of the traffic and onto the narrow, hedge-banked road that wound back to the peace of the hills.

A few trees, even now, stood bare and brown on the hillsides, while others showed the first touches of yellow and green; but everywhere in the valleys oak, ash and beech shimmered with bursting new foliage, vibrant beside the sombre, planted lines of larch and spruce.

Still whistling, Geoff changed down a gear to cruise through the village. He nodded at the cluster of old men on the steps of the Farmers Arms, oblivious to the cold looks that followed him until he swerved past the last house and out of sight. There was scarcely time for a scowl and a shake of the head at the defiled grass of the gypsy encampment before he was rattling over the cattle-grid, then a left and a short burst on the accelerator took him along the dusty track by the oakwood. A startled sheep, wool hanging in clumps from head and neck, sprang clumsily off into the trees, like a wiry little old man on all fours in a worn-out, badly-fitting coat.

Beside the caravan stood a gleaming, metallic-green Ford; a man sat on the bonnet, his head bowed, smoke curling from a cigarette in his fingers. He looked up as Geoff arrived in a whirl of fine dust, and jumped to the ground.

Geoff climbed out and slammed the door, eyeing the stranger through the slowly settling haze. 'Hello there.' His voice was taut. 'Can I help you?'

The man was bigger than Geoff, wearing light but expensive-looking clothing; stylishly cut dark blond hair swept down over one eyebrow from a perfectly straight parting. He flipped away the cigarette butt, his sharp-featured face arranged in an easy smile. When he spoke, it was with a noticeable and familiar accent. 'Hi there. I'm looking for Alver. I'm his brother.'

'Oh, right.' Geoff nodded, relaxing. 'Leon.'

'Correct.' The smile grew broader.

'Yeah. He's mentioned you. Er …is this a surprise visit then? Look, just let me dump this …' Pulling a carrier bag from the passenger seat, Geoff balanced it on one knee while he unlocked the caravan and pushed inside. 'Come in.' He turned and bumped into Leon, who stood in the doorway. 'Oh. You have.'

Leon stepped inside as Geoff bustled around drawing curtains and opening windows. 'Have to keep this place well aired. It can get pretty stuffy, you know?' He sidled past Leon into the tiny kitchen. 'I'm just making up a flask, then I'll take you up to where Alver is, OK? Would you like a coffee?'

'Yeah. Ta. You must be the bloke Alver's helping out then?'

'That's right. I'm Geoff. Milk, sugar?'

'Yeah, both please. So. How's it all going then? These birds?'

Geoff brought through two mugs, pausing at the sight of Leon sprawling full length on his bed, elegant dove-grey leather shoes resting comfortably on his blankets next to the bag of groceries.

'Make yourself at home. Here, this is yours.'

Leon nodded and took the coffee. Geoff went over to Alver's bed, carefully pushing the huddle of bedclothes to one side before perching on the edge. He sipped from the mug, eyes fixed on a point somewhere beyond the caravan wall.

'Well?' repeated Leon. 'How's it going?'

'Oh. No problems. Fine. Should all be over soon.' He stared and sipped, holding the mug with both hands.

'How soon?'

'Another ten days or so. The last one should have flown by then.'

'I see.' Leon was gazing through the window at a silver jet high in the mottled blue sky. 'You can work it all out to the day. Neat.' He turned back to Geoff with a languid half-roll. 'And what about Al? He doing alright? Should be just his cup of tea, this. He couldn't stand being a computer operator, I know that. And the factories ...Christ, how he hates factories. Well. You've seen what he's like.' Idly fingering the contents of the bag, Leon pulled out a sheaf of asparagus, hefting the tight green bundle as if about to throw it.

'I've just bought that,' said Geoff sharply, attention re-focussed.

Leon dropped the asparagus back into the bag, smiling. 'Is he? Doing alright?'

'Yeah, he's doing OK. Been a big help, as a matter of fact. He's enjoying himself.' Geoff took out his tobacco tin. 'I think he'd quite happily stay here all summer if he could.' There was a faint clunk as he prised off the lid.

'Why can't he then?'

'Well, this van, for a start. Belongs to the farm. They'll be wanting it back, after I leave. Smoke?'

Leon's lips curled fastidiously at the proffered tin. 'No ta. That stuff's a bit too rough for me. I'll stick with tailor-made.'

'I must say,' started Geoff, watching as Leon pulled a king-size from a dull-red and gold packet and snapped a gold lighter, 'you don't look much like Alver. I mean,' his eyes lingered for a moment on the darker shades underlying the immaculate blond sweep of the hair, 'I wouldn't have taken you for brothers.'

Smoke left Leon's mouth in a series of spurts as he nodded a throaty chuckle. 'No. Not exactly Tweedledum and Tweedledee are we?'

'And not just to look at,' murmured Geoff.

'How d'you mean?'

'Oh, you just seem … different, that's all.'

'Al's the different one, not me.'

'Yeah.' Geoff's chuckle was uncertain. 'Forget it.'

'OK.' Leon lifted one grey shoe over the other and put a hand behind his head, directing smoke rings at the ceiling.

Geoff's boots banged into the floor as he stood up. 'Better get going then.'

'Yeah.' Leon waved his cigarette. 'Just finish this.'

'Hmm.' Geoff strode past him into the kitchen and began throwing things into a haversack. 'Was Alver expecting you? He never mentioned it.' The caravan rocked gently as he stamped about.

'Nope. Like you said, surprise visit. Thought I'd pop up here and wish him a happy birthday.'

'What?' Geoff's head appeared in the doorway. 'When is it? He never said.'

'That's our Alver.' Leon stretched extravagantly on the bed and sighed. 'The great communicator. No, it's not for a few days yet. The fourteenth. I had a couple of days off though, so …' Swinging long legs to the floor he stood up, flicking ash from a loose, ice-blue shirt patterned with palm trees and breaking waves.

Outside he watched as Geoff locked the caravan door and gave it a tug to check it was secure. All the windows were again closed, the curtains drawn.

'Wouldn't have thought all that was necessary, round here.' Leon gazed pointedly round at the hilly fields and grazing sheep. 'Not exactly Brixton, is it?'

'Yeah, well you'd be surprised.' Geoff was about to continue, but he no longer had Leon's attention, which had wandered to the MGA.

'Nice motor Geoffrey. Been thinking about getting one of these myself. Open top, all that. The ladies go for it, eh?'

Geoff smirked. 'I do alright.' He walked to the bonnet and pointed at the insignia. 'You might get the car, but you'll have trouble getting one of these to go with it. It's – ' Turning to explain he saw Leon had gone over to his own car and was inside, leaning over the back of the passenger seat.

'What do you think of these?' Leon emerged holding a pair of binoculars in one hand, their black leather case in the other.

Scowling, Geoff stumped across and took them, then whistled, his expression changing. 'Leitz. Well, they're the best.' He lifted them to his face and swung them in a rapid, practised arc along the horizon, smiling involuntarily as he concentrated. 'Excellent!' They were now pointing at a sheep twenty feet away, Geoff's forefinger pushing at the focussing wheel. The sheep looked up, slit-pupilled eyes blank, then bowed again to the grass. Geoff handed the glasses back. 'You're better equipped than Alver. He never said you were – '

Leon made a sound halfway between a cough and a chuckle as he lit another cigarette. 'Who, me? As if. You're all train-spotters to me.' He grinned, slipping on a pair of sunglasses. 'Joke, Geoffrey. No, I like a day out in the country as much as the next bloke, fresh air, all that. Long as the pub's not far away.' He lifted the black leather case. 'A present, for Al. For his birthday. If he likes this stuff so much, he should do it properly.'

Geoff nodded. 'Well, you couldn't have done any better.'

'Yeah. That's what the bloke said. Can't remember what his ones are like, but they're bound to be cheapos.'

'They are.' Geoff watched as Leon walked round the open MGA, stepped over the door and dropped into the passenger seat. He made a point of carefully opening his own door, easing himself in and pulling it to behind him. Taking his own binoculars from the glove compartment he flourished them before slipping them over his head. 'The bloke was right. They're the best.'

'Say no more.'

The engine fired, Geoff worked handbrake, gear lever and pedals in rapid sequence, and the red car swung in a tight circle, narrowly missing the Ford.

'That your own?' asked Geoff, when Leon failed to react.'

'What, the old Fiasco? Nah. The girlfriend's.' He flashed his easy smile. 'It gets you there. I'm between motors, as they say.'

They travelled the short distance to the valley in silence. As they were about to get out, Leon turned to Geoff, hefting the black case.

'That's right then, isn't it? The best?' His eyes were hidden behind glossy black discs.

Geoff paused, one hand on the door. Again he tapped his own. 'Absolutely.'

Leon nodded and reached for the door handle.

The shelter was empty.

'He won't have gone far.' Geoff scanned the hillsides, then stopped to pull the notebook free of its anchoring stone. 'Yeah. He's gone to the Sphinx.'

'Oh.' Leon lounged against the wall, blowing smoke. 'Sounds interesting.'

Shading his eyes, Geoff peered to the east. 'It's his favourite spot. See that big rock on the skyline?'

Leon moved to stand next to him, gazed along the pointing arm, nodded.

Geoff raised his binoculars and studied the distant dark crag. 'Can't see him. That's where he'll be though. He won't be long.' Turning back to the valley he swung the glasses in a series of jerks across the cliff-face, from one rock to another, pausing at the ledge. 'Hmmmm. Everything seems to be alright. Want to see the nest?'

Leon nodded vaguely, blank black discs fixed on the east. 'It's not that far Geoff. Think I'll stroll on up there and give him a surprise.'

'Really?' Geoff eyed him sceptically. 'Actually, it's further than it looks. And steeper. These hills take a bit of getting used to ...'

'Doesn't look much to me.' Leon flashed the grin. 'You're looking at a bloke who lives on the second floor.' After a pause to light a cigarette he stepped to the wall and rolled smoothly over, then started up the hillside, brushing at his loose-fitting, dazzlingly white trousers. He turned, waved his cigarette, 'See you later,' and set off at a rapid pace, sheep scrambling to get out of his way.

For a while Geoff stared after the colourful, receding figure, then gave a snort and turned back to the cliff.

Taking a zigzag route to the skyline, Leon reached the crest of the ridge some distance to the west of the Sphinx and sat on a grass-topped boulder to regain his breath. Distant jet-noise rumbled through the air around him. Before going on he took the dark glasses from his face, slipping them into a pocket of the surf-and-palm shirt.

A breeze ruffled the stubbly grass as he strode across it; below him, in the valley, nothing moved in the afternoon heat. The high patterns of cloud had started to diffuse as the day meandered on, drawing a soft, filmy veil over the glare. A dull stain of colour caught his eye high on the grey wall of the looming outcrop: his brother.

Alver sat on a ledge on the face of the Sphinx, twenty feet from the ground, gazing out to the south across the valley.

Leon came to a halt and watched. For a time, on the hills and in the skies, all was still but for the restless wind.

Finally Leon stirred, and picked his way carefully forward through the broken stone scattered across the hilltop. He stopped again just ten yards from the intent figure of his brother, and followed the direction of his gaze, over the valley and beyond, to the marching hills, the knifing precision of rock and rough grass blurring ridge upon ridge, mile upon mile into the haze.

Taking out a bright blue handkerchief, Leon wiped sweat from his forehead and shifted his footing to move forward. Without looking round, Alver held up a hand.

'Hello Lee.' He spoke without turning, still staring into the southern distance.

'Hello Al.' Leon waited a moment, then advanced to the seamed grey wall, which reared to its highest directly over his brother's head. 'Didn't think you'd seen me.' He looked up intermittently from his footing as he climbed, until he was fifteen feet below Alver's booted feet. 'Got yourself a nice seat up there.'

Alver looked down at last but said nothing.

Pushing his hands into his pockets Leon turned away, making a show of studying the view. 'Quite a climb to get to it too. Not much chance of you being disturbed up here.'

Alver's gaze returned to the valley. There was an awkward pause.

'Come to wish you an early happy birthday Al.' He stood, waiting. 'You coming down then?'

Slowly, Alver looked down again at his brother, his face expressionless. His tongue darted from his lips, then he shook himself. Carefully, he eased down from the ledge and climbed to the ground.

'Brought you a prezzy Al.' Leon held out the black case, the side with Leitz stamped into the leather uppermost.

Alver took the case, nodding to himself. His old pair of glasses gave a dull clink as he laid them on a rock and slipped the strap of the Leitz over his head. 'Same as Geoff's,' he observed, with a quick grin.

'Yeah. Best you can get. Top of the range. Geoff says so too.' Leon looked away. 'So. What d'you think?'

'Ta.' A smile forced its way onto Alver's weatherbeaten face. 'Thanks Lee. Be able to see everything now.'

'You like 'em then? I can get another model if you want, no prob, but the bloke said ...' But Alver was shaking his head, the Leitz to his eyes, still smiling his absent smile. Leon lowered himself onto a rock, pulled cigarettes from his pocket. 'Cig Al? Or you still smoking frogs? Right.' He lit one for himself and took the smoke deep, holding it there for a couple of beats before jetting it slowly from his lips. 'Nothing like the open air for really enjoying a fag eh?' Looking down at his feet, he tapped the cigarette repeatedly with a yellowed forefinger, then he lifted his head abruptly. 'You don't mind me coming?'

'No. Course not. Glad to see you.' Alver's gaze flickered over the rocks.

Leon nodded and took another lungful of smoke. 'It's been a long time. Before, when – '

'Isn't this a wonderful place?' Alver made a slow sweep of the valley with the Leitz. 'Can you feel it?'

'Yeah. Really great. I just wanted to – '

'You know what Lee? I've never felt so much at home as I do here. I never have felt at home really, not since we were kids. Not in the right place. Until here.'

A pipit fluttered up from the grass, piping excitedly. Alver looked uneasily around the rocks. 'You're disturbing things. We'd better go.'

They made their way back along narrow, muddy trails scored through the grass over the years by countless cloven hooves. As they plodded, Leon studied his brother's back. A litter of dull red spots showed on the skin where a grubby T-shirt rode above his jeans.

'Lost a bit of weight, haven't you Al?'

'Yeah. Bit, I suppose.'

'Who does the cooking? No, don't tell me - the Geoffrey. Looks the sort. He any good?'

'Vegetarian.'

Leon's eyes rolled. 'Why am I not surprised? Nut cutlets then, all that.' He lit a cigarette, stopping to shield the slim gold lighter with his hand. Alver had carried on walking. 'Hey Al,' he called, 'any chance of a drink tonight? They do have pubs round here?'

Leon rocked back on his chair, one smart grey shoe hooked under the table, and examined the dingy room with its rickety old furniture, its wall of indecipherable notices, the cloth-capped old men in one corner in their shroud of tobacco smoke. 'Ace place Al.' He swallowed beer and grimaced. Alver held out the blue and white pack. 'Yeah, I will have one. Make a change. You telling me you manage to get them round here?'

'No.'

Leon waited, but there was no more. He rocked back to the table for a light. 'Place could do with a juke though but.'

The two of them puffed for a while without speaking, each staring into his own smoke. The celtic burble and domino clatter swelled and subsided in the corner without ever stopping altogether.

'Geoff says you'll be finished here in ten days or so.'

'He means he will be.'

'Oh? How d'you mean?' Leon watched over the rim of his glass.

Alver shrugged. 'I like it here. I said.'

'Yeah, I know. But. There's nothing to do, is there? Once Geoff clears off that's it, isn't it? There'll be nowhere to live, for a kick-off, will there?'

Another shrug. 'There'll be something. Something different.'

Leon began to speak, but stopped and swallowed beer instead. Behind the bar the old barman picked his teeth, holding a finger to the yellowing light to examine the results. He tried again. 'Just thinking about Ma, that's all. I think she's a bit ...well, she worries a lot, you know what she's like.' He rocked forward to grind out the cigarette. 'Spoke to her the other day, on the phone. She said she hadn't heard from you for a while.'

'Is that why you've come?' Alver lifted his glass, eyes locked on his brother.

Leon stared back at him. 'You miserable bleeder.'

Alver's gaze shifted to his beer, then he looked up again. 'Sorry Lee.' He tried a smile. 'Don't get much sleep up here. I get a bit out of it, lose touch a bit. Sorry. You're right, I should ring. Or even go up there to see her.'

'When?'

'Soon. Tomorrow.'

'Tomorrow? How you getting there?'

'Hitch, I suppose.'

Leon scrutinised his brother. 'Listen Al, you don't want to do that, that'll take forever. Drivers nowadays, they ...Look, there's no need for you to slog all the way up there, just give her a bell, she'll be just as chuffed. And what about whatsisname? Geoff?'

'Geoff's got his girl coming tomorrow afternoon sometime. He wants a bit of privacy.'

Leon's jaw jutted. 'What, so he's turfing you out for the weekend?'

'Not really. I wouldn't mind a day or two away.'

'You wouldn't? How about you come back with me then, tomorrow? You can get the train back whenever you like.'

Alver was smiling, as if to himself.

'What is it Al? I'll pay the fare, no sweat. It's your birthday.'

'Thanks Lee, but I do want to see Ma. Something I want to clear up.'

'What?'

'Just something.'

Leon's smile faded. 'There's nothing wrong, is there?'

'Course not.'

Again he waited, but there was no more. 'Hmm.' He got to his feet. 'Same again then?'

'Sure.'

An elderly man wandered in, frail and cloth-capped, and shuffled in a straight line towards the corner and into the bank of smoke. Voices rose briefly in greeting before the subdued burble resumed. Leon returned with two pints.

'So how's the job going Lee?'

Leon shrugged. 'You know what it's like. A job's a job. Drag city.'

'Thought you liked it.'

Leon frowned into the smoky distance. 'I suppose I do, really. I'm good at it, which helps. There's a bit of variety, give it that. Gets you down a bit though, day in day out, always wanting this, wanting that from you. You've got the right idea, keep looking for something different. At least,' he pulled his gaze back to his brother,'it used to be the right idea. Remember when you could do a job for a bit, then pack it in, go off and do something else? Two years was about right. Then, you give it another year, or two, and then you're stuck, cos now there aren't the jobs.' He swallowed. 'How naff is this beer, though but?'

'Are you living on your own now, or ...?'

'Yeah. Well, sort of. There's this girl, Julie. That's her motor outside. She comes round, every now and then, you know. Nothing too heavy.' He glanced idly over one shoulder as a heated discussion broke out in the smoke, then he leaned forward. 'This Geoff. Bit of a snoot, right?'

A slow smile spread across Alver's face and his eyes half closed. 'No, not really. I know how he comes across. You should have seen him to start with, right little would-be chargehand he was. He's mellowed.'

'He has? I like his motor though.' Leon held out his cigarettes but Alver waved them away and took one of his own.

'Lee, d'you ever get back down the east end these days?'

Leon looked away until he had lit up. 'No, not really. No call to. Why?'

'Oh, no reason really. Just wondered if you ever ran into anybody from before. Alex, Mac, anybody ...?'

Leon traced lines in beer on the table-top. 'No. Not for ages. I sometimes think, should I bell them, fix up a night out, you know? Never happens.'

'Not your world anymore.'

'Mmmm.'

'You've moved on. You live in a different world now.' Alver's eyes narrowed, but he was smiling. 'You like it there as well, in your world, whatever you say.'

'I do? Sometimes maybe. Yeah. It's just ...'

'What about your mates, in Kingston?'

'My mates.' The barman looked across without interest as Leon rocked back extravagantly, then returned his attention to the glass he was polishing. 'I see quite a few people, as it happens, mostly from work, for a drink and what have you, yeah. Some of 'em aren't too bad, but I kind of miss the blokes back east, like you say, Alex, Mac and them. Now, it's all clubs and parties, and drugs. Everybody's Jack the Lad.' He rocked back to the table. 'Julie likes the nightlife, wine bars and meals, clubs, all that.

'And you don't?'

'Sort of.' Leon looked puzzled. 'It's what I wind up doing, anyway, most of the time. Tell the truth, I'd be happier just sitting in a decent pub – maybe even this one – but it's always got to be a club, or a party. You get fed up.' His easy smile returned. 'Come back to Kingston tomorrow and you can have a bit yourself, make your own mind up.'

'You love it Lee.'

'Mmmm. It's just that …the number of friends you have seems to dwindle right away as you get older, real friends. You must have found that.' His hazel eyes searched Alver's face. 'I know you never needed people as much as me. I miss having people to talk to, properly. I don't even bother with the football anymore.' Here he broke into loud, theatrical sobs over his pint; there was the briefest of pauses in the clacking of dominoes. 'That's why it's done me good to come up here Al,' he finished simply. 'That is why I came. You can lose your friends but you can't lose your brother. Give us your glass.'

Alver drained the foamy brown dregs. 'I'll get these.'

'Don't be daft. I'm loaded. Short to go with it?'

Alver watched, lips curved in a quiet smile, as his brother waited impatiently for the barman to deal with one of the domino-players. The two old faces studied one another inscrutably as they exchanged long strings of sounds. Leon cut an exotic figure in the dingy room, sauntering through the drabness of which everyone else was a part. He made a loud remark and turned away with the drinks, grinning; the barman blinked rheumy, uncomprehending eyes.

'Taffs,' muttered Leon into Alver's ear as he scraped his chair closer. 'You understand any of that stuff?'

Alver shook his head, smiling. 'Nope. Geoff tried to get the hang of it.' He nodded towards the clattering corner. 'Tried it out on those old duffers one night.'

'What happened?'

'Don't know what he said. Or thought he said. They looked at him like he'd told them tadpoles turned into butterflies.'

'Yeah.' Leon sniggered, then leaned closer again. 'Just think, if you come with me …' he tapped his glass, 'ace beer, decent pubs, meat …you can 'phone Ma from my place …'

'You got a photo of this Julie?'

'Photo?' Leon looked puzzled. 'No. Look, you don't have to worry about that. Forget it. Besides, you'd get along with her fine, even if she was there. She's a good girl, not all mouth like most of them.'

'Yeah. Like I said though, I want to see Ma. Thanks anyway, Lee ...and thanks again for the bins. Really.'

'You do rate 'em, then? I don't suppose smartarse would have them if they weren't the business. I asked around before I got them, anyway. They ain't cheap. Like anything else, it's the name that counts. It's the name you're paying for.'

'Lee, d'you remember, years ago, Dad, on his birthday, plastered, taking us to the side, and telling us – '

'It wasn't his birthday.' Leon looked uncomfortable. 'An anniversary, it was.'

'Was it?'

'Yeah. He forgot it this year, too. Ma was pretty upset.'

'I don't even know when it is.'

'Oh,' Leon gestured vaguely, 'January sometime.'

'Well, anyway, whatever it was. D'you remember what he said? "Never give them your name."'

Leon nodded and took a gulp of beer. 'Gave me the willies at the time. I didn't know what he was on about.'

'What d'you think he meant?'

'Well, don't get married. What else?'

'Hmm.' Alver put down his beer, picked up a small glass of spirit. 'Nice whisky.'

'You reckon? It's some Welsh stuff, believe it or not. I thought you'd be well into it by now.'

'Nope. What's it called?'

Leon swivelled in his chair, leaning back to read the letters from the label on the bottle inverted in its optic behind the bar. 'Hang on, it's upside down.' He held his head at an angle. 'Says S-Y-N, then ... Y, then M-O-R. *Syn-y-Mor*. What's that mean then?'

Alver pursed his lips. 'Let's see ...something to do with a dog?'

Leon sipped. 'Yeah. Glen corgi.'

Alver woke abruptly. For a moment or two he blinked into the darkness, perfectly still, then one hand wandered beneath the bedclothes to rub gently at his groin.

Leon lay on the floor between the beds, snoring in his sleeping bag, invisible in the gloom. Through the erratic rumbles and snickerings wound the softer sounds of Geoff's rhythmic slumber. Tugging at the curtain, Alver looked out at the stars pinned to the cold night sky beyond the glass. *She goes where she likes,* Dawn told him smugly. *They can't control her with their tablets.* She. Her. *The staff, she has ways … they do what she wants.* His own irritable voice, 'If she's so smart, what's she doing in a loony bin?' Blue eyes blinked dully, puzzled. *A what?* Then the slowly returning secret smile. *You wouldn't understand.* The rising double-note of an owl came from the trees around the farm, followed by a sleepy goose-honk. Alver rose sharply on an elbow as stars winked out, then relaxed.

The silent black shape floated through the night towards the oakwood, to hunt mice among the twisted shadows until the light crept back into the world.

10. Dawn

The sheep stood, legs braced against the slope, scrawny body tense. At irregular intervals it gave a dull, barking cough, and a pellet of dung shot simultaneously from the opposite end to bounce among the rocks of the gully several yards away. Between convulsions it stared blankly with heavy-lidded eyes, jaws moving slowly as though chewing grass.

Geoff stood watching from behind the wall, nodding sourly to himself: another barking cough and another black missile curved through the air. Geoff turned away, muttering.

'You been training that sheep, Geoff? Very special' Leon appeared round the wall, dark glasses firmly in place, his grin unsteady; Alver followed.

Geoff glared at them. 'How long have you been there?' He glared at his watch. 'And what time's this?'

'Not so loud there, Geoff.' Leon swung carefully over the wall and sank to the ground. 'Feeling a bit careful.'

'Not bloody surprising. All that banging and shouting last night, I thought the bloody gypos had come back to finish me off. How many did you have, for God's sake?'

'Rather not think about it.' Leon lifted the black discs half an inch above his eyes, then lowered them quickly.

'How about you, Alver?' The bluster had left Geoff's voice.

Alver grinned uncomfortably. 'I'm OK. Just can't stop – ' A ripe, muffled blast split the air.

'Oh charming,' nodded Geoff, one hand fanning. 'What with you farting and the bloody sheep firing crap -'

'Geoff. Let's have some coffee,' Leon cradled his head in his hands, 'there's a good chap.'

'Didn't you just have some with your breakfast? Or couldn't you face anything?' Sighing heavily, Geoff dug out the flask. 'And that snoring …'

'Who?' The dark glasses looked up without interest.

'You. Who else?'

'Noooo. You must have been having a bad dream, mate. I never snore. That right, Al?' Alver grunted, leaning on the wall, head on his hands. 'Anyway,' continued Leon, 'even if I did, it couldn't have been me. I never got to sleep.' He eased back his shoulders, moved his head carefully and groaned. 'That floor's about as comfy as Brighton Beach.' A distinct rumbling sound came from his stomach. 'My poor gut.'

'You should have had something to eat,' snapped Geoff. 'There's plenty of food in.'

'Yeah.' Leon yawned. 'If you're a rabbit. Or a sheep.'

'You're not really the outdoor sort, are you Leon?' Geoff spoke through gritted teeth. 'You come -'

'Look, Lee,' interrupted Alver. 'Hear that shrieking. That's one of the peregrines coming in with a kill. Here, use the Leitz.'

Taking the binoculars, Leon raised them to his dark glasses. He held the position for fifteen seconds, with no change of expression, before handing them back. 'Yeah. Great.'

'They're really something when they fly, aren't they? You see the way he just sort of floated up onto the cliff?'

'Tell the truth Al, I didn't even see the cliff. Feel a bit short-sighted.' Alver farted again. 'Yeah,' nodded Leon slowly, as Geoff's nose wrinkled and he turned away, 'must have been that Welsh dog's piss.'

'You always did suffer, didn't you Lee? It'll pass.'

Leon's mouth twitched gloomily below the black lenses. Geoff's muttered comment was whipped away on the wind.

A buzzard rose in lazy circles beyond the oakwood and was followed by another. The two birds dived and tumbled together, their distant, yelping cries drifting on the stiffening breeze. A frenzy of shrieking broke out on the cliff as the tiercel hovered briefly over the ledge then dropped among the clustering eyasses, leaving them a red, plucked corpse before swinging smoothly back into space.

The wind from the southwest was becoming blustery now, driving billowing grey sheets across the blue. A handful of raindrops spattered into the rock.

'Bug-ger!' Geoff glowered at the racing clouds, puffing furiously at a roll-up. He turned to the huddled figure of Leon. 'Looks as though you'd better be moving soon. Don't want to get caught in that lot.' His thumb jerked at the sky. 'Wouldn't want to get damp, would we? Have you decided which route you're taking?'

'Oh, I found a map in the caravan. Reckon I'll take the coast road south, cut in at … where was it? Some daft Taff name anyway, head for Carmarthen, then the M4, come off around Hounslow somewhere. No sweat.' He searched the pockets of an immaculate zippered navy jacket for cigarettes. 'As to when – that'll be when my innards get back in the groove.'

'Hmm. What about you, Alver? Is he dropping you off somewhere on the way?'

'Yeah. Station.' Alver frowned at the sullen sky. 'Don't fancy hitching in this. Too late, anyway.'

'Well,' Geoff got to his feet, 'I'm off for a constitutional. If you're not here when I get back,' he added significantly, eyes on Leon's bowed blond head, 'I'll see you whenever.' Leon grunted without looking up, and Geoff disappeared noisily over the wall.

After several minutes silence Leon stirred, glancing several times over the dark glasses at his brother before clearing his throat. 'Al, last night. Well … I have been back to the east, just the once. Not long back, as a matter of fact. Had to pick something up.' He paused. 'I saw Dawn.' His forefinger tapped rapidly at his cigarette, and he went on hurriedly. 'Not to talk to. I just saw her going into this house. Near where …' His voice trailed off, and their eyes locked for a second before Leon's gaze fell; he began to brush carefully at his trousers. 'I didn't know if I should mention it, what with …'

Alver stared at him, his face hard. 'You sure it was her?'

'Course …' Leon looked quickly away. 'Yeah. It was Dawn.' He pulled out a cigarette and lit it with the butt in his fingers. 'Just thought …'

'Yeah. That's alright.' Alver turned back to the distant peregrine tracing tight circles over the bracken and rock strewn slopes. 'Sixty six.'

'What?'

'I said that's OK Lee. Let's watch the birds.'

Some time later a rock fell from the wall into Leon's lap as Geoff vaulted clumsily into the shelter.

'Hey, take it easy, Geoff!' He managed a shaky version of his smile. 'I should cut down on the bananas a bit.'

Almost immediately, Alver went for a walk on his own, leaving the other two to sit in awkward silence, Geoff studying the birds and making occasional notes, Leon slumped dejectedly against the rock buttress smoking cigarettes with one hand and holding his head with the other. Finally he shook himself, and began tossing stones languidly at nearby sheep, ignoring Geoff's growls and clucking noises. Pausing between shots, he aimed the dark glasses at Geoff's back. 'Know any good Welsh jokes then, Geoff?' Another clucking noise, louder than before. Leon's smile swaggered back into place.

Alver returned, clambering over the wall without speaking, to take up his usual place at the back of the shelter. Leon pitched a stone aimlessly, all the sheep having left, got slowly to his feet and stretched. 'Right. Reckon I'll hit the road. I've got everything with me in the motor, so I can get straight off.' He glanced at his watch. 'Back in plenty of time for a nice meal, a quiet half gallon of decent beer. Sure you're not tempted, Al?'

Alver grinned. 'I am a bit.'

Geoff looked up sharply; Leon paused in mid-stretch. 'Seriously?'

'Yeah. Why not?' His expression became serious. 'Like you said, I can speak to Ma from your place. I don't really need to plough all the way up there do I? Especially if it's going to piss it down.'

'Great. Manchester's nearly as wet as this place, even on a good day.'

'So you're going to London after all?' asked Geoff warily. 'How will you get back here?'

'Train,' grinned Leon. 'No bother.' He punched his brother on the arm. 'Great stuff. Let's shoot back to the caravan and get your gear.'

'No need. I don't need anything.'

'What about some clothes? Look, you can borrow mine. I've got plenty. Come on then, what are we waiting for? I wasn't fancying that long drive on my tod.' He turned to Geoff, beaming. 'OK Geoff. It'll have to be Yacky dar.'

Geoff gave a curt nod and looked at Alver. 'You'll be back Monday, then?'

'Sure.'

'Well, have a good time.'

'You too.'

Geoff's face finally broke into a smile. 'Next week's the big one.' He shook a fist. In a lower voice, he added, 'While you're down there, give a thought to the sea and the sand.'

'And the sun.'

'Of course the sun.'

Alver nodded, his grin lop-sided. 'Good luck with George.'

The cry of a peregrine sounded over the valley, a thin, rising note. Alver had turned to face the cliff when another flurry of raindrops whipped across the slopes, and he blinked as water ran from his forehead into an eye.

'The birds are saying cheerio to you, Al.' Leon stooped to pick up a final stone, then paused, holding it up against the sky. 'I should be careful, Geoff.' Caught between finger and thumb, scratched lines showed on the dull surface. 'Looks as if you are not alone.' He grinned and winked, then flipped the stone into space.

Geoff watched the two men as they moved away up the long grassy slope: Leon, slim and bright, blond head nodding above his navy jacket, hands gesturing around his muffled voice; and beside him the dark, plodding figure of his brother.

The drive south was uneventful but pleasant. Leaving the coast road, with its cars and caravans, and its view of a long, curving shoreline, they cut inland over gentle green hills, sweeping through lonely, hidden villages with strings of letters for names. Before long they swung onto the motorway, and Leon pushed the accelerator to the floor. The industrial towns of south Wales went by, and the hills that climbed beyond them, distant, sandy pillars with dark plantations crowding at their tops.

'I came over here a couple of years ago' remarked Leon shortly afterwards, 'on a kind of course. That place,' he pointed to the south, to the gleaming, near-silent sprawl of pipes and towers of the steelworks, 'used to be amazing. Just a mass of activity. Clanging, belching smoke, all that.' His head turned slowly as the scene fell behind. 'Maybe it's just their annual shutdown. Looks as if it's on its last legs though. Poor blokes.'

'Wonder if they play tennis.'

'Mmm?' Leon's eyes moved back to the road, the broken lines of speeding traffic.

'Here we go then,' he said some time later as the Severn Bridge loomed against the grey skies. 'Civilization's only a couple of hours away.' The vast, muddy river slid by between greasy brown banks below them. As they left the toll-booth, Leon settled back in his seat and the needle crept around the dial. 'Light us one of your cigs, Al. Can't taste any worse than my mouth does already.' With a whoosh a motorcycle overtook them; two black-suited figures crouched in the shelter of its fairing, bulbous black-helmeted heads bent low. 'Al?'

Two hours later they left the leisurely gallop of the motorway, and the green Ford slowed to a crawl through ordered, leafy suburbs, T-junctions and traffic lights; the road became steadily more congested.

'Refreshing, ain't it?' Leon smiled broadly, waving at the lines of idling machinery. 'That quiet life, it's overrated. All that fresh air. Look at that.' He pointed at oily smoke belching from a bus, and took a deep breath. 'Ah. This is for us, Al. This is the real world.' With a sudden wrench at the wheel, he guided the Ford into the tiniest of spaces at the kerbside. 'Bingo.'

Alver climbed out, moving stiffly, and gazed around as he flexed his legs. 'I'd forgotten what it's like.'

People flooded the pavements between massive buildings, jostling and overtaking like the jam of vehicles clogging the road. Individual sounds were lost in a wall of noise.

'And the smell …' but Leon had gone, pushing confidently into the melee, slipping through like a trout in its stream. He stood in a doorway, grinning and waving.

Inside the restaurant it was dark, quiet and cool. They were led to a table by the window.

'Order whatever you like, Al.' Leon patted his breast pocket. 'I'm well plasticked up.' His eyes narrowed. 'You alright? You don't look too clever …'

'Yeah.' Alver ran his tongue hurriedly across his lips. 'Just feel a bit … washed out. That's all.'

'Soon sort that out. It's all that vegetarian nonsense. No red meat.'

'Have you been here before, then?' His eyes slid over the other diners as cutlery clinked and conversation rippled discreetly.

Leon leaned back in his seat, hair falling in a smooth blond curve as he ran a hand through it. 'Once or twice. I bring Julie here sometimes, when she doesn't feel like cooking. She's a great cook though.' He lit a cigarette and tilted his face to direct a long plume of smoke at the ceiling. 'Go on. Check out the menu.'

Alver picked up the heavy menu-holder and opened it, lips moving as his eyes travelled down the page. He shifted awkwardly in his seat: beneath the table his free hand rubbed quickly at his groin.

'Large vodka tonic, plenty of ice,' said Leon crisply to the waiter poised at his shoulder. 'You Al?'

'Same.'

The waiter withdrew.

'What's it to be then? A pound and a half of raw red beefsteak, in one quivering hunk? Or maybe a lamb's leg?'

'It's expensive.'

'Don't worry about that. Ah.' The drinks were set before them. Leon took his and swallowed half in two gulps. He sucked in his breath contentedly. 'That's more like it!'

A man, shabbily dressed and old, emerged from the crowd outside and pressed his face to the window, then put up a hand to shield his eyes. Alver stared back at him, only feet away, until Leon swivelled in his chair.

'One way glass. Dark from the outside, clear from in here.' He chuckled as he lifted his drink. 'Wonder what he thinks he can see.'

The hopeless face frowned blindly into the glass, blinking, then turned and shuffled back into the moving people.

'Go on, Al. Anything you like. No nut cutlets in this place.' Leon took another menu. 'I know what I'm having. Support the Welsh economy, that's my new motto.'

The street lights had come on when they left the restaurant, holding the grey evening skies firmly away from the concrete, the glass and the scurrying pavements. Leon belched, apologised to a passer-by, and patted his slight paunch cheerfully. 'Not bad.'

'It was great Lee. Best meal I've had since ...' Alver shook his head. 'Can't remember when. Have to come down here more often.'

'Anytime Al, anytime. You know that.' Taking a cigar from his mouth, Leon pointed with it across the street. 'See that pub? Wait in there while I drop the car off, OK? I'll only be ten minutes.' He pressed a note into his brother's hand, 'Two pints of special Al,' and moved off along the pavement, searching his pockets for the keys. 'Ten minutes, OK?'

The bar was large and well-lit, gleaming with lines of glasses and dark, polished wood. Alver took the drinks to a corner table and settled into a chair. After a long swallow of beer he lit a cigarette and turned his seat for a better view of the room.

Most of the other tables were occupied, with more drinkers, mainly men, leaning on the bar. Conversation was subdued apart from the occasional outburst of laughter from a table near the door, where a crowd of young men in the sort of colourful, loose-fitting clothes favoured by Leon leaned forward to catch the words of the gaudiest of their number, an eye-catching figure in mustard-yellow with black and white hair.

When he turned back to his drink Alver caught the eye of the barman, who looked quickly away then picked up a glass and began to polish it. A couple moved across him to the bar, the man bearded, in leather jacket and jeans and a flat cap, his girl in green. Long black hair swayed as she spoke. Again the barman's eyes flicked away then back to the glass in his hands.

Alver's cigarette toppled from the ashtray, spilling a trail of grey across the deep shine of the table. He picked it up and ground it out, then brushed the ash to the floor. For a minute longer he sat watching the door from the corner of his eye, taking quick sips of beer, until his fingers moved again to the blue and white pack on the table.

Two sober-suited men at the next table stared past him into space, sipping occasionally at their drinks, saying nothing. Above the bar a patterned mirror hung askew, reflecting a blank white square of ceiling. Alver's eyes wandered back to the door.

When he glanced up again there was the crash of a breaking glass, followed by a loud chorus of cheers from the table near the door. Alver jerked round as the door opened: it was the old man from the restaurant, head down, making straight for the bar. The man in yellow called something after him and the table erupted once more in raucous laughter.

At the bar the old man's shoulders worked beneath a shabby overcoat as the barman slowly shook his head, a fresh glass gleaming in his hands. Finally the shoulders drooped and the old man made his way quickly back towards the door.

'Sold your paints yet then Harry?' asked the man in yellow loudly. 'Come on, I'll buy you a drink.' His friends had hushed, grinning at one another.

The old man had stopped uncertainly; now he shot a look towards the table, then another at Alver, his withered face blank, then the pub doors were swinging behind him.

Alver stared across the smoky space at the table beyond the doors, which finally swung shut. The crowd had fallen silent again and they leaned forward around the black and white dyed head.

A throaty female chuckle came from nearby as the couple from the bar walked towards the door, talking quietly. The man made a comment as they passed Alver and the girl chuckled again, her eyes wandering over the table, the blue and white cigarette packet, up to his face, briefly, then on, with no change of expression.

He took the packet, pulled out a cigarette, struck a match. *Ah,* said Owen's soft, measured voice, *I see. Dawn has befriended an older woman, just an ordinary woman experiencing similar difficulties.* A swell of laughter. *Patients here are unhappy with reality. This may include those close to them. They may choose to see them differently, to believe things about them which may not be real to you and I ...* Alver dropped the match to the table as the flame reached his fingers ... *a very likeable young lady, I talk with her for hours during the course of a week. There's nothing for you to worry about, I assure you. Nothing real, as we understand it. As I say, it's common enough,* his hands spread, smoke curled from his pipe, ... *in here.* Alver's fingers struck another match and held it to his cigarette as he stared blankly into the flame.

'OK Al?' Leon dropped into a chair, face slightly flushed, and buried his face in his pint.

Alver looked reluctantly from the flame then extinguished it with a quick wave of his hand and dropped the spent match into the ashtray. 'Sure. What took you?'

His brother frowned as he wiped foam from his lips. 'Ten minutes.' He shrugged. 'What's up?'

'Oh, nothing. Must have been miles away.'

The barman had moved to the other side of the L-shaped bar and a young girl stood in his place, mouth chewing relentlessly as she peered at her nails, turning the hand this way and that before holding it out straight, inches from her intent face.

Leon released a cloud of cigar smoke and tapped his glass. 'What's it like to get back to the good stuff?'

'Pretty good.' Alver's grin turned into a yawn.

'Bring your toothbrush? You always did travel light.'

'No not even that, this time. Why, you saying I need it?

Leon looked away and pulled at his drink, then put down his glass and leaned forward confidentially. 'So, what's this woman of Geoff's like then? No,' he held up a hand, 'don't tell me. Meek, right? Mild-mannered? Into yoga, peasant-look, right? Specs, rides a bike? Warm-hearted.' He nodded in agreement with himself. 'Deaf.'

'Nope. You got it all wrong. She's alright, as it happens, Georgina. George, they call her. Bit smart, of course. Student. Blonde, nice figure ... she's got her hooks into old Geoff. Anyway, good luck to him.' Alver raised his glass while Leon sat back, pulling a face. 'Look, Lee, he's alright – '

'I know, once you get to know him. Not my type.'

'Well, you didn't have to keep winding him up.'

'It's that bleeding great handle sticking out of his back. Don't tell me you never gave it a twist.'

'Didn't you have much of a chat with him, then?'

'Hardly. What did you say he's going in for? Computers?'

'Dunno ...' A colourful figure from the table by the door was attempting to gain the barmaid's attention. 'He doesn't really seem that interested in birds, not really. I mean, this study thing, it's dropped right off. At the beginning, everything went into the notebook. He had me doing it all to start off with, but I got fed up.' Leon sniggered around the rim of his glass. 'Now, he hardly bothers anymore. Still, I suppose he knows what he's doing ...'

'People like him always know what they're doing. No need to worry about the Geoffs of the world. Hey, I was reading somewhere about blokes nicking falcons, selling 'em for two grand or something. Thought about you. Could be a nice setup ...' Seeing the look on his brother's face he hurried on. 'Not you, of course. I was thinking of Geoff. He could breed 'em, flog 'em ...'

'You can't do that.'

'Oh.' Leon picked up his pint and looked away across the room. 'If you say so,' he mumbled into an almost empty glass.

The pub filled up suddenly as the sounds of jazz crashed jauntily through the din from a back room. In the bar, voices automatically got louder.

'So what was it you wanted to see Ma about?'

Alver took a fresh pint from his brother's fingers. 'Oh ... nothing much, just ... Look, Lee, have you heard her say much about this bloke Clive?'

Leon shook his head. 'Nope. I've seen the letters, every once in a while, of course. Dad still thinks they're from some woman Ma used to know. It's nothing much though, is it?'

The music ended abruptly and people surged from the back room to cluster at the bar. Alver pulled his chair closer to the table and leaned forward.

'Not really. Seems they used to be very close, though, a long time ago. D'you reckon she's happy, with Dad?'

With a shrug, Leon reached across to take a cigarette from the blue and white pack. 'As much as anybody else, I suppose. He still goes out on his own a lot, though. Drinking. I think she gets a bit fed up, you know what he gets like. She's lonely, I guess, like half the population.'

'Did you know she used to work in a hospital, as a nurse? That must have been about the time she met Dad.'

'Did she? No, I thought she'd always worked in offices, secretarial work, all that … nurse eh?'

Alver studied his brother for a moment through a cloud of pungent smoke. 'Lee. You know when Dawn was in Cathcart House …?'

Leon nodded, his face serious. 'One visit was enough for me.' Drums battered in the back room and were joined by raucous brass and banjos.

'Well, why did Ma tell you she wouldn't go to see her?'

'Didn't like hospitals. Those places, anyway.'

'Yeah.' Alver looked away. Across the crowded room a long-haired youth pushed a large safety-pin carefully through one pasty cheek before a table full of admirers.

'You remember that weird woman got her hooks into Dawn in there?'

'The cult leader, witchy bint? You told me about it –'

'What was her name?'

'Aw. No idea Al.'

'I can't remember.'

'Bugging you?'

'Yeah. She came in the pub once, did I say? Just popped up, when she was supposed to be in there, banged up.'

'So why's it bugging you now?'

Alver shook his head and swallowed beer. Loud cheering and applause sounded from the back room as the band's last number came to an end.

Alver met the man in yellow in the toilets, where he stood in front of the mirror whistling as he shaped his hair.

'You like taking the piss out of old blokes then.'

The hand with the comb stopped. 'Do what?'

'You heard. How about taking the piss out of me?'

'OK, take it easy. It was just a bit of fun …' The drawling voice had taken on a strident note, the face was pale and tight beneath the piebald hair; then there was a shift in tone. 'What's it to you anyway, buddy? He your dad?' Loud again and cocky.

Alver heard the second man at the last moment. He turned and swung in one movement, his fist sinking into soft belly well below the belt. There was a grunt as the man went to his knees then fell forward onto his hands and began to vomit. Alver's knee took him in the side of the face with a dull thud, sending him sideways to the floor where he lay in a ball, legs drawn up under him, retching and sobbing. When he turned back, a mustard-coloured leg was disappearing into the end cubicle. He reached it with a bound and crashed it open with a shoulder. The man had half-fallen over the toilet seat and was holding his arms up across his face as he slumped against the cubicle wall. 'Alright alright!' The voice was muffled by the upflung arms, but loud in the enclosed space.

Alver's features contorted as his fists clubbed the yellow body. 'Slag, fucking slag!' The man whimpered at each blow. At the end Alver dragged him from the cubicle and let him sag to the tiled floor, head hanging over the channel.

He stood for a moment, staring at the trembling body, rubbing the knuckles of his left hand. With a sudden loud hiss water streamed down the cold white face of the urinal. The badger-face head twitched and gave a soft, snuffling moan.

Outside on the street Leon stood talking to a tall, stylishly-dressed man, one of the crowd from the table by the door. When he saw his brother he clapped the man on the shoulder and lurched happily away.

'What kept you? Thought you'd nodded off somewhere.'

'Yeah. Wouldn't be difficult.' Alver put a cigarette to his lips. 'Which way d'you live then?'

Back at his flat, Leon put on a record and slopped whisky into two glasses and over the carpet.

'Y'are Al.'

Their hands swayed towards each other until Alver's took the glass. Leon sat down heavily on the settee next to his brother. He turned awkwardly, his mouth framing words that were swept away on an avalanche of sound from the stereo. Sliding to the floor, he crawled on all fours towards the controls, knocking over his drink on the way.

'Glad you came, Al,' he mumbled earnestly when he regained his seat. 'Glad all that ...' his hand flopped on the settee at his side, '...

glad it's all in the past. OK?' His gaze, intent but unfocussed, was fixed on his brother's face.

'S'alright. Really Lee.' Alver sat at an angle, his torso moving little by little from the vertical toward the warm, dark cushions beside him.

Leon nodded gravely to himself in the ensuing pause, then looked vaguely around the floor at his feet. The rock band battered along. His head jerked up and he manoeuvred himself around again to face Alver, who had reached the cushions and lay with knees drawn up and hands buried between his thighs.

'So you reckon those Leitz then? They're OK, aren't they?' Leon nodded again, one eye almost hidden by a drooping lid. 'Yeah. The best.'

With one final thunderous assault, the stereo noise came to an end and there was a short pause before the machine switched itself off with an amplified click. The low hum of the amplifier and the hissing gas fire intensified the silence. Leon's head nodded once more and he sank sideways to the settee next to his brother.

Alver's lips make smacking sounds as his eyelids fluttered. A huge motorcycle rolled towards him across the sand, its driver's face invisible behind a black visor. Sheep moved placidly to get out of its way, heads nodding in time to their steps, jaws working patiently at the gritty sand. Just when it seemed the vast, black and silver machine would crush him, it stopped. The driver was a girl. She wore a short green dress with yellow boots; long black hair spilled from the black helmet. *You defiled her*. The voice was low and husky. *You soiled her, then abandoned her*. Alver held up a hand to shield his eyes. 'What's your name? I can't see you.' The blank black visor stared. *I can see you*. Pale hands left black rubber grips, fell to white thighs on gleaming metal, slowly lifted the green, silky fabric. A dull reddish flush crept into view as Alver moved forward. And then he was driving, and he felt a girl's arms around his waist, and the huge wheel rolled along a line of footprints. A sheep looked up at the wheel, chewing, became Leon, his hair dark, his face contorted, begging. The machine rolled on and its speed increased. Air rushed over him, turning to smoke, a drifting column of acrid smoke growing thicker and blacker.

He lay in the hot, hissing darkness, staring at a dull orange light. A rattling came from the windows as a bus or heavy lorry rumbled by outside and he eased himself from the settee, crossing the room slowly, feeling his way with hands and feet, until he reached the faint outline of the window and tugged aside the heavy curtains. He stood, swaying and blinking in the sudden light, holding a hand to his eyes as they slowly focussed on a man washing a car in a garden across the street. The faint, tinny blare of a radio drifted up through the Sunday morning stillness.

Turning carefully from the daylight, he re-crossed the room, his boot catching a glass, sending it skittering across the carpet and under the settee. For a few seconds he stared blankly after it, swaying slightly, then stooped to switch off the fire. A car droned by, engine straining for a higher gear.

In the bathroom he squeezed paste onto an electric toothbrush and switched it on, firing blue jelly across the wall. Quickly he switched it off and dropped it into the bath, then scraped a blue smear from the wall with a forefinger and thrust it inside his mouth, rubbing for a few seconds before spitting and rinsing. He took an aerosol deodorant can and lifted his jumper to spray, first at one side, then the other. Finally he held his face close to the tap and splashed water across his cheeks, then wiped it off with a towel. On his way out he caught sight of his reflection in the mirror peering suspiciously at him.

In the big double bed an arrangement of mounds moved almost imperceptibly in time to a muffled snoring.

'Hey, Lee. Nearly twelve.' The words came out in a dry croak.

The snoring stopped, then started again.

'Lee.' Alver leant over and shook one of the mounds, and the snoring stopped again as the body tensed beneath a sky-blue bedspread pattered with cranes and orange chrysanthemums. A muffled questioning noise was followed by the bedclothes being jerked back dramatically. A look of terror drained from Leon's haggard, blinking face, and his head sank back into the sky-blue pillow.

'Wondered who the fuck it was! Must have been having a nightmare or … yeah … you …' He gave Alver a puzzled look, then groaned. 'Bleeding dreams. What's the time?'

'Just said. Nearly twelve.'

Leon's hands reached up to take a grip on the ornate bamboo bed head and he turned a beseeching look to his brother. 'Get the kettle on Al, eh?'

While the kettle boiled, Alver switched on the television. Ten minutes later Leon came in, wearing a dressing gown and carrying two cups of coffee. 'Thought you were doing this.' He glanced at the screen. 'Yeah. Sunday's a complete wash-out. What is this, The Skill of Lip reading? Here. I'll button it and put a record on.'

Alver held up a hand. 'No. Leave it.'

On the screen a trout was coshed on the head and slipped into a bag at a man's waist.

'Hmm.' Leon stood back, arms folded, until credits rolled to the accompaniment of gentle, lazy music. 'Nice song. Heard it before somewhere.'

Alver nodded, still staring at the screen as the music came to an end and a commercial bounded into view. His hand dropped, slowly, and Leon moved forward.

Noise boomed from the speakers and Leon jumped for the controls. 'Christ!' The noise shrank. He flopped back onto the settee with an unsteady grin. 'Wonder we didn't shake the building apart last night.'

'What are the neighbours like?'

'Who knows? They don't bother me ...' He lay back and closed his eyes. 'Got a real thumper. Open a window, Al. The place reeks of whisky.'

Alver pushed open a window and leaned out. A pale smudge had developed in the sky, all that was visible of the buried sun. Swifts screamed and chased one another over the rooftops.

'Look,' came Leon's hoarse voice from the room behind him, 'I'll make some brekkers, right, then we can get off for a drink, sort ourselves out a bit. Got to have something to eat first though.'

Alver coughed and sent a gob of phlegm smacking onto the pavement below, then drew his head in and turned to face his brother.

'I want to pop over and see Dawn first. See how she is.'

Leon's face fell and he looked away in disgust. 'You bastard!' He muttered. 'I bloody knew it! I knew that's why you changed your mind.' He turned back to fix Alver with a cold stare. 'That's the only reason you're here, isn't it.'

Alver returned the look, saying nothing.

'Sometimes I just don't think I know you at all, you ... but I knew. I bloody knew!' He gave a heavy sigh and shook his head. 'Look, Al. Leave it alone. It's been too long. She'll have her own life now. You should be glad you got out when you did.'

'Just tell me where she lives. I'll be back by teatime.'

'Shit! Look, there's some funny people over there, you know that.'

'So?'

'So they might not like you poking your nose in. Look, if you want to get out for a while why not go over to your own place?'

'I'm not going back there.'

'What?'

'They'll have got someone else in now. They know I won't be back.'

Leon looked dazed. 'But what … where are you going to live?'

'That's my worry.'

'You can't go back to Manchester. They couldn't cope, not now.'

Alver's mouth was a hard line. 'Just give me the address Lee, that's all.'

'Alright then.' Leon got to his feet. 'But look, I'll take you over there. I'll wait outside, then if …'

'If what?'

'Well … you won't be long anyway, will you? However it goes. Then I can bring you back. Travel's pretty messy on a Sunday.

'No. Thanks Lee, but I'll be alright. You just tell me where.'

'I'll make some breakfast.'

'Not for me, ta. Just the address.'

'Alright, alright. I'll do it while you're having a bath.'

'Do what?'

'Bath. You know – hot water, soap, all that. Help yourself to clothes, they're in the wardrobe and -'

'Just the address, Lee.'

Leon started to speak, but shook his head and pulled pen and paper from a drawer.

'That's where I saw her,' he said eventually, pointing with the pen. 'That one there. If she lives there …'

'Ta.' Alver folded the paper and pushed it inside his leather jacket.

'Fuck. Sure you won't have a bath?' Leon paused and looked thoughtfully back towards the kitchen. 'Look, tell you what … how about I get Julie round tonight to cook us a meal? She's an ace cook. She really wants to meet you.'

Alver nodded as he turned for the door. 'Sure.'

'Well don't sound so fucking keen. Bastard!' Leon moved forward. 'Wait. I'll get all the gear in this afternoon. More meat.' He put a hand on his brother's arm and produced a ten pound note. 'Go on, take it. Give us it back when you rob your next bank.'

'It's OK.' Alver pushed his brother's hand away. 'Really, I'm alright.'

'Yeah. You're alright.' Leon's smile trembled as he ran fingers through hair that pointed in every direction. 'We're all alright. Go on, don't be daft. You need the stuff round here.' With a lunge he pushed the note into the motorcycle jacket and stepped back inside the flat. He put his head round the door as Alver plodded heavily down the stairs. 'Al?'

His brother turned at the bottom of the stairs and looked up. 'Yeah?'

'Just ... take it easy, alright? And you'll be here for this meal, right? Eight at the latest.'

The lights flickered as the Central Line tube rattled to an impatient stop and the doors slid open. Alver stepped out and turned to watch litter flapping along the platform after the train as it accelerated into the darkness, watching until the rising machine note had passed into silence and the litter was still.

He left the escalator and dropped his ticket in front of a disinterested black face then climbed a flight of worn steps, emerging in a hard grey light where old newspapers scuffled along the pavement and people hurried by, heads bowed and eyes averted.

Adverts hung in tatters from sooty brick walls; boards covered broken windows in derelict factories and abandoned shops. Alver strode without hesitating along the shabby streets, looking neither right nor left, eyes half-closed against the grit that whirled on the niggling wind, his pace unvarying as he turned corners, crossed roads.

At length his steps slowed, he rounded a corner, and stopped. A shop window showed a display of books and magazines and he moved closer, peering distractedly at the covers ranged beyond the glass: sprawling, semi-nude women; inhuman faces dripping blood; white martinet masters with whips, hulking black slaves; a plain white square striped black with the words *Love Beach*; in the glass, the reflection of a man, motionless but for a hand moving slowly at his thigh. Alver turned and walked on.

He slowed again opposite a large, old building, no different to those on either side. A silver Mercedes crouched in the short drive. His feet carried him slowly past, to a bus-shelter where people huddled patiently in the wind. At the last minute he turned to join them, his eyes sliding to the house across the road.

Figures moved in the darkness behind the downstairs windows, then a bus drew up with a squeal of brakes and hid them. People shuffled aboard in silence past the stony black stare of the conductor, then the bell sounded and the grimy red machine dragged itself away. Alver's gaze followed after the whirling fan-belt, then he moved to lean against the bus-stop as two old ladies arrived behind him, breathless and cursing. Across the road the front door opened.

A man in a grey suit came out and walked around the Mercedes, pulling keys from his pocket. As he opened the door he took a cigar from his mouth and glanced quickly up and down the street before climbing in. The silver car rolled out of the drive and onto the road. Still travelling slowly it passed the bus-stop and Alver stared at the square, thick-featured face, the cropped black hair, the neatly-trimmed black moustache drooping to either side of the jutting cigar. His eyes widened and he turned quickly away.

When he looked back the car had gone. He stepped off the kerb.

'Be one along in a minute, dearie', called one of the old women. Her companion muttered something and they both watched as he crossed the road and walked up the drive.

His hand reached for the bell and pressed, one short flat buzz.

A pale smudge moved in the marbled glass, then the door swung open and Dawn stood there.

The golden hair was a tight, blonde cap; mascara-fringed eyes flickered, summer-sky blue, in a face toned and translated by sun and makeup.

'No. Alver?'

He smiled, a slow, spreading smile that reached his eyes. 'Hello Noon.'

Dawn's lips, glossed with vermilion, trembled as she stared at him.

'You look well.' He reached out a hand.

'No!' She backed away. 'What … what … why are you here?'

'Come to see you, Noon.'

Heavy black lashes flickered across suddenly wary eyes. 'No! That's not my name! Don't call me that.' Her face hardened. 'You've got a bleedin' nerve. Come to see me? Come to see me?'

Alver's smile wavered. 'I know it's been a while. That doesn't matter, not really. What matters -'

'What are you talking about? Get away! Clear off!' Dawn backed into the doorway as Alver stepped forward.

'Noon -'

'Don't call me that!' Dawn flicked a chain across the door. She peered through the gap with wide eyes.

'Dawn, I've come a long way. Let me in.'

'In?' Her voice rose almost to a shriek. 'Let you in? After what you did? And leaving me in … that place. You bastard Alver!'

'I didn't, I was told -'

'Beating up my Dad, an old man. Bastard!'

His eyebrows drew together in a slow, puzzled frown; his mouth worked. 'I've missed you.'

Dawn returned his stare. 'My God,' she said slowly, 'what I ever saw in you. Look, come on, what do you want?'

Alver licked his lips. 'Wondered if you wanted to go away. For a holiday.'

The blue eyes blinked slowly. 'Do what?'

'Greece.' Alver's smile returned, hesitantly.

'Are you …? Look, Alver, that was … a lifetime ago. I'm a married woman, I'm … we're nothing to do with each other now, you and me.'

'Married? That man? The one who just left? Do you know what he is? What he did?'

'He's a man, that's what Terry is! A real man, who looks after his own. They do that round here you know.' Dawn's voice had fallen to a hoarse whisper and her eyes slid from side to side as a couple walked by beyond the gate, their heads turning. 'Next to him, you're a child.'

'Dawn, he killed a bloke! I saw him, him and two others. That day I met you. He was there!'

'Course he was there,' she hissed. 'Why do you think I went in the first place? And I used to think you were smart … I can't understand why I couldn't see through you straight away – everybody else did. And that slag deserved all he got, after what he did. And that was nothing compared to what you did to me, the way you … made me dirty, and walked off.'

'I didn't make you dirty. How?'

'I'll tell you, it was a good job you got out when you did. There were people round here wanted to give you some of the same.' Her eyes travelled to his feet and back again. 'I can see they didn't have to bother. Just look at yourself!' The fiery lips curled. 'You look like a bleedin' tramp. All that talk, about how you were different to everybody else, trying to make out you knew what you were doing, and look where it's got you. My God, we get travellers round here look better than you do.' She drew back her face. 'And you stink!'

'Don't talk to me like that!' Alver's voice trembled. His face was drained of expression.

Dawn stared for a moment, then reached to undo the chain and stepped half out of the door. 'Oh Alver.' All the harshness had left her voice. 'What the bloody hell's happened? Do you know, I used to long for this moment, just so I could tell you exactly what I thought of you. I felt like that for ages. I hated you. But now ... d'you know, when I saw you, at first I didn't even know who you were. What's happened to you? You used to be so ...' One hand fiddled with a gold medallion on a golden chain at her throat.

'I'm doing what I was always meant to do.'

'What?'

'Living in the right place, one of the last places. With the birds.'

'Birds?'

'Not birds, *the* birds. Peregrines. Living with them. Right out in the wilds, miles from anywhere, miles from all the crap.'

Dawn stared.

'I found it. I always knew I'd find it. You knew it too.'

Dawn looked up and down the street, hand fiddling again with the medallion.

'Way up in the hills, In Wales. Devil's Bridge -'

Dawn was backing into the doorway.

'That day,' said Alver quietly, 'you weren't there to meet him.'

Dawn lowered her head and ran her hands over her hips, smoothing the silky fabric of a dark blue dress. 'Right, that's it,' she said briskly. 'You don't want to be here when Terry gets back. If he knew -' Her eyes wandered again to the neighbouring houses. There was a movement behind her in the doorway and she thrust out a hand. 'Back indoors Gary!' She pushed the child into the house. 'It's just a mister come to see if we want any odd jobs doing.' As she turned back she blushed and began to speak, then her eyes fell. 'Whatever you saw … that day, forget it. They don't muck about, Alver. Now just go.'

Alver licked his lips then turned and stepped back to stare along the street. 'You see that pub? I'll wait in there until eight o'clock. Right?'

Dawn had stepped back inside and was fastening the chain. 'Why?'

'For you.'

'Alver, please. It's not like that. Look, you don't exist anymore, not to me.'

'I saw Owen the other day.'

A cloud passed across her face. 'You've been back to Cathcart?'

'No. Not there.'

'Where?'

'You know where.'

'Oh Alver,' said Dawn sadly from the shadow of the closing door. 'It's not a damned game anymore.'

'Eight o'clock,' he repeated, but the door had closed.

He was the first person into the pub when it opened at seven, after hours of walking, mile after mile, following the pavements, passing the same places three or even four times. Half an hour later he bought his third drink and changed seats, moving to a table with a view of both doors. Quiet couples sidled in, bought drinks and took places on the opposite side of the room. Eight o'clock came and went, Alver's eyes jumping every time the door opened. A group of men, all in suits, gathered just inside the doorway while their wives sat at a table nearby. Their loud conversation broke off as the door opened, their heads turning and nodding good-naturedly to the three men who stood there. One stepped forward and peered through the smoke, slowly scanning the room.

Alver had crouched below the level of his table as soon as the conversation died, pretending to pick up a fallen cigarette. He edged along the wall, still crouching, pulled open the nearer door and slipped out.

He didn't stop running until he reached the first corner, where he threw himself behind the wall and struggled round to look back. The door he'd left by opened and Terry stepped out, followed by two other large, suited figures. One of these pointed to two streets leading from the pub and the three split up. Alver ran, stooping to stay under cover of the wall, then straightened up and sprinted, his boots pounding the pavement. A woman with a pram turned off the pavement onto the grass as he pelted by. A car hooted as he plunged across the road. He kept running.

After a maze of turnings, cutting through courtyards surrounded by looming blocks of flats, he found himself on a deserted cobbled street where piles of market refuse clogged the gutters. He slowed to a walk, then stopped completely, doubled over, hands on his knees as his body heaved and his breath came in racking sobs. A mangy dog trotted up and looked at him, sniffing, then began nosing in a nearby pile of rotting fruit. A stooped black woman eyed him with suspicion as she picked at discarded cabbage leaves, dropping the better ones into an old sack.

Alver pushed himself upright and looked around, licking dry lips, his chest still heaving. Tower blocks hulked all around against the colourless sky. Further down the street stood a pub, its doors open. He made straight towards it.

On the closed half of the door a sheet of paper had been posted, with the scrawled message *NO TRAVELLERS*. His footsteps quickened as he walked past. *NO DIDDICOYS, NO TRAVELLERS* said the next pub, and *NO TRAVELLERS WILL BE SERVED* the next. Eventually, more than a mile from the cobbled market street, he found a pub with no warning.

He sat in a corner drinking quickly, eyes on the door, glancing up now and then at the barman, who finally moved away to the far end of the bar and took a newspaper from below the counter.

When a group of elderly locals came in, dressed in their best Sunday clothes, he drank up and moved on.

In the next pub he sat for twenty minutes, the only customer apart from two youths at the bar in a long conversation with the barman. For the first few minutes they cast him sidelong glances, then ignored him. On the wall in front of him a sheet listed the winners of a raffle, and he stared at each name, frowning, and at the number opposite each name, his lips moving occasionally between gulps of beer. A young couple came in and sat at the next table; he finished his drink and left.

A short distance away he walked into a tube station, fed coins into a machine and took a ticket. A train arrived immediately. The few other passengers stared silently at the floor.

Another pub, a fierce black and white head swinging on the sign outside: The Falcon. This room was crowded and people lined the bar; one by one young faces looked round and a path slowly opened. His drink went quickly, then another. He pushed outside and stood, swaying, beneath the sign hanging against the dirty orange sky. 'We don't belong here. Not here.' He spoke loudly, slurring the words. The flat black and white face shivered in the streetlight.

Footsteps fell in behind him, skipping to keep up as he lurched off back towards the station. They grew suddenly louder and Alver swung round, fists up. Two black youths in leather jackets pulled up, turned to glance quickly at one another, then ran off. They halted fifty yards away along the street: 'Yo! Dosser man!' then ran on, laughing and slapping at one another.

Another silent, underground journey in a swinging carriage; his glazed eyes followed the line of straps set in the ceiling above him to the end of the carriage, and then on, through a window, to the end of the next, a broken line switching in the empty electric glare. He walked out into the mainline station.

The Asian behind the perspex window averted his eyes while Alver fumbled for notes and dropped them into a steel bowl which swivelled away and then back with a ticket and his change.

11. First flight

The low dark shape slid from the rocky shadows and rippled over the grass, small head swinging restlessly from side to side scenting invisible trails. By a jumble of rocks it paused to test the air, humped hindquarters motionless as the head moved tentatively on a sinuous neck, then it had slipped away again and trembling bracken fronds marked its passage. Momentarily a face appeared, framed by green and grey, a pale feral face blackened with the smudges of a burglar's mask, then it was gone and the bracken shook.

'Polecat,' breathed Geoff, easing carefully back from the telescope. 'Here, have a look.'

George came forward obediently and took his place.

'You'll have to move the scope to your left, very slowly, to keep track of him.'

Gently she pushed at the glossy grey barrel which swung, jerkily, beyond the one pile of rocks among many. 'I … I'm not sure …' she murmured, squinting gravely into the eyepiece.

'No, Georgie, you've lost it. Come on, doesn't matter.' Geoff patted the ground beside him. 'At least you can say you've seen one. Pretty lucky …' he shielded his eyes to watch a buzzard dropping over the skyline. 'They usually only come out at night, must be an insomniac. Alver would have enjoyed seeing that.'

George got up awkwardly from her kneeling position and stretched. 'Isn't it a beautiful day?'

'Yeah. This is the life, eh?' Again he patted the ground, and George came and settled next to him. He draped an arm round her shoulders.

Once more a glaring sun rode high above the valley in a cloudless sky. The air was heavy with the heat and the drone of racing flies. White and blue butterflies floated over the grassy lower slopes.

'Wonder how he's getting on,' mused Geoff. 'Alver, that is.' He glanced at his watch. 'Should be on his way by now.'

'Strange him deciding to go to London at the last minute, instead of to see his parents.' George's words were indistinct as she chewed at a grass stem.

'Not really. That's the way he does things. Spur of the moment.'

'Strange guy.'

'Strange? How? By the way, I shouldn't chew that. The sheep …'

George threw the stem away and spat. 'I don't know, just a feeling. I'm sure he had his eyes on me all the time when I was here before.'

'Well, I can't say I blame him for that. You were a bit better looking than the rest of us.' He leaned across to nibble her ear. 'Not to mention the sheep.'

'Mmm … it's not a nice feeling though. It's as if he's … watching, waiting for you to say something, do something, I don't know.'

Geoff sniggered. 'Well he told me he thinks we're all running around in someone's head, and now you're running around in his and he's … well, I don't know about running.'

'Creeping.'

'OK. Maybe he's not too bright. But he's alright. I mean, when you think of all the pillocks back at university … he seems to fit in, somehow, round here.' His thumb rubbed gently at George's knee. 'He seems to know …'

A jet crashed overhead, and then another. Geoff shielded George with his arm as they both cowered.

'Irresponsible bastards!' he screamed into the din as the sleek missile shapes curved spectacularly away to the east. A muted chatter from the cliff-face grew louder, then stopped.

'Your birds made a noise, Geoff. Aren't you going to -'

'Later.' Geoff was still muttering to himself, staring darkly after the vanishing dots. 'Anyway,' he said pleasantly, turning back to face her. 'Why are we talking about Alver? You don't fancy him, do you?'

George shuddered. 'I don't see how any girl could.'

'Really?'

'Well, apart from anything else, he smells.'

Geoff snorted his amusement. 'Yeah, I know. He ought to do something about that. It's not easy though, in these conditions.'

'You don't smell.'

'Course not. Anyway, he's got a girl. London, somewhere. He has,' he insisted, seeing George's dubious look. 'He showed me her photograph.'

'What was she like?'

'Very good looking, as a matter of fact. Blonde, blue eyes.' He smirked. 'Bit like you, really.'

'He showed you it, did he? Hmm. I wouldn't be surprised if he carries it around with him just to impress people.' Geoff was shaking his head. 'Really Geoff. I'm telling you, I don't think he's had much to do with girls.' She picked at something in the grass. 'That photo's probably one he found, so he could invent a girlfriend.'

'Steady on a bit, Georgie girl. You've only met the guy once.'

George frowned. 'Sorry. I don't know why I'm talking like that. He just ... Let's forget it.'

A few yards away a sheep planted its back legs slightly further apart and lowered its hind quarters to release a watery gush.

George spat again. 'Come on Geoff. Tell me what plans you've got for when you finish here.'

'Oh, priority numero uno - a couple of weeks hanging around a world-class beach in the sun. Probably more. The Med. Greece, maybe. What do you think?'

'Sounds lovely. Who're you going with?'

'We-e-ll ...' Geoff made his eyes roll lasciviously behind his glasses. 'Play your cards right ...'

George disentangled herself from his arms, laughing. 'I thought I'd already done that. Is no-one else going?'

'No. No-one else. Just the two of us. Think of it ... sun, wine, good food ... the beach, the sea, the sun, you know?' He made a low growling sound.

'And after that?'

'After that?'

'What will you do? A career?'

'Oh. Don't worry about that. Just a matter of waiting for the right thing to come along. Something different, a bit out of the ordinary, something with a bit of meaning. Money as well, of course. Can't really see me as a wage slave though, can you?'

George smiled, then motioned with her head towards a sudden burst of agitated shrieking from the cliff. 'Shouldn't you note that down?'

'Mmm? Oh, yeah.' He rolled towards the notebook, scribbled briefly, then rolled back. 'All these people grubbing for money though, and no thought to the quality of the lives they're leading while they do it. Won't catch me in that trap.'

'But what will you do? You must have some idea?'

Geoff's fingers fidgeted in the grass. 'Oh ... plenty ... something in the conservation line. Alternative technology ... agriculture ... plenty of areas ... '

'I wouldn't have thought there was much money in that.'

He reached out to pick a tiny red ant from her hair. 'Depends what level you aim for. I'm not talking about sitting in the rocks for years watching a few birds fly around. That is peanuts.' Taking off his spectacles he peered earnestly at her as he pulled out a handkerchief to clean them. 'I know one or two people, you know. And this,' he pointed to the battered notebook under its stone, 'this is a large stepping stone.'

'But then what? You can't just wait about for something to turn up, not nowadays.'

'I know, I know. Look, take it from me, by the time I'm thirty, it'll be me sending people out to do the peanut jobs.'

George shielded her eyes. 'Thirty. And how old's Alver?'

'What? Well, it's his birthday next week, as a matter of fact. He'll be thirty. What's that got to do with it?'

'Well,' George spoke carefully, 'it's just that I've noticed how you ... you seem to look up to him a bit, that's all.'

'Look up?' snorted Geoff. 'To Alver? Rubbish! As I said, he's alright, that's all.' He pushed his glasses back onto his face and looked away. 'As a matter of fact, I feel a bit sorry for him. I mean, he hasn't got much of a future, has he?' He turned back.

'Oh, I see. I misunderstood.' She lay back on the slope and turned to face him, squinting through one eye in the glare. 'It's so hot. I'd like to just lie here and doze.' She extended an arm. 'Wouldn't you? Let's pretend we're on that Greek beach.'

Geoff's frown cleared slowly. 'Well, it is very hot, you're right.' He grinned. 'I do feel a bit ... drowsy.'

The two figures moved closer in the eye of the Leitz and lay still. Alver lowered the binoculars as a peregrine gave an uneasy shriek somewhere below him on the cliff-face. He swatted at an insect on his cheek and rubbed it absently into his skin.

Slowly moving sheep dotted the grass surrounding the distant, unremarkable smudge of grey rock and the two prone specks of colour; running down from the shelter the slope ended abruptly, cut off from view by the overhang of the cliff before it reached the stream far below. By leaning forward Alver could see the olive fringes of the oakwood straggling up from the valley floor to west. A rustle in the heather made him jerk round, and the anxious rising note of the peregrine sounded again. He relaxed, took a deep breath, and began to inch forward.

The valley wound off below him into the eastern highlands, a deep, curving cleft in the land broken by occasional steep-sided grey fissures leading back into the buttressing hills. He eased himself carefully forward, peering out over the cliff that sheered giddyingly away into space. Poor tufts of grass and threadbare bracken fluttered in the wind, clinging to patches of dark earth running in a narrow broken path down through the crags. At the far end of the path the Fist thrust out over the valley, a massive gnarled jut of rock, and on its knuckles, the falcon. The slaty hunched back remained stock-still as the black and white mask flicked periodically from east to west then back, black eyes measuring the valley and everything in it with glinting precision.

A movement caught his eye as the tiercel floated out into space below him from a hidden perch on the cliff, and his head turned mechanically to follow it; a fixed blue-grey point in a spinning world. The bird drifted on stiff wings, describing a curve, face flicking to his mate, then, with a subtle shift of muscle and feather, hung almost motionless on the wind. The hooked bill cracked open, and Alver's face was buried in the heather before the terrible grating call shivered the air. Moving slowly he crawled backwards, pushing his boots through the woody growth behind him.

Twenty yards into the tangle of heather he stopped and eased over onto his back. For a while he lay there, one arm shielding his eyes from the glare, his uneven breathing threading through the tiny animal rustles, the wind whispering over the moor; then he rolled over onto his side, branches springing up as others yielded, and soon the rise and fall of his chest became steady.

He floated in space high above a rumpled map of the world. Clapping his wings to his body he felt the rush of the wind as he fell into the blue-green haze. Pitiless black eyes glared from striped faces, looming up towards him, then fell with him, at his side. He shrieked, hearing a savage echo on either side. From the valley grew a green rectangle of lawn, and a wrongness. Abruptly he spread his wings, exulting in the delicious, airy shock, then he drifted down beside the alien figure. The face darkened beneath his shadow, the lips trembled.

His body jack-knifed convulsively in the heather as he woke, and he pushed himself to his knees spitting soil and wood. Slowly his eyes closed again as he steadied his breathing, then he climbed stiffly to his feet. He gazed round dully at the silent, wavering brown sea of heather, screwing up his eyes at the sun sinking towards the west. No animal or bird moved. As he blinked down at his watch he saw the dark stub of a tick on the back of his hand, an inch from the raw, bruised knuckles. Frowning, he brought the hand closer, staring at the tiny creature, sweat beading his forehead. Carefully he reversed the Leitz and studied the blackish body, slowly lowering the glasses, and a faint smile pulled at his lips. He let the hand fall to his side. Suddenly he flinched as the air rang with a harsh chatter; the peregrine floated fifty feet above him, an angled black cross against the western sky.

He backed away, half-raising a hand towards the watching bird, then turned to push his way through the grappling heather branches. The tiercel drifted lightly on the wind, maintaining its distance. Another savage, chattering cry broke from the notched bill. Alver stumbled then struggled on, doubling his pace.

With a tiny angling of its wings, the peregrine allowed the breeze to hold it back, and the slowly floundering figure below receded beyond the curve of the moor. The tiercel wheeled, giving a final scream, and with a few shallow, powerful beats drove back towards the cliff in an arrowing glide.

The ground sloped down now beneath his boots, and scrubby green clumps of gorse, spotted with the yellow of fading flowers, straggled through the purple-tinged heather blanket. He slowed his pace, shrugging off the heavy motorcycle jacket and throwing it over a shoulder. As he walked he glanced occasionally at the embedded tick.

A grizzled yellow-brown hare sprang away, black-tipped ears bobbing through the heather. It came to an area of damp green land dotted with straw-coloured tussocks and plunged into the shallow bog without pausing. On the other side it kicked its back legs in the air as it ran, shedding sparkling droplets of water, then vanished back into the rolling brown wilderness. Alver knelt at the body-snug niche in the grass, lined with tufts of fur, and held both hands clasped together inside it.

A jet erupted overhead in an explosion of noise, its approach concealed by the surrounding hills, and Alver fell forward, mouth framing a silent scream, crushing the hare's form, clutching at the earth, gripping roots and thorns.

The grey and olive aircraft slewed round to follow the line of the valley and was gone while its roar remained, crashing and rolling over the moors. Seconds passed before the fading reverberations finally died. A distant angry chatter blew across the heather with the breeze as Alver raised himself on his elbows, trembling. He wiped the palm of a hand across his nose and looked down at the smeared trickle of red. The chattering sounded again; as he lifted his head a black beetle poised on a bleached tangle of gorse spines spread stubby wings and whirred ponderously away across the heather.

'Bloody jets!' hissed Geoff, rubbing his eyes. 'They are absolute bloody maniacs.' He yawned. 'Mmm. Must have dozed off. What's up?'

George sat with her legs drawn up, chin on her knees, rocking gently, staring straight ahead.

'What's up, George?'

'I'd like to go now Geoff.'

'What? There's plenty of time yet.' He peered blearily at his watch. 'Yeah. There is. Plenty of time. There's no hurry.'

'Please Geoff.' She turned to him with a tight smile. 'I'm sorry. I just don't feel very good.'

'Oh, Georgie girl. What is it? He leaned over and slid an arm round her. 'Do you think it might have been the dandelions after all? Couldn't have been, though. I feel alright.'

'It's not that. It must be the heat.' She squinted hopefully at the falling disc of the sun. 'I'm not used to it. Please?'

Geoff pursed his lips but George was already on her feet, brushing strands of grass from her jeans.

'It's really really uncomfortable here.' She rubbed awkwardly at her back, then frowned down at the flattened grass. 'Geoff?'

'Hmm ... Don't like to leave the birds unwatched, not till Alver gets back.'

'Ha!' Her laugh was abrupt and humourless. 'That's a bit of a joke. You haven't looked at them all day.'

Geoff looked bewildered. 'That's not true ... anyway; I was here, wasn't I? That's the main thing. One of us has to be here at all times.'

George poked the ground with a foot then bent to pick up a stone, examining it for a moment before tossing it down the slope and dusting her hands. She cast a gloomy look around the valley and shook in an exaggerated shiver. 'Are you going to take me to the station, or do I have to walk?'

'Alright then, if that's the way you want it.' He got to his feet, shaking his head. 'I don't see why you have to be so sudden about it all.'

'I'm not very well, isn't that enough?'

Geoff clambered into the shelter and began to pack the rucksack. After a moment's hesitation George climbed in and stood beside him, hands thrust into her jacket pockets, eyes moving restlessly over the ground.

'Thought we might have had a flight today,' said Geoff in a brittle voice as he took down the telescope. 'Still, better if it waits until ...' He trailed off into a strained silence. 'Anyway,' he muttered. 'Maybe there was one. Maybe I should have paid better attention.'

A rock rolled past and into the gully as a sheep scrabbled for a footing.

'Right then. I'll just leave a note, just in case Alver gets here and wonders where the hell everyone is.' He wedged the fluttering sheet of paper under a stone and took a grip on the wall.

'Geoff,' said George in a small voice. 'I'm sorry. I really don't feel very well.'

Geoff regarded her coldly. 'Sure.' He swung the haversack over the wall.

The next day's dawn was muted, suffused in the mist that shrouded the hills. A slick of water covered the grass and the few early morning sounds were muffled. After only a few minutes, Alver murmured to Geoff and moved off into the murk to watch the sunrise from the Sphinx. Geoff remained in the shelter, blowing into his hands and stamping, then standing hunched behind the wall, hands buried in his pockets, looking gloomily out into the mist, waiting for it to lift.

Long after the first filtering light had reached the valley the cliff was visible only in fleeting patches. A shadowy shape flickered occasionally through the smoke; disembodied shrieks drifted over the cold, wet rocks. A stone rattled and Geoff pushed on his spectacles, peering into the half-light. Slowly the silhouette of a man emerged, as if coalescing the shifting greyness, accompanied by the deadened tramp of Alver's boots.

'Hell of a morning,' called Geoff cheerfully over the wall. 'What's it like up there?'

Alver smiled, his face flushed, droplets of water clinging to his beard and lank, tangled hair. 'Fine.'

'Fine? As in, no mist?'

'No. As in Fine.' He dropped over the wall in a practised roll.

The shrill piping of several frantic voices fought its way through the mist.

'Weird, hearing them but not being able to see them. Sounds as if they're having eats. Not a bad idea. Ready for a sandwich?' Geoff poured coffee as he chewed. 'Mmm, excellent, even if I do say so myself.'

'Not for me, ta.'

'Mmm. Excellent, banana. You don't know what you're missing.' He smacked his lips appreciatively. Crumbs clung to bristles fringing his mouth. 'So. You haven't really told me how it went in London.'

'Fine.'

'What did you do? Did you manage to see your girl?'

'Yeah.'

Geoff's jaws slowed. 'You did? Oh, great. She, er ... she was pleased to see you, no doubt.' He peered anxiously over the rims of his glasses.

'Yeah.'

Geoff nodded, sipped his coffee and studied his boot as it stubbed itself repeatedly against a rock. 'Great.'

'I told her about the holiday.'

'Oh?' said Geoff uncomfortably.

'Yeah. You know, Greece.'

'Yes yes. And what did she say? Got other plans, has she?'

'Nope. She wants to come. Whenever I say.' Alver smiled into the mist.

'Right. Well, I'll have to see what I can sort out then. Anything ... anything else? Have a good time with Leon?'

There was a slight pause before Alver replied. 'Oh. Yeah. Fine, thanks.'

'Hmm.' Taking a gulp of coffee, Geoff swirled it round a mouthful of masticated peanut butter, jam and banana, then swallowed. 'You did look a bit whacked, last night. As if you'd had a good time, I mean.'

Alver nodded. 'It was good to get back.' He raised his arms in an extravagant stretch, yawning. 'And you? How did your weekend go?' He gazed dreamily at a sheep plodding doggedly through the mist.

'Oh, yeah. No problems. Went well.'

'Did it? I got the impression she didn't really like it here.'

Geoff shook his head, frowning. 'No, no. Don't think so. She's not really the outdoor type, I suppose. Constitutionals and so forth. The weather. But she coped.'

'She coming back?'

'Could be, could be. I told her about our last flight party.' He grinned suddenly. 'Good name for a festival, eh? The Last Flight Party. Anyway, she'll come if she can. She's got a lot on at college, you know? What about Leon? Did you mention it to him? I suppose he'll be wrapped up at work?'

'I mentioned it.' Alver's voice was throaty, cracked.

'Good, good. Well, let's hope he can make it then. The more the merrier. You sound a bit rough.'

'Yeah. My throat's a bit sore.' He coughed and spat, looking down at the yellowish smear of phlegm at his feet with distaste.

Geoff had finished eating and was cleaning water from his spectacles. 'Bloody mist.' He settled them back and went to the wall. 'It's started to lift though. About bloody time. One thing about it though,' he peered warily at the patches of blue appearing fleetingly overhead, 'it's the one thing that keeps those bloody maniac flyboys away.'

Later, as he squatted among dripping thickets of gorse misted with spiders' webs, Alver studied the inflamed areas on his thighs. The redness had advanced about four inches on each side now, and the yellowish-green band at the leading edge had widened. He got to his feet and buckled his belt with trembling fingers, then turned to examine the ground: a shapeless brown spatter melted into the grass beside tight, compressed pellets of sheep dung. Pushing hair from his eyes he turned away.

By early afternoon the mist had shrivelled to almost nothing, a few drifting wisps along the skyline. At the scrape three juveniles stood huddled on the ledge, sparse white tufts of down showing in a few places between the dark, damp feathers. Number One had moved well away and sat awkwardly near the base of the Fist among rusting clumps of last year's bracken striped with new, curling green stems. With slowly increasing urgency, the bird raised itself from the ground and threshed the air, then settled back again, folding its wings clumsily across its back.

'Reckon he'll be away today,' said Geoff briskly.

'Yeah,' replied Alver's wheezing voice, absently. 'He will.'

Geoff darted him a look then took out his tobacco tin. 'Don't see you smoking anymore – oh, I was forgetting, your throat.'

'I've stopped anyway.'

'Really?' Geoff's eyebrows rose, then dipped again in concentration as his fingers fumbled with the cigarette paper. His tongue appeared between his lips. 'You used to say how much you enjoyed those things. Almost thought of giving them a go myself. Well, just let me know if you change your mind. You can always have one of these.' He pushed the crooked, drooping taper between his lips and applied a match, flinching as half an inch of cigarette disappeared in a gout of flame. With difficulty he tugged it free and exhaled, then cocked his head to one side. 'What's that? Can you hear something?'

A distant, heavy drone grew steadily louder and they got to their feet to search the skies to the east. Geoff raised his binoculars. 'There it is. What the bloody hell are they up to now?'

Moving so slowly it seemed impossible it could stay in the air an enormous aircraft, camouflage-painted in writhing olive and khaki, roared majestically up the valley, no more than a hundred feet above the stream.

'A bloody Hercules!' screamed Geoff into the din. He cupped his hands to his mouth. 'Bloody vandals!'

The noise swelled slowly until the air shook, and the outlandish vision at last swept past, below the level of the shelter, moving away to become a brown silhouette that appeared eventually to tilt and slide into the hillside as it followed the curve of the valley floor.

'Don't blame you, mates!' shouted Geoff to the screaming peregrines. 'We ought to get up a petition.'

Alver stared after the vanished aircraft with a look of hatred.

The sun gradually burned away the last traces of haze from the air and the background hum of insect noise returned to the valley. Swallows appeared, hawking flies over the oakwood, skimming the topmost leaves. The three young peregrines sat at the front of the ledge, bills gaping as they dried out in the building heat, while Number One struggled further through the bracken and up finally onto the knuckled rock of the Fist. The full-sized wings spread once again and beat the air. A gusting current caught the clumsy, feathered, body, lifting it inches from the ground, then laid it gently down again.

'Go on, go on ...' Geoff let out a long, pent-up breath as the distant bird settled back onto the rock. 'A whisper away. Or a feather.' He turned to Alver. 'Thought he was off then.'

'He will.' Shrill voices rose feverishly as the falcon drifted across the face. 'Hear it?'

'Mmm?' Geoff had crouched and was squinting into the telescope. 'Excellent view of him, Alver, Number One.' In the magnified eye the glaring mask of the eyas turned in short, abrupt jerks to follow the progress of an insect climbing over the bright pink bells of a foxglove.

Geoff moved back and reached across for the rucksack. 'Last of the coffee, Alver. Want some?'

'No, ta.'

'What's up, you on hunger strike?'

To the west swallows dived noisily around the gliding grey shape of a sparrowhawk before it dropped back among the oaks. Alver turned and focussed on Geoff, smiling as he shook his head. He brushed a greasy wriggle of hair from his face.

Geoff's eyes narrowed. 'What have you done to your hand?'

Holding it up, Alver frowned at the discoloured knuckles and tried to make a fist. 'Oh ... what was it? Mods, yes, the seaside.'

'Seaside? You did have a full weekend.' Geoff grinned, his face eager. 'What happened?'

Alver continued to stare at the hand. 'I did have a tick ... perfect little thing ...' He tugged up his sleeve. 'Must have moved on.'

'Good job. Must have filled up before you could get to the perfume. Next -'

'Listen!' Alver held up the hand, still half-clenched.

Across the valley the tiercel was floating over the Fist, calling softly, a repeated rising note that just carried to the shelter.

'Now,' breathed Alver.

Both of them trained their binoculars on the brown-streaked bundle balanced on the rock. The eyas stood with wings half open, masked face uptilted to follow the slow passes of the tiercel. A gust lifted it slightly, then lowered it back into its crouch. Geoff sucked in a hissing breath. Again the bird tensed, extended its wings, stretched, and then suddenly it was in the air, beating hurriedly in a straight line, threshing to pull itself round, beating back across the face then turning again, the grey shadow of the tiercel all the time slightly above and behind, following with an occasional flick of the wings or tilt of the tail.

Finally the young peregrine pitched into a run of heather, wings and tail fanning awkwardly.

'Bang!' yelled Geoff. 'Excellento!' He punched the air and turned, beaming, hand extended. 'What a sight! Made it look as if there's nothing to it.'

Alver took his hand. 'That's where it all comes together.' His voice was low and steady, although his face was flushed and his eyes were bright.

'One down,' chortled Geoff, 'three to go. Excellent!'

During the rest of the afternoon and the early part of the evening the gawkish brown shape took to the air several times, beating across the cliff-face in impetuous rushes, flapping energetically for each manoeuvre then pitching back into the heather, a sharp grey silhouette never far away. Between flights it would rest before moving to the nearest suitable rock, flapping and scrambling its way over the steep runs of heather and bracken.

At one point both adults arrived with kills, the falcon with a blue-mottled pigeon which was dropped into the shrilling mass on the ledge, the tiercel with a smaller corpse which he dangled above the bird in the heather and then let fall.

As the evening drifted on the valley resounded to almost continual outbursts of shrieking from the cliff. The only periods of relative silence followed feeding, when the gorged eyasses sat motionless on the increasingly white-spattered ledge.

After another hurtling juvenile flight, Geoff reached across and pulled the notebook free of its stone.

'See that? When the tiercel gets close to it, you can see they're the same size. Same light build, you know? I reckon Number One's a male.' He licked the pencil stub, eyes on Alver who pursed his lips and nodded. Geoff began to write. Further down the slope, near the flat, stony bank of the stream, a sheep fell over sideways and lay still.

'Well.' Geoff laid the stone carefully back on top of the notebook. 'I reckon that calls for a celebration. A little drinkie in the Farmers?' He scratched at his beard and grinned.

'Not for me. You go ahead.'

Geoff's face fell. 'Oh. Don't you fancy it?'

'Not really. You go though.'

'Oh, I shan't bother then. Not on my own.' He plucked a flat rock from the wall and rubbed gently at a patch of yellowish lichen, sliding a sidelong glance towards Alver. 'Not feeling too good?'

'No, I feel fine. Just right. I just don't need a drink.'

A crow landed beside the fallen sheep and walked cautiously towards it, pausing after every few steps. The sheep suddenly wrestled into life, writhing ponderously on the ground before struggling upright. After a slow gaze around, its head bent to the grass and its jaws began to move. The crow flapped off back towards its black stick nest in the gully opposite the Sphinx.

Streaks of white cloud had appeared high in the blue, netting it with an almost geometric pattern. Subdued birdsong floated up sporadically from the oakwood; a solitary bee droned by and a sheep coughed: lingering sounds at the end of the day.

'Another one tomorrow then?' asked Geoff after a long, drowsy silence.

Alver shrugged. 'Could be. Can't tell yet. Maybe.' His voice wheezed and fluted in his throat.

'Last sandwich?'

'You have it.'

The shadowy line of evening had already crept over the shelter and on towards the skyline. Small, pale moths moved in lazy zigzags low over the grass and bracken. The flying juvenile had flap-scrambled its way back to the ledge and now huddled against the darkening rock, indistinguishable from its earthbound siblings. In the failing light the two adult birds took up their positions for the night, the falcon near the end of the Fist with the smaller figure of the tiercel just visible near the skyline.

Somewhere to the northwest a cow bellowed repeatedly, a far-off, melancholy sound.

'That's it for today, I think,' said Geoff presently. 'Looks as if it's going to be a cracking day tomorrow.' Hissing his tuneless, cheerful whistle, he began to load the rucksack.

As they trudged towards the skyline Alver lagged behind, then stood for a while on the brink of the valley while Geoff unlocked the car and climbed in.

'Are you coming then? Or are you there for the night?'

The shadowy figure on the skyline slowly descended.

'Come on. No-one's going to pinch them during the night. Let's go get some eats.'

The engine fired and the car swung in a tight circle, its headlights cutting a rippling path through the night.

Back at the caravan Geoff busied himself in the kitchen while Alver lay on his bed, hands behind his head, staring at the stars beyond the glass. A fuzzy reggae beat blared out from the radio as accompaniment to the muffled bumps and clangs from the kitchen and the occasional burst of whistling. Abruptly there came a loud tapping on the door.

The radio noise stopped as Geoff's head appeared round the corner. He shot a glance at Alver, who still lay on his bed, his body tense and his eyes locked on the door. With a sigh he clumped across, turned the handle and pushed.

The farmer stood there, coat buttoned to the throat, peaked cap pulled down tightly on his head. A torch dangled from one hand, its beam playing idly on the grass at his booted feet. Slitted eyes looked out warily from the expressionless, ruddy face.

'Postman brought it.' He held out an envelope. 'Couldn't find you in, brought it up to the farm.'

'Oh,' said Geoff, taking it uncertainly. 'Thanks very much.' He glanced down at the envelope. 'Hope it wasn't any bother,' he called, but the man's back was already fading into the night. One of the pied dogs trotting at his heels peered back suspiciously over its shoulder then disappeared after its master.

'What's this all about then?' he murmured, pulling the door shut. Gas lights hissed and spluttered in the draught. He tore open the envelope and read aloud: *Alver or Geoff. Ring soon as possible. Leon.* He gives two numbers, day and night.' He looked up, frowning, then crossed to where Alver lay on the bed and held out the sheet. Alver took it and slowly brought it over his face.

'Come on then,' sighed Geoff. 'I'd better run you down to the phone box to see what he wants.' Sitting down heavily on the edge of his bed he cast around for his recently discarded boots. When he'd completed the intricacies of lacing them up he got to his feet and reached for his coat. Alver hadn't moved.

'Come on then Alver.'

Alver stared up at Geoff, grimacing, and shook his head. 'I can't,' he wheezed, his voice thin and almost inaudible. He indicated his throat. 'You'll have to.'

Geoff stood for a moment, eyes glazed, then with a curl of his lip he reached for the telegram. 'Alright then. I'll tell him you're sick. Anyway, any other message? Any idea what he wants?'

Again Alver shook his head.

'Hmm. Alright. Won't be long then.' He clumped to the door and pulled it open; searching his pockets for change he shot a last thoughtful look at Alver before stepping out into the night. The car door clicked, then slammed, then after a brief pause the engine roared. Light flashed across the windows and the roar dwindled quickly away.

Replacing his hands behind his head, Alver turned slightly on the bed, back to face the window beyond which the stars glimmered in the cold black sky. His eyes slowly unfocussed; and he was still in the same position, still aimlessly staring, when the sound of the engine wound up again out of the silence, then cut off, and the caravan door flew open.

'You two!' snorted Geoff as he stamped back inside. 'I know he said you weren't identical twins, but really … He just wanted to know where you'd got to, whether you'd made it back.' He stood, hands on hips, waiting for a response. 'He says you were supposed to go round there for a meal, after you'd been to see your girl, but you never showed up. Is that right?' He dropped onto the bed opposite Alver, who rolled slowly to face him and nodded.

'I forgot.'

Geoff groaned. 'Yeah. That's what I told him. He didn't seem all that surprised. More worried about you, I think. Anyway,' he began the business of unlacing his boots, 'I told him you were alright, just had a touch of laryngitis. That OK?' A boot clunked to the floor. 'He wanted you to know he's still eating fillet steak cooked in brandy.' Frowning his disapproval he pulled off the other boot and placed the pair neatly at the end of his bed. 'He'll send me some. Very funny. Another thing,' he said, looking pointedly at Alver. 'I asked him if he could make it to the Last Flight Party, and he said you'd never mentioned it.'

'He was drunk,' whispered Alver.

Geoff mumbled something inaudible as he straightened on the edge of the bed, fingering his beard and eyeing the kitchen thoughtfully. 'Er … I'm actually not all that hungry now …' He glanced at his watch. 'And it is getting on. I wouldn't mind skipping the meal, if you …'

'That's OK. Not hungry.'

'Well, if you're sure. I'll make you something, if … I mean, I've had all those sandwiches …'

'It's OK.'

'Well, righto then, if you're sure.' Again he looked at his watch, hesitating. 'Oh, sod it. I'll make the sandwiches in the morning.' His eyes narrowed as he caught a sudden look of anguish on Alver's face. 'What is it?'

'My arms,' he croaked. They flopped uselessly from his shoulders while his body moved jerkily on the bed. His eyes bulged.

'Here, let me.' Geoff moved quickly across and pulled the arms down to Alver's sides then began to push rhythmically, bending then straightening them across his chest. 'You've had them behind your head too long, that's all. Cut off the blood supply. They're no use without blood.' He gave a short sniggering laugh as he pushed. 'You do look helpless like that. Getting better?' He stopped.

'Yeah.' Alver rubbed each arm in turn. 'Wondered what was going on for a minute ... I thought ... I don't know what I thought. Thanks Geoff.'

'Got to keep the old circulation going, you know,' Geoff pulled of his shirt. He gave a long, luxurious sigh. 'Looking forward to my bed tonight.'

Alver struggled out of his jumper and tugged off his boots, then eased his way into his sleeping bag. The lone blanket slid over the slick nylon and fell to the floor with the others.

'Sweet dreams,' called Geoff quietly. He reached for the tap to turn off the hissing light, then wriggled comfortably between his layered bedclothes.

'Yeah,' croaked Alver. In the sudden dark and silence his eyes glittered with reflected starlight as his breathing came and went in short, fluttering gasps. A howling sounded, faint and far off.

12. Second flight

The following morning dawned cold and clear, the black crags of the cliff crystallizing slowly out of the greyness, becoming grey themselves as the day advanced. Again Alver watched the sunrise from the high, rocky mound on the valley's northern brow. Not until three hours later, when the chill had been drawn out of the hillsides, did he make his way back by the slotted sheep walks to the shelter. He was still several yards from it when Geoff began to speak.

'What do you find to do up there all morning?' His expression was a mixture of exasperation and bewilderment. 'Don't you get a bit ... cheesed off, on your own?'

'Not really.' Alvers's voice was stronger, and very deep, but caught in his throat. He gave a long, dragging cough and spat into the grass. 'I like it there. It's a good place, a good place to think.' Geoff's expression remained unchanged. 'When you're up there,' he continued, frowning in concentration, 'everything's clear ... I don't know. It's a good place.' He smiled, and Geoff's face relaxed as he smiled back.

'I bet you wind up talking to yourself.' Alver looked round sharply, but Geoff had turned away and was peering into his binoculars. 'Well,' he continued in a louder, brisker voice. 'Will we be seeing Number Two airborne today, that's the question?'

'No, not today. Tomorrow, maybe.'

Geoff grinned. 'Confident as always. What makes you think it won't go today?'

Alver shrugged, then pointed across the valley. 'Sixty six.' His slow smile returned.

'Ah.' Geoff nodded slowly. 'Ah yes. Clickety click. Well, we'll see.' He turned quickly, raising his binoculars, as Alver's pointing finger swung to indicate the skyline, where two black spots streaked towards the cliff from the west.

The pigeon jerked to one side but the pursuing peregrine swerved to block its escape, forcing it on in front of the cliff-face to a frantic chorus of shrieks. A brown, screaming shape swung into the air and beat eagerly after them. Dipping and weaving desperately, the pigeon sped on, inches from its larger, relentless shadow.

In the silent, magnified eye of the binoculars, both shapes tumbled and blurred, became one, one awkward shape falling slowly, then rising. The hooked bill of the falcon gaped, uttering a harsh chatter of triumph as she circled with her heavy prey then drifted down towards a grassy slope.

'Bang!' Geoff's eye shone behind his spectacles, teeth showing through his straggling beard in a broad grin. 'Excellent! See the way she herded that piddy in front of the cliff?'

'So the young can see how to kill.'

'Yeah. Looked that way to me. Part of their training. All good stuff,' he murmured as he reached for the notebook. After the entry he got to his feet. 'Right, it's me for a constitutional.'

As he clambered over the wall a lamb sprang out of the shadow where it had been grazing and galloped off in a panic towards the gully, where it fell from view in a clatter of tumbling rock. Geoff's cheerful whistling receded away up the hill.

Alver watched his grimy, sun-browned fingers rubbing in the dirt, gouging arrangements of lines then obliterating them. Closing his eyes he thrust a hand into the diminished litter of small stones and withdrew one. A smile began on his face before he looked, and grew when he did. Reaching across he slid the flat rock fragment among the layered slabs of the wall. As he relaxed, his attention was caught by a small creeping plant, dusted with yellow, winding up through the stamped grass in one corner of the shelter. Rolling onto his belly he studied it carefully from all angles, then examined the magnified view provided by the reversed Leitz.

Twenty minutes later, when the tramp of feet and the whistle returned, Alver was still staring at the tiny, clustered flowers and delicate, trailing, bright green stems.

'Marvellous day, Alver. Make it perfect if Number Two lifts off.'

'I said. Not today.' Alver's voice was a bass murmur.

'Oh yeah. I forgot. Not today,' said Geoff pleasantly, taking out his tobacco tin.

Spreading vapour-trails criss-crossed far away, the only blemish in the shimmering blue sweep of the skies. A cuckoo called monotonously in the heat over the scratchy rattlings of countless hidden grasshoppers. Sheep lay on the slopes or stumped doggedly down their zigzagging trails. Large black flies appeared in clouds, settling over the grass and rocks, while martins and swallows skimmed the ground, following the contours precisely as they fed. A handful of swifts joined them; bigger, darker, their long, slender wings rushing in the heavy air.

On the cliff ledge two eyasses flapped intermittently, spending long periods lying motionless in the powdered dirt of the scrape while their parents watched from nearby perches, the falcon on the Fist, the tiercel nearer the skyline. The second most advanced juvenile had left the ledge, following in the footsteps of the first, and sat several yards away, a misplaced, hunched brown-grey shape in the heather. At intervals the flying juvenile made energetic but increasingly skilful sorties, arrowing across the cliff-face, shrieking, provoking muted replies from the scrape and heather, before executing an abrupt turn and aiming for a perch, to land with wings flapping and claws scrabbling at the rock.

'He's definitely getting better,' announced Geoff, studying the characteristic falcon-shape on a jutting angle of rock to the west of the ledge. 'And the better he gets, the harder it'll be to distinguish him from the tiercel, especially in silhouette, when you can't see the colour.' The distant bird fanned a dark, cream-tipped tail as it reached back to nip between its shoulders.

'Parasites,' breathed Geoff.

Alver made a ragged chuckling sound, then spat.

'What's up?'

'Just thinking. What is a parasite?'

'Well, your friends the ticks certainly qualify.'

'Yeah, I suppose they do, poor buggers.'

Number One made another flight, slightly slower this time and less expensive of energy. Geoff switched his gaze to the bird in the heather. 'Come on, come on. You can do that. It's dead easy.' Pulling loose the notebook he scribbled an entry, rolling a half-smoked cigarette between his lips. 'When that second one goes I'll fix a date for the party. I reckon three will go on consecutive days. What d'you think?'

'Could be.' The words caught again in Alver's throat and he spat once more, rubbing the greenish smear into the ground with a boot.

'Got your voice back, anyway,' beamed Geoff. 'This party? I've been thinking who'll come, and so forth. What about Leon? D'you think he'll come?'

'Nope. He'll be busy.'

'Hmm. On the 'phone last night he said he might be able to get away after all.' Alver glanced up. 'Wants to give you a mouthful, I expect, for messing up his little carnivores' feast.'

'Well, if he comes, he comes.'

'You don't sound too bothered.' Geoff smiled broadly. 'Not his scene, really, is it? Anyway, old Clive'll be here. George, with a bit of luck, Derek. Not James. Nige my brother. His girl, maybe. We need more girls. I'll take photographs, for a permanent reminder of the day ... let's see ...' his voice trailed away as he ticked things off. 'Got most of the food, won't need much ... bit of drink.'

'Geoff. Watch this.'

The flying juvenile, Number One, had launched itself again, and hung uncertainly on the breeze just above the skyline. Slowly it wavered downwards, following the line of the slope, drifting inches from the broken rocks and green-brown patches of vegetation. As it passed over the tapered spike of a foxglove a lemon-yellow foot dropped and snatched, plucking a pink flower-bell neatly from the stem. The bird's body wobbled slightly in the air as the flower was raised to the bill and examined, then dropped.

'Hoo! Excellent!'

The raptorial brown shape swung smoothly back to the skyline on a finely-judged updraught, then repeated the manoeuvre before dropping lightly onto a rock and starting to preen.

Alver's head shook slowly in admiration. 'Did you see that?'

'Not wasting so much energy now,' agreed Geoff, turning to a fresh page in the notebook. 'Much more efficient.'

'Efficient? You make him sound like a machine.'

'Well, it is really, isn't it? A biological machine. We all are.'

'You make him sound like the jets, the - what was it? - the Hercules.'

'Nah. It's – he's – far better designed than that great heap. After all, millions of years of evolution behind it, bound to be better.'

'A better machine?'

'Come on, Alver. Don't be difficult. You know what I mean.' He gave a sudden, short laugh, then repeated the words. 'You know what I mean.'

'Mmm.' Alver's gaze had wandered back to the tiny creeping flower, now dim in Geoff's shadow. He stood up. 'I'm going for a walk. Is your flower book in the car?'

'Yeah.' Geoff looked puzzled. 'Why?'

'They're beautiful. I want to know their names.'

Geoff smiled at him. 'Help yourself.'

Alver walked along the ridge to the west, almost as far as the abandoned cottage in the lee of the hill, then made his way down into the valley again, down towards the rippling olive shade of the oakwood. With the book open in his hand he wandered along the fringes, kneeling to examine the tangled growth, fingering delicate foxgloves and fleshy green bluebells with glowing flowers that stretched away in a scattered carpet beneath the rustling leaves. Lambent yellow buttercups straggled through the gently waving grasses, and pink campions, and further down, hidden in the grass and netting the ground, a myriad of miniature flowers, clustered specks of blue, pink, yellow and white on a green bed. Alver's lips moved as he followed his finger through the listed names in the index.

A tall plant with thick, dull green leaves and tufted yellow flowers caught his eye and he pondered for a moment before pulling a leaf free and nibbling gingerly at its edge. Piece by piece he devoured all of it, his jaws moving steadily faster, then he took another, glancing up occasionally as he chewed, at flitting bird-shapes in the quiet shadows under the trees, alert to needle-thin squeaking notes from the canopy.

When the yellow flowers nodded alone on the stripped green stem he pushed himself to his feet and moved slowly into the wood, treading carefully between bright patches of moss and fallen twigs and the larger branches that lay quietly mouldering among the shadows. There was a faint sound of scuffling as a silvery grey shape flowed in rippling motion along the ground and halfway up a leaning oak, pausing to fix him with bright squirrel-eyes over the curve of the trunk. Alver raised his hand, then moved on. Tiny shadows played among the trembling leaves of the canopy as birds hunted insects, and every now and then the shrill, whispered calls of their young sounded from a dark crack or hole in a knotted trunk. Brown, yellow-speckled butterflies danced together, ascending shafts of filtered sunlight in lazy spirals.

As Alver walked on the burble and chatter of the stream grew, until finally he stepped out onto its narrow, stony margin. Clumps of waterside plants grew in places where soil had built up under the shelter of the overhanging trees. He knelt to study the fluffy pinkish candles of water-mint, reaching forward to pluck a leaf, roll it between his fingers and hold it to his nose. With a faint smile, he popped the crushed leaf into his mouth, then laid himself full-length on his belly at the stream's edge and lowered his face to the rushing water. As his lips made contact he recoiled, then leaned forward again, slowly burying his face and sucking, his eyes shut tight. Pushing himself back to his knees he brushed back dripping hair, then eased down his grimy, stained jeans. With carefully cupped hands he splashed icy water onto his inflamed thighs, watching as it trickled over the discoloured flesh, streaking the hairs of his legs.

Off in the woods two sheep peered over the shoulders of another from the shadowed bracken, three heads springing from one scrawny body, a native viewing a visitor from another world.

'You know,' said Geoff later, 'I don't mind this at all.' He lay wearing just a pair of cutaway jeans, with his legs crossed, and waved a cigarette to indicate the valley drowsing in the heavy afternoon heat. 'Perfect. Well, nearly. Like being in a postcard. The nubile hikers will arrive any minute.'

'Like school holidays,' murmured Alver, in a cracked voice.

'Yeah. Long, hot days. Endless summer.'

'It's not like that anymore, outside.'

'Well, they say you only remember the good bits, don't they?'

Geoff aimed a flurry of slaps at a small spider that scuttled unharmed across his chest. He looked up and grinned. 'This is one of the good bits.'

'It could all be good bits.' Alver glanced at Geoff then tugged out a grey handkerchief and coughed quietly into it, frowning at the result. 'There are still places. Times.'

'Yeah.' Geoff's face was contorted as he inspected his chest. 'Pity. Still, that's the way of things ...'

Swifts screamed high overhead. For the moment the cliff-face was silent.

'Have you been to Greece before, Geoff? Is it like this?'

'Mmm? Oh, similar, similar. Full of Greeks though, unfortunately. You must have seen enough of them in London.' He sat up hurriedly and searched the skies until he found something. 'Nice buzzard up there.'

The broad-winged silhouette sailed in lazy circles hundreds of feet above the cliff, rising on a column of hot air, spiralling slowly up towards an even more distant mote in the blue haze.

'There's a pair of them. Ah, that's the life, eh Alver?' Imagine what it's like up there, looking down on all this. Of course,' Geoff settled comfortably back against the warm grass. 'You don't have to imagine, do you? All your flying dreams, I mean. Have to see if I can imagine one, one of these nights. Or can you have them in the daytime?' He shaded his eyes. 'Oh, they're so far up. Even the birds can't be bothered to chase them all the way up there.'

'When you have a dream, Geoff, you'll know what it's like. You'll be up there too.'

'In spirit.'

'Yes ... in spirit. I think we're all up there, at some time in our lives, in spirit. High up ... way up in the air.'

'Yeah. Right on.' Geoff squinted into the glare. 'And birds - they dream about driving nice sports cars. Every night.'

Alver manage a tolerant half-smile. 'No.' He rubbed at a dull red blotch just above his hip.

'No. A joke Alver. Take it from me, birds don't dream about anything at all.'

'A life without dreams.' Alver stared sadly at the film of blood on his finger.

'Look Alver,' said Geoff deliberately. 'I'm going round to Clive's tomorrow night, to grab a last bath, and something to eat. Are you coming?'

His attention still on his hip, Alver shook his head and continued picking.

'I think you ought to, really.'

'Why?'

'Well, last chance and all that. It's been a while since ... or maybe you had one in London?'

'One what?'

'A bath,' said Geoff heavily.

'Mmm. I went swimming, I think. In the sea.'

'Oh, I see. I think. Look, why don't you come anyway?'

'No, it's alright, ta.'

'What about poor old Clive? He'll be disappointed.'

Alver shifted uncomfortably. 'I'll see him later. When he comes up here.'

'Well, it's up to you of course. I don't see why not though.'

'I'm not going outside. I'm not -'

'Oh, leave that spot alone, Alver, for God's sake!'

Alver looked up, blinking in the glare, and smiled pleasantly.

The day rolled on. Geoff shuffled round at intervals on the slope, presenting his chest to the sun's most direct rays, peering anxiously through sparse hairs at the scattered pink bubbles of budding spots. Alver sat nearby in T-shirt, jeans and heavy boots, the Leitz almost constantly trained on the cliff-face.

The peregrines brought in kill after kill, the falcon at one point passing back and forth in front of the ledge trailing a white pigeon, with the flying juvenile screaming behind her. The three remaining eyasses flapped and shrieked but stayed firmly on the ground.

A single flaring white jet-trail remained in the blue, broadening slowly with the hours, until pink coloured the western sky around a melting sun.

'If it wasn't for that,' declared Geoff, stabbing a cigarette towards the vapour-trail, 'you could believe we were the only people on the planet.'

'It's a long way off. The wake of a boat, on the surface of the sea.'

'Eh?'

'The sea above us. Above the world. It's all like that.'

Geoff grinned uncertainly. 'Yeah. That's why it's always so bloody wet, eh?'

'It's not wet now.'

The plodding call of the cuckoo floated over the valley again, this time from somewhere on the moors, then stopped in mid-note. Activity on the cliff-face had slowed and ceased, and now all six birds sat motionless, watching the light fade from the sky.

'Looks as if you were right after all. Maybe tomorrow.'

'Maybe.'

But the next day was much the same: long, lazy hours in the sun after Alver's return from the Sphinx halfway through the morning, with a gentle breeze from the west taking the edge from the heat. Geoff's routine now revolved around sunbathing in his cut-away jeans on the slope outside the shelter. Occasionally he would rouse himself to scribble an entry in the notebook, scowling with impatience, or sit at the telescope making sketches of the juveniles.

Once again the falcon trailed a kill enticingly past the ledge, and again the three eyasses flapped and shrieked until part of it was brought to them. The tiercel dropped smaller kills straight onto the ledge: a plover, several thrushes, leaving the squabbling young to feed themselves.

Later in the day Alver wandered off alone, taking the plant identification book, and was gone for more than two hours. While he was away a storm passed eastwards over the moors, trembling lines of electric light printed repeatedly on a black lead sky while thunder crumpled the heavy silence. Geoff pulled on a shirt and watched anxiously, but the valley was untouched.

That night as they left the shelter, Alver lagged behind, again standing uncertainly on the ridge, glancing from the valley to Geoff and the car, then back to the valley.

'Are you coming then?'

Geoff waited, fingers drumming the steering wheel, as the vague figure approached hesitantly over the greying grass.

'Don't worry. They've been here for all these aeons; they'll still be here tomorrow.'

Back at the caravan Geoff made a last, unsuccessful attempt to persuade Alver to change his mind, then roared off into the darkness, the car's red tail lights flickering through the trees.

As he opened the door, Clive peered hopefully over Geoff's shoulder.

'Hello Geoff. Thought you might be round tonight. No … no Alver?'

'Nah.' Geoff pushed inside. Behind him Clive closed the door slowly with a look of resignation. He followed Geoff through into the living room.

'Why wouldn't he come?' Clive took a glass from the cabinet, splashed whisky into it, then topped up his own. 'Too tired, I suppose?'

'Yeah, something like that. Cheers.' Geoff took the glass and swallowed. 'He hasn't been all that good, actually, not since he got back from London.'

Clive's eyebrows drew together. 'London?' He pushed back his hair and blinked pink-tinged eyes.

'Yeah. Sore throat, bit of a cold and so forth.' With a sigh, Geoff dropped heavily into his usual armchair. 'That brother of his, Leon, came up. They went back together.'

'Leon? Up here? Oh, you should have let me know, Geoff!' He sat and leaned forward, resting his forearms on his knees. Geoff was gazing at the blank TV screen. 'So he didn't go up to see his mother after all?'

'Nah. Anything on?' Leaning forward he stabbed at the TV controls.

'He's alright though, isn't he?'

'Alver? Yeah. More or less. As I said, he's got a bit of a cold.' The face of a newsreader swam into focus and Geoff shifted to perch on the edge of his chair. 'He's just a bit low, physically I mean. He doesn't eat enough. He'll be alright once he gets back to regular living.'

'Geoff, I think you should have made -'

Geoff held up a hand as a seething mass of people and placards swirled into view. 'Fascists!' he muttered vehemently.

'I said,' repeated Clive loudly, 'you should have made him come with you. I could have fed him.' His knuckles whitened around his whisky tumbler.

Geoff rounded on him. 'Alright Clive, alright!' he snapped irritably. 'I tried. Why are you so bothered? He just wouldn't come, you know? Christ, you know what he's like.' He turned back to the screen, muttering. 'He's old enough to know what he's doing, for Christ's sake. Anybody would think he's a helpless little child to hear you carry on.'

There was an awkward silence, then Geoff got abruptly to his feet. 'I came for a bath, if that's alright.' He strode out and the sound of running water filtered through from the bathroom. Clive stared bitterly at the television where an aerial view showed a coast road jammed with traffic, lips fixed to the rim of his glass.

Afterwards they sat in silence, Geoff eating quickly from a plate on his knee, chopping methodically at the food with a fork, all his attention on the screen.

Clive refilled his glass and stared morosely into it. With a sigh he swirled the whisky gently. 'Sorry, Geoff. I'm just feeling a bit … wound up. Do forgive me. I've been under a great deal of pressure, just lately.' He dragged his eyes from the rolling golden fluid and stole a glance towards Geoff, who stared fixedly at the screen, jaws moving mechanically as his fork dipped, chopped, lifted.

'I'm just a bit concerned, that's all. His mother … I know she wouldn't like to think he wasn't looking after himself properly. In fact she'd be worried sick.' He gulped and swallowed in one movement, and his voice was hoarse when he spoke again. 'You can understand that Geoff, surely?'

Reluctantly Geoff turned, frowning; a lump travelled down his throat. 'Yeah, I know Clive.' The next mouthful wobbled on his fork but he paused, then lowered it to the plate. 'To tell the truth, he hasn't been himself, lately. I used to think he was difficult to get a word out of, remember? Now he just doesn't seem to be with it at all, half the time.' Clive was watching intently. Whisky tilted towards the edge of the glass in his fingers. 'It's probably what I said,' continued Geoff. 'He's just run-down. He really doesn't look after himself, you know?'

'He should come to Bristol,' murmured Clive. 'I could look after him, for a while.'

'Yeah. I don't know … I think something like that is what he needs. He'll be alright once he gets away from this place – I'm not sure it's good for him any more. Still, that's just what he'll be doing in another few days.' He resumed eating, slowly, then stopped again. 'A couple of times I've woken up in the night, and he's been wide awake, just staring out of the window. For a minute tonight I didn't even think he was going to come back to the caravan.'

'Really? Do you mean he wanted to stay up there? Outdoors?'

'It looked like it. It's hard to tell what's going through his head at the moment though.'

Clive smiled wistfully. 'I think he's rather a romantic, under all that hair and the motorcycle jacket. There's nothing wrong with that.'

'Mmm. He's a romantic who could do with a bath. He really does stink now, I'm afraid. I'm not even sure I've ever seen him change his clothes, apart from that bloody jacket.'

'Yes. Food, sleep, a bit of cleaning up. Tell him I'll see him at your little party, Geoff. Tell him he's to come back to Bristol with me for a while.' Clive's face was determined; the pinkish grey eyes were wide and earnest. 'Tell him I shan't take no for an answer. It's all settled.'

'I'll tell him,' replied Geoff, placing the empty plate on the arm of the chair as he stood up, 'but I doubt if he will. He's a bit of a stubborn bugger.'

Clive jumped up. 'You're not going? Please, have another drink.'

'No thanks Clive. Early rise tomorrow. I'd better get off.'

On the doorstep something occurred to Clive and he called out, then trotted to the rumbling sports car. 'I meant to ask you earlier … I had a sketch, just a small one, of a girl. You remember.'

Geoff stared blankly.

'Oh, you must. Alver was looking at it that day I came up to you in the valley. You haven't come across it lying around up there? No?' The sudden animation faded from his face. 'No. Oh well, it doesn't matter really. If you do happen to find it though ... I can't think ... Well.' He stepped back. 'Goodbye then, Geoff. Sorry again about that little ... You will give me a ring, won't you, when you arrange your party? I'll be there.'

Geoff gave a perfunctory wave and pushed the car into gear. Smiling, Clive raised his glass, then the smile died and he peered anxiously at the street of darkened windows.

When the twin red points of light had winked out and the humming note had faded into the night, Clive turned abruptly towards the door of *Diolch I Duw* and collided with the knobbled grey wall. With a grunt of pain he dropped his glass which shattered on the worn grey doorstep. As he rubbed his arm, cursing under his breath, light flooded from an upstairs window of the building next door. For a moment he stared at the scattered splinters glittering as they caught the light. A shadow passed across the lighted square, hovering behind the glass. With a glare and a final muttered curse, he pushed aside the door and slammed it shut behind him.

The caravan was in darkness, an indistinct shape in the shadowy corner of the field as the car drew up and shuddered to a halt. A half-hearted yelping came from the farmyard as the car door slammed and keys jangled briefly. Geoff pushed open the door and stepped carefully inside.

'You asleep Alver?'

There was no reply. Light flared as he held a match to the hissing mantle. Blankets lay in a huddle on the floor beside Alver's bed, as usual, but the shabby red mattress was bare. With a frown, Geoff turned to his own bed, where a torn sheet of paper lay on the neatly turned-back sheets. He nodded slowly as he read: NOT TIRED. NO NEED TO STAY HERE. SEE YOU IN THE MORNING.

Half an hour before dawn the following morning Geoff reached the top of the ridge above the car and paused for a moment looking out over the blurred grey slopes shading off into the gloom. A hand went to his chin and tugged at his beard as he hesitated, then he hitched the rucksack higher on his back and turned east. Apart from occasional rustles in the grass and anonymous clicking night-noises the only sounds were his own laboured breathing and the tramp of his feet.

The night was lit by a full moon and the velvety sky was pricked with glinting stars. Each breath lingered briefly in the air like smoke. After ten minutes he unshouldered the rucksack and lowered it to the ground, wiping a sleeve across his forehead as he peered into the silvery half-light. A long-drawn insect rattle came from somewhere to his left, loud and at the same time far away. Through his Leitz he examined the softened silhouette of the Sphinx, screwing up his eyes with the effort of reading the subtle, shaded tones of grey. Already a paler flush showed in the sky to the east, and a sitting figure was just discernible perched some way up the looming rock.

For several minutes Geoff watched, lowering his glasses periodically to rest his eyes as the light crept over the sky; the figure on the rock remained motionless. Eventually Geoff shouldered the rucksack and moved forward.

At about a hundred yards from the Sphinx he could see the figure quite clearly, sitting with its back to him, facing the east. He looked down as his foot caught a rock, and a thin keening note sounded eerily through the stillness, coming from behind him and to his right. In the instant it took to steady himself and look up again the figure had jumped from the rock and was now moving hurriedly towards him. He stayed where he was.

'Thought I might find you up here,' he called cheerfully, when Alver got close enough.

Alver strode on towards him, glancing back several times over his shoulder.

'Thought you might appreciate some hot coffee and sandwiches.'

'Yes.' Alver's face was pale in the half-light, his eyes bleared as they caught Geoff's for an instant, then he carried on past. As he strode by he thrust out an arm to take Geoff with him.

Geoff remained rooted to the spot. 'Oh. I thought we might sit and watch the dawn from the Sphinx. You're always telling me how good it is.'

'No. We'll go to the shelter. Much better down there. It's too cold, up here.' His words were clipped, and disjointed by the clashing of his teeth.

'Christ Alver, you must be freezing. Come on, let's get you moving. Have you been up there all night? What the hell for? You're lucky I didn't find you as stiff as a board. Crazy bugger.' As they walked Geoff's eyes flicked anxiously from Alver to the broken ground at his feet.

'I had my bag', muttered Alver indistinctly. 'I'm alright.'

Behind the chattering of his teeth his voice was husky and uneven, and the words came in a rush.

'Yeah, sure you are. I wouldn't do it again, though, if I were you. Don't forget, you've only just got over a cold.'

Currents had begun to move gently through the still night air and they carried a faint, ululating sound, like a drawn-out howl. Alver stopped short and turned.

'Just a stock dove, isn't it?' asked Geoff.

A sudden series of shrieks came from the cliff-face and Alver started forward again.

'Are you sure you're alright?'

'Mmm. Just a bit cold, that's all. Soon warm up.' He turned abruptly and managed a trembling grin. 'Another flight today.'

The first tentative notes of birdsong began among the oaks.

Another day of bleached skies and shimmering heat slowly unwound. Rustling, humming life returned once more to the rolling slopes and rock-choked gullies. The pollen of countless grasses and flowers drifted on the whispering breeze; hordes of insects emerged to feed, mate, and be eaten; birds and animals fluttered and scuttled in the relentless search for food, their every waking moment brimming with purpose. The peregrines hunted and killed, feeding themselves and the insatiable predators that would replace them.

Geoff lazed in the sun, head resting comfortably on his hands, one leg hooked over the other. A foot jerked erratically in time to his thin whistle. In the shelter Alver sat propped against the buttress, his eyes closed and his body tense. Every so often his eyelids fluttered and the muscles around his mouth tightened.

'Here comes that tagged kite,' called Geoff.

Alver's eyes snapped open and he moved to the wall, staring intently at the distant silhouette of the oncoming bird. He began to raise an arm, and the kite veered off abruptly, passing from sight behind the long grey ridge marking the southern boundary of the valley.

'Learned to be scared of the birds, I should think.' Geoff smiled to himself, then resumed his aimless whistling. Alver moved back into the strip of shadow at the rear of the shelter.

Later, after the sun had begun its long fall to the west, the falcon brought in a white pigeon with pinkish markings and carried it, wings trailing, slowly back and forth over the ledge, followed at every turn by the shrieking chocolate-brown juvenile, Number One. After six passes the peregrine flexed steely-grey wings and dropped among the frantic eyasses, then swung away unburdened to land on the Fist. On the ledge the pigeon disappeared in a flurry of dark brown feathers. With a scream, Number One dropped into the scrimmage and dragged the corpse clear, anchoring it with a vivid yellow foot as a hooked bill reached in.

Geoff sketched patiently, eyes flicking from the eyepiece of the telescope to the pad on his thigh, marking in the greyer backs and overall cleaner finish of the two most advanced eyasses. At the rear of the scrape the two younger birds sat hunched against the rock, awaiting their turn at the ripped and bloody carcase. Geoff swung the barrel of the telescope slightly to bring them into view, then adjusted the focus. His pencil scribbled notes beside the sketches, indicating the bulkier appearance of the youngest bird, Number Four, and the presence of one or two lingering tufts of down among the rich chocolate feathers of its back. As he worked, the pink tip of his tongue curled up into the dark hairs above his lips.

Towards evening, when the heat and glare had lessened and the ceaseless insect hum had begun to wind down, a silence fell on the cliff-face after another frenzied bout of feeding. After a few minutes Alver jumped to his feet and raised the Leitz.

'Now.' His voice was an urgent whisper.

Across the valley Number Two sat at the tip of the Fist, wings outstretched, trembling in the breeze. Near the skyline the tiercel gave a thin cry and lifted into the air. For another long moment the eyas remained balanced on the rock, teetering on wide-planted feet, and then it was away, lifted into space on the invisible currents.

Geoff's loud whoop echoed among the rocks as the bird circled twice under the towering cliff then crashed into the heather.

'Bang!' Both fists held aloft, Geoff turned to Alver, beaming. 'Excellent! Another male, too, by the look of it. As predicted.' He lowered his arms and rubbed his hands briskly together, then sat on the grass and dug out his tobacco tin. 'Righto. That's our little party set then. Day after tomorrow.' He looked up, a cigarette paper fluttering from his lower lip. 'What do you think?'

Alver still stared across the valley, rapt.

'Alver? The day after tomorrow, for the Last Flight Party. Sunday. What do you think?'

'Mmm? Yes. The day after tomorrow.'

'Excellent. Must get to the phone then, give everybody a bit of notice ...' Hurriedly he cupped a match to his cigarette and pulled out the notebook.

When he'd finished recording the second flight he looked up to see Alver still standing at the wall, gazing with a faint smile at the distant cliff-face. Geoff opened his mouth, then closed it again, chewing thoughtfully at his moustache. After a further moment's hesitation he cleared his throat.

'Alver? I was thinking ...' Alver swung dreamily to face him, frowning slightly with the effort of focussing.

'Why don't you get in touch with this girl, what's her name, Dawn? Maybe she'd like to come along on Sunday.'

The glassiness left Alver's eyes as they narrowed sharply. 'Why?'

'Why? Why? Well, I just thought, you know, she might ... you might like her to come. Don't you think she'd like it here?'

'Of course.' Alver paused. 'You don't believe she exists, do you?'

'What? Of course I do. What on earth are you talking about?'

'That other girl, that ... George.' As he pronounced the name his lips gave a twitch.

'George? What about her?'

Alver gave a thin smile and turned away.

Geoff jumped to his feet and moved to plant himself directly in front of Alver.

'No, come on Alver. Let's have it. What about George?' For a handful of seconds their eyes locked across the wall, then Alver's lifted as a staccato chatter sounded from the cliff.

'What about George, Alver?'

Again the heavy lips twisted into a humourless smile. 'She belongs outside.' He waved vaguely. 'In all that.'

'Oh, come on!' snapped Geoff. His hand made a chopping motion. 'What is all this bloody waffle anyway? Outside? Outside what? It's bloody pathetic! You ought to listen to yourself sometimes.'

The smile trembled as Alver looked off again towards the cliff. Just above the skyline a dark falcon-shape floated, tinted brown in the evening light. A fluttering speck passed nearby and the juvenile lunged after it.

Geoff turned to follow Alver's gaze, then swung back impatiently. His face twisted; with an exasperated grunt he pushed himself back from the wall.

I'm going to the phone box,' he said coldly. 'And George will be the first person I speak to.'

When Geoff returned the shelter was empty. He read the printed note with a sour expression.

'If that's the way he wants to behave,' he muttered. 'Bloody big baby.'

Still muttering he pushed the notebook into the rucksack, then knelt to dismantle the telescope and tripod. When everything was packed in its proper case he arranged the straps carefully over his shoulders. Stones slid under him as he rolled over the wall, and he landed awkwardly on his knees.

'Oh bugger it!' For a moment he remained there, head bowed, hands on his thighs, taking slow measured breaths. 'Stupid bloody place!' He straightened, and wearily began to disentangle the twisted straps. When he stood up again his eye wandered to the indistinct hump on the darkening ridge to the east. Sheep plodded towards it along the zigzagging trail, a straggling line of ghostly, slow-moving shapes in the fading light.

'Bloody big kid!' He turned away and set off briskly up the slope.

13. Third flight

The peregrine allowed the steady westerly breeze to carry it forward a hundred feet above the hills in a slow, curving line. Below, on the long grassy ridge, the small dim shapes of rabbits moved hesitantly through the clumped gorse, alert for the broad-winged silhouette of a buzzard.

Further on a difference registered in the shadows of a familiar rocky mass: a motionless, crouching figure. The peregrine angled swept-back wings, dipped lower. Abruptly the outline of the shape below altered, a pale smudge appeared in it, and the falcon tilted away, swinging in a wide curve to beat back up the valley towards the home cliff.

Alver waved at the skimming grey-and-white shape, then returned his attention to the barred grey feathers between his fingers, turning them in the morning sun, tinting them with a steely blue iridescence. Carefully he laid them on the flat rock at his elbow, one to either side of the enigmatic, ink-sketched face.

The tiercel trailed the limp, black and gold-speckled corpse of a plover over the hillside, pursued by a screaming juvenile which eventually took the kill in a noisy aerial exchange. As the eyas struggled with its burden towards a grassy slope, a second brown shape appeared and chased after it, shrieking frantically.

Geoff looked up from his notes as Alver climbed over the wall. He managed a simultaneous nod and grunt, then went back to his writing. Alver lowered himself to his usual spot, resting against the rocky buttress at the rear of the shelter.

When he'd finished his entry, Geoff spent several minutes leafing through the pages, making small corrections, retracing a word here and there, underlining dates. Finally he stopped, gazed significantly up and down the valley, then replaced the book under its stone.

'Some sandwiches in the rucksack,' he said tersely.

'Ta.' Alver didn't move.

'Coffee, as well.'

'Not hungry, thanks.'

Geoff turned him a cold look. 'You have to eat. You haven't eaten properly for days.'

Alver's smile was vague. A reddish patch, flecked with scales of dry skin, showed through the black bristles around his mouth; it wrinkled stiffly as his lips moved.

After another strained pause Geoff sighed and turned back to face him, his expression resigned.

'Look Alver, I'm sorry if I upset you yesterday. It's just that … well, I suppose we've both been under a bit of a strain, out here.' He broke into a sudden grin. 'I think we could both do with a bit of a rest.'

'Sun,' smiled Alver.

Geoff's grin faded. 'Yeah. Well, anyway …' He glanced towards the cliff at a muffled burst of shrieking. From the sloping hillside below the shelter a sheep stared back, mouth moving idly. 'I bet even the bloody sheep get on each other's nerves up here. Hmm. Anyway, if you want anybody to come along tomorrow, you invite them.' He rubbed a finger along his nose. 'I, er, I rang Leon last night, reminded him about tomorrow. I hope that's alright?'

Alver seemed about to speak, then shrugged.

'He said he'd do his best. Just today and tomorrow, Alver. Let's make the most of it, eh? Enjoy it while it's here.'

'Sure.'

For a brief second they smiled at one another as their eyes locked, then there was another outburst from the cliff, louder this time, as both flying juveniles passed together over the ledge and their noisy, earthbound siblings.

Geoff took out his tobacco tin and offered it, then began rolling himself a cigarette. 'I was thinking, our last night and all that … we should go for a farewell drink, you know? A last celebration, just the two of us.' He cocked an eyebrow as he drew his tongue across the paper. 'What d'you think?'

Alver looked uncertain. 'Oh. I …' He shook his head. 'Not yet. Not out there.'

Geoff paused with a match in his fingers, then leaned over and struck it, sheltering the flame with his hands. He straightened, puffing contentedly. 'Used to take me three matches, when I first came. At least.' Carefully he eased the cigarette from his lips and watched the spreading haze of smoke as it moved over the wall and away. 'I think,' he began deliberately, 'I think you ought to think about Clive's offer, about going back with him to Bristol.' He slid a quick glance towards Alver, who sat facing out across the valley, arms wrapped around his knees, rocking gently to and fro. As he watched, a hand wandered from knee to groin and scratched furiously, then moved back again.

'I think it would do you good to get away … from London, I mean,' he added quickly.

'Maybe,' came the murmured reply. 'When we get back.'

'Back? Oh, yeah. That.' Geoff pursed his lips. 'Well, there are a lot of details to be worked out about that yet. Best not count too heavily on -'

'It'll be alright. Something to look forward to. Afterwards, maybe …' His voice fell to a whisper. 'No rush.'

A jet thundered in low over the hills to the south of the valley. Alver struggled to his feet and gripped the wall, staring intently after the streaking bar of shadow. The tiercel had dropped like a stone from its perch near the skyline and relaxed into a glide, chattering as the roar fell slowly away.

Geoff frowned at the sight of Alver's hands as they grasped the topmost rocks of the wall: knuckles showed white through the grime, those of one hand misshapen and smeared with sores; the hooked fingers ended in broken, blackened nails. Slowly they eased their grip and began to tremble as the tension left them.

The third juvenile, a female, took to the air just after mid-day. Noticeably more bulky and blunter-winged than the first two, it was also somewhat browner, lacking their grey shading on the back. This brought the number of birds moving about the cliff-face to five, and page after page of the notebook filled with Geoff's impatient scrawl.

As afternoon stretched into evening the arrival of fresh kills became more sporadic, and the clamour and bustle of darting blue and brown shapes tapered off. The falcon plucked a collared dove on the slope bordering the gully to the east of the cliff, pale feathers drifting on the breeze to form a straggling, broken line on the grass. After a few ripped mouthfuls the peregrine lifted out over the valley, smears of red blurring the delicately barred cream breast, and fell in a long curve towards the Fist, swooping up at the last second to settle lightly at its tip. All three flying juveniles flopped with varying degrees of clumsiness onto the grass and scrambled, shrieking, onto the red meat.

When the last shrill cries had died away, and the birds sat motionless about the cliff-face or engaged in preening, Geoff turned, on the point of speaking. Alver's head had nodded forward to rest on his chest, and his eyes were closed. Geoff half-turned away, then paused, studying the unconscious face.

Expressionless in sleep, the thick features twitched spasmodically, as if an invisible insect ran repeatedly over their surface. The eyelids fluttered. Pale flecks crusted the insides of the shuttered eyes and clung to the trembling lashes. A wavering trail of sweat ran down the temple, coursing a white line over the greyish skin. Around the slightly parted lips, which shivered periodically, the discoloured area now looked moist, and stippled with tiny points of a brighter red.

Geoff's own face went blank as his brows drew together. His own mouth fell open.

Abruptly the slack face contorted in a sudden spasm and Alver sat bolt upright, eyes wide-open but cloudy. 'It's me!' he blurted in a strangled voice. 'How can that be? All the time …' His head turned frantically as he looked around him, ignoring Geoff who had recoiled and crouched halfway to his feet.

'I can go too,' he muttered. 'I can go too.'

'What is it? What is it Alver?'

With an effort the dulled eyes focussed, and his body sagged.

'You were having some kind of a dream,' prompted Geoff anxiously. 'More like a nightmare. Except it's daylight, of course.' He gave a nervous, barking laugh. 'Hoo! I wondered what was going on.' Moving forward hesitantly he peered into Alver's face. 'Are you alright now? This is what comes of sleeping out, in the cold.'

'I can't sleep, Geoff.' The husky voice quavered. 'I … I don't know how, anymore. Noon couldn't sleep either.' A look of panic crept over his face.

Geoff leaned forward and took a grip of his shoulders speaking slowly and deliberately. 'Look, I'm going to phone Clive. You can stay with him tonight, OK? He'll fill you up with good hot food, and scotch, and put you into a decent bed. You'll sleep like a brick, I promise you.'

Alver blinked, slowly, and lowered his head into his hands. 'I'm so tired Geoff.'

'That's what we'll do then,' continued Geoff firmly. 'I'll get in touch with the local doctor -'

A sudden harsh chatter interrupted and Alver struggled to his feet, pushing Geoff to one side and lurching forward to lean heavily against the wall.

'Never mind that,' insisted Geoff loudly, but Alver had already found the distant, familiar silhouette.

The falcon laboured up the centre of the valley from the east, talons locked in the carcase of a huge pigeon. As she approached the last gully before the cliff-face the crows appeared from their nest to mob the struggling grey shape, but another ringing chatter brought the tiercel screaming in to drive them off. Veering slightly, the falcon passed low over the darkened mound of the Sphinx, and suddenly the pigeon was falling, turning in the air, to vanish from sight among the rocks.

The falcon circled slowly, uttering a long, harsh, crackling scream, echoed by the tiercel fifty feet above her.

Alver swung a booted leg onto the wall.

'Alver, what are you doing?'

'It's alright.' His eyes were fixed on the distant birds. 'I'm alright. I've been expecting that. You go. I'll see you tomorrow.' The voice was still hoarse, but an urgency filled his words.

With a grimace Geoff took a grip on the wall. 'I'm coming with you.'

Alver turned sharply. 'No!' His eyes glittered.

There was a short strained pause, then Geoff relaxed his grip. 'Alright. Suit yourself. If you want to do yourself in -'

'Tomorrow, Geoff. It's alright, really. You'll see.' With that he was gone, hurrying across the slope, ignoring the winding sheep-trails, stumbling in his haste.

Geoff watched him go, his expression uncertain, seeing the scrambling figure recede, hearing the raucous, insistent screaming of the peregrine.

When Alver was a slow-moving dot on the long line of the ridge, and about to merge with the looming rocks, the circling birds fell silent and drifted slowly away towards the cliff.

It was still night when a car nosed cautiously through the darkness towards the caravan, headlights sweeping across grass and the occasional motionless sheep. Clive switched off the engine and struggled out, hampered by a heavy duffel coat of the same inky-blue as the cold night sky. The muffled barking of a dog sounded briefly from the direction of the farm.

Light filtered dimly through the curtains at the caravan windows as Clive rubbed gloved hands together and stamped. He was about to knock when the door flew open.

'Morning Clive. Thanks for coming so early.'

'That's alright, Geoff.' He stepped past Geoff, peering at the cramped, dingy interior, the few shabby pieces of furniture. Nose wrinkling, he crossed to Alver's bed, where he leaned forward briefly to inspect the marred painting of the cliff-face pinned crookedly on the wall above it, then he turned, fixing Geoff with an anxious look.

'What is it then, Geoff? What's the matter with him? You weren't very clear on the telephone.'

'Well, I don't know what it is, exactly.' Geoff scowled as he screwed down the flask-top, the expression exaggerated by the heavy shadows of the gas light. 'He's started acting really peculiarly … won't eat, doesn't sleep, says he's forgotten how to sleep … yeah, I know it's just what I told you the other night, but … well, it's worse. What he says just doesn't make sense anymore, sort of disjointed, as if he's only here part of the time, and the rest he's off somewhere else, you know? Really weird.'

Clive turned away, his head shaking slowly. 'Oh no, no …'

Geoff busied himself in the kitchen, talking in a lowered voice as he packed the rucksack. 'I thought last night he'd come to his senses. I was trying to get him to stay the night with you, see a doctor … Christ, all he needs is a good night's sleep, to break the cycle …' He looked across at Clive as he lifted the rucksack.

'He's up there now then?' Clive turned finally, the lines in his face etched deeper by the dim light. He chewed at his lower lip. 'It's perishing out there, Geoff.'

'Yeah. He's up there. There wouldn't have been any point in going after him last night, the mood he was in. Even if he'd let us find him … anyway, let's go.'

With a practised twist he snapped off the hissing light. They stepped out into the night, the sounds of their movement amplified in the sudden silence.

A redstart in one of the narrow, rock-strew gullies began the dawn chorus with a handful of tentative notes just after three o'clock. Gradually the short, melodious song grew in volume and completeness, and was joined by the plainer, repeated jangle of a stonechat from the scrubby gorse.

A subtle lightening crept over the sky, stilling the furtive rustlings and clickings of the night. A cuckoo, and then a ring ouzel added their voices to the chorus, and with them blackbirds and wrens in the scattered rowans and hawthorns, and the dim oakwood. From the crows' gully drifted the lazy, reeling song of a grasshopper warbler.

Alver studied the girl's face and smiled nervously.

'I'm right, aren't I?'

No reply, but the face said *yes.*

A plain female face, not attractive, not unpleasant. Long black hair glistened in the pearly light.

'I always knew, really. This had to be the way.'

No reply.

He nodded slowly, his smile broadening, then his eyes narrowed suddenly. 'I do … I do exist though, don't I?'

Grey eyes looked deep into his own.

'Tell me your name.'

Give me a name.

Alver shook in a sudden, violent shiver. His teeth clashed in his head. He tried several times before he could speak again.

'You can go where you like, can't you? Anywhere? Through the air?'

Thin, pale lips curved in a faint smile.

'How do you hide yourself from them?'

No reply.

'What's your name?'

Clive's foot stubbed a rock and sent it bouncing with a series of muffled thuds into the darkness below.

'Are we nearly there, Geoff?' His voice was hoarse as he sucked in deep breaths.

'Not far now. We should be able to see it any minute.'

'Do you think Leon will come?'

'I told you just what he told me. He'll be here, but it's a long drive.'

'I do hope he doesn't tell their mother, not yet. No need to worry her unnecessarily. He may just be run-down, after all.' Clive stumbled again and stopped, panting.

Scattered notes of birdsong welled up out of the half-light. Sheep moaned sporadically on the slopes.

'Come on, Clive.'

They started off again.

'You should never have let him stay out here,' blurted Clive after a few more yards. 'He's obviously not in the best of health -'

'Clive. You know what he's like. I tried. Now come on.'

A family of magpies sprang from a twisted hawthorn, swooping off to the north with guttural cries, their pied shapes blurring quickly into the misty stillness.

After a few minutes more Geoff came to a halt and lifted his Leitz.

'Still bloody dark …' A cuckoo began its halting, double-note call. 'Mmm … strange, it shouldn't be as far as this.' He moved forward again.

'We've been walking for ages.' Clive followed, pushing back his hair as he searched the ground at his feet for stones.

'Stop!'

Geoff pulled up so abruptly that Clive walked into him.

'Alver? Where are you?'

A figure detached itself from the ground barely twenty yards away and came slowly towards them.

'What, er … is everything alright?' Geoff's voice was cautious. 'We came to see if … if everything was alright.'

Alver halted, looking from an anxious face to the other.

'Of course everything's alright.' His voice was calm and reasonable. 'Hello Clive. What are you doing up here so early?'

'Hello Alver.' Clive stepped forward. 'Are you quite sure you're … everything's alright? Geoff tells me -' he shot a quick glance at Geoff before continuing. 'He says you haven't been eating properly, and that you couldn't sleep.' He indicated the dim, silent slopes. 'Really, Alver, you shouldn't be out here all night, you know. You'll catch your death. You should have come round to see me, as Geoff suggested. Look,' with a groping hand he found the rucksack on Geoff's back, patted it, 'we've got hot coffee for you, and some food. Let's -'

'Not here.' Alver's voice was still calm, almost a whisper, but Clive stopped short, his mouth hanging open.

'Not here.' He smiled patiently. 'You've missed the dawn. We'll go to the shelter.' He held out his arms, one for each of them, turning the smile to each in turn. After exchanging hurried, uncertain glances, Geoff and Clive turned and began slowly to retrace their steps.

'It's going to be a beautiful day,' promised Alver, drawing in a long, deep breath as he walked. 'Can't you feel it growing?'

Geoff and Clive, each with a guiding hand in the small of his back, looked at one another again. Geoff's eyebrows lifted in a gesture of resignation. The small, silvery sounds of the distant stream trickled through the stillness; as they tramped onwards the first keening note of a peregrine knifed across it.

'Ah,' breathed Alver, smiling to himself again and nodding.

Clive shivered. 'Geoff tells me, Alver, that you've been taking an interest in the wild flowers of the, ah, area.'

They walked on for a while in silence. Clive tried again. 'They are beautiful, aren't they? I can quite understand.' He glanced meaningfully at Geoff, who stared straight ahead, face set in a scowl. 'I do so enjoy them myself. Painting, in the summer months, when everything is in bloom …' His voice began to quaver, and he cleared his throat. 'The heather, especially. Yes I should say that was my favourite, to paint. Such a gorgeous purple … the amount of red, you know, never seems quite the same, from one day to the next … Do you have a favourite, Alver?'

'Oh, they all have their place, Clive.' He stopped abruptly and knelt in the grass. 'This, for instance.'

The light had grown sufficiently to bring the beginnings of colour back to the hills. Between Alver's fingers trembled a button-head of tiny lilac-blue flowers on an erect green stem. 'Love-in-a-mist,' he murmured, stroking it gently.

Geoff made an unintelligible grunting sound and Clive flicked him a questioning glance.

'And this,' continued Alver dreamily. 'Beautiful.'

A cluster of sculpted yellow flowers trailed across the palm of his hand amid pointed green leaves and curling tendrils.

'Heartsease. Can't you feel it? Just to hold it …'

Geoff grunted again. 'I don't think so, Alver.'

'Oh?' He looked up, then got to his feet. 'What do you mean?' he asked pleasantly.

'They're not Love-in-a-mist or Heartsease. It doesn't really matter, but they're not.'

'I think he's right, Alver,' added Clive hesitantly.

With a smug expression, Alver moved between them again and pushed then gently forward.

When they reached the shelter all three clambered inside, and the flask and sandwiches were brought out. Geoff shared the food with Clive after Alver took one polite sip of coffee, frowned with distaste, and refused anything else. Clive began to object but stopped at the pressure of Geoff's hand on his arm.

Shrieks sounded from the cliff-face with increasing urgency.

As he chewed, Geoff picked up the flower guide and leafed through it.

'Here, Alver.' He held the book out, open at a page of coloured illustrations, and tapped one. 'That blue one. A scabious.' Alver smiled pleasantly. Turning the pages, Geoff held the book out again. 'And the yellow one. Vetchling.' Clive turned away to peer at something a long way off.

'Yes. I see what you mean Geoff, but I don't use that part of the book.'

Geoff stared blankly. 'Which part do you use?'

'No.' Alver reached across for the book and turned to the back. 'This is the part. Everything's in there. You don't need that other bit.'

'That's the index.'

'Mmm.' He held open the book with one hand while he moved a finger down the list of names, smiling to himself at intervals.

Geoff turned to Clive, who continued to stare across the lightening valley with a glazed expression.

'Just explain that to me Alver, if you don't mind.'

'It's quite simple, Geoff. My names are the real names. The ones you use … well, they're just forced onto things. Then the things are twisted to fit the names. It wasn't always like that. These are the real names.'

Geoff's mouth opened and closed.

'I say, is that one of the birds, up there?' Clive spoke loudly, without turning, pointing to the crags on the skyline above the cliff.

'Looks like it.' Geoff dragged his eyes from Alver smiling smugly over the open book.

In the rocks opposite a juvenile peregrine had landed and now sat hunched on a spray of heather as a tiny bird fluttered around its head, calling agitatedly.

'Must be right on top of a wheatear's nest,' murmured Geoff.

The wheatear dropped to a rock, keeping up its hard, tack-tacking note, jumping back into the air as the juvenile made a lunge towards it, running awkwardly over the heather.

'Hadn't you better note that down, Geoff?'

Geoff's attention had returned to Alver. He gave Clive a frosty look before pulling out the notebook and pencil.

Some twenty minutes later, after a silence filled with a series of significant glances from Clive, Geoff got to his feet. Sunlight streamed from the sky and the dry scratching notes of the grasshoppers swelled with the heat.

'Just going for a con – for a walk.'

Clive waited a few moments after the tramp of booted feet had receded, then turned from the wall.

'Alver?' Lowering himself carefully at his side, he gave a theatrical groan at the muffled cracking sound from his knees. 'These old bones … you don't know how fortunate you are.' His eyes searched Alver's blank face. 'Did Geoff tell you what I said? About coming back to Bristol with me?'

'He may have.' Alver spoke distractedly. 'I can't remember. Bristol? I thought …'

'Well, I mean it. Come back with me. You said you'd think it over, remember?'

Alver shifted uncomfortably. 'Maybe. There's no rush, is there? Maybe. When I get back.'

'Back?'

'I'm going away.'

'Where are you going? I do wish you'd come back with me. Geoff says he nearly brought you last night. He should have done!' added Clive querulously, then looked quickly away and fumbled for his cigarettes. 'I do understand, you know. This not being able to sleep, and … I once …' a flame flared inside his cupped hand.

'Do you? Really?' Alver frowned in concentration. 'Yes, of course … you did know her. But did you know her name?' He smiled. 'No.'

'Name? Whose name, Alver?'

The drone of a car engine drew closer and stopped, then came the muffled slamming of car doors.

'Good Lord! Can that be Geoff's friends already?' Clive glanced irritably at his watch. 'It must be. It's hardly likely to be a local, not on a Sunday.' He smiled at Alver and drew shakily on his cigarette.

'All these people, eh Alver? Sometimes you wish they'd just leave you alone.' His eyes slid away. 'My poor old bones are still a bit chilled.' He slipped a hand into a pocket of the heavy duffel coat and withdrew the leather-bound silver hip-flask. The top made a metallic creaking sound as it was quickly unscrewed, then Clive raised it and tossed back his head.

'Yourself?' he gasped, wincing as he drew a hand across his mouth. Alver gave an absent shake of the head.

Soon the march of footsteps grew louder, and with it the burble of excited voices. Four heads appeared over the wall, three dark and one blond against the glowing blue sky.

Geoff cleared his throat. 'Alver you all know. George and Derek, you've both met Clive before. James, this is Clive, our local benefactor. Clive, this is James.' He shot a quick scowl at Alver, motioning with his head towards James, who leaned forward over the wall, smiling broadly at the two seated figures. As before he wore a flopping ski-cap similar to Geoff's.

'Yes, yes of course,' replied Clive courteously, slipping the hip-flask discreetly out of sight and getting stiffly to his feet. 'I think I've seen you in the union bar once or twice, haven't I James? I'm very pleased to meet you.' He held out a hand, withdrew it and dusted it against his trousers, then offered it again, smiling apologetically. 'It's very nice to see both of you again as well, George, Derek. How are you both? You must have set out jolly early.' His eyebrows lifted as he made a show of consulting his watch.

'Well,' drawled James in his overloud voice. 'Geoffrey did insist it was all going to be something special, so we didn't want to miss any of it.' His eyes kept wandering to Alver, who smiled at the ground.

There was an awkward pause, then Geoff took a hold on the wall. 'Righto. Let's get comfortable.'

'Oh Geoff,' came George's voice, 'Must we go in there? Can't we stay out here, on the grass?' She looked apprehensively at the weathered, lichen-patched layers of rock, and the shadows between. 'It's such a lovely day, and it'll be much warmer out here. Can't we?'

Geoff hesitated, then relaxed. 'Yeah, why not?'

The four of them laid blankets on the grass and arranged themselves comfortably, falling quickly into a noisy conversation that subsided a little whenever the peregrines made a sortie, then swelled again. Alver and Clive remained in the shelter, where their talk was sporadic and hushed.

So time passed. Piled white clouds built up in the west, loosing wispy strips that passed slowly high overhead. The sun climbed smoothly through the blue. At the cliff-face kills arrived with increasing regularity.

'Everything alright, you two?' Geoff's grinning face appeared over the wall. His attention fastened on Alver. After a quick backward glance he climbed into the shelter and squatted down in front of him.

'Is everything alright now, Alver? You're looking a lot better, isn't he Clive? It's staying out in the open all night that does it, that's all.'

'I'm fine Geoff.'

Gently, Geoff punched his shoulder, then leaned forward confidentially. 'I didn't know that pillock James was coming.' He pushed himself back to his feet and looked brightly up and down the valley, smacking his lips. 'Righto. Well, I'm just going to nip back to the caravan to fetch the eatables. I've made a deadnettle quiche, Clive. Looks pretty good as well, if I say so myself. You'll have to try some.'

Clive gave a tight grin and sent a hand deep into the duffel coat pocket.

'See you soon then.' Geoff paused, straddling the wall. 'Georgie's coming with me, to give me a hand.' He smirked at them both, then leaned back and vanished.

Clive turned to Alver and rolled his eyes, which were dull and slightly bloodshot. 'You can't help liking him,' he whispered, and smiled.

Minutes later an engine fired, its tone sliding as the car manoeuvred, then fading quickly.

'Oh yes.' James' full, resonant voice hung in the air. 'I know just what you mean Derek. Some people do get absurdly upset. But they're simply dead wood, you know? They should be cut away. After all, it's the duty of the young to despise the old – who said that? I forget - so why should anyone be surprised? It's beyond me.'

He fell silent just as a sheep uttered a succession of loud belching noises further down the slope. Clive spluttered as he pulled the hip-flask from his lips.

'I say,' he shouted hoarsely through the wall. 'That's not a terribly kind thing to say, James.'

'Sorry Clive. Forgot you were there.' There was a muffled sniggering.

Clive's mouth worked as he glared furiously at the wall. Beside him, Alver began to raise a hand.

Sighing heavily, Clive turned away and gave a resigned shrug. 'There's no point in getting annoyed. Young people just don't seem to have any compassion these days. To them someone older than themselves might just as well be invisible, or dead. It doesn't matter what they might have achieved, what they might have been through …' His voice became hushed. 'Easy to see why Geoff doesn't care for him.'

Alver's arm fell back to his side. Two jets streaked overhead, curving away to the east and he turned to follow them, his mouth tightening to a hard line.

'Damned nuisance, aren't they?' muttered Clive, glancing from Alver's face to the dwindling silhouettes. 'I know Geoff's always threatening to complain to the RAF or the MOD or whoever it is. Why they have to use a beautiful spot like this …' He chewed thoughtfully at his lip. 'That's a nasty looking sore, Alver, on your mouth.'

Absently Alver brushed dirty fingers across his lips.

'I've got some special cream, back at *Diolch I Duw*. It's very good. You could come back with me …' His voice trailed off into silence as he saw Alver's attention was elsewhere.

More cars were arriving, and distant doors slammed, echoing faintly. Soon the sound of voices approached, and James called out a greeting.

Geoff clumped up, one arm draped awkwardly over George's shoulders while the other cradled a large cardboard box.

'Eats, everybody.'

Behind him came a slim, clean-shaven man in his twenties, with a lively face beneath neatly-trimmed brown hair. He wore faded jeans and a short-sleeved shirt. At his side walked a girl, dark-haired with a round, slightly plump face.

'My brother,' announced Geoff, 'the one and only Nigel. And this is Anice.'

Everyone nodded and said hello, and Geoff brought them to the wall.

'These two, cowering in the shadows, are Alver, over there, and Clive.'

'Hello Alver, Clive,' breezed Nigel, while Anice smiled pleasantly at each in turn, looking quickly from Clive's open, slightly stubbly face to Alver's; their eyes locked briefly before her smile wilted and she turned away.

'Well.' Nigel raised his hands, each of which carried a bottle of wine. 'Who's for a little drinkie?'

'Go on Nige,' urged Geoff. 'Get 'em open.' He withdrew a foil-covered plate carefully from the box. 'Anyone for a piece of this rather excellent quiche?' He lowered his voice as he turned to George. 'Come on, Georgie. I made this specially for you.'

'What's in it?' demanded James.

'Oh you'll enjoy it James, don't worry.'

Derek lay on his side at the edge of the group, his binoculars trained on the cliff. 'What're these two birds up to, Geoff?'

The two eldest juveniles sat together on the narrow, grassy run that led from the cliff's summit to the base of the Fist. As binoculars were rapidly focussed on them, one reached out a foot and clutched at a small clump of dead stalks and leaves, then released it, then clutched again. The second bird did likewise, and for a moment both tugged at the same loose tangle of vegetation, until the first lay on its side in the grass, one long yellow leg fully extended as it patted and snatched.

'Fascinating,' murmured Nigel. 'What're they doing, Geoff? They look as if they're playing.'

'Yes, it is a form of play.'

Both birds now lay in the grass, the ball between them, reaching out to tangle claws in the knotted stalks and tug, straining one against the other.

'Just like a couple of cats,' observed Derek. 'Kittens, rather.'

'Yeah.' Geoff pulled George gently towards him and placed his Leitz to her eyes. 'Look at that, Georgie. Aren't they excellent? Just like a couple of kittens.'

'Mmm.' George peered briefly into the rubber-cupped eyepieces. 'But they look cruel. You can just imagine that being some poor little bird they've caught.'

'Well, yes, I suppose it does serve to strengthen their muscles, improve coordination,' explained Geoff, with a slight note of irritation. 'They are going to have to struggle to survive, you know, once they leave here.' He released her and bent down to pick up the notebook.

As they were emptied, bottles and cans were stacked neatly against the outside of the shelter; green and brown glass glinted with miniature reflections of the sun and sky. Cigarette butts dotted the beaten grass around the gaudy tartan blankets, and smoke drifted in a hazy, almost unbroken stream over the shelter and on over the shimmering slopes.

'What did you think of the quiche, Clive?' Geoff's voice was now loud and boisterous.

Getting politely to his feet Clive held up a hand to shade his eyes. 'Very interesting, Geoff. Yes, thank you very much. Dead nettles, you say? Not had them before.' With a tight smile he lowered himself back to his seat.

'I threw mine to the sheep,' chortled James. 'That one.' He pointed to a motionless, pasty shape by the gully's edge. 'Hasn't moved since.'

Geoff gave him a wintry smile, but James' attention had returned to the motoring magazine on his lap, on which he balanced a plastic cup of wine.

'Think we'll see a kill, Geoff?' asked Nigel. Anice glanced sharply at him.

'Could be Nige, could be. Let's ask Alver. He's the expert nowadays.' Holding his plastic cup carefully, he thrust himself to his feet and strode to the shelter.

'Are you two still cowering in the shadows? Come on come on, don't be antisocial. It's lovely out here.'

Clive looked at Alver. 'Oh, it's alright, really Geoff. We're quite comfortable here, aren't we Alver?'

'Alright, alright.' Geoff wiped sweat from his forehead and pushed it through his tangled hair. His face was a glowing pink. 'Nige wants to know if we're going to see a kill, Alver. What do you say to that?'

Alver's face, streaked now with grimy sweat marks, became thoughtful. One eyelid trembled uncontrollably. He stood up and fixed his attention on the cliff, then looked at Geoff.

'Yes.'

'Oh, well, that's it then.' Geoff lurched away, nodding. 'You're alright Nige,' he bellowed, 'Alver predicts a kill, so that's that. Just a matter of waiting.' He moved back to his place on the rug next to George, still clutching his drink.

Clive smiled and winked as Alver sat down, and gave a mock salute. Shrieks filled the air as the juveniles sighted an adult bringing in food, the urgent, elemental sounds mingling with raucous laughter and argument and the clinking hiss of ring-pull cans.

'Geoff doesn't seem to be getting much of this down in his notes, does he?' whispered Clive. An insect moved slowly across his forehead, turning over and waving tiny limbs as it became trapped on a wriggle of hairs bound together by sweat.

Suddenly a new voice cut through the burble, which stuttered to a halt.

Geoff made brusque introductions. 'Everybody, this is Leon. Leon, everybody.'

'Leon!' gasped Clive, struggling to his feet. 'Thank God!'

Leon stood looking down at the others with an amused expression, hands thrust into the pockets of his usual dazzling pair of white, loose-fitting trousers. A pale grey shirt, equally loose-fitting, was open to his chest. A girl was approaching down the hillside, moving awkwardly under the weight of a heavy shoulder-bag.

Spotting Clive, Leon stepped lightly over George's prone body and thrust out a hand.

'Hi. You must be Clive.'

'Leon. You can't know how pleased I am to meet you at last. I'm so glad you could come. Please ... do come in.'

Leon turned to the girl, who had just arrived and was looking uncertainly at the figures sprawled in front of her on the blankets. She gave a quick smile as Derek said hello.

'Come on, Doll. Come and meet Big Bro.'

Leon vaulted over the wall and turned to help the girl and the shoulder bag. She wore a bright, canary-yellow blouse and white trousers like Leon's, which she brushed fastidiously after negotiating the rocks. A long mass of blonde curls shook rhythmically as she flicked away dirt.

'This is Julie. Julie, this is Alver. And this is Clive.'

Clive reached out, waiting until she offered her hand, while Alver gave a slight nod, smiling pleasantly. 'Julie. Real name Doll.'

'Correct.' Leon pulled a pack of cigarettes from his breast pocket, easy smile in place beneath his dark glasses. 'Smoke Clive?'

Clive took a cigarette and leaned forward as Leon snapped his lighter.

'Doll was the cook the other night, Al, remember?' The dark glasses fixed Alver through a cloud of smoke as Leon straightened.

'Mmm,' said Alver vaguely. 'I remember.'

'So where were you? What happened?'

'I needed to be here.'

'Fine, fine,' nodded Leon. 'Only it would have been a good idea to let us know. Anyway, doesn't matter now. We enjoyed ourselves, didn't we Doll?'

Julie was inspecting rocks in the corner, brushing away soil as she prepared to sit.

'Doll?'

She looked up. 'Yes. A shame you didn't come, Alver. It was lovely.'

Leon continued to stare at her.

'Er … you must come for a meal, Alver anytime.'

A burst of laughter filtered through the wall, then Geoff's voice drowned the others in a fit of coughing.

Leon gave a quick twist of the mouth. 'I spoke to Ma as well.'

'Oh, did you?' blurted Clive, who had been gazing dully at his feet. He looked at the faces turned towards him, and cleared his throat. 'I mean, I hope everything's alright, up there.'

'Everything's fine.' The dark glasses stayed on Clive for a second, then shifted back to Alver. 'She says you never did get in touch, Al.'

'Oh … I meant to. I will, soon.'

'That's what I told her. She said to wish you a happy birthday and she'll keep your present until you go up to see her.' Leon eased himself into a squatting position in front of Alver. 'Geoff tells me you haven't been feeling too good.'

'Geoff's wrong. I had a cold, that's all. There's nothing wrong, really.' Wide, unfocussed eyes stared into reflecting black discs.

Leon's eyes fell to Alver's injured hand, which he lifted gently, nodding at the sight of the swollen knuckles.

'This didn't have anything to do with a bloke with stripey hair, did it, in the pub? Black and white?'

'Black and white? No.' Alver pulled the hand away. 'No, not black and white.'

Geoff's voice cut in. 'Suppose you'd like a drink.' He dangled a half-empty wine bottle by its neck. 'All the food's gone though …'

'It's OK Geoff, we've brought our own.' Leon motioned to Julie, who lifted the shoulder bag and held it out to him. 'Cooked flesh,' he said as he took it, 'Nice,' beaming up at Geoff who disappeared with a grunt.

Julie arranged a cloth carefully on the ground, removing stones with the tips of red-nailed fingers and dropping them over the wall. There was an occasional clink as one slid over the slowly growing pile of cans and bottles.

Leon peeled foil from a roast chicken. 'Come on Al, real eats at last. You too Clive, unless you're,' he paused dramatically and jerked a thumb over his shoulder, 'one of them.'

'I beg your pardon?'

'A grazer.'

'Oh, no. No, certainly not.'

'Doll. Pass us that wine.'

As plates and glasses were passed round a whoop from outside brought them all to their feet except Julie, who glanced up then went back to arranging knives and forks on the tablecloth.

At the western entrance to the valley, beyond the oakwood, a fleet of about twenty racing pigeons had appeared, moving in tight formation towards the cliff. Over the trees they lost height suddenly, still driving east in a rough wedge, following the course of the river.

The compact silhouette of the falcon swooped down on them, swerving to split off a bird paler than the rest and snatching unsuccessfully at it twice before circling back to the cliff-face, where three juveniles flew agitatedly back and forth, shrieking, while the fourth flapped and squealed on the ledge.

James made a loud comment and snorted with laughter.

'Tough cheddar that, eh Al?' Leon turned his brother a questioning look. 'Reckon they'd like some of this chicken?'

'Just keep watching, Lee.'

The falcon had returned to the point of her attack, passing over it in a long, low glide. Suddenly she dived, and a pale shape broke from a clump of bracken and dashed out over the river. Instantly the darker, heavier shadow of the falcon was after it, grabbing once, twice, again and yet again, thwarted each time by a last, desperate swerve. The tiercel streaked in, lunging at the pigeon twice as the falcon eased into a smooth upward curve taking it above the two tumbling shapes. With a final effort, the pigeon darted vertically skywards, tiring visibly, and the falcon overhauled it quickly, snatching it from the air and falling with it towards the green slopes above the stream, bill gaping in a long, savage chatter.

'Bang!' bellowed Geoff ecstatically.

On the distant grassy bank the falcon leaned forward, and with a snap of the notched bill broke the pigeon's neck.

'What did I tell you?' beamed Geoff, turning towards James, both fists clenched above his head in triumph. 'Fantastic killers!' He lowered his arms slowly at the sight of George's pursed lips and lowered eyebrows, but his jubilant grin stayed in place. Derek chuckled to himself and looked away, lifting his binoculars to watch the peregrine tearing feathers from the limp body.

Laughter and loud conversation resumed with a rush and everyone settled back except Alver, who remained at the wall running his tongue over his lips, eyes on the swatch of green where the falcon worked. Leon reached up to tug at his arm.

'Come on Al. Grub up.'

'Not hungry.' But he allowed himself to be pulled gently back to his seat.

'I should have something Alver,' urged Clive through a mouthful of chicken. 'Geoff says you haven't eaten for days.'

'Geoff's wrong.'

Leon looked across at Clive, then shrugged and tore loose a chicken leg. Alver, watching, poked idly with a grimy fingernail at a sliver of red lodged between his teeth.

'This is more like it,' said Leon, belching softly as he lifted a bottle of wine. When he'd taken a long, gulping swallow he passed it to his brother, and belched again. 'Pardon. On the way up here we tried to get a drink, didn't we Doll? I couldn't believe it. Every pub was shut.'

'Yes,' observed Clive sadly. 'It's a Sunday, you see. I'm afraid this is a dry area.'

'Talk about the land time forgot.'

Clive nodded. 'They had a vote, not too long ago. A local man of the chapel campaigned for alcohol to be available only on prescription. Thank you Alver.' He lifted the bottle to his lips.

'Where does this bloke live, Mars?' Leon looked bewildered. 'Christ, the stuff ought to come in the morning, with the milk.'

As they ate and drank, Leon's eyes constantly slid towards his brother, who sat placidly, saying nothing, touching neither food nor drink.

Eventually Leon finished, licking his fingers noisily and smacking his lips. 'Lovely grub, Doll.'

'Yes,' agreed Clive. 'Thank you very much Julie, ah ... Doll.' He smiled hesitantly at the girl who sat in her corner busily cleaning her fingers with a napkin.

'You're welcome, Clive.'

He nodded gratefully, his smile growing.

'Well, Al. You're coming back with me and Doll tonight, OK?'

Alver started to speak, but Leon held up a hand. 'No buts. It's all fixed. That right Doll?'

Julie licked pink lips and nodded.

With a sigh, Alver closed his mouth and gazed affectionately at the three people beside him.

'There.' Leon grinned suddenly. 'That's settled then. Right, let's have one of your smelly fags then to round off the meal.'

'I haven't got any Lee.'

'Oh? First time I've known you run out. What you smoking then? Geoff's vegetarian sheep dung? Here, have one of these.'

'No thanks. I don't smoke now.' He got carefully to his feet and began to search the sky. Almost immediately the air throbbed with the approach of a jet, and Leon and Clive stood with him, squinting into the glare as the overwhelming noise rushed towards them. Outside Geoff was waving a fist, his words drowned in the roar. The huge shape flashed overhead, blotting out the sun for an instant. Alver's pointing finger followed as it shot away, slanting down over the hills while its thunderous wake rolled over their heads.

'My God,' murmured Clive in Alver's ear.

The streaking shadow flashed behind a long grey bar of hills, and a smudge of black smoke dawdled into the sky a second later. The roar careered away towards the curling smoke as they watched open-mouthed, then a dull thud sounded through it. A chorus of chattering cut across the fading, rumbling echoes, then excited voices broke out all at once.

'It went down!' gasped Geoff. 'Bloody hell!'

'Quick!' quavered Clive. 'Somebody -'

George's voice trembled in a long inarticulate moan of disbelief.

'The phone.' James spoke in a loud, deliberate voice. 'I'll go. The jet was on its own, they probably don't know what's happened. Geoff, mark the position on your Ordnance Survey map for me. Quickly!'

Geoff looked round frantically then thrust his cup at George, slopping wine in a spreading red swathe across her jeans. Ignoring her wail he fell to his knees at the rucksack, dragging out its contents until he found the map.

'No chute,' observed Leon quietly. 'Bloke's a gonner.'

James dashed off up the hillside, the map flapping from his hand.

Across the silent hills the ragged line of smoke had crawled eastwards, fading to invisibility over the miles.

'Poor man,' whispered Clive. 'Poor, poor man.' He fumbled in his pocket, blinking tear-filled eyes. 'His poor family.'

Leon gave a long sigh. 'Nothing we can do, Clive. That mate of Geoff's should be at the 'phone soon. You never know, anyway. Chances are he wasn't married, no kids.' He took a pull from the wine bottle, then held it out, eyes still on the distant smoke. 'Here, have some of this.'

Clive lowered his flask and took the bottle with his other hand. 'He had a father though. A mother.'

Geoff sat with an arm round George, talking softly to her as she stared blankly to the south and the crawling black line above the hills.

'That's put a bit of a dampener on things.' Leon took a cigarette from Clive, pulling out his lighter and snapping a flame from it in one smooth motion. He glanced round then lowered his voice. 'Geoff's girl seems a bit bowled over. What about you, Doll? You alright?'

Julie looked up from a plate of chicken and nodded. She eased blonde curls from the sides of her face with the heels of her palms, holding her greasy fingers carefully out of the way. 'Terrible, isn't it?' she mumbled.

A peregrine chattered as it brought in a kill.

'Horrible things!' George's outburst was sudden and shrill, then she started to sob. Geoff's voice sank to a murmur as he cradled her in his arms, rocking gently back and forth.

Derek, standing just beyond them, looked towards the shelter and raised his eyebrows.

'Come on,' urged Leon. 'I think everyone could do with a bit more wine.'

Eventually James returned, striding up to announce in an authoritative voice that everything was under control, that he'd given their names and the address of the university to the police and that they would all be interviewed about what they'd seen in due course.

'They're sending a car out here straight away, of course, after they've alerted the base. Expect the RAF will send a chopper.' He gazed at the fading smoke. 'Not much we can tell them though.'

Slowly conversation picked up, and as more drink was brought out the atmosphere relaxed. Geoff held a plastic cup, coaxing George to take sips as her sobbing subsided. Leon went over to talk to James and Derek, vaulting lightly over the wall, a bottle in one hand, then turning to help Clive help Julie over.

'Oh well Alver,' said Clive, sitting down heavily beside him. 'It's been quite a day, one way or another.' He fumbled to unfasten buttons at the neck of a navy blue shirt. The drooping curve of greying hair was now dark with sweat and plastered immovably to his forehead. He leaned over to tug the hipflask from his pocket.

'Are you sure you wouldn't … I thought you liked whisky?' With a quick tilt he shot the hot liquid into his mouth and swallowed. 'Yes,' he repeated, screwing the cap noisily back into place. 'Quite a day.' His eyes narrowed, and he lifted himself slightly to peer over the wall.

'Look,' he whispered, bringing his face to within a few inches of Alver's, 'I was going to give you this later …' His eyes were glassy and tinged pink, and rolled slightly as he spoke. For a moment they stared with wavering intensity into Alver's face, then he swayed back to rummage in the duffel coat, pulling out a long, rather crumpled brown envelope.

Leon's voice came loudly from the other side of the wall, and there was a burst of laughter.

'Good old Leon. You're lucky you know Alver, having a brother like that, a good down-to-earth …' Clive gave a crooked smile, then looked down at the envelope. 'For you. For your birthday.' With the words he smoothed the worst creases from the paper, then held it out. 'I hope you don't mind.'

Alver took the envelope, ran a finger along the letters of his name, written in flowing, elegant script.

'Thank you.' He tore it open clumsily and stared at the notes that spilled into his hand.

'I hope you don't mind,' repeated Clive anxiously. 'There's a hundred pounds. I …' but his voice trailed off.

Alver's eyebrows drew slowly together. 'I … don't understand.'

'Don't give it back.' Clive spoke in an urgent whisper. 'Please take it. You may need it when … well, wherever you go next. It's of no use to me.'

'You hardly know me.'

'Don't say that!' The bloodshot eyes looked earnestly into Alver's, and his hands reached out to close around Alver's hands and the banknotes held loosely within them.

'We know each other, you and I.'

Alver looked puzzled for a moment, then broke into a slow smile. 'Yes. Of course. We both know. I understand now.'

Stones clattered as they fell from the top of the wall and Clive looked up to see Geoff leaning heavily against it. Hurriedly he withdrew his hands and dragged a florid handkerchief from his pocket.

'Hello Geoff. Everything alright out there?' He buried his face in the gaudily-patterned square of cloth and blew noisily.

'Hmm? Oh yes, everything's just fine, out here.' His gaze shifted from face to face. 'What about in there?'

'Oh, fine, fine. We're alright, aren't we Alver?'

'Yes. Fine.'

Geoff glanced over his shoulder, then leaned forward. 'Why don't you come out? George was a bit upset by that jet thing, understandable, but she's OK now. Come and join in. Don't be antisocial.'

'Yes. Yes, alright. We've just been having a little chat, that's all … I hope no-one thinks … Come on, Alver, let's join the others.'

Alver had pushed the money back into its envelope, which he jammed into the pocket of his jeans.

Outside everyone sprawled in the sun in a rough circle, and they shuffled round to make room without interrupting the noisy conversation. Everyone stopped and looked up a second later as two olive helicopters clattered overhead, then a third, painted yellow, moving in a steady line towards the southern hills.

'They're a lot faster than the police,' observed James loudly, glancing at his watch.

'They shouldn't be long.' Geoff pulled off his spectacles and rubbed a hand across his eyes. 'It's quite a drive.' He pushed the spectacles firmly back into place, then raised George gently from his lap and got to his feet. 'Let's have a look at that bloody last bird.'

The telescope was trained on the ledge where the fourth eyas still squatted resolutely. Geoff crouched behind it, then straightened and scrambled back to his place with an exaggerated groan of exasperation.

'You reckon it's a female do you Geoff?' Leon lifted his sunglasses, squinting in the glare. 'Never ready when they should be.' He winked at George, who gave a frosty smile. Leon grinned as the dark lenses slid back over his eyes.

Clive had fallen into a preoccupied silence. Every so often he raised heavy-lidded eyes in response to an extra-loud remark or burst of laughter, grinning faintly, then his head drooped again. Suddenly he straightened.

'Oh, Geoff! I completely forgot!'

Everyone stopped talking and looked round. Geoff frowned. 'Well? What is it Clive?'

'Ahem. Well, I was talking to a man in the village the other day. He'd been drinking in the Farmer's Arms. Or was it …?' His eyes dulled momentarily, then he shook himself as Geoff gave a short, impatient cough. 'Anyway. Apparently some men came in, strangers, and started asking about peregrine falcons, were there any nesting in the area?'

'Buggers!' exclaimed Geoff softly.

'Londoners, this man said they were. Cockneys. Mind you, to most of the locals any *Sais* is a Londoner, unless he's a Brummie.'

'And every Londoner's a bloody cockney,' added Leon.

'Quite. Anyway, I thought you ought to know, Geoff.' Clive licked dry lips, and the faces turned away.

'What d'you think they're up to Geoff?' asked Derek.

'Thieves,' he replied heavily. 'Bound to be. Still,' he waved towards the cliff, where three eyasses chased one another along the skyline, shrieking furiously. 'They've left it a bit late if that's what they're after. They're probably regular villains … obviously don't know a thing about the birds. The real buggers know how to find their own, they don't go round asking. Clive. Did anyone tell them anything?'

Clive's head had nodded forward again.

'Clive?'

'Mmm? Sorry, Geoff. Just … thinking about something …'

'Did anyone tell these cockneys anything?'

'Well, this chap thought not, but he claims they were buying drinks for everyone, and he said he wouldn't be surprised if, on the quiet … This place, this nest, is very well known locally, after all.'

'Hmm.' Geoff half-turned to scan the hills. 'Thing is, they wouldn't know they were too late until they got here, would they?'

All eyes followed his to the broken grey skyline.

'Well well, east end villains,' mused Leon. 'Just like home, eh Al? And the police. Never here when you want them.'

'They will be Leon,' growled Geoff. 'Give them a chance.

Gradually conversation turned to other things, and Geoff's visits to the telescope, after becoming briefly more frequent and of longer duration, soon tailed off again. Only Derek turned away occasionally to search the cliff-face and hills.

Attention was diverted every so often when the tiercel took off on long, aerobatic flights over the valley, twisting and looping through the air with two or sometimes all three juveniles screaming in his wake. Sunlight caught the slaty blue feathers of lower back and rump as the slim, dagger-winged shape slipped in and out of the frantically pursuing brown eyasses.

Craneflies emerged in enormous numbers as the sun slid inexorably across the endless blue sky; frail, gangling bodies carried eastward by the thousand, followed by swooping martins and swifts. Songbirds left the shade of the trees in fluttering sorties to snatch the helpless insects.

Leon began to organise a sweepstake for the nearest guess to the time of the flight of the last eyas. As he cajoled and argued with the others, Alver leaned across to Clive, whose chin again rested on his chest. The long, almost white hairs at the side of his face hung down like blinkers over his eyes.

'There were three of them, weren't there?' whispered Alver.

'Mmm?' Clive's head twisted jerkily round, one bloodshot eye peering dazedly through a screen of hair.

Alver drew back and nodded, looking satisfied. 'There's no need to worry though. I can go anywhere now. They don't know that.'

Clive rubbed his eyes and pushed the hair back into place; he stared blearily at Alver and smiled apologetically. 'I'm sorry, Alver. What was that? I must have nodded off for a second. Not used to these early starts.'

Alver got to his feet. 'I'm going for a walk.' For a moment he stood there, shielding his eyes as he watched the others arguing loudly over the size of the bets.

Groggily Clive pulled himself upright and dusted himself down. 'Would you mind if I came along? I could do with a walk myself.'

'Sorry Clive. You can't come.' The sweat-streaked, blunt-featured face wore an expression of regret. 'Maybe afterwards …' He turned and began to climb towards the skyline.

'Where you going Al?' shouted Leon, pen and paper poised in his hands, a cigarette dangling from the side of his mouth.

Alver halted and looked back. 'I'll see you soon. I'll see you all soon.'

Wriggling the pen further into his grip, Leon plucked the cigarette from his lips. 'Make sure you do,' he called. 'We haven't had your bet yet. And you're the expert. What time d'you think?'

'Six minutes past six.'

'Oh, very definite,' grinned his brother. 'I like it!'

With a wave of his hand, Alver turned away and plodded on.

At the Sphinx he climbed to the broad ledge where he usually sat and pushed a hand carefully into the crevice where it met the main body of the silently crouching stone beast.

14. Last flight

On the eastern side of the shelter, downwind of the others, Clive knelt miserably in the shadow of the buttress, wiping his mouth with the brightly-coloured handkerchief. When he'd finished he folded the cloth neatly and returned it to his pocket, then piled stones carefully over the yellowish mound of vomit. Steam rose gently through the miniature cairn. He paused, listening to the uninterrupted babble from beyond the shelter.

'Bloody dead nettles,' he muttered bitterly, starting to rise, then he sank wearily back to his knees. His body sagged as he groped for the handkerchief again to wipe away the tears that suddenly filled his eyes.

Leon's voice rose above the others. 'Four fifteen then, Derek. You can't change it now, it's in the book. Come on, let's make it worthwhile. A fiver each, you're all rich students, you can manage that.'

Peregrines shrieked faintly in the background.

Alver clawed at the ragged neck of his T-shirt as sweat poured down his face. The worn material tore and pallid, sweat-slicked skin showed through the rent. A crow called hoarsely from a leaning hawthorn higher up the sun-baked gully. As he climbed on the bird called again, drawing a reply from its mate circling warily overhead. A rock, loosened by his boot, crashed and clattered behind him. Three young crows watched from their nest, filmy lids sliding over expressionless eyes as they shuffled round on the black pile of twigs to keep his struggling figure in view. The harsh cries died away as he finally hauled himself clear of the gully and rolled onto his back, panting, at the edge of the rustling brown sea of heather.

When his breathing had steadied he rolled back to look down at the steep-sided, rock-filled fissure and swallowed, running his tongue nervously over dry, white-flecked lips. With each sucked lungful of air a muffled scraping sounded in his chest. Tearing off the T-shirt he crawled a few yards into the heather and, lifting off the Leitz, lay face down, arms outstretched, fingers curling and uncurling around the tough, woody stems.

A faint, grating scream hung on the air for an instant, and his body tensed. He got to his knees. A curlew broke from the heather with a loud yelp and beat rapidly away, long curved mandibles parting as it called again and again. Much closer, a lizard flickered almost invisibly across a great flat stone, a shadowy suggestion of movement.

He got shakily to his feet and examined himself. Apart from weather and dirt-browned arms, and a patch at his throat, his skin was white. Two ticks clung to him, one among the spreading sores of his chest, the other on the sunken flesh below his ribcage. Bending quickly he scooped up the Leitz and moved forward, swinging his legs high over the tangled heather. After a few such clumsy strides he flung himself down and ripped frantically at his laces, tugging off the heavy boots and struggling upright again to hurl them far out over the waving brown and purple sea. His fingers worked at his belt, and he stepped out of the tattered jeans, emptying the pockets before sending them after his boots. Soiled underpants and socks followed. His eyes travelled from the damaged hand at his side to the muddy scarlet stain between his legs; black crusts of dirt showed between soapy white toes.

Naked, with the Leitz bumping at his chest, clutching the contents of his pockets, he clambered on through the grappling heather.

'Excuse me, but does anyone have any more wine?' Clive looked hopefully at the flushed, smiling faces. He fingered the empty flask in his pocket. 'I should have brought some myself – I meant to – but I was in such an awful hurry this morning. It slipped my mind. It's on the cabinet, at home ...'

'Have some of this.' James held out an open can of beer. 'I've got a long drive back, and I've had more than I should already. Like one or two others,' he added with a nod towards Geoff, who stood arguing loudly with Leon. 'Here, take it Clive. Might as well put it where it's most needed.'

'Thank you. Thank you, James. This heat ... makes you thirsty.' He took the can graciously. 'Still no sign of the police then?' As James turned to look towards the hills, Clive raised the can and swallowed greedily.

'Well,' Leon announced loudly, making a show of consulting his watch, 'I'm afraid that's goodnight to your bet, George. Shame.'

George's lips twitched and she glanced sullenly at Geoff.

'Who's next?' Leon examined the list. 'Five-forty-five's the number, Geoffrey is the name. Could be you Geoff, could be. Sweating yet?' With a sudden frown he looked again at his watch, then peered to the hillside beyond the shelter. 'Wonder what's happened to our Al?'

'Oh, I shouldn't worry,' murmured Geoff, squinting into the telescope. 'He'll be up at the Sphinx. You know, that big rock he was at last time you came. He spends hours up there on his own. He's happy there, and it's warm now. As long as we collect him before we go ...' His voice trailed away as he made a deft adjustment to the focussing. 'Well at least she's moved off into the heather. That's a start.' His gaze dropped briefly to his watch. 'Come on you lazy bugger. You've only got a couple of minutes.'

Leon lifted the sunglasses and stared towards the distant hump of the Sphinx. 'Yeah ... think I'll just pop up there and see him. He's probably fallen asleep. Back in a minute, Doll.'

Julie lay a few yards away on a blanket, sunbathing in a tiny black bikini. Her blouse, trousers and shoes lay next to her in a neat pile. She looked up, shading her eyes. 'Don't be long, Lee.'

'Would you mind if I came with you, Leon?' Clive got to his feet, swaying slightly. He raised a hand to his forehead and winced.

'Course not Clive. Let's go.'

With a long, gulping swallow, Clive drained his can and went across to place it carefully on the pile of cans and bottles by the wall, then straightened slowly and began to follow Leon up the hill.

'Hang on a minute!'

They both stopped as Derek got to his feet, stroking the focussing wheel on his binoculars. Everyone turned towards him, drawn by a note of urgency in his voice.

'There's some people over there, to the west of the cliff. Three men. They're making towards it. Look.'

'The bastards!' whispered Geoff. 'It's those cockney bastards of Clive's, the crooks, got to be! They're going in a dead straight line – they must know just where the bloody nest is. Thank God there's only one eyas left. She should be able to scramble out of their way, even fly.' He swung the binoculars back towards the cliff and fingered the sheer grey face into focus. A movement on the skyline caught his eye, and his forehead creased. His eyes strained into the Leitz.

'Bloody hell!'

Treading carefully, Alver placed one foot slowly in front of the other as he made his way down the narrow, scrubby trail between the massive walls of rock. Below him the angled face of the cliff fell away into haze. He paused as a peregrine drifted past at eye-level, much closer than ever before, black and white mask turning to fix him with a cold, black stare. The tearing bill cracked open and a deafening, jagged scream shattered the silence.

Alver raised a hand then moved on, clutching at sun-warmed knuckles of rock as the path slanted downwards.

A second sleek grey shape swung into view, and both peregrines floated slowly before him, hanging against a hazy backdrop of grey and green. Each in turn split the air with the terrible, shattering shriek of alarm.

Finally he reached the root of the pitted grey mass of the Fist. He stood there panting, sweat coursing over his naked body.

Cautiously he placed a foot on the warm rock, then walked slowly out along it. The eyasses had joined the adult peregrines now; screaming silhouettes flickered in and out of the air around him.

He turned his glance downwards. Far, far below, a still, pale smudge lay at the water's edge. Slowly he lifted the Leitz. Twisted white limbs swam into view, a body sprawling and broken. A trail of whitish marks led to it over the blurred ground. As he lowered the glasses he swallowed, his head moving slowly from side to side, his eyes wide.

Two of the peregrines had left him, and dived now at three figures, dwarfed by distance, moving over the valley floor below him, directly under the cliff. Alver's breath came in ragged gasps as he looked from the approaching figures to the pale, wrecked body. Inching his feet round deliberately, he turned back to face the cliff, and knelt on the weathered rock. As he laid the things clutched in his hands down carefully, a shadow passed over him, and all sound was eclipsed by an overwhelming grating scream.

The plain, oddly vague face looked up at him, the staring eyes searching his. To either side he laid a barred grey feather; they gleamed suddenly blue in the sunlight streaming over his shoulder. Taking the purple-patterned notes from their crumpled envelope he spread them on the rock beneath the staring face; they rustled and shifted in an eddying current of air. Holding them down with one hand he lifted the strap of the Leitz over his head and placed them on the fanned notes. Finally he crushed the envelope in his fist, staring for a moment at the swollen knuckles, then threw the balled paper into the bracken.

Confident now, he turned and walked back to the tip of the Fist. Below him three dark figures hurried along the bank of the stream, and beyond them, moving down the long slope across the valley, more figures, rushing towards the water where small, slow, lazy waves pulsed rhythmically. He smiled at the tiny figures and waved. His mouth opened, but the only sound was an ear-splitting scream.

One savage masked face after another swept towards him and veered away as the peregrines skimmed the air yards from his staring eyes. The rushing sounds as their bodies clove the air mingled with the relentless barrage of screams.

Alver's eyes narrowed as he concentrated. His face became rigid, every muscle straining with effort. Beyond the twisting shadows, beyond the rock, beyond the sky itself, a vast printed pattern of stars glimmered for an instant.

For a last time he looked down, at the wandering line of footprints scuffing the sand, at the three figures following them. A face tilted far below and a faint howling sounded in his ears. He raised a hand to the swooping birds, to the distant nub of rock beyond them. The cacophony in the air around him swelled, and with an effort he followed the flashing shadows.

Six.

His body tensed.

www.ingramcontent.com/pod-product-compliance
Lightning Source LLC
Chambersburg PA
CBHW031108260626
47172CB00001B/276

* 9 7 8 0 9 5 6 8 6 7 5 1 3 *